The Secret Chronicles

Evalesco

By: J. L. Nicholls

A man's face is his autobiography.
A woman's face is her work of fiction.
~ Oscar Wilde

For Daddy; for Mother; for my sixteen year old self, and for you...

Happy Reading.

CONTENTS

Prologue

It was winter in the Marsh Village. A light snow fell on the peaty wetlands, although the warning of a greater storm sent most running home to stoke their fires.

Experience told them a stiff nightcap and a book would see them through the deluge, and the majority would heed that remembrance, remaining blissfully unaware of what the night had in store.

Unfortunately, not everyone would have such luxury.

Far from the belly of the village, atop an exposed hilltop, a manor waited. Shards of twilight seeped in through the shuttered windows, saturating the large rooms in a dusky haze, and faint shadows sat among every corner, as if prisoners within the isolated walls.

In the vast library, a small grandfather clock counted down the seconds, its tick muffled by pages of books stacked along numerous shelves. Inanimate by nature and ignorant to the intruders present, it knew nothing of the dust being wiped from its face, followed by the mantel it stood upon and the fireplace it protected. If it could talk, it would speak of the matter the intruders stole to take form, how they flickered excitedly – an occasional lick of fire or droplet of water falling from their masses – only to disappear before the manor felt their touch. It would say that they were no louder than the scampering of mice feet: exploring, waiting, but growing increasingly impatient for the coming hours.

For soon the selected one, the one whose destiny would shape their own, the one being born upstairs at that very moment... would change everything.

Far above, waiting in one of many bedrooms, all present heard the commotion. Although aware of the position they found themselves in, the impatient energy rising from the depths of the manor fuelled their increasing anxiety.

"Do not be afraid," a soft voice assured from a grand bed.

A doctor and his two midwives looked to the origin of the voice, acknowledging a slight woman behind a sheer veil hanging from the canopy above. She faced the large bay windows, the murky horizon looming beyond, and when she spoke, her lips trembled with the exertion of labour.

"You know they won't hurt you," said a different voice, the tone rough and leaden with fatigue. "They're just waiting."

As if in answer, a thud sounded from the pantry below, startling the doctor as he dropped the cold compress in his hands. He grabbed it from the floor and handed it to one of the midwives before wiping his brow with his sleeve.

"Maybe so Charras, but their presence worries me. I feel the pressure on my shoulders enough; I do not want to fail you." Casting his gaze towards his patient's bulging stomach, he added, "both of you."

More clattering erupted from below, followed by a glass smashing somewhere in the kitchen, spurring the midwives into action. Tending to the pregnant woman, they dabbed her moist forehead with cotton cloths and soothed her whimpers with hushed words.

"She's nearly there doctor," said one, pulling back the veil so he could see for himself.

Leaving them to their task, Charras rose from his station and walked towards the windows, staring out into the gardens below. A frost rest on the ground, the promise of winter's embrace once an affair his wife celebrated, now serving as nothing more than a hollow reminder of the cold nights ahead.

"It's time," he murmured, loud enough for all to hear.

He didn't turn to meet their reactions, wishing the events to unfold quickly before he changed his mind... again. It was enough to hear the shuffling of feet and whispers of decision to confirm that everything would soon be in place.

The doctor removed his gloves, his patient's dilation confirmed. Then, rubbing his forehead to dull the stubborn ache, he stood to face Charras. "Eight centimetres," he said.

A glare sliced through the twilight, its ferocity such that he bowed his head and returned to his duties. "She is doing well," he assured, following it with a half nod over his shoulder.

Charras immediately withdrew, compelling himself to turn around and look into the gloom. In the distance, a storm crept closer, the threat of chaos on the winds something he could almost taste. Its power filled him, stirring fear and sadness in his gut – emotions he knew he needed to bury lest he act foolishly.

With a breath, he shook them off, daring a glance at his wife – his gracious Isalize – as she bravely accepted her fate, something he'd never done. Stooped over her, the doctor continuously checked her progress, his expert touch an empty comfort.

"Remember the stories old friend?" Charras asked, his voice barely audible over the storm's growl. "Remember how as boys we would spend hours listening and then pretending we were the heroes of each tale?"

From the bedside, the doctor turned to face him. "Old friend?" He contemplated the words before smiling. "Yes, we were young and foolish once. If only we knew those tales hid a darker future than they promised, perhaps then we would not have listened so eagerly."

Letting out a bitter laugh, Charras said, "I do not believe that you would be here this night if you truly thought that."

The doctor shrugged. "I am here to repay a word, my father's to you. He promised that when you called, he would deliver her, yet in his death that promise passed to me."

Charras shook his head. "You are here because you still live in hope, even if you have turned your back on what you are."

"Something most would have accused you of, not so very long ago."

With a grunt, Isalize sat up, halting the midwives attempts to help her. "Things changed, quite obviously," she said, allowing the resulting silence to give the doctor enough time to look ashamed.

"Forgive me Isalize, I do not wish to pain you further," he said quietly.

"Then do not fight, please…" Unable to finish her sentence, she took a breath and fell back into the sheets. This time, she allowed the midwives to help her.

His heart heavy, the doctor looked towards Charras silhouetted in the windows diminutive light. His focus was firmly on the gathering storm, fists balled and shoulders hunched. "I know this isn't easy for you," he said tentatively, "and I do not expect you to understand the reasons we have chosen to live our lives the way we do, but please know we do not do it for ourselves, but for our son."

Still staring towards the horizon, Charras sighed a sigh of one long suffered. "We are Mages. Our duty is binding, even to those who are outcast."

"Perhaps," the doctor replied. "But this is not the time to argue it. The elements are near."

Allowing the warning to hover purposely, he addressed the midwives in turn, directing them to obtain bowls of ice and water while he found and ignited a candle himself.

With them gone, the subsequent lull stabilised the tension in the room, while outside, the storm approached, its pressure ironing fields as it neared – the atmosphere ablaze with energy.

"Charras?" said Isalize, her voice weak as it cut through his thoughts.

He took a breath and walked to her side, resisting the urge to snatch her away into the night. Leaning down to kiss her clammy forehead, she feverishly took his hand in hers, releasing a soft grunt in an effort to smile.

"Promise me you'll love her," she said. "Promise me you won't blame her."

Charras brought her hand to his lips, her skin amazingly cool for what she was undergoing, and nodded. Then embracing her, the sorrow that passed between them was private.

It was only when the doctor returned they parted. He felt like an intruder, a spectator in a moment not meant to be shared, and he watched patiently as Charras kissed Isalize's forehead and pulled back to look into her watery blue eyes.

"I'll wait for you," he said, retreating slowly.

In his place, the doctor and his midwives gathered at the foot of the bed. Standing centrally, the doctor held the ignited candle towards Isalize, his hands steady. Then, wetting his lips, he began to sing, the midwives promptly adding their voices to the ethereal melody as it echoed through the room.

"Vivere, crescere, nascere."

On the bed, Isalize stirred. Clutching the sheets as she arched her back, pain seizing her in preparation for delivery, her agonised cries were soon lost to the noise of rattling windowpanes, the storm raucous as clouds tumbled overhead in anticipation.

Charras knew what needed to be done, and edging his hands towards the clasps, hesitant at first, but then decided, he forced the windows from their locks.

Fierce, hungry wind howled for attention as it gained access, dancing around the furniture and claiming its territory. It found its target on the bed, circling Isalize as she delivered her baby – before snatching the newborn and holding her within its swirling form.

Isalize's chest heaved, her breath shallow, but she was thankful nonetheless, glad she had time to see her daughter. *At last*, she thought, and with a small sigh of relief, escaped peacefully into death.

Charras watched her go, overcome with grief as he witnessed her leave existence – his existence. If it were not for his baby's screams puncturing the air, snapping him back to reality, he would have crossed over with her in a heartbeat. Instead, he was doomed to live.

There was no time to grieve, nor even think as a burst of flame from the doctor's candle shifted the attention. Crumbling to his knees, he raised it high above his head, the flame still burning brightly through the tumultuous noise and wind. It caught the particles circling the infant, sending a rush of fire to engulf her that expanded into a cocoon, then just as quickly folded to form a ring – a careful flame disintegrating her umbilical cord and cauterising the tip.

A heartbeat passed before the midwife on the doctor's right also fell to her knees. The water within the basin she held streamed out to join the circle of fire, extinguishing the flames as it traced a path. For a short while, it created a smoke screen that hid the newborn and polluted the air with acrid damp and burnt earth.

Then the haze dispersed, leaving only a gentle flow of water, and in seconds, the ice from the bowl of the remaining midwife flew out to join it.

Charras couldn't take his eyes off what was happening. He couldn't move either, his limbs immobile as he watched the fragmented shards dazzle like crystals within the current, their gentle bobbing soothing his daughter's cries as she watched them circle her. Wide eyed, her bare arms flailed as she reached out to grasp one, accidentally upturning so she lay facing the ceiling. She didn't seem perturbed, happy to gurgle and bounce in her protective bubble.

But then the water suddenly changed its course, arching upwards before plunging into her open mouth, leaving the remaining ice to mould together – particle upon particle – until it completely encased her and lowered to the floor.

Unsure what he should do, Charras had no time to react as the storm outside peaked and the tremendous noise became unbearable. As the only one left standing, he too crouched down and covered his ears.

It was just in time; for a second later, the pressure within the room heightened to such a degree that it felt as if the walls shook. Cracks appeared along the ceiling, the fractures expanding and groaning as the foundations threatened to crumble. And just when it seemed they would yield, a huge crash roared from outside, followed by a flash of light as a bolt charged through the window and struck the block of ice – shattering it into tiny pieces around its captive.

She instinctively opened her eyes, staring up at the bolt lowering towards her lashes. Then, breaking off into two forks, they hovered above her pupils, no more than a hairline breadth between. She blinked once and the light disappeared beneath her lids.

It was quick then, almost quicker than it began; the storm ceased and the song ended, leaving ringing in the ears and dryness in the mouths of all present. A bitter odour hung in the air, the taste of sulphur and smoke cloying and unpleasant.

Not that any paid much attention. Sat beneath the haze, the open windows slowly filtered the pollution out, which they ignored in favour of making sure they survived unharmed.

It was only when a lamp flickered on, its broken shade lying meters away, did the destruction in the storms wake become apparent. Upturned furniture littered the floor and a thick layer of ash covered every surface, while the cracks along the ceiling and walls were highlighted by the beam, as well as burn marks in the dishevelled rugs, shattered glass, and the white faces of all present.

Behind a crushed chest of drawers, Charras slowly stood up and wiped his eyes with his sleeve. Searching for his daughter, he saw her cosseted within the ice ring and made his way over, touching the doctor's shoulder as he passed.

Reaching where she lay, he bent down to pick her up, surprised as a force resisted his touch, although quickly relinquished, somehow knowing his right to claim the gift it sheltered. He scooped her into his embrace, united with the warmth of her tiny body, and was instantly surprised by the strength of emotion within him. It was unlike anything he'd ever imagined, anything he thought he would feel when she finally arrived. But he couldn't help it, an instinct taking over that made him promise to always protect her, to make sure she knew happiness even though seconds ago he was certain he would never know it again.

When she stirred and opened her eyes, he had to stop himself gasping as her mother's sapphire gaze stared back at him. "Incredible…" he murmured, peering over to where Isalize lay.

Making a decision for his daughter's sake, he slowly made his way across, placing her next to Isalize's breast and uniting mother and baby. He stood back then and watched with disbelief, denial swearing that they both merely slept, each recovering from their traumatic ordeal. Soon they would wake and his family would be whole, ready to build their future together…

How sorely he wished it so. But as reality dawned and he was left in the cold, he succumbed to the darker truth.

Brushing an ice blonde lock from Isalize's face, he stroked her cheek. "We did it," he whispered, gently picking their daughter back up and taking her away.

The presence of death was no place for a baby.

Standing once more by the window, looking out at the rising day casting the hills a pale blue and green, Charras wondered how much time had passed.

Burying Isalize had been the hardest part of all. He still imagined she would be cold, the doctor and midwives having wrapped her in nothing but a flimsy white robe as they lay her to rest in the gardens outside the manor. It was only as they performed the rituals, enabling her spirit to pass into a true death that he accepted the strange finalisation; a chapter ended. There was no going back now.

"Charras?"

Almost forgetting that he was not alone, he faced the doctor as he approached, his manner uncertain. "There is no need to be wary, you are being released from your word," he grunted.

The doctor said nothing, bowing his head as Charras prepared the casting. After several moments of silence, he felt the firm touch of a hand on his crown and he held his breath.

"*Dicio*," Charras said – the word of power. "*Incendiī-Anima*." His Mage name followed. "*Dissolvo*."

As the final word escaped into the room, sparks materialised and twisted off the doctor's scalp, disappearing into the air to be lost in an instant. Once they subsided, he raised his head and ran his fingers through his hair, checking if any remained. Other than a few singed ends, he was satisfied.

"Thank you."

Charras nodded. "You have repaid your fathers word with honour."

"Then let me leave you with my blessings, for this night and the nights that follow."

Looking towards the cot where his daughter slept, Charras made his way over. "And how desperately we need them… Now she is here, we know a war is coming. In a decade, all of our world will know the same."

"Then we must prepare. I will still fight with you, know that, but our son will be spared."

Fatigue stopped Charras disputing the doctor's immovable sentiments. Instead, he gathered his daughter in his arms and returned to the window, his brow heavy and shoulders forward.

"She looks like you," the doctor ventured. "She has Isalize's eyes, but the rest of her belongs to you. Has she got a name?"

"Indeed, but I will not speak it until the time comes for others to know it too."

The doctor nodded. "Very well, until then… old friend."

"Until then."

And with that, he was gone, the soft click of a door shutting marking his departure. In the silence that followed, Charras felt the inevitable well of grief. It threatened to engulf him, a vast chasm of emptiness rising in his chest – despair he hadn't known before. If it were not for his daughter stirring in his arms, reminding him of his responsibility and his alone, he often wondered what he would have done in that moment.

Peering down to meet the already familiar gaze, the vibrancy contrasting the gloom, he felt the anguish lift. A gurgle escaped from the small rosebud lips he already knew so well, and he lowered his forehead to meet hers.

"It starts Charlize."

1

Untamed

Charlize was hot as she lay in bed, her white sheets shimmering like the surface of a tranquil lake. Morning peaked above the window ledge, a crack in the curtains casting a beam on her face and she reached up to shield her eyes. *Finally* she thought, kicking the sheets from her body. She watched as they crumpled to the floor, before following them and idly pacing her room.

She wasn't usually restless, but today was her birthday, which meant presents. It also meant something else, turning ten an age her father said was extremely important – apparently too important to explain – only shaking his head when she asked why.

Consequently, she became unable to sleep, which led to being unable to concentrate on anything more useful than daydreams, her mind full of potential surprises as the rising sun bathed her room in golden light. It painted soft shadows across the walls, and she contented herself with picking out shapes and faces for a while. But soon, even that grew dull. So, crossing her immaculate cream carpet, she drew the heavy curtains aside and peered into the dawn.

Cold slapped her cheeks instantly, the south-westerly breeze fierce, but she paid it no attention, instead listening for the crow of a particularly tardy cockerel.

"Henry, you're late again!" she called, searching the faint light for her adopted friend.

The resulting feeble caw helped her spot him. Standing atop a headstone in her back garden, his feathers ruffled around his neck as a more enthusiastic wake-up call dislodged from his throat.

"Much better!" she assured, resting her elbows on the window ledge and putting her head in her hands.

The sight of Henry clutched to the marble stone, lonely amongst the static graves, reminded her of her father's words the day before.

'Tomorrow is an important day, it is your Awakening.'

Somewhat bemused, the tone her father used more frightening than his words, his awkward attempts to reassure her made little impact.

'Come,' he said when her eyes grew wide, 'I'll show you.'

Indicating that she should follow, they stepped from the kitchen door and into the hazy garden light, wandering over to a grave and standing before it. Made from a rare marble – purple and red snaked across its surface, the headstone glittered in the dappled rays of the afternoon sun.

As she always did, Charlize knelt beside it, motionless as a sense of warmth crept through her body. It settled her until a sudden jolt severed her from the moment.

Finding herself suspended in her father's arms, his expression worried, she made no objections as he pulled her away, her vulnerability in the open air something he remained cautious of.

'Your mother was strong Charlize,' he said hesitantly, 'her mind as well as her spirit.'

He shifted her weight onto his hip and carried her towards the safety of the manor.

'Do not be sad,' Charlize said, curling her fingers around his dark hair.

With a soft snort, he flung her across his shoulder, tickling her feet as she pounded his back and shrieked with delight.

'Stop it father, stop it! She doesn't want me to go!'

Freezing, Charras held her tightly, scanning the grounds for any sign of danger. Once assured nothing lurked, he jogged the rest of the way to the manor, pulling open the kitchen door and easing Charlize into a chair at the table. Then, bending down so they were face to face, he cupped her chin.

"Who doesn't want you to go?"

She pointed at her mother's grave, aware she'd done something wrong, and said nothing more as her father stood up and put his hand in front of her face.

'Stay here,' he said, storming from the kitchen.

Charlize felt the resistance surround her, the familiar glow of her father's protection rendering her incapable of movement even if she wished it. All she could do was watch as he marched back to the grave.

The sun was setting, bathing the garden in an orange glow and masking it in a calm quiet he clearly didn't feel. He patted the earth beneath the headstone, closed his eyes, and tried to sense a presence within, but found nothing, as always.

'Rest in peace Isalize,' he murmured.

Catching his stare as her father faced her, Charlize sensed fear, its heavy pulse radiating towards her as he watched her strangely. Without knowing where it came from, she frowned.

'But she can't.'

Shaking from her malaise, Charlize shut the window. She hated her father being upset and the memory of the previous day only confused her – although most things confused her, her father's general disposition to answering questions with questions rarely satisfying her curiosity.

She thought of this as her stomach growled, hunger signalling it was probably time, and walking to her door, she slowly opened it, careful that it made no sound as it shut behind her. She then tiptoed along the corridor, avoiding the threadbare runners, their stitches worn and prickly on her feet, and wondered for the thousandth time why her father refused to replace any of the manors furnishings, despite their age or erosion. He did always say that memories were the only things a person truly owned, but then again he often bought liquid amber that he forbade her to drink. (Not that she liked it anyway – it burned her throat and made her dizzy).

Turning into another corridor, Charlize passed several unoccupied rooms on her left and right. Although it was the main wing, many of the rooms were no longer in use. Once, after her father found her playing in what used to be her Grandmother's quarters, he explained that she should respect the remnants of her late relatives. She just couldn't understand – if they were no longer alive – why she couldn't make use of them. He never did explain it, and to this day, the rooms remained locked.

She passed them now with mild interest, their hidden secrets a mystery she often guessed at. Charlize knew there were toys and trinkets beyond their doors, their prohibition only fuelling her desire for them, but she quickly dismissed the notion of their seizure as she reached the first of several portraits.

Hung in oak finished frames, generations of her family sat glaring at each other. She didn't think much thought went into what their relationships might have been like in life, for whenever she passed, she felt as if she intruded some sort of showdown – an eternal staring match with no victor – and she always bowed her head in apology for the interruption.

Upon reaching the 'safe zone' Charlize straightened her neck, trod lightly to the nearest door, and pressed her ear to it. Able to hear her father's soft breathing and confirm he still slept, she walked to the end of the corridor where a large window stretched from ceiling to floor, the thick pane of glass revealing the rich landscape of the manor gardens. She placed her hands on it and stared onto the estate below.

Golden rays swept across the grounds, the winter morning waking the glistening frost. It highlighted the sheep grazing idly on the dewy grass, while in further fields cows roamed unhurried, mooing happily as they gathered for breakfast.

"Pretty," Charlize murmured, taking a last glance and peeling herself from the cool glass.

Then, making her way down the stairs to her left, resisting the temptation to slide down the polished wooden banister, she skipped the second to last step, its creak embedded in her memory, and walked to the centre of the lobby – a circular room carefully crafted to accommodate huge paintings. The intricate scenes of nature, portraits, and civilisations all moulded into the bow, and Charlize stood in admiration, as she often would – many hours having been lost to the masterpieces. Her favourite was an illustration of a silver-maned mare. Black spots freckled down her muzzle and she dazzled with the chrome paint used to capture her.

Amongst the paintings stood five glass-paned doors, each leading to elsewhere in the manor. Charlize opened the one nearest her – a large closet – and placed her icy feet in a pair of white slippers. Then, walking through the lobby towards the kitchen, she passed beneath an archway set back from the stairs.

The kitchen was darker, at odds with the lobby, and once her eyes adjusted to the faint light, she checked the clock hanging above the stove. It read five minutes past seven. She was early.

Knowing to wait, she took a seat at the table and rest her elbows on the large oak surface. She didn't notice the fridge opening at the exact moment she passed – seemingly of its own accord. Blissfully unaware, she proceeded to pass the time by admiring the carved woodwork that made up the majority of cupboards. Usually, she could pick out at least one new detail, the homely kitchen her favourite place in the manor. She revelled in the moments before she began breakfast, waiting every day until fifteen minutes past seven precisely. Her life was one of discipline and routine. Everything had its place and everything had an order. Although curious and energetic, she knew the consequences of her disobedience well.

A few minutes passed, along with a new discovery in the form of a carved rosette, but still Charlize grew bored. Tapping her fingers on the table, she twisted her head to check the time, suddenly noticing the fridge door was open and spilling light onto the wooden floor. With an eye on the clock, she got up to close it, assuming her father had forgotten to do so the night before.

As she touched the cool metal, she didn't expect the jolt that flung her hand backwards. Shaking it vigorously, attempting to stem the violent current coursing through her nerves, she stood in shock.

✤

Charras woke after a disturbingly restless night. Lying in bed, he listened to the familiar groans of the ancient manor.

It had been his home his entire life. When he and Isalize married at just seventeen, it then became their home, a haven from the world they shied away from. The stone used to create the foundations was ancient, hewn from the same rock castles were formed. Then, years later, when the original foundations failed, renovation occurred in the form of bricks, plaster, and insulation.

Throughout the generations, several inhabitants of the huge building added their own uniqueness to the décor, it soon becoming a quirky home of painted landscapes and portraits, intricate ironwork, timeless heirlooms, extravagant woodwork carvings, and several items of mismatched furniture. Although it held a distinctive jumble of adornment, somehow nothing looked out of the ordinary.

Charras laid his mark on the manor days after he and Isalize moved in together. Inheriting the skill from his father, he carved the elaborate mantelpiece that now sat above the fireplace in the sitting room. All who saw it commented on the skill, and not to be outdone, Isalize – a keen tailor – made cushions that rest elegantly on the four settees in the same room, embroidering another to match the antique rocking chair sat offset to the hearth.

Not that they often had guests. Far from her own territory, Isalize had built a home with him in the Marsh Village, their relationship an abomination to the Mage community. Outcast, few took kindly to them, yet within the walls of the manor, none of that mattered.

Pushing himself onto his elbows, Charras rubbed his face, forcing out the memories of what could have been. The air on his back spurred him to flip the sheets from his body, and swinging his legs to the floor, he stood up; pulled on a pair of trousers; grabbed a shirt off the back of a chair, and tugged it on as he made his way downstairs.

Reaching the bottom, he was surprised to discover Charlize sat at the kitchen table, her head in her hands as small sobs escaped from beneath a layer of dark hair.

Knowing to approach with caution, he trod carefully. "Charlize?" he asked gently.

She took her hands away from her face and swivelled in her seat, her head still hung towards the floor.

Charras closed the gap between them and knelt down beside her. "What's wrong?"

Raising her eyes to meet her father's concerned expression, she sniffed once. "I burnt the toast."

Charras smiled with relief. Tilting his daughter's chin up, he glanced over his shoulder to take a quick look at the charred remains of their toaster. "At least it isn't the stove," he teased.

Charlize failed to see the funny side, more annoyed that he couldn't understand her problem. "It wasn't my fault; I just put the bread in the toaster when sparks came out of my hands!" Noting how he still smiled, a rage of contempt washed over her. "You don't believe me!" she yelled, shoving his broad shoulders to no avail and jumping down from the chair.

She didn't get far. Refusing to allow petulance triumph, Charras grabbed her around the waist and swung her in the air, only moments of stubbornness passing before she began to laugh vivaciously and forget her grievance.

He lowered her to the floor. "Happy birthday little one."

Charlize stretched her arms around his waist, attempting to join them behind his back, and peered upwards, her father's unshaven face smiling back.

"Shall we open your presents?" he asked.

Before she could respond, a strange surge ripped through her body and a dull pain pushed against her eyes as something escaped from them. Collapsing to the floor, she curled into a ball and closed them tightly, not daring to open them again.

Charras saw her eyes illuminate and dodged the strike just in time, the bolt darting past his shoulder to hit the stove, ironically, and smash the front door into tiny shards. Looking out of the kitchen window, he saw storm clouds gathered in the sky. Irritated he hadn't noticed them sooner, he walked over to shut the blinds, yelping as a cold hand gripped his ankle and sent a sharp shock to the bone. Bending down, he managed to peel his daughter's fingers from his limb.

"I'm sorry father!" she cried.

His flesh bubbled as the ice burn spread, and hobbling over to the sink, he grabbed a towel from the rack below it; ran the hot tap; soaked the towel in scalding water, and wrapped a makeshift dressing around his wound. Incendiī ran in his blood and the heat would heal.

When it was suitably numb, he made his way over to the bundle that was his daughter and leaned over her. "It's okay Charlize; you can open your eyes."

She shook her head.

"Open them," he coaxed warmly.

Lifting her head slowly and turning away from her father, she opened her eyes and blinked several times. With the floor inches from her nose, she choked out a sob.

Her father's hand appeared under her chin, but she refused to take it, instead sitting up with her back to him.

"It's your untamed power," he explained. "Elements you will learn to create and control. Today is special for you because it is your Awakening. This is the day when you recognize your power and learn how to use it." Pulling over a chair, he sat on it and sighed. "Do not be afraid of me, I will explain everything."

With deliberate effort, Charlize turned to face him, listening as he bore news she couldn't quite grasp.

"Over the next few years I will teach you all you need to know," he said. "I will teach you about our way of life, about being a Mage. We live in secret Charlize, and the world we inhabit is different to the modern day outside these walls, different through the eyes of the Ungifted we walk among. We protect those without power, for that is our duty, and it is our duty from birth."

Charras stopped when he noticed the bewilderment in his daughter's eyes, glistening with the threat of more tears. Holding out his arms, she clambered up from her sitting position and onto his lap. "You are not alone in this," he reassured, "although your purpose is unique. But I'll be here with you through it all, until the end."

Charlize sat gaping at her father, shocked and terrified by his words, but intrigued, infused with a fresh curiosity she'd not known before.

But to Charras, her reaction to the words he tried to put so delicately provoked a previously dormant realisation in him. The next years were not going to be easy, unlike those that had gone before. Charlize was no longer a child. She had much to learn.

In a moment of selfishness, he felt grateful. The coldest truth was yet to come, and he was not the one to tell it.

2

Awakening

Following the trauma of earlier, Charras trod lightly, hoping no more bursts of energy would surprise him. Luckily, Charlize maintained her calm and they washed and ate without mishap.

The afternoon did not continue in the same fashion however, much to Charras's chagrin. Charlize's newfound power caused her more distress than he first thought it would. Only the toaster, the stove, and a porcelain mug had befallen her untamed status, but the way she lamented the damage seemed otherwise. It took all of his reassurance to stop her grounding herself, and after what seemed like hours of apologies and bleeding fingers – Charlize having attempted to piece the mug back together – Charras retired to the library, managing to coax his despondent daughter to follow.

Once inside, her face quickly brightened as she saw her presents stacked on and next to his favourite chair. She produced a smile he thought he'd never see again and ran over; hurriedly sat down; crossed her legs, and blew on her fingers to extinguish the flames that had ignited. Then, gently wiping the ash from her nightdress, she ignored the look of concern on his face and gazed expectantly upwards.

"Are you ready?" he asked, holding her first present at a safe distance.

Nodding, the curiosity burning within her eyes, Charlize received the first red wrapped gift. She turned it over in her hands and tore the paper to reveal a puzzle box. She loved puzzles.

"Thank-you," she said, grinning widely.

Charras nodded, committing the delight she expressed to memory. Then, passing her the remaining items, he watched as she uncovered a stack of colouring pens; a new pair of shoes; a dress; a skipping rope, and a large dollhouse. With each item, her face grew redder and her excitement threatened to spill over. But he relished it. Content to sit reading while his ten-year-old played with the items of her dollhouse, enraptured by the miniature furniture, he wished it could be that way forever.

And yet slowly, as he knew it would, the weight of duty soon pressed on his shoulders, the dreaded moment unavoidable as its call prickled along his conscience.

With a deep breath, he reached behind him and pulled out the final present.

Charlize looked out from a bedroom window of her new toy and immediately noticed the package in her father's hand. He hadn't said a word, sitting composed and thoughtful as she crawled across the floor and positioned herself at his feet.

"Is that for me too?" she asked, meeting his gaze.

At first he didn't say anything, tightly holding onto what he seemed reluctant to give to her. Then, with deliberate effort, he handed her the gold wrapped item, resisting her pull only slightly.

With excited interest, she tore the paper hiding her gift and pulled out the contents, soon frowning with the disappointed recognition that it was a book.

Stroking the blood-red leather, ribbed and cool, she traced her fingers along the patterns and writing etched in gold, coming to rest on the title: 'Book of Becoming.'

"It's what you'll learn from," Charras explained. "I'm afraid your teachings start here."

Charlize didn't say a word, her curiosity piqued as she gently opened the book, its spine groaning as the pages parted. They were a deep cream, thick and smooth, and all of the words were of the same golden hue, faintly shining as she turned to the first page and read the inscription.

"This book belongs to the Āetis. If you are she, place your palm upon me. If in false faith, I will destruct until returned to thee."

Knitting her brow, Charlize looked up at her father for guidance. His expression remained unidentifiable, so she turned back to her book, the decision hers and hers alone. And yet, somehow, she knew there was no going back.

Suspending her hand above the page, a moment passed; an intake of breath; a pause… and then she brought it firmly down on the writing.

The book responded instantly, the words tingling beneath her palm, their brilliance prickling up and down her fingers as if they were scanning for verification.

"Father… look," she whispered, gasping as her hand began to glisten, the same gold as the text creeping up her wrist and along her arm.

She watched with fascination as her entire body ensconced the magic, her breath quickening and heart beating furiously as a previously dormant energy awakened within her.

It seemed to emphasise the blood pumping through her veins and arteries, blood that suddenly felt active – energised, and gliding into a standing position, her father towering above her as he led her to a chair opposite his own, he plied the book from her hands and placed it on the coffee table, waiting for the transition to end.

He didn't need to wait long. With laughter in her throat, the radiance soon dimmed and absorbed into her skin.

"I can feel it now," she said, her voice soft.

Charras smiled and leaned over to pick her book back up from the table. "Then let us read together," he said, opening it at the second page. "It will answer all of your questions."

She didn't acquiesce at first, unable to settle.

Still bonding with the energy, she was getting used to the freedom of the once suppressed power – a power she'd always had but been unaware of. It was strange to think she'd ever been without it, that the strength she felt so naturally used to sleep in her belly, a suppressed entity. She felt as if she'd aged several decades, not just awakened, but also transcended. It was a part of her – a recognised inner-soul – and she was a part of something so huge that she could barely comprehend it.

Time passed like a gentle wave, each wave readjusting her composure until she grew calm and still.

When she felt like herself again, she climbed onto her father's lap and began to read aloud, tracing the words with her index finger and causing them to glow beneath her touch.

Asking the meaning of words she didn't understand, or an explanation of a sentence that made no sense, she soon found herself engrossed in the world she was born, the origins of the Mages unfolding before her.

Every Mage had a book of their own, passed to them on their tenth birthday to ignite their Awakening. Full of stories, lessons, and spells, it explained a Mage's purpose, what it was they fought for, and most of all, what they fought against.

It was only when the doorbell rang, its harsh tones resonating through the library, Charlize jolted from her serenity. Her heart pounding against her chest, reality striking a fist in her stomach, she immediately felt on edge. She remained wary even when she slipped off her father's lap as he got up to greet their visitors. Having never left the manor or its grounds alone, her social skills were derelict. On the rare occasion's she'd defied her father's rule, usually in pursuit of animals, strange things always happened, and usually something dangerous. So she quickly learned that leaving unaccompanied was never a good idea.

With that in mind, she followed close at her father's heels as he entered the lobby and continued out into the foyer, reaching for the polished bronze handle of the front door and pulling it open. He looked out across the driveway, his gaze coming to rest on the figures stood at the bottom of the path behind the large iron gates. The smaller of the figures, a boy no older than Charlize, held his finger poised, hoping to press the bell once more. Not that it would sound, only alerting the manor's residents if they were in, and even then, only the rooms they occupied.

With no need to squint, Charras knew immediately who the visitors were. "Come!" he called. "You are welcome."

A protection spelled around the house momentarily disintegrated, allowing the visitors to open the gate and walk up the apple-tree lined path. Stopping to admire a collection of bare dwarf weeping willows set back from the stone, only the boy continued onwards, running to stand in front of Charras.

"Hello sir," he said, holding out his hand.

Impressed by his manners, Charras took the significantly smaller hand and shook it, surprised by the grip. When he let go, the boy offered the same to Charlize, who frowned and sunk further into the house, staring at him from behind her father's back.

The boy scrunched his face and crossed his arms before turning to his mother as she came to stand by his side.

"Christian, meet Charras and his daughter," she introduced.

Shooting a menacing look at Charlize, Christian flinched as his mother tapped his shoulder. "Apologise at once," she scolded. "I saw that."

Red faced, he lowered his head and mumbled a 'sorry', grimacing further as Charlize still said nothing, merely staring at him wide eyed.

He looked up at his mother, about to plead his case, but stopped when she shook her head. He immediately realised there was something 'different' about the girl – the same way his mother explained his neighbour's daughter Molly was 'different' when she cut off her own hair and glued it to her gerbil. Instantly relaxing, he thought nothing more of it as his father joined the group and lifted the mood instantly.

"Hello old friend," he greeted Charras. "Tell me, how long has it been?"

"Exactly a decade Theo," Charras replied warmly. "Come inside, it looks as if a storm is brewing."

He ushered them into the lobby and took their coats, hanging them in the closet and engaging in small talk as his guests admired the paintings. They declared their favourites after seconds of deliberation, Charlize glad to see Christian's mother liked the horse too. She didn't voice this though, content to hang back and remain a spectator while the adult's interacted. Her main interest was to find out why her father allowed them into the house in the first place – especially considering they didn't bring food or post.

"Charlize, come and meet Leanne and Theo, two very dear friends of mine," he said to her after a while, shepherding her so she stood in front of the strangers. "She's a little shy," he apologised, nudging her forward.

Leanne and Theo both smiled kindly and held out their hands for Charlize to shake. Tentatively, she did so one by one, as she'd seen her father do with Christian.

Then, with the formalities over, she stood back and attached herself to her father's shirt, avoiding eye contact with anything but the inhabitants of the paintings.

There was further idle chitchat before her father bent down and spun her to face him. "Take Christian upstairs to play. I'll be up in a while."

Taken aback, her stomach fluttered strangely, unused to her father wanting to be apart from her. "I don't know what to play."

"I'm sure you'll find something, please, do as you're told," Charras said.

Without watching, he heard his daughter skulk upstairs, an increasingly bemused Christian following behind.

Once out of sight, the adults turned to each other.

"She's grown somewhat in ten years," Theo said brightly. "She doesn't remember me yet, but she won't for some time. She will always stick in my mind though – make no mistake. When I sleep, I still dream of her birth. It was incredible."

"Yes, it was certainly eventful," Charras agreed. "Shall we sit down?" he offered, having no intention to relive a night he hadn't spoken of for ten years.

"That would be lovely," replied Leanne, spinning to enter the sitting room.

Quickly surveying her surroundings, admiring the familiar uniqueness, she secretly noted how little had changed since her last visit. Then, shifting her admiration to Charras, she saw that he hadn't changed much either. His muscular frame still caused a recurrent ripple to dance up her spine – an effect she'd experienced since they'd known each other. Intensity exuded from him, his olive skin matching his dark features and marking him as an obvious Incendiī-Anima Mage, the elements of fire and air a compliment to his physique and presence. Even so, he retained his awkwardness, a shyness that made him smooth his dark curls away from his face and balance precariously on the edge of the settee, as if ready to escape at a moment's notice.

"How are you Leanne?" he enquired, breaking off her stare.

A flush reached her pale cheeks as she collected herself. "I'm alright thanks, how are you though? It's her Awakening today is it not?"

Charras nodded in response, admiring his friend's wife and her strong features, recalling with sadness the last decade devoid of her company.

Age had graced her well, time allowing her to retain several attributes he remembered so well. Two streaks of white at the front of her blonde hair now sat at shoulder length, no longer reaching the base of her spine, while her full lips still imitated a smile even when her mouth relaxed. The rest was pure Fulgor, with typical dark eyes and pale skin, along with a personality infused with infectious optimism and positivity.

"You look well, even though it has been far too long since we last saw one another," he said.

"Indeed," Leanne agreed, "far too long." Then, suddenly noticing his bandaged ankle, she pointed at it with raised eyebrows.

Charras cleared his throat and shuffled on his perch. "Yes, a minor mishap. She's been sparking all morning."

Leanne leaned forward and checked the bandages. "You must be more careful, she could easily kill you, even at this age. She may only be ten, but her power is ferocious. Be careful not to frighten her."

"I can handle her."

"She is not Isalize; she does not yet have the control."

"She's already learning."

Theo stood, ending the dispute as he made towards the door.

"Where are you going?" Leanne asked, sitting back up.

"Is Christian safe?" He looked to his wife and then to Charras.

"The power is now active, she will not spark unless she has a scare," Charras assured his friend, ignoring his daughter's comparative to a ticking time bomb.

Theo instantly relaxed and sat back down. "I'm sure they're both having fun, Christian's temperament is calmer than even mine."

Charras chuckled. "I fear Charlize's is like my own also."

It doing nothing to ease his worry, Theo forced a smile nonetheless, rocking on his heels and silently promising to keep a more vigilant ear for any peculiar disturbances.

Minutes passed as the three of them sat in relative unease, until Charras suddenly jumped up and dashed out of the door. Heard clattering about in the kitchen for some time, he returned to the sitting room leaden with biscuits and a tray of tea.

"Apologies, I don't have visitors often," he said, placing the tray on the coffee table and counting out the accompaniments.

Running back to the kitchen to collect sugar and milk, he returned faster than before and clumsily put them next to the teapot, easing himself onto the settee and ardently gesturing for them to help themselves.

Leanne shot Theo a quick look, and then leaned forward as if to tell a secret. "Where are your mugs Charras?"

"Damn it," he cursed, stomping out to collect the chinaware.

Theo chuckled quietly, stifling his mirth as Leanne laid a quieting hand on his knee.

Appearing a few moments later, Charras handed them each a mug, waiting in the doorway to see if there was anything else he'd forgotten.

"Would you like one?" Leanne asked.

Placing his cup on the table, Charras settled himself back down as Leanne proceeded to make them each a drink, her conscience kindly ignoring the absence of a teaspoon.

When they each held a steaming mug, doubling up as a welcome distraction, they began to relax.

It wouldn't last long.

Words didn't come easily to Charras, the silences between polite chitchat serving as an excuse to take a sip from his mug. But he knew it was merely a thirst-quenching buffer, a satiating delay to conversation doomed to become awkward. For it was no coincidence his old companions chose to visit that day.

Ten years from the day of Charlize's birth had passed, ten years devoid of the company of his friends as they dutifully stayed away. It was a risk for Mages to know of the Āetis before their Awakening. Unprotected without their powers, therefore vulnerable to the threats the Mages fought, their whereabouts needed to stay a secret from those who wished them harm.

Hard but necessary, the sacrifice to their friendship confirmed his trust in them.

"Tell me why you are really here," he asked. "This day could have been any, I am sure you have not missed me so much a few days would have made a difference."

Theo shook his head, his smile hiding sadness. "Do not be so sure old friend. For one, it was nice to remember where you lived, like a light-switch as my memories of this place came back to me. There is so much we've wanted to tell you in the last ten years, but try as we might, we could never remember your whereabouts." Theo clasped his hands, his tone sombre. "The Marsh village is changing. The world outside this Arx is growing darker. Of course you have more than enough to contend with, with Charlize at home and the importance to her cause."

"Our cause," Charras corrected.

Theo and Leanne exchanged meaningful looks.

"No longer, as you know," Theo replied.

Sighing, Charras sank back into the cushions. "Then this is why you are here, to confirm your absence completely?"

Leanne pursed her lips and then shuffled forward slightly. "Remember at school when I was picked on by those nasty Ungifted girls for being different?"

Charras furrowed his brow. "I don't understand what that has to do with anything."

"Well," Leanne continued, "you and Isalize were my friends throughout school. You introduced me to Theo and you looked after me. I'll never forget the time those same girls cornered me for having white streaks in my hair, threatening to cut them off! It was Isalize who jumped in and scared them away."

"Please Leanne, your point?"

Huffing, she clasped her hands. "My *point* is, as friends we should stand by each other, whether we agree with the decisions each of us make or not."

"You are feeding your son to the wolves my friends. He'll be helpless. He won't be like the Ungifted, for he'll be unbecome, stripped of his birthright. His light will draw them and you will have left him defenceless."

Leanne shook her head as Theo held her hand. "Our son must be protected; he will have no part in this war. We have given him the chance to choose his own path."

Incredulous, his anger towards his friend's naivety seething within him, Charras balled his fists. "Too many Mages are turning from the cause; we cannot bury our heads in the sand, for eventually, our heads will be *theirs*. Pretending they do not exist only means they grow stronger."

"We will still fight," Theo assured him. "Christian will not. His ignorance will make sure of it. The war has not yet reached the Marsh Village Arx. It will be many more years until the protection around this area feels the full weight of breaches. Hopefully by then, Charlize will have ended this."

Leanne cooled the two Mages by placing her hands in the air as a sign of surrender. "Let us not argue. Charras, we can change the fate of our son, if you could do the same for Charlize, would you not try?"

Charras shrugged but did not answer, his pride hindering his admission.

"Of course you would," Theo answered for him. "We all would."

Standing from the settee, Charras paced the room. "It seems we have much to discuss tonight. Please, stay and let's eat."

Leanne smiled as the tension eased. "That sounds like a good idea."

3

Stormy Relations

Silence filled the room as Charlize and Christian sat on opposite sides of the bed, both staring at whatever wall faced them. Neither spoke to the other, Christian having given up once Charlize finished showing him her presents, refusing to let him play with any of them. Thinking it would be nice to read to him instead, she had tried to find her book – which had mysteriously gone missing after dinner – but to no avail.

So instead, they sat ignoring each other. Bored.

It caused Christian the most discomfort, unaccustomed to girls being quiet. The fact he couldn't make any sort of mess also disturbed him, forcing him to consider the kind of parent Charras was. One that didn't allow fun... that was for sure.

"Did you have a nice day then?" he said in another attempt to break the silence.

Charlize nodded, although continued to pick out patterns in her curtains. "He was reading me a story before you arrived."

Struggling to make eye contact, annoyed how she persistently looked away, Christian gave up. "Oh, well that's nice," he mumbled.

Her face hot, Charlize felt thoroughly overwhelmed by the strange boy in her room, wishing he'd leave and not come back, while Christian was utterly convinced she spent most of her life in a cupboard. Either that or she really was like Molly, even though she didn't randomly scream and throw things at him.

Deciding to test his theory, he let out a long sigh and stood up. Walking to the dresser and picking up a stack of colouring pens bound in elastic bands, he rummaged around and found a page of plain paper. Then, positioning himself on the floor, he flicked off the pen lids and drew the tips across the length of the sheet, the colours merging to cover the white with swirls and circles.

Throughout his undertaking, Charlize watched intently, Christian's creativity astounding her. When he finished, she gasped.

"That's beautiful!"

So, she wasn't like Molly, Christian thought. Molly would have been outraged if he touched her things, especially if she'd already said no.

Pondering this as he put the pen lids back on, he sat cross-legged. "Thanks," he said, watching as Charlize picked up the paper and traced her fingers along the colours. "Don't you draw pictures too?"

She passed him back his artwork and shrugged. "No, I write stuff," she said, certain her talents could never match his.

Dissolving into laughter, Christian found the concept strange. His parents always encouraged his creativity, hanging every drawing he gave them around the house, especially on the fridge. Why anyone would choose homework over painting seemed silly to him.

"What's so funny?" Charlize demanded, deciding that being laughed at was not something she enjoyed.

Unable to stifle his mirth, Christian put his hand over his mouth. He wasn't sure if it was because he spent the last two hours staring at a wall, or if being subjected to the boredom of Charlize had sent him crazy, but no matter what he tried, his face still turned red and his mouth still opened as hysteria racked his body.

In response, Charlize got up and put her hands on her hips. "My father told me I was special, you do not laugh at someone special!" she said hotly, baffled that for some reason, this only made him laugh harder.

"Stop it!" she shouted, pushing his shoulder and feeling instantly satisfied when he stopped making noise.

Immediately standing up, Christian straightened his back, noting that he was only slightly taller than she was. "My Dad says that everyone is special, no matter who they are." He puffed out his chest to reinforce the point.

"Well that's a lie. *I'm* a Mage."

"I don't even know what that is," he said with a scoff, although his chest deflated and he crossed his arms.

"We're –"

Grabbing her neck, Charlize began to splutter and cough, unable to force any more words out. A surge of fire scorched the back of her throat and she closed her mouth.

"Are you okay?" Christian asked, perturbed by how red her face had turned.

She shook her head and took a deep breath. "I… I can't tell you," she mumbled, rubbing her neck.

"You're weird."

Snapping her eyes towards him, her brow darkened. "And you're a nobody!" she yelled, making to push him once more.

"Don't!" Christian countered, shoving her instead.

Charlize missed the bed as a spark shot through her arm and she landed unnoticeably hard on the floor. Clambering up and shaking it out, a strange tingling fizzed through her nerves as she ran to the door, yanked it open, and hurriedly shut it behind her.

Before she took another step, a shout sounded from downstairs, freezing her to the spot. With a quick look at the closed door, confirming no pursuit was about to engage, she wondered why the manor had suddenly turned hostile. *Maybe father was right*, she thought. He always said strangers were dangerous.

With no desire to face Christian again, Charlize decided to figure out the source of the commotion. So tiptoeing her way towards the argument, keeping to the evening shadows as they masked her progression, she reached the stairs and slowly descended.

When she got to the bottom, she noticed that the only light available sprung from the glass of the sitting room door, and aiming towards it, snuck along the lobby walls and crouched just out of sight. From there, she was able to eavesdrop on the conversation within.

"It's ridiculous!" Charras shouted again.

"Calm down," Theo coaxed, trying to settle his fellow Mage as they stood nose to nose. But finding himself grabbed by the jumper and pulled closer, he knew the words fell on deaf ears.

"Did you learn nothing the night Isalize died?" Charras spat at his captive. "Did I not tell you a war is coming?"

"Calm your temper," said Leanne sternly, placing a hand on Charras's large shoulder.

Ignoring her request, he tightened his grip, his fiery gaze desperate. "My daughter needs all the help she can get."

A jolt stabbed along his arm, followed by the sensation of hot pins prickling through his muscles – a warning – and he instantly let go of Theo. Twisting his head to face Leanne, her eyes midnight black, he knew she would strike again if he gave her cause.

"Respect our choice Charras. You don't have to agree, but you need to respect it." Her voice shaky, she added, "Isalize would have."

"Do not speak of her."

Although he spoke sharply, his temper calmed and he dropped his hands, leading Leanne to do the same as her eyes returned to their normal brown.

Finding the settee and slumping back into it, he placed his head in his hands and took a few breaths, mumbling an apology as embarrassment replaced rage.

"Let me explain it to you calmly old friends," he said steadily, lowering his hands from his face. "She is the first female Āetis we've ever known. She will have prejudice against her, anger and betrayal in abundance. Do not be like those who will judge and fear her. Do not fuel their fires by joining them in keeping Christian away. Let him fight with her. You are my best friends, my family. Stand united with me." Gesturing for Leanne and Theo to take a seat, the friction in the sitting room heightened when they refused.

"You know nothing that is certain; we do not even know our own fates for sure. We have the power to change things if we want, twist them at least," Leanne said confidently. "Keeping my son away from our dangerous world is not to harm your daughter, but to keep him safe. It is our choice, as many Mage parents who have spent their lives fighting for freedom would agree. Our world hurts far more Mages than Ungifted. Is it so wrong to also protect those we love, not just the loved ones of others?"

Leanne knelt and rubbed Charras's hand, affectionately beseeching him. "I just want what's best for my son. I want him to grow up normally, to learn the ways of the world himself. I do not want him to follow a path already decided for him, especially not one where he suffers. I know that Charlize has no choice, but Christian does, and we want him to follow the path he carves out for himself."

A heavy ambience descended on the room, the atmosphere fraught with unsaid words, each knowing they would make no difference to the thoughts of the other.

Heaving himself from his malaise, Charras rubbed his eyes, the white slightly bloodshot with fatigue. "The war will come," he warned. "Every Mage must be prepared to fight."

Exasperated, Theo spoke next. "We've been fighting a war all of our lives. I will not burden my son with the unknown and the fear of it. He will make a choice based on what he believes to be true. And when, *if*, the time comes for him to fight, he will. But in the meantime, I want him to grow up in what relative peace we have left."

Charras knew it was hopeless. Getting up – dismissing the guards Leanne and Theo reactively put up – he walked over and stood by the bay window.

Outside, dark storm clouds loomed portentously in the sky. Watching them for a short while, he barely noticed as Leanne joined him, a gentle embrace closing around his waist as she nuzzled under his arm.

"Let us be friends again," she said. "Whatever happens, let us not lose each other. We made a promise remember?"

A rueful sigh escaped Charras's lips. "I do. But the promises of four sixteen year olds did not prepare us for this."

"Nevertheless," Theo piped up, coming to stand with them. "We've been through worse."

"Going against the teachings was once a risky game I could play, but no more," Charras replied. "However much I wish it otherwise."

"I know," said Theo. "And we will still fight alongside you and Charlize; trust us in that. It is only Christian who must be kept away."

"So you will go against the Sky itself?"

Nodding, Leanne looked past Charras to the elements beyond. "Maybe it's time someone did."

The lobby seemed darker as Charlize's heart raced. Her head full of nonsensical words, she left the haven of the wall and made her way back upstairs, the air a little chillier, the shadows somehow more suspicious.

Passing the window, she paused to touch the glass, troubled how it glimmered with a frost obscuring it completely. Wondering when the temperature dropped, she pressed her cheek against the cool pane and listened.

In the distance, a storm rumbled, still many miles away. She didn't know how she knew that, but even so, an ominous feeling turned in her stomach.

Peeling herself away, she ran to the end of the corridor and carefully opened her bedroom door, wary that Christian was still angry. But finding him sitting on her bed, his shoulders hunched and head drooped towards his stomach, she felt relieved and took a step into the room, standing a cautious pace inside.

"You come to push me again?" he asked miserably.

Charlize shook her head and softly said, "No, I've come to say sorry."

He turned to look her in the eye, and realising she was sincere, nodded his acceptance.

Charlize figured it was a good sign and walked to the foot of the bed. She waited for him to look up, but when he didn't, guessed it was because his chin was still heavy. So, instinctively lifting it, as her father did whenever she sulked, she probed his face with interest. Even though he frowned, he didn't push her away, his own intrigue matching hers as they distinguished the differences between each other.

He had the darkest brown eyes Charlize had ever seen, contrasting her bright blue, while his hair was the lightest blonde she'd ever seen, the soft waves thick and unruly, or as she suspected, un-brushed. Her own hair was a dark chocolate, and holding a few strands up to his fair eyebrows, she compared their colour. When that was determined, she dropped his chin and picked up his arm, holding her own against it and noting how her olive complexion seemed darker against his pale, almost dewy one.

"You haven't met many people have you?" Christian asked, worried the probing would never end.

"I have met a few, when father takes me out sometimes," she replied, giving him back his arm.

"Why not more?"

Shrugging, she lowered her eyes to the floor. "I don't really know."

Before Christian could say anything else, the door opened and they both jumped as if caught doing something naughty.

Leanne stepped into the room with a large smile adorning her face. "Have you had fun?" she asked, marginally concerned by their proximity.

Speechless, Charlize merely nodded, unable to look away from her father's friend, certain she was the most beautiful person she'd ever seen.

Planting a kiss on her son's cheek – which he wiped away furiously – Leanne turned to her admirer, staring back into the eyes regarding her so intently. She didn't want to see it, for it saddened her to do so, but the likeness was there, an undeniable fact – Isalize positively shining from the eyes of her daughter.

They wore the same expression, what she called Isalize's 'doe face', a face she made whenever she saw something that fascinated her, such as the first time she met Charras. The deep blue of her irises would sparkle and widen, and Leanne would hear of the subject for days until the obsession concluded.

A tugging on her sleeve stopped the lump forming in her throat and she found her voice. "Yes sweet heart?" she addressed her son.

"We're staying here aren't we?" he said, a frown forming on his brow.

Leanne ruffled his hair. "We adults have a lot to discuss. It's alright; Charlize will look after you, won't you dear?" She smiled at Charlize who nodded dumbly. "Wonderful. And your father tells me you can show Christian to a spare room?"

Charlize nodded again, words lost. Leanne exuded warmth, a promise of comfort, nurture, and a host of all other things she was sure her father instinctively lacked – a barrier between them that had existed for as long as she could remember. But Leanne was different, softer somehow. And it was only when she left, disappearing back downstairs, she snapped from her reverie.

"I'll show you to your room," she said to Christian, storming ahead and leaving him to trudge after her.

The room was two doors down from hers, past a painting of a rustic rocking chair that she swore sometimes moved, and before the creak that always got her in trouble, its loud groan a deafening signal when she was trying to sneak around.

Ignoring the painting as she passed, deciding not to scare Christian, but promising to catch it out next time, Charlize opened the door to her old room and turned on the light.

The bulb dim as it hung morosely above the familiar single bed, she waited for her eyes to adjust before clearing several past toys from the sheets, littering the floor with them instead.

"How did you know you were staying tonight?" she asked once finished, clapping her hands free of dust.

Christian shrugged. "I dunno. I'm a good guesser."

"Maybe you're psychic," she suggested, ushering him out of the room and back along the corridor.

Skipping down the stairs and waiting for him at the bottom, his reluctant footsteps soon joining her, she proceeded to knock on the sitting room door. The resulting bellow of her father bidding them to enter made her turn the handle, just as Leanne and Theo returned from the library. Their expressions initially downcast, they quickly lightened as Christian ran into their arms.

"I think it's time for bed little one," Leanne said, stroking his head as he buried it in her chest.

"But it's scary here," he mumbled.

Leanne and Theo smiled at each other. They were aware of the lingering presences, the marks of Mage's past carved into the æther. The walls had memories, whispers of history, and their son was Fulgor; of course he could to sense their remnants – Fulgor were closer connected to the æther than the other clans.

Readjusting Christian so he faced her, Leanne bent down and cupped his chin, their eyes locking. "Tell me what could hurt you while we are here?"

"Only my mind's bad intentions and my made up inventions," he replied with a smirk.

Leanne tapped his nose. "Precisely."

"And cats," Charlize chimed in, her hand still clutching the door handle. "Cats come into the house and attack you sometimes. We don't know how they get in though." Almost falling through the door as it swung open, her father loomed above her, his expression cautionary.

"That's quite enough."

"But it's true."

"I said, *enough*."

Charlize's eyes flashed and she crossed her arms. "Fine. Goodnight father, I hope you sleep well."

Swinging on her heels so her entire back turned from him, she met the amused expression of Leanne. Their eyes connected and she instantly felt that she understood. Her dark gaze possessed the ability to penetrate her, read parts of her that she didn't even know she wanted to share. Leanne saw her, really saw her, as if nothing separated their minds, and somehow, Charlize knew that she impressed her, that she reminded her of someone very dear.

A hand on Leanne's shoulder snapped their connection, leaving Charlize a little dazed, and when she looked up, she saw that Theo offered the distraction. He tilted his head to Leanne's temple and she closed her eyes, a brief exchange of affection, although enough for Charlize to know that whatever Leanne had seen greatly upset her.

"It was nice to meet you," she ventured, holding out her hand.

Laughing, but not unkindly, Leanne bent down so Charlize's face was inches from hers. "Goodnight sweetheart," she said, pulling her into an embrace and planting a warm kiss on her cheek.

It was an unusual moment for Charlize, having little experience in the way of overt affection. Directing a quick glance at her father to see what he made of it, he appeared quite contented, causing her to wonder why he'd never done the same. Reasoning that his friends might just be the odd sort, she found herself shifted into Theo's embrace, although he didn't offer the kiss she expected.

She quickly deduced it must be something only girls did, and curtsying once before leaving the sitting room, she beckoned for Christian to follow and proceeded to lead him into the bathroom. There, she found and passed him a spare toothbrush and they both cleaned their teeth and washed their faces, briefly laughing as cotton from fresh towels stuck to their damp cheeks.

"It was like a Grandpa beard," Christian surmised as Charlize walked him back upstairs and towards their respective bedrooms.

They reached hers first, and turning to say goodnight, she hugged him and clumsily kissed his cheek before disappearing into her room and shutting the door.

Christian stood there for longer than he should have, blindly staring ahead and wondering how he'd managed his first kiss without saying a word.

4

Vrealâ

Lightning sounded and Charlize awoke with a fright. Hugging the duvet to her chin, she let the quilt protect her, and roving her eyes around the room in an attempt to make sense of the shadows, she yelped as her door opened and a small figure entered.

"Are you okay?" the voice of Christian whispered.

He walked towards her bed, his hands outstretched, and Charlize noticed that his skin took on a vague glow, enabling her to see him in the dark.

Another crash sounded outside and she jumped a little, hurriedly patting her bed and shuffling over so Christian could climb in with her. He wasted no time, tucking the sheets around him as he sat bolt upright, arm linked with Charlize's as they both stared at the closed window, each sensing a violent storm and fearing it.

"It's close," Charlize murmured, her tone amplified in the dark.

Christian knew it too. He'd never dreaded something like it before, intuition telling him the storm was dangerous, but his senses offering no further insight than that. So, slipping off the bed, he bravely walked towards the window.

"Christian… don't…" warned Charlize, her voice worried. But he ignored her, taking a breath and pulling the curtains aside.

Peering into the gathering storm, he looked beyond the boundaries of the manor. Lightning flashed high in the sky, sharp bolts striking the ground and churning the earth into sludge and clay. Angry, it seemed intent to cause damage, although Christian quickly noticed that the elements didn't touch the grounds within the gates, as if an invisible barrier stopped them from coming too close.

He stood mesmerised, watching and waiting for some climatic event to reveal itself, wondering which would win: the storm or the protectors of the manor…

Charlize must have thought it too, for she joined him a few moments later, her presence welcome as they watched the battle rage together. At one point, they clasped hands without realising – an instinctive comfort; their innocence unclouded; their bond unchallenged. They stood and knew that the storm wasn't natural, that something threatened their safety, and that they knew all of it without a single lesson.

A particularly intense rumble of thunder drew their attention, the lightning that followed suddenly turning and hurtling towards the window, and they both automatically dropped to the floor, tense as they waited for the bolt to crash through.

Yet nothing happened.

Charlize was the first to lift her head, reaching out and shaking Christian. "It can't get us," she whispered.

Without a word, he stood up and brusquely shut the curtains, blocking out the violent elements. Then, pulling Charlize to her feet, he dragged her back to the bed and drew the warm sheets around them both.

"Shall we get our parents?" he suggested when their hearts resumed a normal beat.

Lifting her head only slightly, Charlize listened as the distant rain hammered like an unsynchronised drum beat, calling to her from behind the curtains. "No. Let's wait," she decided.

Christian wasn't sure of the hour when he woke, only aware of the fear clenched in his gut. Wrestling with the sheets, he managed to kick them off and roll onto the floor after them, a short struggle ensuing before he clambered up and scanned the room.

His fears confirmed, he darted towards the bedroom door and flung it open, wildly sprinting across the hallway and banging on every door he passed. He only stopped when he reached the window.

Ice blocked the glass, the dark haze proving that whatever presence raged outside the boundaries had finally broken through.

Panic rose in his throat, and spinning on his heels, he bolted down the stairs, skidding at the foot and barely catching the banister to stop his fall. Righting himself, he continued through the lobby, under the arch, and into the kitchen – darkness enveloping him like an old friend. The shadows hid him from sight, and as his eyes adjusted, he saw an open door ahead of him. It let in the chill of the night, the cold wrapping itself around his ankles and coaxing him forward.

He didn't know where he was or how he knew to get there, only aware of his footsteps as they echoed in his ears, nothing but adrenaline fuelling his bravery as he reached the door and curled his fingers around the frame.

With a breath, he peered into the unknown.

The storm that seemed ferocious before now held nothing in comparison. It was as if the very Sky itself was at war, the chaotic storm clouds twisting and crashing into one another, rolling overhead like a blanket of trepidation. Watching in awe, Christian felt overwhelmed, a mere ant beneath the vast sky looming above.

Flashes of lightning darted within the matter, highlighting the huge raindrops charging to the earth, and another flash burst, illuminating the sky as a rogue bolt suddenly changed direction and pummelled to the ground instead. It exploded behind a static set of headstones, drawing Christian's attention and forcing him to witness the destruction created in its wake.

Ravaged, the gardens resembled a marshland, the once sombre headstones now lying shattered or upturned. Amongst the rubble, a patch of white lay inches from where the bolt struck – an oddity within the mud soaked surroundings – and when Christian looked harder, he realised it was Charlize.

Hunched on all fours, motionless and drenched, she didn't seem concerned with the bedlam around her, staring intently at whatever lay beneath.

Christian's worry quickly turned to fear. One way or another, he needed to get her back into the manor – that was his only purpose. He had to ignore the alarm bells ringing in his head, ignore the peril he faced, and ignore his sheer helplessness against the might before him.

Decided, he clenched his fists and stepped into the storm.

The noise, somehow muffled within the manor walls, suddenly erupted in his ears outside the haven of the kitchen. The wind howled and shrieked, taking his breath with it as he curled into a foetal ball, no match for the elements as his thin blue pyjamas quickly soaked to his skin.

He knew he was under attack, as if the storm knew he was there, warning him to retreat. But he refused to listen, instead fighting to keep air in his lungs as he got to his feet and pushed forward, the mud oozing between his toes wet and cold.

Shielding his eyes, just able to pick out the white in the darkness, he tried to call out, but the wind carried his voice away; so he cupped his hands over his mouth, withstanding the vigour of air as it ruffled his hair into a frenzied mound. Still he refused to budge. Even as the rain continually pounded the earth he stood upon, and even as it changed tact, easing off and turning into snow, he stood firm. There was no going back now.

As the soft flakes fell onto his skin, Christian hugged his shoulders, shivering beneath their cold kisses. Through the drift, he realised the slower fall gave him a better view of Charlize, and looking towards her, he could finally see what held her attention. A new chill shot through his spine, and he had no time to react as a voice called to him in the distance, the source from the direction of the kitchen – the door he'd just come from. Swinging around, he managed to make out his mother's face, bright and full of concern. She was yelling something, but he couldn't hear her through the clamour.

He chose to ignore her and turn back to Charlize, holding his hands in front of his face as he pushed through the curtain of snow. It quickly changed to hail, the aggressive chunks slicing at his body and scratching at his cheeks, causing him to stumble and fall.

Only determination to save his new friend drove him onwards.

"Come back!" he called, his voice audible this time.

A slight shudder rippled through Charlize's torso, although she remained lost in whatever held her absorption, fixated on the dirt beneath as if she could see the corpse below.

Christian reached her moments later, bending down so his face was level with hers. "Charlize?" he said again, wiping his stinging cheek and flinching as his sleeve drew blood.

She suddenly snapped her head up, sniffing the air, and then slowly turned her head so their eyes locked.

She smiled. "Foolish boy, very foolish."

Realising it wasn't Charlize who spoke, Christian's heart plunged to his stomach. "Wh…who are you?" he stammered, unable to animate his limbs.

Her eyes flicked across his face, searching the dread spread across it. "My name is Vrealâ," she replied, the words hissing in his ears, "a name worthy – a name born. Isalize is no more, a mere parasite, a name worthless of the Minae."

Evil dwelled within her; Christian could see that, her eyes colder than the air around them. Without knowing how, he forced himself to stand and back away from the demon.

Charlize also stood, her limbs awkward and twisted as her body jerked forward. "Where are you going?!" she screeched into the storm.

A mocking laugh carried on the wind, following Christian as he ran. The rain returned and slammed to the ground harder than before, although he couldn't help but notice it eased where his footsteps landed, even as the darkness drew closer. With a quick glance over his shoulder, he saw the stationary figure of Charlize, waiting like a ghostly apparition in the incessant downpour. He pushed onwards, running through the churned mud of the manor grounds, aiming for his mother and the protection she promised.

It wasn't long until the kitchen doorway emerged before him and he saw her on her knees. She was clutching her hands to her heart, her face worried as she searched for him. Behind her, his father crouched so he could secure a grip on her shoulder, while Charras towered above them both, his large bulk filling most of the remaining space.

Quickly, their silhouettes became more distinct – Christian's tireless run paying off as they noticed him and began shouting, although he still couldn't hear what they said. Driving his limbs harder, he reached outwards, almost there, his mother's open arms torturously close, and with one last leap, slammed against a force and collapsed backwards in the mud.

He lay there for a moment, disorientated, until the cries of his fretful mother forced him to pick himself up and brush himself down. Then, slowly, he walked towards the door and placed his hands on the area denying his safety. Sensations of cold, strong air resisted his touch, driving him backwards, and in a moment of terrifying clarity, he realised he wasn't being allowed to enter.

"Mum?" he said, his eyes wide.

Looking into her face, Christian saw unadulterated fear. He pounded his fists frantically, only to continuously meet with friction, and eventually held them still.

"Let me in!" he pleaded, "Why won't you help me?!"

Tears fell down Leanne's face as she watched her son. "Sweetheart, I can't, I'm sorry," she uttered, mirroring her hands on his. "You have to run now. Run as far away as you can. We will find you."

Taking a step back, Christian felt a well of betrayal manifest in his gut. Leanne stood too, a sudden urgency in her eyes.

"Run!" she shrieked.

With the hairs on the back of his neck prickling, Christian turned around.

On her hands and knees, Charlize crawled towards him, a slight grin on her face as she edged closer to where he stood.

"No more running," she warned, before folding to the ground.

Christian watched in horror as she landed face down in the mud. Starting towards her, he stopped in his tracks as she flipped onto her back and screamed – a blood curdling sound that made him cover his ears. She twisted in pain, her body heaving and shaking as she scratched at the mud and grass around her. Then, abruptly sitting up, she stared straight into his eyes.

An internal struggle ensued as she fought to maintain eye contact, fighting the urge to give herself to whatever writhed within her, and without thinking, Christian ran forward, skidding on the grass and landing on his hands and knees for the second time that night. As he lifted his head, he let out a choked scream and spat the muddy water from his mouth.

Above Charlize, a hazy shadow coiled and swirled like steam evaporating from her skin. It forced her body to rise with it, and suspended in mid-air, seconds passed before it broke free, leaving her to fall back to the ground with a sickening *thud*.

Immobile where he cowered, Christian stared at the mist as it developed features, the first a pair of ice blue irises that perforated the darkness, the cornea pallid as threads of red veins knotted the white. Below, a fissure materialised where a mouth should be, emitting such a hunger that Christian lay mesmerised, knowing the deadly vacuum would swallow him if he strayed too close.

Taking on corporeal form and stretching out her bald elongated limbs, Vrealâ shook her head and let out a shriek of delight. "Now, to finish this," she said in a voice that almost sang the words – at odds with her appearance.

Moving to where Charlize lay, she bent down and pushed her pitilessly. Then, looking up to the Sky, raised her arms. "I walk!" she screeched, "fear me now, for you will soon know the reasons I exist!"

The storm clouds growled as if in answer and Vrealâ smiled, her mouth a sinister hole of glee. She glared at Charlize and then back to the sky, holding an arm outwards and pointing a talon at her prey. "Let me show you."

The threat rang hard and sweet in Christian's head and he clambered to his feet. Launching himself towards Charlize, a blind concern for her safety discarding any notion of retreat, he ran through the everlasting storm and neared where she lay. He ignored Vrealâ towering above her. He didn't even notice her turn as he approached, only realising as she took hold of his throat and hurled him back to the earth without a hint of exertion.

"Very *very* foolish boy," the demon sang, pointing back at Charlize and mumbling words beneath her breath.

Overhead, the sky ignited and a thunderbolt impaled the dirt inches from where she stood. Vrealâ jerked her head upwards, watching as the storm leered menacingly, and bared her toothless mouth. Then, sweeping her hand upwards in a gesture of power, the rain gathered in a torrential stream, curling from her feet and up the length of her mass. Once it reached her head, she disappeared, leaving the water to fall back to the earth.

Christian stared at the spot she'd just been, disbelieving, and then up at the sky to watch the clouds swirl above him. Lightning danced within the vapours, zigzagging in rebellious pattern's as they loomed uncontrolled and turbulent. Thunder rumbled, echoing through the air as its foreboding tone rebounded through the skies, and suddenly Christian knew, a realisation thumping him in the stomach as he struggled to his feet, ran to where Charlize lay, and grabbed her arms. He tugged her towards the manor, attempting to pull her to safety, and as the thunder deepened – a warning, he somehow realised the only option left to him.

Without wasting a moment, he arched his body so it protected Charlize's and turned his head to face the Sky.

It wasn't long, a mere moment before a hole opened within the mass and the ferocity of lightning prepared its attack. Christian knew it was too late to save them both, yet he also knew he'd take the assault better. So, holding his free hand towards the Sky and gripping Charlize's with the other, he cried out as the bolt, dazzling and fierce, broke from the chains of the storm and hurtled towards them.

His outstretched hand received the strike, sending him careering through the air to land on the grass several paces away. With his senses blurred and the distant screams of his mother distorted in his ears, immense nausea washed over him and he gave into the urge to die quickly.

5

Sparked

The kitchen was soundless. Only the ticking of a clock passed any notion of time, its lonely drum a bleak reminder of the minutes that passed.

Dying down to nothing more than a bitter wind, the storm no longer waged, the devastation left in its wake the only proof it ever occurred.

Charras sat at the table with his head in his hands, while Leanne and Theo hunched solemnly opposite. Silent in their grief, they each absorbed the shock, repeatedly replaying the horrific events in their minds. Each time they tried to find a different outcome. But whatever conclusion they reached, the facts remained. Broken and bloodied, their children lay lifeless in the library, a protection spell weaving gravely around their dirtied bodies, while the warm leather chairs masked their cooling skin.

Charras lifted his head from the table, his sadness radiating in the deathly quiet. "I need to reinforce the protection spell," he said, standing. "It was broken…"

Leanne touched his hand. "It can wait; first we must finish the rituals." Turning away in her sadness, she clutched her chest as deep sobs racked her body.

Anguish flared in Charras's expression and he too turned away, striding over to the kitchen door. He gazed out to where they'd run moments before, racing across the wet grass and mud to the bodies of their children. Once again, he saw Charlize's pale face as he gathered her weightlessly in his arms and carried her back inside. Every step was strained, fretful, and acutely aware that the bundles they held were dead.

"The doors, this was planned," Theo said, intruding his thoughts. "Isalize –"

Cut short by Charras grabbing his shirt and pinning him against the back of his chair, he held his hands up in defence.

"Don't you dare say it," Charras warned.

"I'll say it," said Leanne, standing so her mouth was inches from his ear. "She's been taken by *him*, she's being used by *him*. *He* has waited for her this entire time."

"Shut-up," Charras growled, tightening his grip on Theo.

Leanne didn't listen. "You know what Isalize was, you know how strong, you know how valuable she'd be, *his* prized possession."

"She changed."

Letting out a bitter laugh, Leanne wiped her face. "She buried her potential, yes, but only for you, only so she could have you. That darkness was still in there."

"You're wrong."

"Our children would say differently."

"Enough!" Theo bellowed, pushing Charras away. Holding his arms between both heated Mages, he took a few breaths. "Please... We must not fight each other; we must be united in this."

Waiting a few moments, he dropped his arms.

Charras put his head in his hands and bit his lip, and bowing her head, Leanne held onto her husband's arm. "You're right, we shouldn't fight, but we have to face the truth."

"Isalize would never kill her own child," insisted Charras, his voice hoarse.

Shaking her head, Leanne sat back down. "Not the part he isn't interested in, but you have to accept that Isalize –"

"Is Inferus-Malus's dead hand?" The name drew cold into the room and Charras immediately regretted saying it.

Rubbing his throat, Theo spoke carefully. "The evidence is undeniable. This is the end. She walks, and the only person capable of destroying her lies in the other room with my son. We need to warn our communities, send word out to all who'll hear it. The Āetis is dead."

"No," Charras uttered, his body shaking.

"We must –"

"No."

Leanne squeezed her eyes and wiped her face before standing to embrace Charras, putting her cheek to his. "It's over," she whispered.

"No," he said again, pushing her away and pacing the kitchen, clasping and unclasping his hands. "Why did it take ten years for her to materialise? Am I the only one who saw the essence rise from Charlize?" He paused to look at his friends. "How long has this been planned by *him*?"

"How can we answer that?" said Leanne, her face taut. "It wasn't supposed to happen like this, it is not what we foresaw."

"Nothing is certain," Charras spat bitterly – "just another clause to the duty of a Mage. Live in a constant state of vagueness."

Disappearing into his dark thoughts, he remembered the white matter twisting off Charlize as she hovered in the air; he remembered the hours spent keeping her from her from Isalize's grave, fearing the dark effect it could have. Each a disconnected memory, but he knew they held answers.

"Charras," said Leanne softly. "Come, we have pressing matters to attend to. We must –"

"We must find out the reasons for this night! Why Charlize was killed before she could destroy those she was destined to!"

"My son took the bolt," said Theo sharply, "after he tried to save her."

"He merely got in the way and killed them both."

Hurt flashed across his friend's faces and Charras was instantly sorry for his outburst. Shaking his head, he sank down next to Leanne.

Her eyes swollen and haunted, he closed her in an embrace. "I'm sorry," he murmured. "He was brave; there was nothing he could have done. Rogue magic is impossible to predict."

Nodding, Leanne faced Charras. "This is why we wanted him away from our world." Her eyes empty, she stood once more. "We must send their spirits before it's too late. The rituals must be done."

Without another word, she vacated the kitchen, leaving Charras and Theo with no choice but to follow.

They entered the library, its dim light disappearing behind the endless bookcases, and Leanne turned on the lamp between the protected children before turning to observe her son. His bloodied face bruised and dirtied, she covered her mouth with a quivering hand and stroked the matted hair from his forehead. Theo immediately crossed the room to embrace her, gathering her in his arms and stroking her hair as she buried her face in his neck.

Charras watched them for a short while, realising he'd forgotten what two people in love looked like. It was odd, how grief brought people closer. The bonds that tied them seemed unbreakable, even at their most fragile. But their love always had been effortless – unlike his and Isalize's...

He lowered his gaze, knowing he couldn't put it off any longer. His brow heavy, he approached Charlize, towering above her as she lay limp and cold on the chair. Although the mud distorted her considerably, she seemed peaceful, and taken back to the night of her birth, when she lay sleeping in her mother's arms, he'd imagined then that Isalize would open her eyes at any moment.

Ten years had passed, a decade gone and still Isalize's eyes remained closed. So he found it odd that he thought the same now, that somehow Charlize would wake from whatever slumber had taken hold. He never could comprehend death, even though his duties revolved around it, and with a breath, he reached out and placed his hand on his daughter's forehead.

Closing his eyes, he searched with his mind, feeling along the edges of her broken spirit. It felt like shredded paper, disconnected fragments that had once been whole. He knew he had to draw it out, but the minute that realisation entered his head he recoiled, losing the nerve to touch it. Instead, he listened to the racing thud of his heart, rendering him incapable as he tried to calm his breathing.

"That's enough now," Leanne said, her face wet. "Leave me to finish this."

"I can do it," said Charras, searching for his daughter's pulse, hoping to find a reason to wait. Quickly becoming desperate, he repeatedly checked for a sign; a breath; a murmur – injuries that proved to be false. But each time he found nothing.

Wringing his hands together, he took another breath and squeezed his eyes shut. When he opened them, he allowed Theo to guide him from the room, leaving Leanne to perform the duty of their birthright. She knew he didn't have the strength and he was grateful for it.

Closing the library door, its aged oak creaking upon its hinges, time almost slowed as the metal locked together, sealing both father's outside. It was almost exactly as the click sounded a small spark erupted in Charras's gut. He exchanged anxious glances with Theo, who'd felt the same, and the two men froze. Through the silent anticipation, they eagerly awaited another sign, praying that their imaginations weren't playing twisted tricks.

Then, suddenly, as it seemed their fears were correct, a flicker of life erupted in the pit of their stomachs. Sprinting back into the library, almost breaking the door handle in their urgency, the two men fell over one another, landing in a heap on the floor.

Leanne laughed through her tears as she rocked Christian in her arms. "They're alive," she mouthed in astonishment.

"But how?" Theo asked, gaping in wonder towards the sleeping children.

"They're being protected," Charras said surely. "The Sky…" Trailing off, he bounded over to the chair protecting Charlize and scooped her up. Cradling her in his arms, he kissed her forehead and smeared some of the dirt. When she stirred, it took all of his effort not to shout out.

"It's okay, I've got you," he whispered, replacing her on the chair where the enchantments could heal her. Then, turning to his friends, he said, "We must let them sleep. Come, we need a drink."

They checked the protections several times before they left, the three parents searching and testing for any weakness – up until they resolutely confirmed their security. And upon doing so, vacated the library and shut the door behind them, all smiles as they breathed in the air of the lobby.

Hand in hand, Leanne and Theo put their backs to the wall and sank to the floor, while Charras disappeared into the kitchen and returned with three glasses and a bottle of whiskey.

They sat for some time without saying a word, enjoying the beating of life in their hearts and stomachs. The manor groaned as it settled for the night, the thuds and sighs disturbing enough to keep them alert. But as the malt worked its way through their blood, they slowly found themselves relaxing.

"Our plans remain the same Charras," Theo said after some time. "He will not become a Mage, this night makes that final."

"They are connected," Charras replied. "It is not that easy."

Leanne rested her head on her husband's shoulder. "He's right," she said softly. "Let them be friends, no more."

Charras reached over and squeezed Leanne's arm. "A compromise at least, thank-you."

"I fear it is their connection where the problem lies," Theo said, rubbing his temple with his free hand.

Leanne hushed him. "You know as well as I do that running away will not solve this. They will find each other somehow, and the circumstances may not be as amicable if we have no part in it. Perhaps if we learn their importance to one another we can prevent it." She entwined her fingers in his. "We will find a way."

Charras said nothing as he rest his head against the wall, the conversation between Leanne and Theo knowledge he wasn't privy to. He didn't wish to pry, only caring that whatever their reasons, he and Charlize would have them around. For that alone he was grateful. Then, snorting with amusement towards his own thoughts, he beamed at his companions.

"What is it Charras?" Leanne asked, the corners of her mouth involuntarily tilting upwards.

"Nothing is certain old friends."

The library was warm as the children slept. Outside, their parents sat slumped against the wall, empty tumblers in their limp hands as they dozed deeply. They would stay there and guard the entrance until morning.

Inside, as the dark rest softly, like a blanket waiting to be pulled off at dawn, it masked the faces of the sleeping children. Only the boy opening his eyes disturbed it, a yellow glow emanating from his pupils as his gaze gently lit the girl's face opposite him. It highlighted her peaceful slumber, and satisfied with her safety, he closed his eyes once more.

Only the moon caught the smile that creased his mouth.

6

Womankind

Charlize woke from the midst of a nightmare. Sitting up, she clutched her heart as it pounded furiously. *It was just a dream* she told herself, rubbing her chest as she looked around her bedroom. Warm against the autumn backdrop, she focused on the light filtering through the break in her curtains. It immediately calmed her, and leaning forward on her elbows, she brushed the hair off her face. *You have to stop this* she scolded herself, although the slowing of her heart was a welcome result.

Nightmares had been a common occurrence throughout her life – to varying degrees. But even so, their effect never failed to take her by surprise. Sometimes, she would wake so drenched in sweat, she could have sworn that she'd run the length of the Marsh, while at other times, she'd wake up in different parts of the manor with no recollection of how she got there.

She shifted her gaze to stare at the paintings hanging on the walls. They depicted landscapes of valleys; rainforests; mountains, and hillside blooms – recently the more gripping since her father promised she would one day see the beauty they captured.

Living in a countryside village, the sites were limited. Her integration into society had not been vast and she shied away from the company of others, finding them strange and difficult to talk to. It became so that even in the streets of her homeland, she was an outcast to those who did not know her secret identity. She cared little however, knowing one day it would be time to say good-bye anyway.

A bird chirping caught her attention and Charlize stretched, yawned once, and threw the sheets from her lap. Climbing out of bed, she vaguely caught her reflection in the full-length mirror, only stopping for a closer inspection as she noticed a patch of blood on her nightgown. Rolling her eyes, she ran downstairs to use the large bathroom.

Leanne had explained the cause of the bleeding to her months before – a concept she found horrifying, and recalling the embarrassing shopping trip she'd endured – her father having recoiled at the very idea, she pulled open the small drawer next to the lavatory. It held the necessities she needed.

Half an hour later, she emerged from the bathroom, shaken but satisfied with her first attempt. Showering had helped, and wrapped snugly in a towel, she decided that it really wasn't a big deal. In fact, there was nothing to it, and she allowed herself a smug smile as she made her way back upstairs.

Reaching her room, she opened the door gently, glad the hinges made little noise due to their recent oiling. She hoped her father hadn't heard, his prying an unfavourable habit at the best of times. His intentions, although always through concern, often left her feeling inadequate and adolescent. And in this instance, she was quite sure she could handle herself well enough.

With that thought in her mind, Charlize pulled on a white shirt and a pair of black leggings, finishing it with a green wool jumper that complimented her skin. She ran a brush through her long waves to smooth out the knots and idly noted a few blemishes that added a red tinge to her complexion. Home schooling had given her the basic knowledge to know it was hormones, and Leanne had assured her they would disappear once she got older. The truth was: she didn't care. Her appearance mattered little to her considering the reasons she existed in the first place.

Even so, she appeased Leanne's assumptions of her vanity, her influence the only maternal nurture she had. And that, coupled with her ability to keep her father in check meant they'd grown quite close.

Leaving her room in less of a hurry, she descended into the lobby, slipped her feet into a pair of slippers, and walked through to the kitchen. Her father was already there and humming jauntily to himself, his state of wakefulness before midday an unusual occurrence.

"Good morning," she greeted.

Charras turned from what he was doing. "Good morning Charlize, how do you feel?"

Her cheeks flushed. "I feel fine, thank-you." She peered over his shoulder at his attempt to make breakfast and added, "What are you trying to cook?"

Gazing down at the pan of scrambled eggs, Charras stirred the yellow slosh a little more. "Can't you tell?"

"Father, you hardly ever cook, why now?"

"Your suspicion offends me, you should be pleased," he said.

"It depends," said Charlize flatly. "Why are you cooking?"

"We have many things to discuss and celebrate today. I thought you would be pleased, have you not seen yet?"

Aghast, Charlize stormed from his glare and sat at the table, staring at the wall as she composed herself.

"I'll take that as a yes," Charras said, hiding his hurt as he took the scrambled eggs off the hob and separated them onto two plates. "Enjoy," he mumbled, placing one in front of her.

Charlize poked the soggy attempt with her fork. "I'll get the toast," she said, jumping up to grab the slices from the toaster.

She buttered both slices and passed one to her father, all the while avoiding his increasingly puzzled gaze. Able to hear the wind knocking a branch against the window, it served as the only interruption until they cleared their plates, when she thanked him, hurriedly wiped her mouth, and disappeared into the sitting room.

Left to put the dishes in the sink, Charras pondered his next actions, unsure of the appropriate behaviour when such events took place. Deciding to ring for help, he picked up the kitchen handset and dialled the familiar number long committed to memory. It rang three times before Leanne answered, her cheery voice resonating down the phone.

"Hel... *hold on Theo I'm on the phone...* Hello?"

Charras cleared his throat. "Leanne, it's me. Sorry to bother you but –"

"Hello Charras! How are you?"

"Fine… thank-you," he replied. "It's Charlize. Things started well, but she's quickly become hostile."

"Not everything is because of her blood, she's a teenager."

"Even so, I think she needs to talk to you," he said.

There was a pause before Leanne said with a titter, "Well put her on then!"

Feeling foolish, Charras called Charlize. After a few seconds, she emerged from the sitting room and dragged her feet into the kitchen.

"It's Leanne," he told her left cheek.

She perked up marginally and uncrossed her arms to take the phone, staring at him for a few moments until he understood he had to leave.

"Teenagers indeed…" he grumbled.

A soft breeze tickled the back of Charras's neck, contenting him as he sat reading. The windows were open and the presence of his daughter had been lurking outside for some time.

Once she hung up the phone to Leanne, he had given her the broach she'd been so suspicious of, allowing her some privacy as she opened the parcel and read the letter inside.

Passing it over had been hard, the gut wrenching reminder that Isalize was not there to do it herself fresh in his thoughts. The only heirloom she owned, she wanted Charlize to have it once she finished her initial teachings. Heavily pregnant at the time, she wept silently as she wrapped it in gold leaf – the same way she received it from the mother she'd also never met – and kissed the package before placing it in Charlize's cot.

Charras drove the memory away and put his book down, turning to the door. It was obvious his stubborn child debated whether to enter or not, her shadow loitering beyond the glass, and clasping his hands together, he waited for the outcome of her indecision.

The battle finally won a few moments later, she entered the library and sat in the chair opposite, avoiding his gaze by adamantly staring out of the window behind his head.

After a moment of painful quiet, Charras leaned back in his chair and sighed. "I did not realise your situation," he said apologetically.

"You are not a woman, so you would not know my situation all that well," Charlize replied.

"I see Leanne has educated you appropriately. Is everything… alright now?"

Grimacing, Charlize nodded. "Everything is fine father, thank-you for asking."

The flush of her cheeks was enough for Charras to know the conversation had ended. Glad of it, he allowed himself to acknowledge her maturity, puberty achieving its intention. No longer a young child who required protection, at thirteen, she was already becoming a woman. Frightfully similar to her mother, the same strength and determination burned within her, her innocence lost the minute she discovered her purpose. To those who did not know, youth would deny her power, but to those who did, there would be no doubt she was the Āetis. Fire raged in her sapphire eyes, and although her controlled behaviour kept the energy at bay, it oozed from her, ever eager but always patient. Just like her mother.

Assured, Charras made a decision. She was ready.

Silently contemplating the phone call with Leanne, Charlize analysed the nerves in her stomach. They were curious bugs, materialising over situations she considered juvenile. There seemed to be no cure, no amount of telling herself she'd dealt with far worse. It was inevitable; her father would make sure of it. Next term, she would begin attending secondary school.

That wasn't even the worst part; she also had to go with Christian. This worried her immensely. She and Christian weren't the best of friends, 'toleration' a modest description of their friendship dynamic. They had nothing in common, and her unpopularity was an established but ignored fact between them.

The only likeness they both seemed to share were night terrors, and from what they each shouted out when asleep, they were similar. To combat her fears, her father would tell her stories to calm her and they always helped. So, one night, when their parents had their monthly gathering and forced Christian to stay over, she heard him shouting out and tried to sooth him with such a story. Unfortunately, the words lodged in her throat and he awoke to find her choking. His response was to tell her – rather rudely – to get out of his room.

Upset, she discovered from her father that she couldn't speak to him about the Mages because he'd never had an Awakening, and was therefore unaware he even held power. Before then, she didn't understand why the adults argued so much. Now, she was unsure whether she was jealous that Christian escaped his fate, or sad that he would never discover it.

Sighing quietly, a fresh wave of guilt washed over her as she fiddled with her mother's broach. Beautiful, and obviously valuable, a gold paisley design outlined the engraving of a feather within its centre, the barbs zigzagging outwards to touch the small diamonds and rubies encrusted along its edges.

"Did she wear it?" she asked.

Charras cleared his throat. "No, she felt the right wasn't hers."

"Why?"

Choosing his words carefully, he spoke quietly. "It is very powerful and your mother felt only one with ultimate power should wear it. Study it and you will see why."

Charlize cradled it in her palms. Nothing immediately drew her attention, just the overwhelming sense that her mother once studied it the same way she did at that moment. "I feel like she's still here sometimes."

She knew her father wouldn't answer, talk of her mother almost forbidden, and she promptly pinned the broach to her blouse. It didn't particularly suit her outfit but she liked the feel of it next to her heart. Then, looking through her lashes, she caught the expression on her father's face. His eyes were glazed slightly as he silently fought whatever demons surged within him.

"Forgive me," she whispered, realising her mistake.

Snapping his eyes to her face, Charras composed his features and rubbed his temples. "Nonsense, you are bound to be curious."

"Not if it causes you pain to think of it."

Silence followed as Charras considered his daughter. Long ago, he'd made the decision never to tell her of Vrealâ's origins, glad nightmares remained the only reminder. Yet the secret meant the mere mention of the hybrid caused an uncontrollable anger to swell within him, his stomach thudding so hard he sometimes thought it would break free altogether.

He was certain though – Charlize would never know the ultimate threat lay within the reanimation of her mother. He shuddered to think of the consequences should she ever find out...

Charlize watched her father refocus and silently promised to never cause him undue pain again.

"You may as well tell me, Leanne already did," she said, changing the subject.

Charras frowned before he realised what she meant. "Ah, yes. I know you hoped you could stay here and be home schooled forever, but there are things I can't teach you, things you need to learn for yourself."

"But what if I'm not ready?"

He shook his head. "I have taught you our ways. You know everything about the history, the magic, and the control. You are more than ready."

Wondering why the same bugs fluttered in her stomach, Charlize realised they'd risen to her chest. She clutched it and sucked in some air. Then, breathing out, she said, "Father, I hardly know anyone; everyone knows each other around here, but not me. Other than the shopkeepers, the baker, and a few of Christian's friends, but that's hardly anyone. I couldn't possibly be expected to remain discreet when I am so obviously different and out of place."

"You are being hypothetical."

"I am not! We rarely leave the house. Anytime I do, I am either ignored or called names."

"Take a breath."

Obediently taking a breath, Charlize sat back in her chair.

"These are all the reasons I need you to do this. The Āetis should not fear the mere thought of socialisation."

"I don't fear it; I just don't know how to do it."

Peering at her through half raised eyebrows, Charras sighed. "I know I've worked you hard these past few years, but it was for the utmost of importance. I'm giving you the chance to see the world outside your front door. I need you to see what we fight for."

"I know what we fight for."

"Knowledge is one thing, but understanding is another. Do not think I ignore the apathy in you."

Opening and shutting her mouth, Charlize had no argument so decided to keep it closed.

"I need you to do this."

Shrugging her shoulders, defeated, she nodded. "Of course father."

Not convinced, Charras held out his hands, beckoning for Charlize to give him hers. Doing so, she looked at the floor. "You are the most important Mage to have walked for some time. The fate of this world lies on your shoulders and I realise the pressure you must feel. But you walk blinded, as if nothing but your loyalty to me guides you. I need you to fight for humanity, not for duty. How can you do that if you shut it out?"

Although angered, Charlize knew the truth in his words. With a bitter taste in her mouth, she absorbed the dreaded certainty that she would have to learn – whether she wanted to or not.

"I promise I'll try," she said, standing up and making to leave the room.

"Wait."

She turned around. His face set, her father stood by the alcove and stared at the raindrops obscuring the window.

"Before you go, I want to see how much you've learned," he said. "The teachings from me end here if you complete the test."

Charlize wanted to say something but faltered, knowing from the past three years of experience that whatever test she underwent wasn't going to be easy. "I haven't revised," she argued weakly.

"Then it's the best kind of test," said Charras, gesturing with his finger for her to follow.

Moving through the library, passing by the vast collection of literature, they reached the very end – a dusty corner where two bookshelves met side by side. Charras studied the array of hardbacks, each leather-bound and clearly old. He scanned his index finger down the spines of each volume until he found the one he was looking for.

A dusty addition of *'Bindings for Beginners'* poked out a fraction more than the rest, and taking the book from its residence on the shelf, it revealed a lever.

"When I took the test, my father said to me that if you search for the answers you seek, you generally find them." Charras pulled the lever down and the bookshelves opened inwards to reveal another hidden door. "This library holds the answers to everything you seek, you only have to look."

Charlize nodded her understanding as he laid a coercing hand on her shoulder. Then, guiding her to stand in front of the hidden door, defined only by a faint light that traced the edges of a frame, he released her and stood back.

"Knowledge is one thing, understanding is another, but practise is the ultimate test. This library taught me how to teach you, this test will show you the truth only you can discover. If you pass, I've done my job well."

Charlize placed her hand on the wood. "I'm ready."

7

The Test

Alone in the dark library, Charlize let her nerves reveal themselves. Stretching out her fingers, she called upon her energy, the surge an immediate comfort. Then, speaking her full name aloud, as instructed, she held her breath as the door evaporated – a brilliant light swallowing the imitation.

Reaching up to shield her eyes, she stepped through.

The atmosphere changed abruptly, the warmth from the manor disappearing, as well as the light. A musty aroma replaced the mature scents of age, although she couldn't fathom the source, and holding her hands out in front, the dark swallowed them.

She waited for a moment and listened to the sound of her breath as she inhaled and exhaled the cold from her lungs, certain it billowed in front. There was no other noise, nothing to give away where she was, and wrinkling her nose, she couldn't place the odour either.

With only curiosity feeding her courage, she took a step forward.

Slowly, images awakened from wherever they slept, emitting a soft light to form a detailed forest within the darkness. Differing shades of green made up a vast array of trees and shrubbery, their imagery impressive as they loomed upwards and branched outwards, like several ballerinas' posing en pointe. But Charlize knew none of it was real, the room she'd walked into a memory, as clear as the recollection depicted, which in this case was a vivid one.

When all grew still, she looked around her, quickly discovering that she could discern the edges of the walls, cleverly disguised by a fake night sky that changed its shade every few seconds. More than a little impressed, she found herself so busy admiring the skill that she almost tripped over what she sought.

She looked down to examine the device that bruised her toe. It was a small prism like object, formed of three triangles slotted together. Made from glass and infused with properties of ice, Charlize knew it as an Amici – a memory containment and projection device. Her *Book of Becoming* had explained the property of magic to her only a few months ago, and she recalled with added respect how it took a highly accomplished Mage to achieve what she witnessed. To focus every texture, detail, and character into one thought, before transferring it into the Amici, required extreme mental concentration and often took years to perfect.

The memory could be of anything or anyone. Sometimes, Mages conjured images of passed loved ones, driving themselves to distraction in their grief. At other times, Amici's had a more practical use, projecting events in an attempt to solve a mystery or seek an answer. Their use could also be sinister, cases reported of Mages confining an enemy and projecting a memory that drove their captive insane. In the wrong hands, they were dangerous objects.

Charlize bent down and brought her face closer to the Amici. A haze surrounded it and a light breeze wafted against her nose, but she could still make out the memory within – a condensed mixture of sheer colours that only made sense when projected.

Her father said they were an art piece of the brain. Although, unlike some art, even when it was complete a Mage could add to it and strengthen the imagery, but only if it was their own creation. If tampered with by another, the memory could become corrupt or lost altogether.

To ensure this never happened, a Mage generally spelled an individual protection around their work, and Charlize smiled as she touched the blur circling the Amici and felt the resistance of air. *Anima* she thought. Then, putting her hand through a tree trunk, she confirmed her surroundings weren't real.

Happy with her cleverness, she continued onwards, soon reaching a wall covered with imagined foliage and creepers. Scouring the bricks inch by inch, she quickly became impatient when no door revealed itself.

"Hello?" she called, standing back and folding her arms across her chest.

There was no response, and rubbing her arms to encourage circulation, her teeth soon started to chatter, their noise amplified without solid mass to muffle them.

Irritated her father lacked the foresight to suggest an overcoat, she decided to ignite a flame. With a short incantation, she held it in her palm and squeezed her fingers together, absorbing the warmth and directing it through her skin.

It helped, although she could hear her father's voice in her head scolding her for not maintaining her strength. *Well* she thought, *I couldn't possibly be expected to freeze.* And besides, the spell wasn't strong enough to drain her significantly; it really was a matter of self-preservation.

"Excuse me miss?"

Charlize immediately extinguished her flame and span to face the owner of the voice.

"You really should maintain your strength."

The voice was polite and belonged to a plump man of short stature. He wore a deep red and gold waistcoat over crisp cream linen trousers, his quaint clothes implying he must have been quite rich, and even though his face blurred slightly, his strong features still shone through: bright rosy cheeks accompanied by a sharp moustache that pointed out towards his ears.

"Are you a memory too?" Charlize asked.

The projection studied her before answering. "I am who your father believed would be best suited," he replied.

"How are you here?"

"The same as you are my dear girl. When you leave this place, so will everything else. This test is personal to you; your father merely provided the details." His voice crackled slightly as his features flickered. "This test is an ancient spell within our family, and it is within it you can speak to the dead."

Charlize stepped back, looking about her for any sign of trickery.

As if unaware she wasn't paying attention, the projection continued speaking. "I am Nicholas Chaparral. I am your Great-Grandfather. I have been awaiting your arrival; I hope you find it to your satisfaction."

Charlize nodded her head mechanically. No threat seemed imminent, so returning her attention to her ancestor, she looked him up and down.

"My father did all this?" she asked.

"He learned the skill from your mother, a better artist than he."

"My mother?"

"Yes; your mother Isalize."

Charlize smiled. So… her parents were artists.

"This is highly sophisticated for something so old," she said, knowing the insult as it left her lips and clapping a hand over her mouth.

The projection of her Great-Grandfather said nothing, the corners of his mouth rising in what she hoped was a smile.

After a few moments of agonising embarrassment, he spoke. "Thank-you Charlize, although you know as well as I that magic is unchanging, becoming no more and no less. It is solely a Mages responsibility as to how accomplished they become. Evolution is unique to the individual."

The apparition of Nicholas moved two branches from the foliage-covered wall, exposing another door. Moving so he blocked the entrance, he flickered and faded before returning to his more lucid state. "Your first question is a simple one. Name each Mage clan and the properties they possess."

Nicholas waited as Charlize looked behind her and then back at him, evidently puzzled. "And then what?" she asked.

"And then you go through to the next stage," he replied.

Gathering her thoughts for a few moments, she prepared her answers, silently praying that all the questions were as easy.

"The Fulgor Mage," she started. "Their properties include creating and controlling lightning." She paused, wondering if this was enough.

Nicholas nodded and gestured for her to carry on. "The Aquāe Mage: their properties include creating and controlling water. Incendiī Mages can create and control fire; Glacies Mages are able to create and control ice, along with its varying properties, and the neutral Anima Mages can create and control wind, air, and breath."

Finished, Charlize waited for Nicholas to inform her she was correct, although she knew she was.

However, he didn't move from the door.

The reason dawning on her, she lowered her voice. "The Āetis. One born when the need arises; they are the only Mage capable of controlling all of the elements." She looked away from her ancestor and to the floor, her earlier bravado diminished.

"Yes, very good," Nicholas said. "And what is their purpose?"

"*Ducere Aetas*."

"Which means?"

"To lead an age."

Standing aside, he let Charlize pass.

The same light as before appeared, outlining a door and shrouding her in warmth. She squinted to counter the brightness, stepping through, and it ebbed away to reveal a poorly lit room, the source a grimy lantern hanging from a low ceiling.

She was in some sort of cell, the grey stonewalls windowless, the masonry aged and fragile as damp made a home within the cracks. In the centre, three quaint school chairs sat in a row, each with a desk attached, although they were much larger than usual and held an air of stateliness.

Charlize was reminded of a book she'd read where the heroine was punished with doing homework for three days in a chair much the same – a cautionary tale her father often repeated when he found her face down in her books.

As she made her way across, her footing careful against the uneven concrete, she hoped he hadn't finally followed through on his threat…

An X taped crudely to the floor made her stop. Clearly an addition and not a usual resident, she stepped onto it, jumping as three figures appeared in the chairs. They vanished the minute she leapt backwards, her hands to her chest as she caught her breath, and quickly discerning the box was a trigger, she felt foolish as she tentatively stepped back on.

This time, she didn't cry out as the three figures reappeared. Their faces were familiar, Nicholas making another appearance as he sat in the middle chair, garbed in the same clothes as before, while either side of him were the faint faces of her Grandmother and Great-Grandmother, each dressed accustomed to their era.

Charlize squeezed her hands together and waited. She had only heard of her ancestor's, all on her father's side, through stories. She'd never thought about her demeanour upon meeting them, believing that, naturally, the portraits on the landing would be her only introduction.

"Well, go on and speak child," the projection of her Grandmother said, interrupting the silence.

Charlize immediately unclenched her hands and spluttered a hello as the projections leapt into life, their animated chatter sounding through the cell in a chorus of babbles.

The first sentence she distinguished was her Great-Grandmother's: "Welcome my dear," she greeted, "how are you?"

"Very well," Charlize replied, bowing her head.

"Your modesty fools only you child, the pressure must weigh heavily upon the shoulders of one so young." Her face flickered and waned, but even so, her gaze remained sharp as she peered at Charlize over the top of her thin glasses.

"I am as well as I can be," she tried again, finding herself frightened to lie. "My father wishes to send me to the secondary school within the Marsh village. I think this test is to prove to him I can defend myself."

The figures each murmured between themselves before addressing her. "This test is irrelevant to your schooling; it only measures your ability, and your father's ability to teach you," they said in unison.

"He is a wonderful teacher, I assure you!"

Nicholas held his hand up for silence. "Your father feels attending school will give you a greater understanding of the Ungifted and their ways. But he will not allow it if he feels you may be in any danger away from the manor." Charlize began to protest but Nicholas raised his hand once more. "Show us what you have learned fairly, with no other intent than to prove your skills."

Rubbing her neck, Charlize nodded, her plan thwarted.

"Very well," said her Grandmother, "let us begin. The prophecy I trust you know?"

"Yes," she confirmed, recalling the age-old script to mind.

"One day a woman and a man,
shall be born from separate a clan.
Both an opposite, dangerous mixed,
together in love, a future's fixed.

The power will lead us into war,
after their path tells them what for.
And if this heart is proved untrue,
the world will suffer until born anew."

Charlize took a breath. The pressure often weighed in her heart after each recital.

"You must not worry," Nicholas assured her. "That time is yet to come."

"Indeed," said her Grandmother. "You may not understand the prophecy as of yet, but you will child."

"Yet if I fail, the world will suffer. I know nothing now, how will I know when I do?" Charlize asked.

Her relatives lingered in silence as they prepared an answer. Again, it was her Great-Grandmother who was the first to speak. "It is vague. Many things can happen from now until then. The questions you mustn't ask yourself are how or when you'll know, because you may never hear the answers. You must only ask what feels right."

"But what if I'm wrong? I am the Āetis; the mistakes I make effect everyone."

"*If* your heart is proved untrue…" Nicholas reminded. "If you follow what you believe to be right, then you will know where you must lead."

Brushing her hair behind her ears, Charlize said nothing more, her understanding no greater than it ever had been.

"Let us continue then," said Nicholas. "Name each Minae and their known forms."

A cool shiver rippled up Charlize's spine as the tone in the room darkened. The light flickered in the sombre ambience, and it was as if the air itself listened to her next words.

"The Ghul," she began. "They come from the deep controlled by Inferus-Malus. They are male Minae, formed from the malice of men who have committed deeds of darkness during their life. They possess incredible strength, but tend to carry weapons of whatever nature they find, otherwise using their sharp teeth and sheer bulk to overcome their prey. The Ungifted see them as misguided mutes, brutal forms of humans who attack the innocent. A Mage sees them for the rotting beasts they are."

Charlize froze as a Ghul appeared from thin air and stood stationary behind the chairs of her ancestors. It didn't move as its twisted face glared at her, the malice behind its bloodshot eyes the only mortal imitation.

"Continue," Nicholas urged. "He will not harm you while we are here."

While we are here, Charlize repeated in her head, figuring what happened once her ancestor's disappeared.

"Wraithart," she said, pushing her fear aside. "They are feminine or masculine forms of creatures that have been unable to pass through the veil. Most we do not notice, thinking them to be stray cats or dogs, wild beasts or deranged animals having lost their minds. They can walk through walls and change their form at will. And not all Wraithart's are malevolent. To an Ungifted or a Mage, they can act as guidance, and in return receive a true death from the Sky."

As expected, a Wraithart in the form of a large brown bear walked through the wall and stood beside the Ghul, their heights equal.

Charlize stared in awe. She had only encountered one Wraithart in her life – that of her neighbour's cat. When it came to her in the street one day she brought it home, the neighbours having gone away. Little did she know that it had died several months earlier. Two scars on her arm remained a constant reminder of the evening it attacked her – right before her father stormed into the room and re-killed it.

Much speculation as to why Wraithart's held no allegiance to Inferus-Malus was a common debate among Mages. Some thought he had no need of them, while others believed there was a direct correlation between an animal's welfare in life, to the behaviour it would display in death.

"Charlize… continue," Nicolas said, breaking through her musings.

"Sirenaris," she said promptly, straightening her back. "They are female threats – tortured souls retaining their original form from their life on earth. They are malicious when alive, slaves of Inferus-Malus when dead. Known to travel in packs of three, the gift of enhanced beauty grants them the ability to lure the Ungifted with whatever cunning they can; for only a Mage sees them for what they are – decomposing, ugly, and lacerated – with no sign of former beauty covering their bodies."

Charlize watched the deformed figure of a woman emerge from mid-air. Lank matted hair framed yellow sunken eyes, which stared unblinking, and a putrid smell emanated from her wrinkled flesh, covered by nothing but dirt and flora. She scraped her broken ankle along the concrete to stand beside the bear, flicking back and forth from her true form to the naked perfection of the human body.

The only constant feature were the talons at the tips of her elongated fingers, their brutality documented by various books in her father's library. Charlize shuddered as she recalled those that had pictures…

She cleared her throat. "An Achak and Akuji are both female and male lesser forms of Minae, forced into slavery by Inferus-Malus. He shreds the light from its dark counterpart as the spirits cross into the in-between – the æther – and sends only the darkness back to earth where they destroy more souls of the living. Commonly seen as wisps of light if they are an Akuji, or vague imitations of the human shape if they are Achaks, Mages and the Ungifted alike can see them. They are the most common form."

Two balls of energy appeared next to the Sirenari. One morphed into the transparent shape of a man, while the other, nothing more than a sphere of energy, glistened hazily. The shapes brought a chill to the air, their presence freezing the movements of those around them, even the other Minae.

Charlize clutched her throat, attempting to warm the ice crystallising and stealing her breath away. She knew the illusion merely demonstrated the effect each threat had on the Ungifted, but she still gasped and drew in a lungful of air as it warmed.

"Shadowlan," she croaked. "They evolve from an Akuji or Achak. To do this, the Minae must obtain the spirits of five children. This gives them a darker energy and more sinister power." She coughed a little. "Able to possess the bodies of Ungifted, a Shadowlan can animate them as if they lived, taking over the life of that individual. What makes them different to their lesser forms is their intelligence, and the fact the host body doesn't need to be alive. Cases reported of horrendous crimes – where a father or a mother kills their own children and then themselves – shocks communities. As Mages, we know the truth and recognise the deeds of a Shadowlan."

Nicholas clapped his hands as he looked eagerly to his companions. "Splendid," he beamed, ignoring the Shadowlan appearing behind him and causing the room to ice over once more.

It was true to its name, materialising as a shadow would, a dark mass with two dots of deep red where eyes would formerly have been. Charlize wrapped her arms across her shoulders as she recalled how the demons would scavenge the dead or dying as carrion would a carcass, even entering a grave or body of an innocent just to absorb their essence.

"Why are those Minae behind you?" she asked, afraid of the answer.

"Pay them no attention," her Grandmother replied. "Now, tell me, who is Vrealâ?"

Charlize snapped her head up, wide-eyed, not wishing her to emerge like the other Minae. "She won't…?"

"Of course not, she is an isolated case," Nicholas assured.

Wary nonetheless, Charlize spoke carefully. "She is Inferus-Malus's right hand. Not many know much about her, generally regarded as a myth. But the assumption is that she is a new form of Greater Minae – a rare darkness long believed to be extinct. As one prophecy spoke of my existence, another told of hers:

When anger seeps through spirit dead,
turning her against her blood.
She will rise and command the sky,
until the blood she bore should die.

When the war is waged and won,
when good or evil is overcome.
Then begins a future new,
of love or hate through and through."

Ringing her hands together, Charlize grimaced and waited. No other form materialised, her gut turning with the expectation, and she eventually let out a sigh of relief. Then, gazing across the faces of her family, family she never thought she'd meet, she could have sworn she saw sympathy in their hazy expressions.

"You're so real," she murmured, almost to herself.

"Sometimes reality isn't always what we see before us," Nicholas replied kindly. "A memory can create a personality, even if it's within the limits of what that person knows it to be. Your father is highly accomplished in this art."

"But less of that," her Grandmother interrupted. "Tell us. Prophecies thousands of years old, made by the first Mages on this earth are still coming true. Why?"

"They were readers of course," Charlize said, pushing her earlier fears aside. "The first Mages of this earth, created by the Sky to fight *Inferus-Malus* and his Minae, were able to decipher the stars, the messages within them, and even connect to it through meditation. Whatever they learned they enclosed in a chamber where the Orbis – the window to the Sky – also resides."

"Yes, well done child, now for the last question," her Great-Grandmother pressed, as if time was running out.

Standing from their seats, all three members of her family bore their stares into her, as if awaiting a momentous event.

"Why do we fight?"

With the last question delivered, Charlize succumbed to the inevitable. For deep down, she knew that what happened next would be crucial.

The answer ready in her mind, she began. "We fight to protect humanity; we fight for the freedom of our race, both in life and in death. We protect the Ungifted by keeping them safe within the Arcēs, safe from the Minae infested wastelands outside each Arx and the truth of what the world truly holds."

Suddenly transported to three years ago, several days after her bruises healed and warmth returned to her heart, she recalled her father's face.

Sitting on the bed, the sheets cold as he tucked her in, he turned his eyes downward. 'It's time now,' he said, before opening her book. 'Let us go back to the beginning.'

And they did, for that was when it started.

8

The Beginning

In the very beginning there was the Sky and everything in it. The Sky was pure and knew nothing of good or evil. It watched the earth being born and came to love the planet and its development, casting a nurturing force upon it, delighting in the beauty, wonder, and life the planet was able to hold.

Yet, in the balance of things, a darker, more sinister force was born unto the planet. This caused the parallel of opposites, and in its entirety existed merely as a dormant force.

Only when life, when awareness and intelligence surfaced and the planet developed beings with consciousness, did the dark force awaken completely. Soon, the energy wanted control of the planet it infected, imploring the Sky to grant it power beyond its purpose.

When the Sky – sensing the destructive and malevolent force within – refused, the darkness challenged the Sky to a fight upon the earth where it could prove its worth. The Sky accepted the challenge and became earth bound.

Fighting for several suns and moons, and causing much destruction upon the planet, the Sky finally conceded, impressed with the dark energy and its knowledge of power. Granting it control over all that was dead, the Sky knew no further harm could effect what was already dead, and it returned its watchful stare above the earth.

Angered by the pitiful prize, the darkness retreated below the ground where it lay in wait, endlessly plotting its next move.

Time rolled forward; the earth healed and developed a new kind of 'Being,' ones with more intelligence than anything the planet had ever seen. This new race grew quickly and the darkness was attracted to it, walking among the strange creatures and learning the truths that lay within each of their hearts. It found both its own essence and the essence of the Sky within them, discovering that when the beings died, they left behind a unique energy – unlike any the darkness had encountered. Although their host bodies were gone, the power and the soul did not rot in the ground like the rest of the flesh. The essence, the spirit, the power in each 'Being' retreated into the Sky, and the Sky took them warmly, allowing them eternal rest among its stars.

All of this the darkness watched, only interested in its own essence within each Being. It seemed the more of it they held, the more earth bound they were. Even in death, the spirits took longer to reach the Sky. Yet the brighter the essence, the more welcomed it seemed into the Sky's embrace – as if the weight it held on its way upwards was lighter than those who had lived lives corrupted by darkness.

One day, when sweeping across a golden desert, the darkness saw a Being fall. Curious, it swooped down to examine the transition into the Sky.

As the essence rose upwards, the darkness reached outwards and found it was able to grasp it. Delighted, it bonded with the energy and traversed into a place between life and death called the æther. Here it returned to its original form, intent on taking control by using its gift of all that was dead.

Now, every spirit that transcended into the æther would belong to the darkness, and with the dead, it would build an army, ripping the Sky's influence from each essence and sending only the darkness back to earth. As the malevolence on earth grew, so would its strength, until eventually it could take control of the planet it was born unto, the planet that it felt rightfully belonged to those bound on it.

The unnatural shift in the balance of things caused a great upheaval on earth, and the Sky felt its shudder across its night. Even so, many years passed as misery engulfed the lands, the greedy, bloodthirsty, and violent becoming the most powerful. Evil grew and malice reigned, fields of red replacing pastures of green.

It was only when the bloodshed had gone too far and the Sky lamented the destruction caused, it attempted to placate the darkness, now named 'Inferus-Malus' by the intelligent 'humans' who occupied the planet.

As the Sky knew it would, Inferus-Malus refused to relinquish his powers, rejecting another offer to fight for compromise, and ignoring any suggestion of trade or treaty. Unable to touch him in the æther, the Sky had no choice but to retreat, only able to watch the planet plunge further into darkness.

When it seemed hopeless, light almost a fallacy, the Sky once again became earth bound, taking on human form to walk the land for the last time. It took on a beauty so real that those who saw it felt such compassion it took their breath away, and none recovered.

The word quickly spread. Hope suddenly filled the hearts of those who'd almost given up, and the Sky rejoiced. It believed that it could fight back, that as long as its light remained in the hearts of those who nurtured it, Inferus-Malus could never truly rule.

How wrong it was.

Raging through the æther, Inferus-Malus ripped spirit after spirit until all light cowered from his touch. With more darkness than ever before tainting the earth, the Sky prepared to fight back, making a decision to force Inferus-Malus and his dark magick's away from the crossing place into death; to re-join the dark spirits with their light counterparts, and to return the now unnatural world to its former balance before it wilted and died.

To do this, the Sky infused gifts into five men it deemed worthy. The gifts were weapons against the dead, destructive elements from the very earth itself; one man for each element, able to create and control the gifts they possessed and the properties unique to each of them. With their will, be it from a natural form, such as rain for the man with the gift of water, or an unnatural form via creation, they could manipulate the degree of destruction. The stronger, more accomplished, and hardier the conjurer, the fiercer the power within them.

Upon the annihilation of Minae, only their natural essence remained.

Through the Mittere ritual, the men of power released it back into the Sky, reuniting the darkness with its light, allowing it the freedom to cross over into a true death.

Thus the Mages purpose was set, and so it was they lived."

9

First Battle

A buzz hung in the air once Charlize stopped talking, the electric pulse palpable as her ancestors each agreed that she was prepared. Having surpassed all expectations in her knowledge, she was ready for the final test.

"Congratulations," said Nicholas. "You have the knowledge, now prove the skill."

Without warning, Charlize felt herself lifted from the X as her ancestors disappeared. The light diminished to nothing, darkness encasing her, and in the silence, a cold chill ascended her spine.

She wasn't alone.

The rasping breaths of the Minae were the only indication of where they stood, eerily unmoving, and frantically attempting to distinguish the figures, she watched as a strip of light appeared in the far right corner. It traced the outline of another door, and aiming blindly towards it, almost tripping over in her urgency, she broke through the forms of the Wraithart and Sirenari, their foul stench so potent it was almost unbearable. She held her breath to stem the nausea and pushed her shoulder through the door, landing heavily on the other side.

Moonlight ensconced her – a delightful freedom – and with only the beating of her heart drumming in her ears, the familiar feeling of air on her cheeks brought a much needed revival.

She gulped in a few extra breaths, time pressing, and sat up, letting her eyes adjust to the faint light. In an instant, she knew she was on a battleground.

Her realisation of what was happening sent a short shock of panic through her spine, and rising to her feet, she took a few tentative steps, taking in the vast abandoned amphitheatre surrounding her. It was barely distinguishable beneath a half moon and mass of brilliant stars, but she could see moss and lichen blanketed the aged ruins, whereas half of the central space lay flooded with water – the moon's reflection the only indication.

Charlize wondered how deep it was and made her way to the edge, bending down to touch the water with her index finger. Poised as it immediately hardened, a wave of white and blue rushing outwards to crack and groan under the sudden pressure, the cold hit her first as the amphitheatre frosted over. She rubbed her arms, cursing her lack of warmer clothing, and waited for the impending attack.

It was sooner than she expected. The hairs on the back of her neck stood on end first, and she saw the shadow careering towards her only when it came within reach. She ducked just in time, her feet giving way so she skidded across the ice and balanced further inwards than she liked.

"Damn it," she cursed.

Darkness aided the Shadowlan. Made of the night, its natural ability of mute stealth meant it was the trickiest Minae to defeat. The crude apparition would hide until she seemed distracted and then take its chance to rip away pieces of her essence – until nothing but a shell remained.

She shuddered at the thought and threw her arms upwards. "*Fiat Ignem.*"

Jumping as something brushed past her shoulder, she span to face it, just as the fire she called burst from her body. Her mind momentarily distracted, she fought to keep it under control, using her will to cast it outwards and form a ring. Then, sinuously, she forced it to expand and stretch so the amphitheatre stood ablaze.

The sheer size of her arena now apparent, Charlize crouched and waited, knowing the Shadowlan would soon reappear. It wasn't long until she saw it. With nowhere left to hide, it darted in frantic sweeping motions and juddered backwards each time it hit the ring. Upon finding no escape route, it changed tact and tore towards where she waited.

She took two deep breaths. On exhalation of the second, she rose to her full height and charged forwards – subsequently falling into the now melted ice. Although it was only knee height, the shock of cold was distraction enough to allow the Shadowlan to tear through her body, the iron grip chilling her blood as it took hold of her essence.

"*Dicio*," she rasped, calling on the word of power.

Unable to possess a living Mage, the Shadowlan withdrew from her body and the cold instantly dispersed, replaced by an almighty surge of magic that spread from her heart to every extremity. She stretched her fingers, reenergised, and focused on the relentless Minae as it zigzagged strangely, rushing forward and doubling back, only to switch its pattern on the next round – presumably trying to confuse her.

Still kneeling in the water, and with little patience left, Charlize bit her lip and plunged her hands beneath the surface. "*Presteris.*"

The incantation cut strongly through the night, the water stirring violently as the spell sounded with her authority. It twisted into a powerful maelstrom and she directed it around the edge of the arena, smiling as it washed the moss and dirt clean, the loose rocks crumbling into dust. Then, getting to her feet, she squinted against the spray blurring her vision and the wind throwing her hair about her neck like a scarf. But her intentions were satisfied and the Shadowlan's spirit descended into a pile of faint sparks.

She clapped her hands to release the spell and the whirlpool broke apart. Then, reabsorbing the remaining energy, she forgot to dodge the returning water and winced as it drenched her.

"Oops," she mumbled, wiping the hair from her eyes.

With a quick shake of her limbs, she ran to where the Shadowlan's dishevelled spirit still flickered and held her hand just above it. "*Evincio*," she whispered.

A simple command, the body of water in her palm expanded like a balloon and stretched over the essence, capturing it within its protection. Then, clasping her hands in a prayer stance, Charlize whistled the simple tune that had been with her all her life – a mere four surreal notes only a Mage could produce.

The binding lifted into the Sky, forming a beautiful azure sphere the size of a tennis ball, and picking up speed, it left the earth to join its counterpart – wherever it belonged.

Freeing a spirit always settled the Rester, which was the name for a Mage who performed a Mittere. When the essences of defeated Minae returned to the Sky, the anger and malice left with them. And so, for a few short moments, Charlize felt at peace.

She took the chance to assess her strength, knowing she had to conserve it lest her magic weaken in her exhaustion, and taking a few breaths, she was happy to note she only felt a small difference. Nevertheless, she decided to be cautious, and clapping her hands, she reabsorbed the fire still burning brightly around her and plunged the amphitheatre back into darkness.

Although smaller spells could be released permanently – the drain on a Mages energy dependant on their skill, mastery, and blood strength – it was never wise unless necessary. Charlize only knew of one such need: the protection around the manor. Her father reinforced it daily, adding parts of his energy to fortify their defence. Yet to do such a thing in combat could be akin to suicide.

With the light lost and the cold penetrating her bones once more, it wasn't long until the atmosphere changed, violence piercing through Charlize's calm as she sensed two approaching Minae.

There was no sign of them where she stood, so lifting her head to sniff the air, she gagged as sulphur burned the back of her throat – a sign of greater threats, and knew she needed to run.

She wasted no time. Sprinting away from the stench, she didn't stop until she reached a ledge of rock, grasping the side and turning to observe the Ghul and lone Sirenari edge their way dissonantly towards her.

The Ghul carried a giant cleaver in his burnt olive hand, his appearance similar to a corpse that had been rotting in a grave for some time. He stomped towards her without caution, his deformed face scrunched in concentration as low growls and sighs escaped his frothing lips. He seemed unaware the Sirenari staggered close at his heels, her sharp talons glinting in the moonlight.

Charlize didn't hesitate to lift herself free, glad to escape any form of hand-to-hand combat. Against a Ghul or Sirenari, martial arts were almost useless, their physical strength too immense for most Mages to match. So, aiming for optimum ground, she climbed with added fervour.

It wasn't easy. To find footholds within the shaky rocks required her full concentration, something made difficult by the vicious noises from below, and she slipped several times, catching her knees on the rocks and ripping her leggings.

It was only through sheer perseverance she eventually felt high enough.

The air was marginally cooler, a chill that cooled the sweat on her brow as she caught her breath. Then, steadying herself on the edge of a shattered step, she dared a glance at the pursuing Minae.

The Sirenari had reached the ledge before the Ghul, and although her snapped ankle hindered her progression, she was still agile, using her sharp claws to ascend the ridge instead.

Charlize sighed and pushed onwards, scrambling over the remaining hurdles to land in a stall. She quickly pressed herself against the upper tier wall and secured her footing.

Weather and disrepair had flattened the earth, leaving mere dust and stones in a small clearing that plunged off into a sheer drop – an uncertain step a fatal fall. But she ignored the danger and shuffled along with tentative footsteps, dislodging debris that tumbled fore-warningly into the void.

She continued until she found another clearing, this one piled with rubble head height, and releasing her held breath, dived into the shadows of the first mound. There, she waited.

Minutes passed before Charlize heard the Sirenari nearing – an unmistakable short stamp followed by a drawn out scrape as she dragged her broken ankle along the ground. Thinking fast, she shifted through various spells in her head, trying to settle on one that would wield enough power to overcome the greater Minae, but still leave enough of her energy to battle the Ghul.

She quickly decided to use her Aquāe element, the water close and therefore the stronger instinct. So, holding out her palm, she whispered a small command, only to suddenly notice that the clearing had fallen silent.

Dread thumped her in the stomach. Frantically reabsorbing the waters' energy, Charlize forced herself to her feet and lunged forward, her hands tight to her ears as she darted through the maze of rubble, her footsteps landing without care as she scrambled over, under, or around each obstacle, intent on putting as much distance between her and the Sirenari as she could.

But then, with the cry of a thousand trapped souls, the greater Minae opened her jaws and screamed.

The noise carried so much anguish, fury, and desperation, that tears sprung down Charlize's cheeks involuntarily, the sheer magnitude of the wail against her eardrums a torturous ordeal. It left her with nothing but the desire to sink to the floor and cry. And that's exactly what she did, sobbing and retching at the same time, unable to muffle the sound but desperate to escape it.

Looking urgently about her, she saw nothing more than rock and ruins, their collapsed foundations offering a bleak shelter. She silently wished for a miracle, her teeth hard against her lip and hand on her chest, unsure how much more she could endure.

It was a trick; she knew that. Sirenari's had the ability to emulate the suffering of their victims, their dying cries mimicked and magnified for the unfortunate to hear – a poison of the senses. And yet, knowing this held no cure. She didn't know many who could hear the last moments of the deceased and tolerate it.

A flash of orange invaded the corner of her eye and she immediately put her guard up, her attentions refocused as the same blur made itself known. It made its way to a dip in the earth, and in doing so, revealed what appeared to be a hidden entrance sat behind a long eroded archway.

Charlize hoped it hadn't seen her. She didn't have the will to recoil, and was still unsure if what she saw was a mere trick of her mind, or it was indeed as real as she hoped it wasn't. But then, as its amber eyes fixed on her, she finally accepted that a tiger did indeed sit before her.

"Interesting…" she murmured, the rare cat a specimen only seen in books.

It made no attempt to reach her, instead choosing to study her with interested eyes, its tail wagging from one side to the other – a hypnotising motion that reassured Charlize the Wraithart held no threat.

She shuffled towards it, stopping when it stood up, stretched, yawned, and then walked towards the entrance of the ruins, turning only once to make sure she followed. She did so without question, descending into the vestiges of the vomitorium and the reprieve they promised, continuing until she was deep enough to release her hands from her ears.

Although the ringing didn't diminish entirely, the rush of relief was a welcome high, and loosening her clenched jaw, she rubbed the subsequent ache and examined her surroundings, damp and mould rising to invade her nostrils.

The light almost entirely lost, she considered the tiger before her against the threat behind her and cast a quick spell to aid her sight. Her hand now an orange flame, she held it above the Minae.

"Where have you brought me?" she demanded, her voice louder than intended in the tunnel.

Of course it didn't answer, only responding by tensing its powerful jaws and squinting as the light dilated its pupils. That was enough however; for in that moment, Charlize saw something familiar – a distant memory, but enough to make up her mind.

Not that the tiger cared. It was already sauntering away in its golden form, and she could do nothing more than follow as they delved further into the ruins.

They continued their journey for some time, navigating through the maze of obstacles and dead end's, the Wraithart never faltering in its seamless transition through the amphitheatre, determined, as if it were looking for something important.

It was only when Charlize began to think they were lost, the endless tunnels all morphing into a monotonous continuation of the same, the Wraithart suddenly dug its claws into the earth. She immediately held up her hand, its light revealing a network of surrounding dungeons, the conditions varied but compact. There was no room to manoeuvre easily among the remaining rusted bars and doors, and if there were an ambush, she'd be an easy target.

Cursing her stupidity, she thought fast. Knowing she needed the element of surprise, she let the flame guiding her way grow hotter. Currently distracted, the Wraithart held its nose to the ground, sniffing deeply, back turned, and open to attack.

Charlize sensed her chance, aiming her arm and taking a breath, calling words of fire to her mind as she phrased the spell in her head.

But no sooner had she done so, something stopped her.

The Wraithart was behaving strangely. Stopping at each intact cell, it rubbed its nose against the door before moving onto the next, its whiskers twitching and tail ruler flat, an alertness that kept Charlize following closely, curious.

Finally, it settled outside a particularly sturdy cell, the dirt beneath cleared away as if someone had been there recently.

A small growl echoed through the dank corridor as the Wraithart used its large paws to force the rusted iron from its hinges, flattening it with an almighty *bang*.

Charlize swiped away the resulting dust and peered into the dark chamber, avoiding the tiger as it strode forward to sit on the fallen door, content to stay there and clean its paws. The only light currently between her fingers, she held them high above her head and covered her mouth with her free hand. Then, moving to stand next to the tiger, she quickly noticed a blotch of red hanging in the furthermost corner. It was shrouded in shadow, and on closer inspection, she realised the red was in fact a robe, the dirtied material hanging beneath an indistinguishable mass.

"Hello?" she said, taking another step and further realising the tangled mass was actually hair.

Still facing the wall, the matted head jerked up. Bony arms reached out and grabbed the robe around its shoulders, pulling it taut as its head twisted to look directly at the intruder.

Charlize immediately shrank back, the close proximity a new experience and one she wasn't fond of.

The prisoner was a girl, the wear of time causing her skin to constrict her bones and her eyes to sink and turn sallow.

"You shouldn't be here," she warned. "Better to run away."

"Why?" Charlize asked, instinctively holding onto the fur of the Wraithart.

Moving suddenly, the girl flew towards her, shoving her against the old stone and cutting her head. Blood thrummed from the wound, which made Charlize cry out – cut short by a cold grip around her neck that began to constrict. She flailed her arms in an attempt to shove the girl off, but the iron hold showed no sign of easing.

She had only two thoughts then. The first was that she couldn't make a sound, and the second was that everything currently happening was all a test – none of it was real.

Even so, the fingers around her throat felt real, and the swirling in her head as her consciousness slipped away also felt real... but surely it couldn't be, her father would never allow it... would he?

Closing her eyes, Charlize listened to the sound of her own futile struggle. She wondered if she succumbed to the promise of shortcoming oblivion she would wake in her warm bed having failed the test. As the tiger roared, she wished with all her might that it were the case. Even as the grasp loosened and she fell to the floor, she prayed that when she opened her eyes, familiar surroundings would embrace her and the nightmare would be over.

Needless to say, it was not.

Spluttering as she drew breath into her lungs, Charlize gazed about her. The same cell surrounded her, although now it housed a version of the girl in a twisted heap, her head severed from her neck completely. She didn't know where the head was, but she guessed the Wraithart had eaten it.

She rubbed her throat and looked over at it sat once more, resuming the cleaning of its paws. A patch of red on its breast confirmed her initial guess.

"Thank-you..." she said breathlessly.

Briefly pausing its grooming, the golden eyes focused on her face, watching with the same intelligence she'd seen previously. Then, as if bored by their interaction, it yawned widely and lay down.

Charlize smiled despite herself. For some reason, the Wraithart's company put her at ease, and crawling over to the body of the girl, she reached outwards with her mind.

She quickly found the Achak within and bound it, performing a Mittere and sending it through the cell and into the night Sky. The fleeting reprieve on her senses was welcome and she took several deep breaths – until the Wraithart stood and strolled from the chamber.

"So soon?" she mumbled, although followed regardless.

In half the time it took to reach the dungeons, they found the exit and escaped above ground, appearing on the opposite side of the amphitheatre.

The cool caress of the night air allowed Charlize to suck in a breath and shake off the closeness of the cell. Sweat beaded on her forehead and top lip, which she wiped away, all the while maintaining her stare on the Ghul that still hammered at the rocks in the distance. *Stupid brute* she thought.

Deciding what her next move should be, she called a spell to her mind, at the same moment the tiger morphed to become the bear she'd seen earlier in her test. She shrank back, immediately on guard, although was still close enough to see the fur bristle across its arched back and watch as it opened its snout to growl loudly. She put a finger to her lips, but the Wraithart didn't listen and the Ghul soon turned and spotted them.

"Great…" she grumbled as the demon began to sprint towards them.

Seemingly unperturbed, the bear stood on its hindquarters and growled again, before falling to the floor and scraping the dirt in front. Then, with no time for Charlize to react, it charged towards the Ghul and collided with it moments later, merging into a jumble of ferocious energy – all teeth, flesh, and fur.

When it became apparent the bear was no match for the greater Minae, Charlize felt a tug of loyalty, a spark that charged her compassion, and she ran to assist her unlikely friend.

She didn't get far before an almighty pain seared down her back and she fell to the floor.

Her hands instinctively stopped her from hitting her head and she turned to face her attacker, the gleam of something sharp catching her attention first. She didn't need to see the Sirenari to know it was her, but as she stepped from the shadows to reveal herself, brandishing her weapons high above her head, Charlize still felt nauseous. The tips of her right talons were marred with the blood and flesh of her back, which the Sirenari carefully licked clean, her free talons poised to attack should she have need, and Charlize could only watch in horror, immobilised as she drew air through gritted teeth – violent sensations of hot pokers rippling along her spine.

Her vision blurred and the world spun. She attempted to shuffle backwards but the Sirenari soon noticed and sprung another attack, this time gouging the earth inches from her foot.

"Torquere," she uttered in desperation, kicking out as she dodged another blow.

Using all of her energy to stop herself passing out, she didn't attempt to evade the Sirenari when she lunged again, luck the only ally keeping the inches between them. And before she could push it further, the element she called lifted her free from the ground.

Safely atop the tornado, the harsh winds beneath a cacophony of destruction, Charlize brought them under control and managed to sit cross-legged, not daring to stand while her back remained torn. There, she used her will to steer the funnel towards the Sirenari.

It took more effort than she first thought it would, her head dizzied and heart pounding in her ears. The world seemed to wane and lose clarity, a surrealism replacing the harsh reality of her situation. And if it were not for the Sirenari's temper getting the better of her – having ceased her predatory circling to slash at the tornado, she often wondered if she would have succumbed to her injuries.

But with teeth bared and eyes aflame, each of the Minae's strikes ricocheted violently, her infuriated screeches, hisses, and repeated attempts – only to suffer the same result – angering her further by the minute.

Charlize felt their every touch, watching patiently as the demon, clearly long starved, became more careless and less adept with each swing. Then, sensing her chance after a particularly severe backlash, she swerved the funnel abruptly and managed to knock the Sirenari's shoulder, causing her enough instability to be dragged into the updraft.

The screams that followed made Charlize close her eyes, a strange pang of guilt stabbing her in the stomach as she maintained the energy crushing her captive.

Seconds later, she felt the resistance falter and knew all that remained was a pile of embers.

She lowered herself to the ground; found her footing clumsily; hurriedly performed a Mittere on the defeated Minae, and then spun to aid the Wraithart.

But it was too late. She hadn't taken another step before a roar echoed through the amphitheatre and she realised the Ghul had won. It continued to strike the Wraithart with its cleaver, connecting heavy blows that caused the bear to whimper and grunt in pain, its attempts to escape futile as it lost the use of its legs.

Without thought, Charlize pointed at the brutal victor. *"Dicio, Āetis, Aqua et igni interdicere homini."*

The command hit the Ghul like a bullet, constricting him where he stood. Growling, he fought the binds, edging towards her as his eyes bulged beneath the pressure. Steam evaporated from his putrid flesh and froth seeped from his rigid jaws as he wrestled against his fate. But Charlize fought to assert her will, tightening the bind by clenching her fingers, forming a fist, and drawing it towards her stomach. She didn't once take her eyes off her captive, and it quickly went in her favour, her strength far stronger than the Ghul's desire to walk.

With one final snarl, he tumbled to the ground where he twitched and succumbed to the inevitable, disintegrating into the tight sphere surrounding him. The air twisted within the binding, securing the essence, and then darted into the Sky.

The hold on her will relinquished, Charlize caught her breath. Unsure how much more was to come, aware she'd lost a lot of blood, she listened to the deafening silence that surrounded her, the ringing in her ears so loud she almost didn't hear the whimper of the injured Wraithart. Her body sore, she staggered to where it lay and slumped down beside it, observing its weak and shallow breathing.

Once again, she was confused as to why sympathy filled her, and after a moment's hesitation – and against all instinct – she cautiously reached out and stroked the bear's long snout.

"You were great," she whispered, doing her best to ignore the fatal wounds gouged in its chest.

Another whimper rumbled in its throat and it turned to look her in the eye. For the third time that night, Charlize saw intelligence within its gaze. Then, with a sigh – as if the weight of a thousand men escaped from its body, all fell silent once more.

The rapidity a slight shock, Charlize shakily stood up as she prepared the final Mittere. Holding her hands above the Wraithart, she opened her mouth to whistle, but before she made a sound, the Sky parted just a fraction and cast a beam of light between her thumbs. She didn't dare move them, watching in amazement as thousands of orbs circled slowly within the beam, splashing everything they touched with a golden hue.

Drawn to another movement beneath her, she looked down to see the Wraithart shrinking, its massive form morphing into the shape of a much smaller creature – one with lustrous golden fur covering its entire body.

Charlize dropped her hands and fell to her knees, reaching out to stroke the head of the Golden Retriever – its true form. Startled when it suddenly turned to lick her hand, she had no time to react as the light disappeared and she was finally alone.

"Bye," she murmured into the dark.

And then she fainted.

10
Home

When Charlize opened her eyes, hair obstructed her view, the wet strands draped messily across her face. Wiping them away and rubbing off the excess moisture clinging to her skin, the memories came back to her in patches.

Refusing to acknowledge them just yet, she lifted her stiff neck before quickly replacing it. With a groan, she realized she was still in the amphitheatre, and the soft splashes she could hear were not from her father running a bath, but from a breeze causing the flooded surface of the arena to ripple.

Shivering against the cold, she committed to sitting up, rubbing her neck as she watched dawn break over the broken stalls. It cast a faint light upon the dusty earth.

"*Dicio, Āetis, Inardesco.*"

A bright orange and yellow flame flared in her palm, the heat warming but also draining the last of her dwindling energy. Fatigue washed over her and she closed her eyes once more.

"I wouldn't do that yet." It was Nicholas's voice. "You may not wake again for weeks, even months."

Charlize opened her eyes and looked up at her ancestor smiling down on her. "They were real. You made me fight real Minae," she accused, finding her anger quickly.

Nicholas stopped smiling. "We didn't make you fight Charlize. This room was merely a place to show your skills, which you did. You chose to fight."

"I had no choice, they would have killed me!"

"Then you did what you needed," Nicholas said simply. "This is a test of strength and weakness; your father trusted your ability."

"And what if he was wrong, what then?"

"The point is that he was not."

Charlize frowned and tried to stand, before quickly realising it was unwise. "Lucky for him then," she said, sitting back with a sigh.

"Perhaps. But if you had a choice, what would you choose?" Nicholas asked, his question seeming odd.

"To go home," she replied impertinently.

As if oblivious to her contempt, Nicholas continued. "Do you want a purpose or a choice?"

Huffing, Charlize forced herself to her feet, wincing as sharp waves of pain jolted through her back. Her legs shaky as she steadied herself, she searched for an exit, forlorn when none seemed obvious.

"Do you want to fulfil your destiny or do you want to choose your own path?" Nicolas asked, following her as she hobbled away. "Many changes can be made to the future. Every action has a reaction. The future is uncertain; each purpose is a rough outline. That is how things are. We can only follow what we wish to, and sometimes, what we need to."

"I don't know," Charlize snapped, stopping in her tracks and facing her ceaseless inquisitor. "How can I answer you?"

"What does your heart tell you?"

"My heart?" She stared at the projection as if it had a fault. "I don't understand all this talk of my heart!"

"You will," Nicholas assured her, tilting his head and raising his hand in a gesture of goodbye.

And with that, he was gone. Although with his departure came the sun.

Closing her eyes as the day shrouded her in warmth, Charlize basked for a little while. Time had gone so fast she'd hardly noticed the fight had lasted most of the night. It felt as if lead sat atop her lids, but she heeded Nicolas's warning and forced herself to open them, glad to see a door like the others stood before her, a welcome opening in the middle of the arena.

With one last look over her shoulder, she gratefully stepped through and left the strange world behind.

A familiar smell hit her first, although not one she expected to receive.

Unsure why she'd ended up there, she climbed over the shoes and pushed through the coats towards the glow of her safe home. The door of the cupboard swung open and she spilled into the lobby, falling to her hands and knees as the artificial light bathed her in security.

Feeling more delighted than she could ever remember being, tears of elation fell down her face, although she wiped them away, determined to leave her bloodied body as the only trace of her ordeal.

To make sure she wasn't dreaming, she slowly got to her feet and touched her hand to the painting of the horse, its energy greeting her fingertips and promising her their truth. Whoever had painted the mare had loved her very much and Charlize could still feel each tender stroke that went into capturing her.

Footsteps originating from the library broke through her reflection, and her stomach re-knotted as her father threw open the door and came to stand in front of her, his face an odd picture of both elation and worry.

"You're back," he said, his voice steady but strained.

Facing him without a word, Charlize didn't know what to say, only able to stare as anger; betrayal; yearning, and disgust all wound themselves into a bitter knot and sank to her stomach.

"That was some test," she said finally, her voice hoarse.

Nodding, Charras held up his palm. "And yet a necessary one."

Charlize's eyes flashed with anger, but she said nothing as she matched her palm, her father's elements registering down her hand and along her arm, confirming he was who he said he was. By the look on his face, he was satisfied she'd come back herself also, albeit a mangled version…

He held her at arms length and stepped back a pace, staring at the bruises covering her body, his face a blank canvas. Unsure what to say, if there was anything he could even say, he turned on his heels and walked towards the kitchen.

"Let's get you cleaned up."

Charlize followed slowly, passing through the lobby with caution, each step revealing a new ache and pain shooting through her body. When she reached the arch, she stopped to catch her breath and placed her hand on the wall to stem the spinning in her head. A portrait caught her eye and she subconsciously clutched her throat.

Charras doubled back to join her, standing in front of the same portrait of him aged twelve. He held a golden bundle in his arms, a grin on his face as if he were the happiest boy alive. Warming at the memory of his only pet, their ownership heavily restricted, he became concerned when he noticed Charlize's tears.

"Come now," he hushed, reaching out to her.

"Don't," she snapped, shrugging him off. "I'm fine."

Stunned, Charras withdrew his hand, following her silently as she hobbled into the kitchen and sat at the table. There, she pulled up the back of her top and revealed the extent of her wounds. Among the various bruises and superficial cuts, three deep welts sat side by side along her spine, dirtied and oozing. He couldn't tell how infected they were but he knew they needed immediate treatment.

"This will sting," he warned, swallowing his concern and pulling out the required equipment.

It was necessary; he knew that. He had to make sure she could protect herself. There was no other way; the Hetairia Doman – the government of the Mage world – expected it and they already doubted his abilities in training her. If he could not prove himself they would take her away and she could suffer worse tests, or even punishments for her small rebellions he kept a secret. No, she was safer with him, happier at least…

And yet, even with a snapped ankle the Sirenari had been a match. He dreaded to think what could have happened if they'd been present in their pack.

Stop it he scolded himself. *She is strong like her mother*.

With that thought guiding him, he proceeded to clean the Sirenari's handiwork, letting the warm antiseptic seep into the wounds and clean out the dirt and infection. Then, using his Incendiī element, he forced the welts to scab.

Throughout it all, Charlize bit back gasps of pain, although her demeanour showed no signs of softening. She refused to complain or flinch, instead staring at the floor as if it held answers, her knees hugged to her chest as she balanced stoically on the wooden chair.

She knew; Charras was sure of it. For weeks he'd been slipping out to collect the Minae, retaining their every detail in his mind before transferring them into the test as memories. He hoped their presence there would explain their presence on the battleground. Yet due to the Wraithart, he hadn't fooled her. If only he'd known the bear that stalked their house had once belonged to it.

Securing the last dressing, he pulled her top back down. "All done."

Immediately standing from the table, Charlize limped towards the arch.

"He was a good dog," Charras said, stopping her in her tracks.

She turned slightly and nodded once. Then, without a word, she vacated the kitchen, leaving behind a chill that Charras would never forget.

11

Older

A fire burned serenely in the sitting room. Its flickering light emanated from the hearth and danced along the furniture, casting honeycomb flecks on the face of a young woman. Her long dark hair hung down from the settee, reaching the floor, and her hand dangled limply on the soft cream carpet.

Suspended in the cool dawn, the manor awaited her next movements. Outside, a jackdaw crowed, its harsh caw signalling to others that the worm it caught beneath a bog rosemary shrub belonged only to him. It had taken him all morning to find it, waiting as the damp earth from last night's rains had dried enough to reveal the worms' position, and he wasn't about to forfeit the juicy morsel now.

The ruckus caused by the competition made Charlize flick open her eyes, stirred from a nightmare as the terror that gripped her subconscious rebounded in her waking thoughts. Allowing a shiver to vibrate along her spine, she quickly crawled across the carpet to stack more wood onto the fire, the warmth soon soothing the memory away.

It was always the same one: the face of a broken girl, the glazed eyes of a person who had once been alive – hair lank and lacklustre… It had taken her a long time to realise she'd been fighting herself.

She plunged her hand into the flames of the fire and forced herself to think of the mundane. It helped to ease the frequent darker thoughts, the technique something her Hetairia Doman councillor tried to teach her. He called it '*an aid to escape the worries of the Āetis affliction.*' It often helped after a particularly bad dream, but only if she mastered it. So, taking a deep breath, she crossed her legs.

Okay, you can do this. Breathe deeply. Centre the flow of air. You are one with the breeze… you are the air… flowers bloom beneath your feet… There are fields stretching for miles in front of you… fields of space…

space that stretches beyond the Arx of Marsh Village, the world on the other side of the Arcēs… the dangerous world you will soon discover on your pilgri' –

"Dammit."

Swatting the fire, Charlize got to her feet. She was leaving for her pilgrimage in a few days, a fact she couldn't get out of her head, regardless of how desperate her meditation. Not that she should be calm. Her eighteenth birthday was just two days away, a milestone for every Mage that signalled the commencing of their journey. It would see them dwelling in each Haunt to learn the ways of each clan – a tradition upheld since Mages came to be. Its aim was to unite them without prejudice, fear, or diffidence; to bring together their cultures and declare themselves brothers and sisters bonded in their magic.

But of course, Charlize knew its real aim was to make sure that when war waged, the Mages did not stand divided. If they had a hope of winning, they would have to fight alongside each other. And seeing as her birth heralded the coming of that war, it was her job to make sure they all got along…

Luckily for her, that day was yet to come, whereas currently, it was a day of celebration. Finally, after five long years, she could say goodbye to her secondary school. She wasn't sad and the goodbyes wouldn't be difficult. Her class was small so she had made few friends, fewer still because those who did not know her true identity thought her to be strange, while those who did felt inferior. Polite interaction was all she knew, unable to share in the frivolous behaviour of most of her classmates. No one bullied her – not that they hadn't tried; it just quickly became obvious that taunts didn't affect her, which meant it wasn't fun. But it also meant she was the anomaly of the class, having no place in any of the circles.

The chime of a clock pulled Charlize from her thoughts and she rubbed her eyes. Getting to her feet, she left the sitting room and crept through the lobby.

Twilight swallowed the manor, the early hour harbouring a slight chill, and pulling open the bathroom door, she gently closed it behind her.

It wasn't unusual for her to be up early, often unable to sleep for long periods of time – a fact she tried to hide from her father. Fortunately, the manor was big enough to shield her night-walking antics from him, for although his concern for her safety had lessened throughout her schooling, he retained an air of vigilance over her whereabouts – something that often infuriated her.

She turned on the taps and proceeded to run a bath. The warm water helped to calm her, and once the lavender suds reached the middle of the tub, she stripped to her bare skin and immersed herself, casting a quick Aquāe spell that allowed her to breathe underwater. Then, sinking below the surface, she soon fell to sleep once more.

Awaking from her slumber, refreshed and resembling a prune, Charlize broke through the foam surface and stood from the significantly cooler bath. Wrapping herself in a large towel, she left the bathroom and made her way upstairs, morning finally broken as eastern light streaked into the manor.

She entered her room, which was immaculate as usual, and dressed quickly. Then, tying her long hair in a loose bun – paying no attention to the unruly strands refusing to stay confined – she checked the time on her Fulgor powered clock. It read 7:15. With a gasp, she rushed downstairs to the kitchen where she busied herself making breakfast. Christian would be arriving in less than an hour and she still had her father to feed...

Charras awoke to the smell of bacon and eggs frying expertly on the hob. Although they were in the comfort of their own home, Mages lived much like the Ungifted, their aim to keep their race a secret of the utmost importance. The practise indoors made it more natural outdoors, and it wasn't wise to risk exposure, even in the security of your own walls.

He sat upright in the warm leather chair, a soft blanket falling from his shoulders, and noted how Charlize must have laid it across him the night before. Rubbing his groggy head, he recalled the discussion they'd been having before fatigue took over. It was crucial they finished what they'd been talking about.

After a few attempts, he managed to heave himself into a standing position; silently curse his imbalance; shuffle from the library; cross the lobby; enter the kitchen, and ease himself into a chair at the table. There, he put his muffled head in his hands.

"Good morning father," said Charlize. "You're just in time, here you go." Placing the plate of eggs and bacon in front of him, she held her hand to his forehead. "You're burning up, more than usual."

Charras waved her off and picked up his knife and fork. "Thank-you," he mumbled.

Charlize nodded and finished pouring the freshly squeezed lemon zest into a cup of hot water. "Drink this, it will help your cold." She placed it in front of him. "I won't be back until later so make sure you drink plenty of it." She then pointed towards the kettle on the stove.

Charras stared at the mug as if the virus mocked him from beneath the citrus waters, making Charlize shake her head and slide it closer. "I've added honey for sweetness. It will help it go down, so make sure you drink it all. You'll feel better I promise. And your Incendiī will burn it out in no time."

With a grunt, Charras devoured his plate of food in less than two minutes, before eyeing the mug and sniffing the steam coiling above its brim. Taking a small sip, he immediately placed it back on the table and avoided the scornful expression of his daughter.

"There have been further breaches, you must stay alert," he said to the table.

Having finished the washing up, Charlize wiped her hands on a towel before pointing at the mug. "Drink. Christian will be here any minute so I can't make sure, but I'll know," she warned.

As she passed him on her way out, Charras grasped her wrist. "Promise me. No more heroics, you come straight home the minute your classes are over."

His eyes were dark and red rimmed, but Charlize knew not to argue. Bowing her head, she gently pulled away from his clasp. "Of course father, as always."

He nodded, signing a gesture of thanks for his breakfast, then grasped the concoction that promised to ease his suffering and brought it to his lips. From beneath his brows, he watched as Charlize disappeared back upstairs, her pace quickening when the clock chimed for eight o'clock.

He knew his words fell on deaf ears, but he hoped their warning would stay in her mind the next time she thought to lead a small class of underage Mages into the fray of several Achak and Akuji. He'd endured several angry calls from parents for weeks afterwards, it mattering little that their battle had been an impressive success.

Upstairs, Charlize desperately tried to recall where she'd left her final assignment, the last one she'd ever have to hand in. The doorbell rang loudly, echoing through her room, and she heard her father get up to answer it, shortly followed by muffled greetings. A quick shuffle through the papers on her desk revealed the reports hiding place – tucked neatly beneath a pile of chalk drawings – and sighing with relief, she shoved it into her folder; grabbed her bag; ran back downstairs, and pulled on her coat as she met Christian in the lobby.

"One day I'm sure you won't be late," he said, standing back as Charlize rushed to haul her bag over her head and pick her folder back up. "Oh no, wait, this was your final chance."

She ignored him, opened the door, and ushered him out of the manor. "I'll see you shortly father!" she called over her shoulder.

A soft grunt found its way to her before she shut the door firmly behind her. It was the best she could hope for.

Christian was already in his car as Charlize struggled to the bottom of the driveway and through the voice-activated gate, which was wedged open again – despite several requests for it not to be. Kicking away the stone, she scowled at him through his window and walked around to pull open the familiar red door and ease into the passenger seat.

Once settled, she sat with her belongings on her lap, there being no other place for them amongst the garbage on the back seat.

"One day you'll stop wedging the gate open," she said.

"Oh well, I guess we both blew our final chances."

Neither looked at the other, eyes fixed dead ahead. It was not their decision to go to school together every day – it was their parents, forced upon them since they were thirteen. If it were not on the bus, then it was once Christian learned to drive five months ago, his hope of freedom short lived. Fortunately for him, Charlize didn't say much. Any attempt at conversation quickly ended in awkward silence, which he believed had everything to do with the fact she didn't own a television. Cut off from the world of entertainment made her dull.

"You can explain why we're late again," he mumbled once they'd been driving in silence for over ten minutes.

"It was only two minutes; perhaps if you drove faster we'd be there sooner."

Christian frowned and Charlize continued to stare out of the window. That was the end of their communication for the duration of the journey. Neither had much more to say to the other, and it had been that way for years.

The large school loomed ahead as Christian pulled onto the grounds. Parking in a bay closest to the school gates, he immediately got out of the car, leaving Charlize to struggle once more. She shoved the door open with her foot and climbed out, but upon slamming it behind her, dropped her folder and scattered several loose papers across the gravel. With a heavy sigh, she bent down to pick them back up.

"You're such a klutz," said Christian, walking over to help her.

"Don't, I can manage," she snapped.

"Fine, sorry," he said with a grunt, holding up his hands.

Charlize gathered the remaining rogue sheets and got to her feet. Then, swinging her pack on her back and hugging the folder to her chest, she mentally prepared herself for her last day, gazing towards the school as she watched a boy with shaggy brown hair bound over, a smile on his dimpled face. He instantly took her bags and put them over his shoulder.

"Thank-you Elliott, I see manners aren't quite dead," she said impertinently, aiming the comment towards Christian.

He responded by rolling his eyes and throwing his keys into his bag, before sauntering off to join his friends. They stood standing in the alcove of the grounds bus shelter, all sharing in the delight of their last day of secondary education. Each of their faces held excitement, the promise of their futures a novel concept. Charlize felt a stab of envy, the promise of her future far less uncertain.

"How many did you borrow?!"

Returning her attention to Elliott, she shrugged. "Eight in the last term, I promised to return them today."

"Well, let's not disappoint Miss Lewis."

With a last glance towards the bus stop, Charlize took a deep breath. "No, let's not," she murmured. Miss Lewis was a tough Librarian, her strict regime within her walls notorious to all and unfortunate to those whose ignorance was soon corrected.

Charlize followed Elliott, walking by his side as they ascended the stone steps of the red brick building. Together, they stepped through into the reception area where several corridors forked out like tree branches. Each led to a separate subject area the prestigious institution offered, a piece of concept art in the form of a tapestry nailed into the wall above each section.

Marked quite apparently by the different shades of maroon on each uniform, the blazers signified the year a pupil was in – the darker the shade, the older the student. College year allowed students from the age of seventeen to wear their own clothes, as long as they wore white and navy and still donned the badge of the Marsh Village, which was a sycamore leaf.

Six entrances led into the school, and each corresponded to the house pupils were allocated. The entrance Charlize and Elliott came through stood at the very front, the Birch Wing, and a mural of the same tree greeted them as they made their way through a corridor decorated with equations and the face of Einsteiner, a famous Glacies Mage (or mathematician – depending on who you talked to).

They were no further than a few feet from their classroom when Christian and his large social group pushed past them, running ahead as a tennis ball darted back and forth between them. They laughed meanly when the ball managed to hit several first years on the head, even though they attempted to duck from the flying hazard, and Charlize rolled her eyes in contempt. The game provided nothing but proof to her silent accusations of immaturity.

"Luce! Catch!"

Standing a pace away, Charlize watched her fellow classmate reach out with her hand as the ball flew towards her. She missed the catch and Charlize instinctively caught it instead, her quick reactions drawing the attention she usually avoided. Silent accusations bore into her as the Mages of her class hushed respectfully.

"Wow, that was lucky!" Lucy remarked excitedly, unaware of the sudden tension.

Charlize lowered her eyes and placed the ball in her bag, allowing Elliott's grasp on her arm to guide her away from the stunned audience.

"That was impossible," she heard a boy she knew as Adam whisper.

Looking up momentarily, she managed to catch Christian's bemused expression before she quickly averted her gaze. His dark eyes always seemed to hold her attention, their kindness able to switch to scorn quicker than she could say *Dicio*.

"Go easy Charlize," Elliott murmured as they found their desks.

Putting her head in her hands, she sighed. *Idiot* she cursed herself, staring at the tarnished wood beneath her elbows. She only looked up again when their teacher, Mr Hammond entered. Without a word, he walked up to the board at the front of the class and held up a red marker pen, slowly writing two words:

'LAST DAY.'

Cheers and shouts rang through the classroom until Mr Hammond hushed them. Then, pushing his glasses up his elongated nose, he cleared his throat.

"Now, to those of you who chose to stay on for your A-levels, the next year is an important one for you. It will be time to choose your University. I understand many of you have decided to take a gap year, to either go to neighbouring villages for travel, or to work and earn money. Some of you are perhaps just going to leave education for a while. This is your decision and you alone can make the right one. Therefore, for this reason, today's class is a small one. We will spend the majority of it finishing your work for the final moderation, to then end our day with a light discussion of everyone's future plans." Pausing, he peered through his thick black frames to the expectant class. "Then you don't have to see me again."

Smirks and murmurs of *'yes!'* rang quietly through the room.

All of this Charlize ignored. Staring silently out of the window, she lost herself to the light drizzle that teased the window ledge. There would be no university for her, no gap year to return from. She would travel to five points of the earth, to a world outside the isolated comfort of the Marsh village. She would meet her fate and never return from it; the Āetis, her great destiny; her duty; her birthright... Yet, no matter how hard she tried, she couldn't focus on anything but the end. No matter how glorious her title, she couldn't meet her destiny with a smile. There was no question of running; nothing in her fought the inevitability; she would carry out her duty for the greater good, and because, by some twisted clause, she was the only one who could…

"You okay?"

Blinking, Charlize turned to face Elliott, his question penetrating her thoughts. She nodded once and turned back to the window. Throughout her absent-mindedness, the rain had picked up speed, heavy droplets now hammering against the glass.

"It's raining," she said. "It always rains."

"The forecast said there would only be a mild breeze today," Elliott replied. "Where has it come from?"

Charlize didn't know. She had an idea, but she couldn't be certain. Squinting in an attempt to pick out the source, threads of ice began to weave in the corners of the window, the droplets noticeably louder as they turned to hail and began to bounce off the glass. The room darkened as the light was lost and all attention turned to the sounds of the *tap-tap-tapping* that grew urgent and aggressive.

"Charlize…"

It was Mr Hammond's voice. She looked up to see him casting, his hands outstretched either side of him as he used his Anima to send the Ungifted of the class into a somnolent trance. They each stared ahead, frozen in time, suddenly unaware of the barrage against the windows.

Charlize looked at Christian, his floppy blonde hair obscuring his brown eyes – half shut and dreamy. She often wondered why he was still affected by the castings, assuming that his dormant energy must stunt his natural immunity to magic in some way.

Only five Mages retained their awareness. They all stood from their desks and looked at Charlize, who was already standing and heading for the door.

"Wait, let us come with you," Elliott said, following her.

Charlize shook her head. "Not today, I can't put you at risk again in such a short space of time."

"That's our choice."

With a quick look to Mr Hammond, who was concentrating on keeping the Ungifted under control, she sighed. "Ok, but just you Elliott."

She didn't hang around to see the looks of relief on the remaining Mages faces.

Out in the corridor, the smooth cream floors were cold to the touch. Each of the windows were threaded with webs of ice and a biting chill had descended on the school – or at least in the wing Charlize occupied; she wasn't sure where else was effected.

"What do you think it is?" Elliott whispered. Not because he had to, but because the stillness seemed to call for quiet.

His warmth next to her was a noticeable presence in the cold and Charlize was grateful for his company, although she would never admit it. "I'm not sure, we're either dealing with several Achak or Akuji, or we've got a Shadowlan again."

She didn't need to look to know Elliott tensed. Their last affray had been a Shadowlan and he'd felt the grip of their icy fingers, just as she had several years earlier. He'd described it as being like they intruded parts of him that had no form. For days after, he couldn't shake the residue of cold, even though he wrapped himself in blankets and drank tea with honey every few hours. His mother had been the first and the last to speak out to her father, and Elliott hadn't been allowed in school for two weeks.

"You don't need to stay, I can't handle this alone," she said, meaning it kindly but saying it brashly.

"No Charlize, I must conquer these fears. Otherwise, what kind of Mage will I become?"

She nodded. "Very well, follow me."

They walked through the blue tinged corridors at a gentle pace, ever alert as the hail sliced at the windows. If they were made of normal glass, and not reinforced with ice enchantments of their own, they would lie shattered and exposed. But the Arcēs were built with the threat of destruction around them. Even the smallest Arx was designed to withstand a potential siege.

Turning into another corridor, this one decorated with murals of Silver Birch trees, the pale bark further chilled the air, causing Elliott to suck in a breath that made Charlize flinch and turn to him. And then, all at once, a shadow darted past them, close enough that the pull of its form drew them in, but far enough away that Charlize managed to slam them both against the wall and release a ball of flame that shot in the direction of their attacker. She missed, but the fizzle of fire lit a path that warned the Minae from returning.

"*Shadowlan*," Elliott croaked.

"You really don't have to stay," Charlize replied, attempting to soften her tone this time.

He shook his head and she saw his stubborn resolve. She wouldn't argue with it, not unless she wanted to cause offence, which she certainly had no intention of doing.

"I think it went towards the library," she said instead, stepping away from the wall. There would be many hiding places and Minae favoured crowded spaces.

If Elliott was scared, he did well to hide it. Broadening his chest, he led the way with a determination that hadn't been there before.

They crossed into the reception area, the lamp on the desk having switched on – an automatic response to the dim – and it illuminated the receptionist, her body slumped and head to her chest. As Charlize got closer, she spied the protection weaving around her and waited until she saw the characteristic heaving of shoulders that reassured her Katrina – as was her name – still breathed.

Elliott on the other hand was already continuing onwards, his right hand out and ready to cast. He would not be caught off guard again....

Charlize hurried to catch up with him in the Oak wing; its twisting corridor intended to mimic the reach of the grandfather tree's knowledge – an apt place to house a library. She stopped once more to peer into a classroom of tenth graders. They sat in the same way as her class had, with eyes dead ahead, eerily unmoving and silent while their teacher kept them entranced. Those who were Mages looked over to her framed in the door's window, relieved to see her face and know the threat was being dealt with. Some even gave a nervous wave, which she responded to with a small nod before carrying on towards the library.

Knowing without seeing that her guess was right, she tried to ignore the slight jubilance in her stomach as she caught up with Elliott, rounded the corner, and witnessed how the library door was completely frozen and impenetrable to Ungifted.

"You were right," Elliott murmured.

"It was the most plausible place," Charlize replied, placing her hand on where the seal between the casement doors would normally be. She could feel the shift in depth, the energy used to create the barricade weaker where it had nothing but itself to secure it.

"Stand back," she warned, pointing at the place she'd marked with condensation.

Elliott didn't need to be told twice. Giving Charlize her space, he watched as she threw her hair back from her shoulders, the lean muscles in her neck tensing as she secured her footing and mumbled an incantation. Then, with the speed of a whip, she sliced a lattice of sparks the length of her arm into the ice fortification, following it with a blast of air that made it shudder, the ice crumbling as the doors screeched across the polished wooden floorboards. They juddered to a stop wide enough for three people to pass through.

"Impressive," Elliott smirked, coming to stand by her side.

Charlize shrugged, although she silently agreed. However, her father always told her that outward confidence wasn't socially acceptable, so she kept it to herself.

The library was a warm and mildly dusty room, the burnt oak furnishings and wooden panelled ceilings designed to give the visitor a sense of being inside the hull of a tree. Even the bookshelves were placed in carved hollows, each recess delicately lit with small yellow bulbs screwed into the 'branches' so it looked as if they sparkled at a distance. With no particular order, high backed chairs of greens, browns, mustard, and mahogany sat sporadically beneath over-lamps, their necks extended so they offered small breakout areas to read or convalesce. Some clustered around tables stacked with more books, their patchwork cushions long faded or frayed – likely due to the many hours spent housing students gossiping or discussing recent findings and intrigues.

Miss Lewis often burned sandalwood incense to disguise the fusty aroma, and she'd insisted on brewing coffee in her open office in the middle of the library, claiming it would further sweeten the lure of learning, (although the rumour was that the faculty was too scared to refuse her) and Charlize looked towards it now. It was shaped like a tree stump, burrowed out in the middle to leave enough depth for the ridge to double up as a countertop. She walked towards it, certain Miss Lewis would have been around at the time of the attack. (No one had actually seen her outside of the library, it being rumoured she permanently resided in the school).

Peering over the counter, Charlize looked down at the desk littered with stationary; a wire phone; a small flat computer, and a half-eaten wheat biscuit. Then, scanning her eyes over the swivel chair, she noticed a broken mug on the floor, the contents of a freshly poured coffee staining the floorboards.

"Is she here?" Elliott asked, his voice holding an edge of concern.

Charlize shook her head. "No. But she was, not long ago."

He walked towards her and looked down at the same scene. "Follow me; I know where she'd hiding."

Mildly wondering how he would know such a thing, Charlize followed Elliott as he led her towards the farthest part of the library. There were books cordoned off in a shallow hollow with no light, and a warning sign to the left saying: 'NO UNAUTHORISED ACCESS.'

"Perhaps we shouldn't," Charlize said, disliking the idea of breaking a rule.

"It's fine," Elliott replied, ducking beneath the brown tape and beckoning for her to follow.

She didn't move at first, a lifetime of following the rules meaning she felt a stiff resistance to violating one so obvious.

Elliott must have noticed as he held his arms out and gesticulated that all was well. "She keeps all the history and magic books here, the ones the Ungifted shouldn't see. We can pass because we're Mages. We're allowed in here, I promise."

"Then why am I just hearing about it now?"

"I honestly don't know Charlize. I thought you of all people would have known about this area. Perhaps you would have sooner if you spoke to people more often."

She thought that it was a fair assumption. Besides, for as long as she could remember the hollow was restricted. Miss Lewis said that if anyone wanted a book from its collection, they would have to explain why in detail. Luck would have it that she never needed a volume from its capacity; her father's library held every answer she sought, even some she didn't...

"Ok," she said. "Show me where you think she's hiding."

Ducking beneath the tape as Elliott had, Charlize put her back to the nearest wall and crossed her arms. She shifted uncomfortably, constantly looking out to the library as if she were afraid someone might catch her rebellion. To distract herself, she busied her mind by watching Elliott put his hands either side of a central shelving unit. His face set, he used all of his weight to push against it, adding pressure until it finally budged across the floor and clicked against an unknown stopper. Then, throwing off the newly exposed moss green rug, he revealed a set of stairs, gesturing at them with triumph.

Having forgotten her earlier discomfort, Charlize's interest was piqued. She peered into the hole and held her hand just above it. A cool breeze met her skin and she curled her nails into the flesh of her palm.

"It's down there," she said.

A shiver brushed her spine, and turning to Elliott, his eyes wide, she saw he felt the same. He immediately cast a flame in his palm and readied his Anima. He would blast it forwards at the right moment should he need to.

Charlize nodded towards him, took a breath, and circled a protection around herself. "Be alert," she said as she began to descend the stairs.

She reached the bottom without pause. All was dark, any light that may have been available swallowed or broken by the ice crystallised along their surfaces. Her breath was cold, and even though she couldn't see, she knew a thin layer of frost covered everything around her.

"Show yourself," she murmured.

The chink of something falling responded, and she cast a fireball in its direction, only to illuminate the face of Miss Lewis as she lay on a bed made of two mattresses. Rushing to her side, Charlize immediately checked for a pulse.

It was there, faint but unmistakable.

"Miss Lewis? Miss Lewis, are you okay?" she asked, shaking her shoulder.

A small whimper responded and the weathered librarian opened her eyes, blurry and confused as she looked up at Charlize holding an orange hand above her head.

"What, what is the meaning of this?" she said, her voice weak but still sharp as she attempted to sit up.

"You've been attacked, a Shadowlan… have you seen it?"

"A Sha –" She was sitting now and holding a hand to her side. "Yes. Yes, I do remember. Why, it came at such a speed I had no time to react."

It was only when Charlize thought to ask of any relatives she could contact, she realised the rumours were true. Miss Lewis did live in the library. From the limited light her hand was giving off, she was able to discern a small stove in the left-hand corner. Next to it sat three mismatched chairs surrounding a wooden table, which had a shelf built beneath – currently home to a few dishes and mugs each stacked neatly across its breadth, and in the opposite corner, a chest of drawers doubled up as a bookshelf.

"Can I get you anything?" she asked. "Is there someone I can –"

She didn't finish her sentence before a force sent her careering into the wall above Miss Lewis's bed, who she accidentally kicked in the shoulder as she passed.

"Apologies!" she called before landing on the pillows with ease – the protection absorbing most of the impact.

She then proceeded to give chase.

"Elliott, it's coming!" she shrieked, reaching the bottom of the stairs as the Shadowlan shimmered its way through the opening.

Taking the stairs two at a time, she darted through the hidden hollow, breaking the tape at her waist as she spilled into the library – only to quickly find herself gathered into Elliott's arms, his face a picture of elation.

"Charlize, I did it! I did it!"

It took her a moment to collect herself and resume a normal breath. But then, letting a smile cross her face, she looked over Elliott's shoulder to the Shadowlan's energy gleaming against the floor, a rainbow of colours that told her it was fresh.

"You did excellently, well done!" she said, freeing herself from his grip and putting a hand on his shoulder. "Now to send it."

He nodded once and strode confidently to its side. But as he opened his mouth to begin the Mittere, a howl of anguish came from the hidden hollow.

"Destruction! Vandalism!"

Charlize looked over to see Miss Lewis's chin wobbling as she shook with rage.

"The sheer mess in here! Oh how will I ever clean this up? Look, look what has become of my library!" She shook her fists. "Out, both of you, I will deal with this!"

Elliott lowered his arms, shooting Charlize a quick glance as he backed away from the spirit. If they didn't know about her tragic living conditions, they may have been more inclined to argue. But as it was, they felt a stab of pity. The library was her home, a place she usually felt safe, and now the attack would forever be associated with it.

"Of course, Miss Lewis," Charlize said. "Please, let us know if anything can be done to aid you."

There was no response, and as Elliott and Charlize began walking back to their classroom, the school returning to its normal luminescence, they acknowledged their newfound respect for the grouchy librarian.

12
Fuel

The bell rang and the class said their goodbyes to one another before slowly siphoning off, whoops of joy ringing through the corridors long after Mr Hammond vacated – curiously the first to leave. Only Elliott, Lucy, and Charlize remained in the classroom. Not by choice, but out of concern, for the goodbyes were all too much for Lucy and she hadn't stopped crying for over twenty minutes.

Staying to make sure she didn't hurt herself, Charlize was concerned that the mascara bleeding into her eyes was a hazard. There had already been an awkward moment when Lucy hugged her, declaring their friendship more important than Charlize believed a handful of conversations in four years could ever possibly be. But even with this new revelation, comfort wasn't something that came naturally to her. So, in an attempt, she tucked her supposed friend's short blonde hair behind her ears.

"You will be fine Lucy, you are full of energy. People like that," she said, patting her shoulder.

Lucy sniffed and nodded. "When will you come home? Oh Charlize, you're my only friend around here." More black tears sprang down her face.

Behind her, Charlize felt Elliott tense. Attempting to smile warmly, she shrugged. "I'm not sure how long father wants to travel for."

The lie was easy. Although she knew it was the last time they'd see one another, allowing Lucy the reassurance that she wouldn't lose a friend, however recent, seemed the right thing to do. Luckily, it wasn't long until Liam, Lucy's boyfriend, came to collect her, and with one last snivel, she waved her last goodbye, allowing Liam to dry her tears with his sleeve.

In the resulting empty room, Elliott turned to Charlize. "You leave for your pilgrimage next week," he said, not really asking a question.

Charlize nodded, touching the hand of her Incendiī-Anima friend, the same clan's as her father. "We'll see each other again, I'm sure, for you'll leave for your own in three months – and already with a tale to tell."

Elliott nodded. "I'll have to address you as Āetis then."

"We will never need such formalities," Charlize reassured. "Besides, it is rude to speak to me using that name. It sounds like a curse. Unless you meet with me in formal circumstances, we shall always address each other by our first names, not our titles."

With a lop-sided smile, Elliott sat on the desk Charlize propped herself against. "I think I can do that."

After a few moments of pause, he took a deep breath, exhaling slowly. Suddenly looking nervous, he spoke, his voice softer. "With this last day ending, and our future beginning and all of that… stuff…" Charlize waited, her eyes meeting his. He smiled and shook his head. "I just wanted, I mean, I want to say – keep well."

"Keep well," she replied.

Elliott moved closer and put his palm up to face her. Automatically knowing what to do, Charlize placed her own palm against his, as was the traditional greeting of the Mages. The contact allowed the sensations of each clan to surge through skin-to-skin connections. It helped Mages recognise each other, noting the elements within their acquaintance. Deemed rude to ask or even speak openly about the complexities of magic, unless a context called for it, the palm greeting was a safe way of communicating their kin.

"You would have seen me before I left," reminded Charlize, aware they hadn't severed their palms.

Saying nothing, Elliott moved closer, maintaining a peculiar amount of eye contact with her, as if the situation required an action she couldn't fathom. It was only as he leant forward she realised what was happening.

Still refusing to relinquish her palm, too courteous to do so first, Charlize watched as Elliott tilted his head. She'd seen Lucy kiss Liam once, but it looked messy and awkward. Having never kissed a boy, she wasn't sure it was something she was interested in trying… Although it didn't seem like she'd have much choice, as dangerously close, she was able to see Elliott's true eye colour for the first time – a light chestnut with a green circle around them. She thought how nice they were, but soon lost all concentration as his lips pressed against hers.

His eyes now closed and blurred, she didn't know where to look. Fortunately, it didn't last long; Elliott pulled away and sat back up after only a few seconds.

"Yes, I probably would have," he said softly.

"Would have what?" Her mouth was dry.

"Seen you before you left."

"You still will," she reminded, slightly more legibly.

With both adolescents not quite sure of their position, they sat quietly. It wasn't bad Charlize thought, not at all what she was expecting. There was a distinct lack of spittle, and Elliott's chin was dry and devoid of lip-gloss – not that she wore any. It was a success; she was sure.

"I should probably go," she said quietly, standing upright.

"Me too."

Both a little shy, they picked up their bags before facing each other once more. Elliott smiled and pulled Charlize towards him, preparing an embrace, but caught off-guard, she stumbled forward and landed on his toe. She immediately jumped back and apologised profusely. There was another pause as they stared at each other, and then Elliott laughed, causing Charlize to smile – again out of courtesy – for she wondered what was amusing.

"Keep well," Elliott reiterated, laughter still in his throat as he held his palm up in a gesture of apology.

Charlize mirrored hers against his. "Keep well."

"Are you ready?" a sharp voice asked, cutting through the moment.

Snapping her head up and dropping her hand, Charlize turned to see Christian standing in the doorway. Wondering how long he'd been there, she stepped back a few paces and composed her face. "Yes, of course," she said.

The heat rose in her cheeks as Elliott made to leave. They exchanged a few kind goodbyes before he patted Christian on the shoulder and disappeared along the corridor, soon out of sight.

Alone, Charlize waited for Christian to say something, uncertain of the expression he'd adopted, his intensity only causing her cheeks to flush further.

"Are you coming?" he asked.

"Yes… I was just… saying farewell," she replied.

Christian didn't respond, instead turning to march towards the exit, barely acknowledging her as she followed and fell into step at his side. They reached the end of the corridor and he shoved open the thickset doors leading to the car park, his lonely pride and joy surrounded by the numerous white marks of empty spaces. Running up to it, he opened the door, threw his virtually empty bags onto the back seat and waited for Charlize to do the same. When she didn't, he looked back to see her staring up at the school, a whimsical expression on her face that stopped him from calling out. There was something about her posture that silenced him, and dipping down, he made himself comfortable in the driver's seat. He didn't start the engine, waiting and watching as Charlize shook herself from whatever moment she was having. She turned around, her face embarrassed, and quickly walked to the car and got in.

"I'm sorry," she said.

Christian shrugged and waited while she fiddled with her seat belt, her immaculate bronze skin and large eyes suddenly clear to him. He frowned, confused by a sudden feeling he couldn't quite place, and tried to figure out why the girl who held a countenance of ethereal arrogance suddenly seemed so vulnerable to him. He found himself strangely wanting to comfort her – a girl he saw as nothing more than a burden his parents forced on him; a girl that no matter the weather, a grey cloud seemed to stalk her.

"Are we going to go home?" she asked.

Her voice brought him back down to earth. It annoyed him. Her sickly sweet tone always seemed fake and strained, her air of propriety now completely broken since her little incident with Elliott moments ago. It confirmed his suspicions that she wasn't the princess she made herself out to be.

"Are you sure it's your home you want to go to?" he said with a smirk.

Charlize didn't move. "Have I done something to make you think otherwise?"

"I'm sorry, I must be mistaken, does Charras know his daughter sneaks around and kisses strange boys?"

The flush rose to her cheeks once more. "That is none of your business Christian. Besides, Elliott is not a stranger; he is less of a stranger to me than you."

"I could see that."

Pulling her long coat around her knees, Charlize frowned. "Why does it matter to you?"

Christian shrugged and put his hands on the steering wheel. "I find it amusing you pretend you're some sort of holy virgin, while the entire time, you're anything but."

Charlize opened and shut her mouth before finding her rage. "That is an insult beyond what I thought you capable! Please, take me home."

"You're right, forgive me, I only wonder at the reaction your father would have to such a revelation."

Charlize was incredulous, her heart beating faster than she could remember for a long while. Unable to do much more, her eyes darkened and she sat back in her seat, crossing her arms and staring out of the passenger window. If her father discovered her moment of curiosity he would be ashamed. Swearing to never find cause for such weakness again, she prepared to placate Christian.

"Please, do not tell him," she said as softly as her bubbling wrath could manage.

Sighing, Christian relaxed his grip on the wheel. "It's no big deal, it was just a kiss. I don't see why Charras would care so much."

"Then why would you threaten to tell him if you thought so?"

"I suppose I like to see you squirm."

"That's not very nice."

"*I'm* not nice? Ha! I'm not the one who doesn't let you near boys."

The slur on her father's character was enough. "Do not speak of things you know nothing about. It is improper for me to have relations with any man; I wouldn't expect you to understand. Besides, I have neither the time nor the inclination."

"Does Elliott know that?"

Guilt rippled up Charlize's spine. "I was curious, it was a mistake."

Raising his eyebrows, Christian guffawed. "That's flattering."

Charlize glared at his cheek but said nothing. She knew better than to push the issue, his furrowed brow an indication of his mood, and she thought to herself how easy his emotions were to detect. She turned away and looked down at her hands.

"The first time we talk for more than five seconds and we end up arguing," Christian said with a sigh. Then, turning his body towards her: "It's weird, I have grown up with you, yet I know nothing about you. You're like this statue I see in the park. It's there, but not alive, you know?"

The words hit her like ice. For more times than she cared to remember, Charlize longed to tell him why they were distant, why they couldn't be close. Yet, if she were honest with herself, even if he did know, there would still be distance between them. For years she'd felt the mental walls building around her and of everyone else she came into contact with. Mostly she didn't mind, the chance of a true friendship a concept too painful to endure, knowing the likelihood of them being short lived. But never would she feel the freedoms of those around her, the happy-go-lucky bonds that made Mages and Ungifted alike smile, the cherry on a cake baked with ash and bone.

"If that's how you see me, then why do you suddenly care about it now? You've treated me with nothing but distain our entire lives."

Christian straightened his back against his seat and looked out of the windscreen. "I don't know," he grunted after a short time. "Maybe I'm getting sentimental."

The joke fell flat – the same way conversations always did when they spoke for more than a minute.

With a nod, Charlize pursed her lips. "Maybe."

The low rumble of the engine disturbed the silence as Christian finally pulled out of the school gates. With the moors blurring into a succession of colour, Charlize said her farewells, convinced the picture of her journey to and from school would never be forgotten, able to recall every detail of the small town at a moment's notice if she so wished. For even in the Arx there were places out of bounds, high-risk danger areas meaning that tried and tested 'safe' routes kept being re-established, the trails worn and trodden. Of course accidents happened, curiosity a curse that meant walking the marshes deemed you as brave as a patrol officer by Ungifted, or as stupid as a gnat by Mages.

She thought of the time Christian proved his 'bravery' by wading into a flooded Marsh wearing only his wellington boots, undershirt, and trousers to rescue a stranded kitten. He was only fifteen and had been heralded a hero by all – none less than Geraldine Tilderberry whose tabby it was. When he returned to school after surviving a subsequent bout of flu, she'd been quite taken with him, the obsession lasting for many years afterwards.

Of course, what they weren't to know was Charlize's part in the rescue. While Christian boldly stepped into the muddy waters, she'd secretly warmed and slowed the flow beneath his feet. It wasn't noticeable enough for him to suspect anything, but it was helpful enough that when he recounted the details to his parent's, she wouldn't be scolded for letting him put himself in danger.

With a hidden smile at the memory, she peered at Christian out of the corner of her eye. His stern expression and set jaw told her he still mulled their conversation over.

"I haven't ever meant to offend you," she proffered.

Keeping his eyes on the road ahead, Christian managed a slight smirk. "I think we're both guilty of the opposite."

All warmth leaving her body, rendering her unable to argue further, Charlize kept her expression stony, a strange feeling in her gut as she concentrated on the rolling countryside. As she folded her arms across her chest and twisted her body towards the door, the car came to a sudden stop. She turned to Christian as he thrust his door open, got out, and slammed it behind him. She then watched as he paced back and forth on the tarmac, apparently ignoring the rain soaking his clothes.

Bemused, she followed suit, holding a hand above her head to ward off the rain. "What are you doing? Have you lost your mind?" she yelled.

Christian didn't know where the surge of anger had erupted from. He put his hands either side of his skull and tried to stop his brain's internal conflict. *You were almost rid of her!* **Yes, but she has been your friend forever!** *She's NOT my friend; she is a cold and heartless statue!* **But you are protective towards her; you care deep down.** *I would care more if she didn't annoy me beyond all reason.* **Ah, but look at her blue eyes, they hold more compassion than you give her credit for…** *The only compassion she knows is towards animals.* **You don't know that, you've never asked!**

"Yes, I think I might have," Christian mumbled. He looked as if he was about to vomit. "It's crazy…"

As dusk began to creep from the sky, Charlize looked around them, worried about the exposure they faced. They were only able to rely on the Arx around the Marsh Village to keep them safe. "A little," she agreed. "Come on; let's go home, I'm sorry."

Christian ignored her and continued pacing. "No, it's crazy how, until you know you won't see someone again, it's then you want to know everything about them."

Catching her breath, Charlize stared mutely as Christian waited for her reply. With the car separating them, she held onto the doorframe, lost for words. Her breath billowed outwards and she found herself wondering when the temperature dropped. Then, in the distance, a light shone, invisible to the eyes of an Ungifted. It flashed once, bright and strong, before diffusing in a shower of sparks.

Another breach she thought to herself, certain that Mage's were already rushing to fix it. She wondered what it was, which Minae had attempted to gain access. The occurrences had started happening more often, and Charlize knew the safety of the village was in jeopardy.

"You're right, this really is crazy," said Christian, ducking down to get back in the car.

Breathing a sigh of relief, Charlize didn't waste any time doing the same, and once they were both inside, she locked the doors, wiped the wet from her face, and waited for Christian to start the engine.

Instead, she found herself locked in eye contact once more.

"Do you think, if we talked more, we'd be like you and Elliott?"

Again, another jolt churned in her stomach. "Perhaps," she replied after a second of deliberation.

Christian shook his head, sending droplets against the interior windows, and scoffed. "I don't think so either."

Where the droplets slid down the glass, a faded light refracted and caught Charlize's attention. In the daylight, it was almost invisible, but in the evening haze, she could make out the outline of a person. "Let's go home," she said, more urgently than she meant to.

There was a pause where she was convinced Christian was about to lose it again, but then composing his features, he turned the key in the ignition. With a strange whirring noise, the engine sputtered once and died.

"Crap," he cursed.

After another two attempts, the soft roar of life rang through the automobile, the sound like sweet music to Charlize's ears as they sped off, leaving the Achak far behind.

As they made progress, the two teenagers sat warily, a new episode in their relationship opened up, but neither able to talk about it. Gazing behind her, Charlize made sure nothing pursued them, before turning back to the front and easing her grip on the chair.

The rest of the journey was in silence, and it had been that way for years.

The roads narrowed and Christian pulled onto a cobbled drive as he noticed his mother, bright and beaming from the roadside. He rolled down the window as she came running towards them.

"Hello sweetheart, hello Charlize, how are you both?"

Lightened by the sight of her favourite person, Charlize smiled. She hadn't seen Leanne for ages. Both she and Theo worked in the lighthouse off the coast, so they were rarely at home until late.

At times, they were away for weeks, leaving Christian with a Fulgor carer called Latharia. Their absences were a great source of gossip amongst the Ungifted, and a source of amusement to the Mages. Tales ranged from the trials of 'that poor boy Christian with the absentee parents' to 'that Latharia, she's a dodgy character, there one minute and gone the next. It's witchcraft if you ask me.'

Of course, the truth was, Latharia lived in the next town, only accessible via trains secretly guarded by Mages. There was no other way to get around. Cars mysteriously stopped working along the border of the Arx, and walking the marshy moors on foot had you deemed insane. Superstition kept the villagers safe, for the protection not only stopped any but the living in, but it wouldn't let them out either – not withstanding incapacitating fear anyway.

So it was that those who wished to expand their horizons fell prey to the disparaging label of 'strange folk.' Although the trains allowed such a freedom, poor Latharia and Christian's parents suffered the hushed accusations more than most.

"Very well thank-you. It's good to see you, you look well," replied Charlize.

"Just the same old same old," said Leanne, grinning widely as she leaned through the window and kissed both teenagers on the cheek. She smelled of orange blossom. "Let me give you this."

Receiving a letter, Charlize turned it over on her lap. "We'll see you tomorrow though, won't we?" she asked.

"Oh of course!" Leanne confirmed, rubbing Charlize's cheek with the back of her fingers. "I just wanted to give you time to read this before you left."

The meaning dawning on her, Charlize nodded and folded the paper into her coat pocket.

A few revs of the engine signalled Christian's impatience to leave and the car soon began to roll backwards. "I won't be long," he assured his mother, reversing out of the driveway and back onto the main road.

Charlize watched as Leanne became a dot in the distance. A strange feeling crept up her spine. She wasn't sure, but she could have sworn it was sorrow.

13

It Begins

The next few days passed quickly with various preparations. Due to the recent heightened Minae activity, the protection spell around the manor doubled. Leanne's letter had explained the breach was an infiltration of Sirenaris – two groups of three. Hungry, they'd scavenged the border, relentlessly slicing at the protection barrier in an attempt to gain access. Failing, they feigned death.

An Ungifted, known to be one of the 'strange folk' was walking his dog when he came across what he saw as naked maidens. Upon reaching out to them, his hand passed the barrier, but before he could recoil in fear, a Sirenari managed to snatch him forward. They used him as a bridge to cross into the village, meeting the sentry Mages a little while after.

Leanne went on to write how they managed to fell two of the Threats, but the remaining four escaped with the Ungifted in tow. There was no time to deal a mercy blow, and the dog couldn't be called upon to give chase, for he'd died protecting his master in the initial attack.

The news saddened Charlize. Although her father tried to hide it from her – in some backwards attempt to ease the pressure – she knew the world outside the Arcēs was crumbling. The light of the cities, towns and villages wasn't enough to stop it, and their influence grew weaker day by day.

When she was little and the borders of the village still seemed so far away, she used to ask her father why the world was so big. He would smile and tell her that one day it wouldn't seem that way. And he was right. The Marsh village shrank every year she grew, until quickly, it became stifling. Now, when she looked at the borders from her bedroom window, she felt like a prisoner, and what struck fear into the hearts of every Ungifted when they looked out at the wasteland beyond only intrigued her.

Sitting on the window ledge in the sitting room, Charlize sighed. Gazing out at the night sky, she wished she could join the stars. She smiled, imagining what the busybodies of the village would say if they saw her take-off for the clouds. If anything, it would give their accusations of witchcraft a measure of truth...

A flash burning in the distance caught her attention and she felt her stomach plummet. Just a week ago she'd attended a meeting where all the available Marsh Mages gathered, joining to discuss how to strengthen their defences in light of recent events. After a lengthy debate, the decision to create a new barrier was finalised.

Then, in the dead of night not three days later, six groups of Mages walked to each strategically plotted site and positioned themselves just inside the original barrier. On the signal of a lightning bolt, they each combined their protection spells to create the new Arx.

It presented many risks, for while no Minae could now come within a ten-mile radius of the barrier and still walk, the energy it left in its demise could take days to find, meaning it grew weaker until it faded to nothing. The spirit lost, its counterpart would be unable to pass on. None knew what happened to the other half of a severed spirit, but the consensus was it could be nothing good.

The larger cities used the same Arx configuration – although they had the resources to do so, having more Mage's to spare and employ as 'trackers' – but in the Marsh village, there just weren't enough of them.

Creating the new upgrade also meant the first one needed destroying. This left the village open to attack during the hour it took to complete. Throughout the transition, every house was on full alert and teams of Mages scoured the streets nightly, searching for any threat that may have broken through. They called it a 'Code Black' and the Ungifted were oblivious to it all.

In the midst of all the chaos, Charlize had attended the school leaving party, the goodbyes quick and easy, made easier by the fact Christian barely said two words to her. They seemed to settle quite comfortably into the same routine they'd always had: ignoring each other whenever possible.

Leaving the window ledge, Charlize glanced at her packed bags. Her father had completed the majority of it, his flu forgotten as he distracted himself by filling the rucksacks with dry foods and tins, very few travelling clothes, and limited sleeping equipment. He was taking the heavier load, and in a moment of defiant inspiration, she'd already concocted a spell that made the pack lighter. By using the Anima element of air, she enchanted the bag so it floated slightly, easing the weight. Her father didn't approve, but she felt it was fairer that way, leaving him to mumble to himself about the dangers of exposure.

Charlize walked over to the roaring fire, uttered a quick protection for her hair, eyebrows, and lashes, and then planted her face in the flames, attempting to soothe her jumbled thoughts. Careful to avoid the same fate of her last jumper, she made sure she didn't lean close enough to encourage a spark.

It was hard to imagine where she'd be the same time next week, and the only clues on offer were in the paintings that adorned the manor. None of it seemed quite real yet, although she wondered if it ever would. Sometimes she thought her entire life was a form of surrealism. She even imagined that an Āetis before her came up with the form, the type of art speaking to her more than any other. There seemed to be an untold story waiting to be heard in it, the delicately drawn and disjointed images that came together to represent a subconscious thought – broken and yet somehow profound – an entirely freeing form to enjoy. She found herself looking at the works and wondering if she dreamed or stood as awake as she believed she was in that moment. She wanted to get into the mind of the artist, to unlock their ability to be so unshackled in their thoughts, so alive in their dreams. She both envied and admired them, and at times, hated them for their beautiful reminder of her own inadequacies.

Perhaps, she thought, that was another reason for the rift between her and Christian. He was a remarkably accomplished artist, especially in surrealism, but he didn't know it, and her praise often made him grunt and turn red.

And then there was her father. He tried so hard to fight her apathy, often reminding her of all the wonderful things she would soon see, of all the wonderful people she would soon meet, of all the wonderful experiences she was yet to feel, and of all the wonderful things she'd have to leave behind...

A loud *hiss* sounded in her head and she span to face the room. Outside, beyond the window, she saw the sparks of another breach. *Something got through* she thought, running into the lobby and out into the foyer. She threw open the front door and gazed across the driveway. On the horizon, a flare of blue signalled Mages were dealing with the breach.

"Strange..." she murmured, turning to go back inside.

A sharp yelp made her stop. Squinting against the haze of the half moon, she saw a silhouette outside the gates. Shadowed hands clung to the iron railings, as if they were somehow the only security left to them.

Their face obscured, Charlize stepped forward. The safety light flicked on automatically, illuminating her pathway and shrouding the figure further in shadow. A bitter air swirled about her head, and as she got closer to the wheezing figure, it dawned on her that it could be a trick.

"Who's there?" she called into the night.

A distant sob echoed from behind the bars and Charlize turned to alert her father. He would know what to do.

"Charlize," a small cry rasped.

The voice stopped her in her tracks. Turning back to the gate as two bloodied hands pulled themselves from the ground, she took a sharp intake of breath.

"You are welcome," she called urgently, releasing the barrier so it would allow the figure to pass through the boundary.

Running to the gate, Charlize wrenched open the smaller entrance and caught the unsteady mass as they both collapsed onto the gravel. With a wave of her hand, the bars swung shut.

She sat cradling the badly beaten victim as she looked about her, suspicious of another breach. But the air tasted fresh, and noticing the familiar red car parked at an awkward angle, she looked down at Christian.

"What happened?"

"They need help," he choked, his face twisted in pain.

Charlize nodded. "Okay, but let's get you inside."

She pulled him to his feet and led him into the safety of the manor, her father there to meet them with an expression matching her own. He took Christian's weight as Charlize bundled them into the lobby, and lying him on the floor, it quickly stained red as he writhed about.

"Easy," Charras murmured, pinning down Christian's hands to stop him pawing at his chest.

"I'll be right back," Charlize said, leaving to fetch warm water and antiseptic.

She returned with the prepared kidney dish and a first aid box, and passing the amenities to her father, stood back as he crouched over Christian.

"What happened?" he asked, his gruff voice even.

"I'm not sure," she replied, folding her arms across her chest. "The breach was being dealt with…"

"Phone Leanne," he said, not looking at her.

Christian began to shake violently, his eyes rolling into the back of his head as he smeared more blood across the floor, the ruby stark against the white. Turning him onto his side, Charras held him steady. "Go," he growled.

Charlize forced herself to look away, spinning around and running into the kitchen. The dark masked her whereabouts, but she didn't need the light to know where the phone was. She grabbed it off the wall next to the fridge and punched in Leanne's number, holding her breath as she waited for the familiar ring.

When the mocking drone of a cut line greeted her instead, she dropped the receiver, barely catching it before it hit the floor. Clumsily replacing it, she ran back into the lobby.

At first confused as to where Christian and her father had gone, her gaze followed the trail of blood to the library. She found it odd that she caught herself thinking how it would need cleaning, the smell of sweat and blood somehow calming her to the point of indifference. But then she remembered the blood was Christian's and she pulled herself together and made her way towards the soft light behind the door.

Her father was scouring the many shelves when she entered; she could tell by the soft thuds that pulsed down the walkway. "The line is dead," she called.

Charras poked his head from one of the middle sections and locked eyes with her – his face stern as an unspoken decision passed between them.

"I'll go now," he said. "I'll ring three times when I come back."

Knowing she had no choice, Charlize nodded. Slowly walking to the chairs where Christian lay, she sat down opposite him and studied his haunted face. A frown creased along his forehead and his body was still and silent, having finally passed out.

A strange déjà vu hit her, but before she could place it, her father touched her shoulder.

"Look after him," he murmured.

She nodded and then listened as he left the manor, the door closing firmly behind him. Silence followed, and without him there, she felt on edge. The library was vast and welcoming, but the secrets hidden within tempted her curiosity. On more than one occasion she'd uncovered something that burned her, and she soon realised that sometimes, there were things she'd rather not know.

Christian murmured something in his sleep and swiped at an unknown assailant. His eyes tightly shut and fists clenched, Charlize noticed that he was still bleeding, his cream shirt damp and dirtied. She jumped up, almost glad of something to do, and disappeared back into the kitchen to fetch more medical supplies.

When she returned, he was wide-awake.

Twisting his head to face her, Christian's eyes held the same fear as when she first found him. She took a few tentative steps in his direction and breathed a sigh of relief as his expression flooded with recognition.

"I'm going to take a look at you again," she said, placing the medication on the table. She bent down to touch his forehead, which was hot and clammy. "Is that okay?" she asked, wanting to make sure he understood.

Christian nodded.

"Okay," Charlize said, helping to ease him forward.

She lifted up his top slowly, taking deliberately deep breaths to encourage his, and when the shirt gathered at his neck, she pulled it over his head and discarded it on the floor.

His bare chest exposed, she quickly found the cause of the bleeding – a deep laceration beneath his right pectoral that oozed with sinister intention.

A welling in Charlize's throat took her by surprise and she forced it back down to her stomach, figuring she hadn't eaten enough, and focused all of her attention on inspecting the cut, making sure she didn't accidentally cause further injury. Her father had cauterised and sewn the wound quickly, but Christian had scratched away the stitches and exposed threaded ends. *Even so*, she thought, *the bleeding should have stopped*.

Bringing her face as close as she dared, Charlize soon realised there was something wrong. *The wound isn't natural*. Then she saw the cause. Glass-like shards multiplied as they buried deeper, the fragments fighting the cauterisation to keep the wound exposed. *Ice...* she realised. Ice was deadly to a Fulgor, even an unbecome.

There was no time to waste. She put her fingers in the antiseptic water, away from Christian's sight, and closed her eyes. A spell immediately came to her and she recited it in her head, something most would never dare try. Heat spread through her fingers and she let it escape into the water before sitting back up and bathing some cotton wool in the mixture.

"This will help," she promised, pushing Christian into the back of the chair and holding his shoulder firmly.

In theory, the Incendiī element of fire would counteract the destructive element of Glacies, halting the deterioration of the wound so it could heal properly. Her father's cauterisation hadn't been enough; she just hoped it wasn't too late.

Christian gasped in pain and grabbed the sides of the chair as she worked to clean the infection. He bit down on his lip with every stroke of the cotton, which Charlize did her best to ignore despite the nagging pull in her stomach, and she idly wondered if a midnight snack would suppress the strange twinges...

However, by the time she was done, it taking a little longer than she anticipated, all thought of food was completely forgotten. The remaining ice destroyed, an open wound was left and ready for new stitches.

"I'm sorry," she said, preparing a fresh needle.

Clenching his teeth, Christian withstood the pain with grace, enabling Charlize to finish quickly and tie a bandage around his chest to hold the dressing in place. She then turned her attention to the superficial cuts on his face and hands, wiping them clean and feeling satisfied that the antiseptic achieved its purpose.

"There," she said, "all done."

His eyes were already bruising and he needed a plaster where a puncture wound dented his arm, but other than that, he was relatively unharmed, much to her relief.

"Thanks," Christian mumbled.

"Can you walk?" she asked softly.

He held out his arm and Charlize wrapped it across her shoulders. Then, slowly heaving him up, she led him into the sitting room, glad as he managed the last few paces by himself.

"At least that's something," she said with false enthusiasm.

She watched as he staggered over to an available settee, but gently taking his arm, guided him towards the fire and sat him on the rug in front of it instead. Then, pulling over a footstool for him to lean against, she sat herself opposite.

The flames crackled quietly in the hearth, their heat a consoling presence as she stared helplessly at her broken companion. "Father's gone to help," she said hesitantly.

Dismayed when Christian began to shake violently, her attempt at reassurance unsuccessful, Charlize stared at him with wide eyes as he broke into retching sobs, his body heaving with obvious trauma.

She surprised herself by reaching out and stroking his arm. It was cold to the touch.

"Let me get you a jumper," she said, standing from the rug.

Christian shook his head and wiped his eyes. "Don't go."

"But you're cold…"

He looked up at her, his dark eyes meeting hers, and she could no more argue than tell a dog to walk on two legs.

She sat back down. And this time, when she reached out, she did so more assuredly, securing Christian's hands in her lap and entwining her fingers in his.

They stayed that way, holding each other's gaze, lost in the support of one another for the hours that passed. Nothing stirred and nothing changed, the fire the only witness.

Leaving the Strike household, Charras pulled his overcoat up to his chin, refusing to allow the cold entry. He closed the gate behind him and turned when two villagers approached.

"They've gone," one called.

He nodded. "So have Leanne and Theo."

Shock and fear drenched the features of his companions, their faces distorted in the faint moonlight.

"So it is true what they say. She's real...?" the other uttered.

Clenching his jaw, Charras nodded again.

"What will you do?"

He looked towards the house of his old friends, the darkened windows already lonely. "I'll find them," he promised, more to himself than his cohorts. He didn't need to look to know they disapproved.

"What of Charlize and her purpose?"

Letting out a grunt, he squared his shoulders. "Her purpose will not change tonight, nor in the mornings that follow. Christian has a right to avenge his parents."

"Is it the boy you seek revenge for, or yourself Charras?"

His eyes alight, he bore them into the shorter of the two Mages. "Your backs turned on me and Isalize even quicker than they turned back when Charlize was named the Āetis. If revenge ran in my blood she would not exist, and I would have reached the Sky long before you knew her name."

"Forgive my friend, he does not hold his tongue so well with gin," said the smarter Mage.

"He would do well to watch it," growled Charras, turning to ascend the hill back to the manor. "Vrealâ was here tonight, she hid for days," he shouted over his shoulder. "The village was compromised right beneath our noses. None of us are safe. Be prepared."

14

As Fate Lays its Path

Faint embers provided little light, the remaining protective flicker shining on the two figures asleep on the rug. Hours had passed until fatigue washed over them and sleep called from a place of exhaustion, their heavy lids no match for the heat and quiet.

Christian was the first to wake, his eyes roving around the gloom as he tried to figure out where he was. His heart skipped a beat as the doorbell rang three times, with only the third chime rousing Charlize, and he swallowed dryly as the memories flooded back with a vengeance.

"It's my father Christian, I'll be back in a minute," she assured, glancing at him quickly.

His arm fell from her body and confusion crossed both of their faces, unaware they'd fallen asleep embracing.

Charlize chose to ignore it and got to her feet. She crept into the lobby, dark immersing the room, and for a short moment, felt disorientated. She listened to the dull thuds of heavy footsteps trudging up the driveway, their presence further reassuring her it was her father – the only other person who could pass through the barrier uninvited – and the resulting knock on the door made her throw it open with relief.

His familiar face was expressionless as he stepped through into the warmth. Cold night air clung to his overcoat, contrasting against his flushed cheeks, and without his meaning to, they exchanged glances, long enough for Charlize to notice the pain etched in his eyes. She held her hand to her mouth, stifling the sudden welling in her gut, and followed him into the sitting room.

Christian sat up immediately, sucking in a breath as a wave of pain beat against his chest – the harrowing events of the night taunting him with veracity. He clasped his side and tried to stand, growing frustrated at his inability to do so.

Charras ignored him and swept past to stoke the fire, pushing him back down with a kind but firm hand. He said nothing more until the light in the room was sufficient to see one another clearly. (He would have ignited the Incendiī lamps, but he didn't have matches to disguise his element while doing so).

Then, taking a seat on one of the settees, he put his hands on his lap and leaned forward so Christian could see his face properly.

"I have been to your house," he began. The fire *snapped* behind him, the hungry flames engulfing the fresh wood as Christian listened intently, fearing the next words he may hear. "I tried to find your parents," he continued. "I need to know what happened; for although the house spoke of horror, it did not speak of death. I searched and they were not there."

His chest heaving, Christian sighed loudly as a tremor shuddered up his spine. Then, lowering his eyes to the floor, he squeezed them shut. "I woke up because I heard my Mum yelling. The house was cold and there were voices. They were saying things I didn't understand. I couldn't hear my Dad so I crept downstairs…" He took a breath and scrunched his lids tighter. "He was on the floor in the front room… he wasn't moving. Mum was over him, holding his head on her lap. She was pleading with them about something."

"Pleading with whom?" Charras asked carefully.

Christian shrugged and opened his eyes, although continued to stare at the floor, lost in his own dark thoughts. "They were big, two men. There was a smaller one, a woman, but she had a black cloak on. I didn't see her face, but she spoke. It sounded familiar… Her voice was soft, almost tuneful… but it was *so* cold, as if she knew nothing of compassion or love. She said she'd find me and kill me, but if my parents told her where I was she'd spare them."

Charlize crouched down next to Christian so she could hear him clearly, intrigue masking her fear. *Vreală* she thought to herself, *it has to be.*

Christian didn't notice her presence as he continued to relive his ordeal. "My Mum told her that I didn't know who I was, that it didn't matter – to leave me alone." He wrung his hands together. "One of the men hit her; he hit her really hard; it looked like he burnt her... I lost it then; I ran in; I was stupid. They hit me too. I fell and crawled over to Mum, but she was screaming at me to run. It gets so hazy then... A fight broke out and all I can remember is managing to run out of the house. Mum's words were the only thing I could hear, ringing over and over in my head: '*Find Charras; tell him to teach you, you must fight back...*'

Lifting his head, Christian wrapped his arms across his shoulders. "So here I am."

Charras nodded and sat back.

"Can it even be done?" asked Charlize.

There was a few seconds of pause, a stillness that seemed to signal the universe switching, a twist on the dial of change, and then Charras rubbed his forehead, sighed, and stood up. He took off his coat; draped it over the rocking chair; disappeared from the room, and returned with a plain blue jumper. He handed it to Christian and waited while he pulled it on with difficulty – it being several sizes too large – and then held out his hand.

"Come with me," he said.

With slight trepidation, Christian let Charras pull him to his feet, wincing as his stitches tightened and pulled at his skin. He didn't complain, even though the throbbing in his chest made him nauseous, and he followed Charras back into the library where he and Charlize were ushered to the glass coffee table and told to sit. He did so without question, watching as his parent's closest friend proceeded to produce three tumblers and fill them with a fine single malt whiskey.

"Drink this, it will warm you," he assured, pushing glasses into the hands of both him and Charlize.

She didn't drink hers as she glanced at Christian, waiting to see what he'd do first, and not wanting to lose face, he sniffed the liquor and tentatively took a small sip, screwing up his nose as oak burned the length of his throat.

Charras managed a half-hearted smile and sipped his own malt as he considered his new charge. A swelling grew across the left side of his face, the punch he'd received enough to knock out the largest of men. Yet somehow, Christian had stayed on his feet. He wondered if it was the adrenaline or his mother's spell that spared him a blackout. Whichever it was, it had certainly saved his life by enabling him to get to safety. But then, Christian didn't know what he was capable of. Charras had seen the boy's bravery and endurance once before, a night he'd relived too many times to count – trying and failing to solve the mystery of how two dead children came back to life. They were connected, that was for sure, and Charras couldn't help but wonder at the timing of things, with Charlize leaving for her pilgrimage the next morning and the disappearance of Leanne and Theo the day before their children would never see each other again. It seemed like a plan rushed into completion with a severe lack of grace.

Decided, he said to Christian, "I do not believe that tonight was a coincidence. Your coming here was meant to happen, even against your parent's wishes."

With a frown, Christian placed the tumbler of ash back on the table. "I don't understand."

"You won't, not for some time."

The wind howled outside the manor, the eerie atmosphere that enveloped inside providing no comfort. Charras poured himself another drink, the amber liquid almost in slow motion as it flowed into the glass.

After another swig, he lowered his voice. "I need you to make a choice. You can come with us and learn what we know, or you can stay here and wait for your parent's investigation to begin."

Charlize opened her mouth to protest but Charras flicked his wrist, instantly silencing her with a vacuum of air.

The spectacle unseen by Christian, he eyed Charras suspiciously. "Learn what?"

"A secret." He gestured towards the bookshelves in the library. "One that will open your eyes to the world around you in a way you have never known before."

Wriggling where she sat, Charlize released the spell on her face with a counter hex but said nothing, instead choosing to cross her arms and scowl at her father.

"I don't want to be alone," Christian replied.

"Even if by choosing to come with us you put yourself in more danger than you ever thought possible?"

"What kind of danger?

"I can't tell you that yet," replied Charras simply, taking yet another sip of his whiskey and twisting the tumbler so the liqueur swirled against the glass.

"Then how can I make the right decision?"

"You can't, but you have good instincts. Learn to trust them."

The advice was blunt and infuriatingly lacking in details. Christian weighed up the options, only knowing one thing for sure: he didn't want to wait until whatever wanted him came back. His parents were missing and he intended to find them, even if that meant leaving the village. But there was something he wasn't being told, he was sure of it. Charras's talk of fate put him on edge, for if the old man truly believed in that sort of thing, then did he think the attack was meant to happen? If so, did he really want to travel with a man who thought such things? Everyone knew that destiny was a myth; you made your own fortune. The nut-jobs who thought that choices were merely the means of creating a path to your pre-ordained fate made him laugh.

He looked at Charras now. He didn't seem like a nut-job, but then, when he thought of Charlize he wasn't so sure…

They each sat for some time in their own private thoughts. The minutes ticked past and the bookshelves creaked as the pressure in the air changed several times – mainly due to Charlize's impatience and frustration. But eventually, after a gruelling twenty minutes, Christian sat forward.

"Just like that?"

Charras nodded. "Just like that."

Christian picked up his whiskey and took another sip. His opinion still unchanged from his last experience, he put it back down. "Then I want to learn, whatever it is you're talking about. My Mum told me to come to you and she's not been wrong about much before."

"But he's too old!" Charlize blurted out before Charras had the chance to stop her. He lowered his gaze onto his persistent child and narrowed his eyes.

She ignored him and stood up. "Father, it has never been done before, we do not know the effects it could have!"

"Settle Charlize," he warned.

Sitting down obediently, she did not however, settle. "If he stays here then he is safe at least," she argued.

"Safe?!" spat Charras.

"Safer than he'd be if he came with us," she shot back, matching his glare.

Taking her drink away, he leaned forward in his chair. "We both know that the world is crumbling around us Charlize. Our defences have weakened considerably over the last decade. At least with us he can be protected."

"That is a burden I feel I have the right to decide!"

Charras shook his head and with steady words said, "The breach tonight was not an entry. Do you understand? Nothing got in; it was already here."

Taken aback, the very idea alien, Charlize frowned. "But how?"

"Probably when the new barrier was being formed; we knew the risks."

She shook her head, unable to digest the thought. Then, speaking with hesitance, she said, "But they were undetected, why weren't they seen?"

Deciding how to answer, Charras tapped his fingers against his glass. With a quick sigh, he put it on the table and clasped his hands. "It is what you believe it is."

Cold rippled down Charlize's spine, making her reconsider another swig of whiskey. "Then the breach and flare signalled both their departure and their resolution? The barrier got confused…" She fell into silence and sat in disbelief.

Having never seen her silenced so easily, Christian looked at Charras with new admiration. "If it is my choice, then I choose to come with you. The rest will follow in time."

Charras acknowledged the decision with a tilt of his head and stood from his chair. Disappearing into the depths of the vast library, he returned with a book identical to the one Charlize received on the day of her Awakening. He placed it on the table with purpose and sat back in his chair.

"This is yours," he said to Christian.

They all stared at the red leather book – bound in gold and etched with gold writing – as if it might explode at any moment. It made Christian uneasy as he picked it up and held it in his lap. Acutely aware of his companion's eyes boring a hole into his skull, he was unprepared for the sudden surge in his stomach. Every hair on his neck stood on end as he stroked the cover, the words alive beneath his fingertips and desperate for recognition.

"Open it," said Charras.

Without question, Christian turned the first page. The sheets gleamed up at him with bountiful energy, bright and – he could have sworn – happy to see him. *"The Book of Becoming,"* he said aloud.

Turning the page, he read the first inscription.

'I am held only by the Mage Christian Strike. If you are not he, then this book will destruct until returned to thee.'

Slowly turning another page, the curiosity burned inside him as the paper sparkled and warmed to his touch, as if greeting an old friend.

'I can teach you everything you need to know before your pilgrimage. I can tell you stories – stories of destinies completed and destinies yet to be fulfilled. I will teach you about the magic, the secrets of our race, and the

history. I will bind your knowledge to your bloodline, and in turn bind you to the duty of a Mage.

We fight the Minae that walk the earth, protecting those in need of protection. The war between our worlds is on-going as we wait for the end to come, our final rest.

This is your chance to learn. Do you wish to?'

Not taking his eyes from the book, captivated with wonder and intrigue as his fellow Mages sat expectantly, Christian held his hand over the page.

"Think," came Charras's voice from somewhere in his vicinity. "You cannot go back."

How can I now though? Christian considered. With the magnitude of wonder hidden within the pages he held, why would he want to anyway?

The same voice warned him again, but he brushed the words away as one would a shiver. Of course there was no need to worry, nothing to fear, for every answer he sought lay in the seductive book of secrets...

"I'll learn," he promised.

15

Memories

$\mathbf{S}$olitary among the books he considered friends, Charras shuffled in his seat. The turn of events gave him much to deliberate. Now Christian would be joining them, their plans had to change; certain rules would have to be set. Although they seemed indifferent towards each other, and Charlize knew her place, he was well aware that young passions could ignite if proximity allowed it. If that happened, then the effects could be catastrophic. But then, he struggled to think of any real love that didn't end in tragedy…

Pouring himself another dram, he put the half-emptied whiskey bottle back on the table. Then, sinking into the cushions, he rubbed his temples, trying and failing to block the convoluted memories. Yet they haunted him, fiercer than Sirenaris stalked their prey.

He downed the tumbler of aged malt and focused on the burn in his throat, knowing he couldn't fight for much longer. The silence always failed him, its lonely state lending an ear he didn't ever want. He closed his eyes, trying to concentrate on thoughts that wouldn't lead him to *her*.

But of course, as he knew she would, she quickly emerged from the labyrinth of his inebriated mind.

Standing in the kitchen humming to herself, Isalize emptied the last of the merlot into two wine glasses. They'd purchased the bottles from a vineyard in a French Arx called Aquitaine-Gironde, a popular Mage holiday destination. She and Charras had visited earlier that year, a place she yearned to live, should policy allow it, but they'd waived that opportunity by daring to fall in love. The Hetairia Doman would no more grant a foreign citizenship to outcasts than allow them a say in their politics. To the Mage community, their choice made them less entitled than Ungifted – which is what they pretended to be in order to travel in the first place.

It had become a game of sorts, a new identity in each town they travelled to until they reached their desired destination. They would do it forever if money afforded them the luxury, but Charras's job as a teacher and her job as a tailor meant they had little means.

Crossing the lobby and entering the sitting room, Isalize passed one of the glasses to Charras. "We've run out again," she giggled.

He took a sip, smiled, and placed the merlot on the hearth, just out of reach of the flames. Then, standing to his feet, he turned up the radio, listening as bolero floated through the speakers. The music rushed through his head, its melody an itch in his body that wanted liberation, and he walked over to Isalize, bowed low, and held out his hand.

She pertly placed her glass next to his and took his offering, laughing as he hauled her into his arms instantly.

"M'lady," he murmured, steadying her against his chest.

Isalize smiled and bent her head into his neck, swaying gently even though bolero reached its crescendo and blared into distortion.

Spinning her once, Charras brought her back into his embrace, his nose to her cheek. "I don't think we're doing it properly," he said softly, biting his lip as Isalize kissed his throat, her lips cold against his hot skin. He reached up into her hair and bent her head so he could see her face.

She looked up at him with her lips slightly parted. "I don't think we do anything properly," she whispered, lightly brushing her mouth against his.

Breathing her in, Charras stared into her sapphire eyes, their bright expectancy always melting him into utter defencelessness. He kissed her lightly, holding himself back as their initial contact flared against their lips, fire and ice colliding with intent. Then, before he could react, Isalize pulled him to her, her mouth pressing hard against his, the elements having no choice but to bond and allow them to touch. She clawed at his shirt and ripped it off, gasping as he pulled her to the floor, his deep kisses penetrating the deepest layers of her skin. He pushed himself between her legs, letting out a grunt as she clutched his buttocks, urging him, before forcing her hands into his trousers and spurring him to kick them off.

Free, Charras reached beneath her dress and found her underwear, tugging it towards her ankles as he pressed his hardest against her thigh. Then, facing her, he kissed her again, eager but playful.

"I love you," he murmured, adoring the flush in her cheeks whenever he said it.

But she didn't respond. She stared up at him as if he were a stranger, her eyes glazed and hollow.

"Isalize?" Charras said, immediately pushing himself into a sitting position and gently touching her arm. She remained frozen and continued to focus on the ceiling.

"Isalize?"

When she still didn't respond, Charras clasped her hand, shocked as she recoiled from him.

"Isa? —"

"I have to go," she said.

She stood to her feet and staggered from the room. Charras let her go while he pulled up his trousers and caught his breath. He watched the fire die down and listened to Isalize's footsteps march across the landing, their thumps fading and intensifying as they stormed about with assured resolve.

When he'd collected himself enough to concentrate, he followed the racket, finding himself upstairs. A faint light emanated from their bedroom and he walked towards it, pushing open the half-closed door.

Isalize paced the room, her blonde hair swept off her face as she packed clothes into a suitcase, her cheeks wet and eyes puffy.

"What are you doing?" Charras asked.

Without looking at him, she continued to pack her belongings.

"Answer me."

When it was clear she wouldn't, Charras put his hand on the suitcase, bending so she had no choice but to acknowledge him. She avoided his gaze, gently removed his hand, and placed it on the bed.

"What's happening, where are you going?"

Isalize pulled the case to the floor and attempted to leave, gasping as Charras pinned her against the wall. "Let me go," she whispered.

"Not until you tell me what the hell is happening," he said, grabbing her face so their eyes met.

She touched his cheek and bit back a well of tears. "I can't be with you anymore."

"Why? What did you see?" he asked, searching her face.

Her lip trembling, she gently took his hands in hers. Kissing his fingers lightly, she pushed him from her, sending him flying against the wardrobe with an elemental force. Then, without haste, she picked up her suitcase and left the room, closing the door behind her with finality.

Charras rubbed his head, clambered to his feet, and yanked the door open. He raced down the stairs, hands out, and sent a vicious fire careering towards the front door that engulfed it in flames.

Isalize immediately shrank away and fell back into the lobby. She turned to him with an agonized expression. "Don't do this; I don't want to fight you!"

"Then tell me why you're leaving?!"

He stepped towards her, his hands held in surrender, but stopped as she pointed a finger at him.

"I love you," he said, his eyes pleading. "Whatever it is, we can get through it."

With a bitter laugh, Isalize lowered her hand. "I can't bring a child into this world."

The revelation rang through the lobby, rendering Charras immobile. He forced his arms to his sides as he digested the words, and clicking his fingers, extinguished the fire. The blackened door crumbled into ash.

"That's why you're upset?" he uttered, noting how she shook where she stood. Wary of sparking her anger, he kept his distance. "We both agreed we would never do that," he said gently. "I didn't know that's what you wanted."

"It's not," Isalize spat, balling her fists.

"Then what?"

She stared at the ceiling and took a deep breath. Then, wiping her sleeve across her face, she dried her tears and met Charras's brown eyes, saddened by the longing within them whenever they fought.

She looked away. "Some things we can't help. But I can stop this if I'm not around you. Good-bye Charras."

Before he could react, Isalize created a blockade of ice between them. He cried out to her and pounded on it, sending fireball after fireball in an attempt to destroy it. But his endeavour was hopeless; she had always been the stronger one.

By the time he broke through, she was gone.

Choking on his whiskey, Charras swallowed it down and rubbed his eyelids. Then, leaning back in his chair, he pulled the blanket around his shoulders.

Tonight he would not go to bed, her essence left in every inch of the manor but the library. It was only between the books and his liquor cabinet could he ever escape her, and even then, only for a short while.

16
Movements

On the early hours of the morning, Charlize watched the sun rise beyond the sleepy hills. Standing in the peaceful garden, she allowed the breeze to wash through her hair, stirring in her the realisation it was her final hour in the manor.

The events of the previous night constantly intruded her thoughts, managing to find a way to her stomach and sit there like lead. It fluttered in a way she was unused to, the strange position she found herself in a huge contrast to what she initially expected.

She was not just the Āetis beginning her pilgrimage; she was one who also brought an unbecome with her. Not only was it illegal, it was unheard of. A Mage had never started the teachings at such a late stage in life, and although she was exempt from the laws that bound her race, having an unbecome journey alongside her would gain no favours should anyone find out.

Clasping her birthday gift – a delicate tear shaped diamond necklace, no larger than a pea and hung on a thin silver chain – she absently fiddled with it while she sat on the dewy grass. The properties of such a precious stone were renowned in the Mage community, with many wearing such jewellery to aid them in battle. With slight satisfaction, Charlize thought her own seemed finer than most.

A light breeze stroked the back of her neck and she shivered against the subtlety, continuing to read the words on her mother's headstone in front of her, although it was long committed to memory.

Moments later, a pattering of carefully placed footsteps alerted her senses, but she pretended not to hear as the culprit neared. They stopped a little way behind her, as if trying to keep some distance, and allowing the perpetrator to decide their course of action, glad of the interruption to her thoughts, she soon grew bored when they didn't budge.

"I couldn't sleep either," she said, still not turning from the grave.

Bemused and slightly impressed, Christian emerged from the shadows and sat next to her, hugging his knees to his chest.

"Does any of it make sense?" he asked after a short silence.

Charlize considered him for a moment. "My father was careless allowing you to learn so late."

"Oh, wow, thanks. Positive thinking; I like that about you."

Furrowing her brow, Charlize wondered why Christian felt the need to attempt constant inopportune humour. "Do you know why we learn when we're ten and not any older?" she said.

He shook his head.

"A ten year old is on the cusp of awareness; the world around them becomes a possibility. They listen, learn, and explore more each day. Can you remember listening to faerie-tales, wishing that they were true?" She didn't wait for the answer. "You're still susceptible to the fact that magic truly exists. It enables you to believe. If you don't honestly believe in what you hear or see, if logic doesn't cloud your judgement, then you won't reject what you hear."

"So what if I don't believe?"

Charlize shrugged, sighing as she also brought her knees to her chest. "The Ungifted who have seen our ways end up in institutions. That is why we live in secret. You are a Mage Christian; you are a part of this world as much as the rest of us. Your parents didn't want you to become a Mage because of how dangerous it is, what it may mean for your future."

"You didn't answer me."

Shaking her head, she looked away. "It has never been done before."

Before Christian could probe further, the kitchen light came on and Charlize turned to watch her father through the window. His face was drawn as he prepared their bags and executed the various other tasks that needed completing. He wouldn't leave until the manor was secure, but there was a sense of finality about his demeanour that touched a nerve.

"He looks angry," Christian said, echoing Charlize's thoughts.

She turned to face him and noticed how the sun's stark rays lightened the blonde in his hair, the wavy mass of no particular style cropped high on his head. His dark eyes squinted against the blaze and he held up his hand to shield the beam, enabling her to see random patches of stubble along his jaw.

She met his gaze and he pulled a face, which made her abruptly look away.

"You need to lighten up," Christian said, although his voice wasn't mean.

"Lighten up?"

"Yeah, you know, live a little, laugh, try to remember that life doesn't need to be so serious all the time."

"How could you say that after what's happened?"

The mood darkening again, Christian let out a breath and dropped his head. Charlize immediately regretted her outburst, but said nothing, even as he starting plucking out random blades of grass and she could feel their energy disperse like little pin pricks in her mind.

"I don't mean serious things aren't happening right now," he said after several moments of silence. "I just mean you don't need to wallow in misery. Things can always be worse."

More than a little confused by the sentiment, Charlize remembered that he was a Fulgor Mage – typically positive and optimistic. But he was also naive, and the road ahead of him wasn't full of rainbows and happy endings, however nice it would be to believe otherwise.

She kept that to herself though, glad his grass mutilation had stopped and reluctant to give him cause to start it again.

"Someone asked me a question once," she said instead.

Propping himself on one elbow, Christian looked up at her face, the light obscuring her features.

"I was asked if I wanted a purpose or a choice," she continued.

"Seems like a strange question… what did you say?" he asked, watching how her face tilted to the left as she considered how to answer.

"I didn't, I have no idea. I have never thought about the decision I'd make if I had the choice; I've always known my path."

"Sounds organised."

Charlize laughed softly. "You could say that…" She laughed again, a noise that both surprised and warmed Christian to hear. But it was fleeting, for seriousness soon crossed her face once more. "I believe that one day I will know the meaning. If you search for the answers you seek, you generally find them." She gave him a telling look and he smiled with understanding.

Charras appeared in the doorway to let them know breakfast was ready, their appetites whetted as the scent of smoked mackerel wafted through the door in his wake. They got to their feet, although Charlize held back while Christian went on ahead. It was her last chance.

Folding her arms across her chest, she looked out beyond her garden. The sun had fully risen, illuminating the Marsh Village in a swathe of gold – the hills, marshlands, and sporadic townhouses all cloaked in its nurturing glow. It looked peaceful, sleepy, ever hiding the danger that lay beyond, and searching above the horizon, she found the edge of the Arx, pinpointing several elemental surges across its surface, their presence confirming their protection.

She stared for a little while, saying her silent goodbyes, confident in the remaining defender's ability to protect her home. For her, the time to leave had finally arrived. She was about to embark on the journey she'd prepared for for over eight years. Soon, the Marsh Village would be a distant memory.

So she found it odd that she caught herself reaching out to her mother's headstone with sadness in her heart. It stood amongst her ancestors where it always had, and the same emptiness swallowed her whenever she glanced at it.

Isalize
1970-1990

Devoted mother and beloved wife.
May you rest in peace for all eternity.

It was almost lunchtime when Charras was ready to begin their journey. He'd redistributed the necessities in each bag between the three of them, and with the weight greatly reduced, he was almost glad of the extra pair of hands Christian offered. Although, what he was happier about was the use of his car. Conscious of the road ahead, and the possibility they may need more money than the Hetairia Doman allocated, Charras had sold his motorbike days before, having no further use for it. There was a main pickup service in the Marsh Village, but the vehicles couldn't drop them off at the border without failing, meaning they would have had to walk on foot to the underground train station beyond the Arx. It had better links to the towns closest to their first stop, and every Mage embarking on their pilgrimage from Marsh used it. Now it would be a shorter trip with less risk of Minae exposure.

In the car, Charlize and Christian settled into their seats and pulled on their safety belts. They watched as Charras closed the gate behind him, checked, and re-checked the protection, sniffed the air around the boundary, and paced back and forth along the outskirts of the gated driveway with his fingers splayed.

"What's he doing?" Christian asked. "Why is he poking at thin air?"

"He's checking the protection barrier is secure before we leave. The manor needs to be protected," Charlize explained. "Can't you see?"

Christian shook his head and continued to stare in mild bemusement. "He looks like a madman," he meant to say to himself.

Charlize huffed and looked at her father. She saw the usual thin line of white air and orange fire spinning around the manor, as it always had. The protection domed over the entire grounds, like a miniature Arx, but only the strip was visible. Mages preferred it that way, wishing to see the sky above their heads when they sat in their gardens or popped out to fetch the newspaper.

"You must be having side effects," Charlize justified. "Until you believe we are in fact Mages, then perhaps our world will not reveal itself to you."

Not liking the sound of that, Christian tried to concentrate, narrowing his eyes in an attempt to see whatever the protection barrier was. But he didn't know what he was looking for and quickly gave up.

Having finished his inspection, Charras marched over to the car and manoeuvred his large body into the small back seat. He squashed one of the rucksacks against the opposite window as he made himself comfortable, and then pulled his belt on once he'd settled.

Christian thought how large he looked, his head slightly bent so it didn't hit the roof and his knees almost reaching the head rests on the back of the chairs. *It's a good job I cleaned* he thought… Even if he had little choice when Charlize passed him a bin bag and wore a telling frown earlier that morning.

"Okay Christian, we're ready. Head towards the school and I'll guide you from there," Charras said, leaning to the right so he could straighten his neck.

With a nod, Christian turned on the engine. He took a last look at the manor when something dawned on him. "Is *that* why we always had to wait at your gate? The protection barrier wouldn't let us pass?"

Charlize nodded. "That's why most houses in the village have gates. Many of us live among the Ungifted protecting them."

"What about at night? What protects them then? You can't keep people prisoner in their own homes, surely?"

"Of course not, the protections we put on our own homes are to keep us safe and shield our secrets. The Minae are drawn to our light more than the Ungifted's, and if we die, there would be no one to protect the village. It's the way it must be."

"So better an Ungifted casualty than a Mage?"

Charras cleared his throat and Charlize looked down at her hands.

"I see..." Christian murmured.

"It's not like that," Charlize said, brushing her hair behind her ears. "Casualties are rare. And it is as you say; we can't very well keep people prisoners in their own homes. This is the best we can do."

Christian nodded and put the car into first gear. "So how many villages are like this?"

Charras leaned forward and the car creaked slightly, the suspension groaning under his weight. "Throughout the world there are places which are protected. The Marsh Village is just one in thousands; the Minae aren't native to Britain. London naturally has the highest security, all of the major cities, and then every town and village with a postcode. The Minae walk freely everywhere else, although many try to breach the barriers and gain access in various forms. That is why many Mages live among the Ungifted and not in their respective Haunts."

"Haunts?"

Forgetting himself, unused to talking to an unbecome, Charras explained. "Every clan has a homeland, their domicile. They have their own way of life where the majority of Mages populate, generally of pure kin. They are called Haunts, and we will be visiting each of them on our journey."

"Pure kin... Those with one power right? Double kin's are those with two?"

"That's correct," Charras confirmed, impressed at the information Christian had retained from only one quick lesson that morning. "Double kin's are commonly found in Ungifted areas, where Mages of opposite powers mix frequently."

"So what about triple kin's, or quadruple kin's?"

Charlize took a sharp intake of breath. Then, composing herself and forgiving Christian's ignorance of the etiquette surrounding talk of such things, she replied, "They are not regarded as Mages, for the magic that runs in their blood is diluted. Their power is weak and they are therefore classed as inferior. It is illegal to cross-kin in such a way."

Thinking that sounded stupid, Christian grimaced. "So you have to choose someone from your own clan to fall in love with?"

"Love?" It was Charlize's turn to look confused. "Being a Mage isn't about love, it's about the greater good. As Mages, we know our duty and we know what we must do to keep our race strong. To love is fortunate indeed."

Charras winced at his daughter's words and swallowed his retort. Hearing her talk of love in such a way made him feel hollow. After all, his love for her mother was the only reason she even existed. Luck and foresight chose her as the Āetis, for in any other circumstance termination would have been kinder, her birth a crime that would have imprisoned him and Isalize. In his darkest moments, Charras wondered if it would have been a kinder fate.

Christian pulled onto a dusty road and out into the main street. As the scenery blurred into a mumble of colour, he was keen to continue their discussion.

"The Minae, they're the monster things the *Book of Becoming* first tell you about aren't they?" he asked, as if he'd been reading a comic.

"Indeed, you will encounter one at some point, which is why you must stay with myself or Charlize at all times," said Charras. "There will be many days where we walk unprotected, with only ourselves as defence. They are attracted to larger places, such as cities, but it's near the Haunts we'll encounter them the most."

"Why?"

It was Charlize who answered. "As I said before, they crave the light within a Mage more than they crave the blood of an Ungifted. We are descendants of the Sky and we hold its light in our veins. The Minae are also descendants of the Sky, although only the part of darkness. We believe that a consequence of their split mean they naturally desire a reunion with their other half. Unfortunately, we're the next best thing."

"I see," Christian said, putting his foot on the accelerator as they reached a long stretch of road.

He quietly contemplated the revelations as they headed for the train station outside the village. Until that morning, he was unaware that there *was* another train station outside the village, only knowing the Marsh trains that connected to the next major town twenty miles east.

"So, why are we visiting the Haunts?" he asked after a long silence, and because the whirr of the engine was beginning to make him sleepy.

Soft snores drifted from the back seat and Charlize realised her father wouldn't be the one to reply. "When a Mage turns eighteen, they all undertake a pilgrimage. They can go to any Haunt first, and in any order, but they must lastly end up in the Fulgor Haunt."

"That's lightning isn't it?"

"Yes," Charlize said. "It is designed so each new Mage can learn the ways of every clan, and more about the Mages as a whole. The Fulgor Haunt is where the Orbis lies protected. It represents the Sky, which is what created the Mages in the first place. It alone can tell you your destiny and the part you play in the on-going fight against Inferus-Malus. It hopes that by doing this it can decipher when the Ultimate War will be waged and which side will win."

"I remember that part…" Christian murmured as he digested the information.

"There is a lot to learn," Charlize reiterated, "it takes time."

Opening his mouth to ask another question, he quickly shut it as the car juddered and swerved, coming to a standstill on an expanse of road he didn't recognise. He clutched the steering wheel and caught his breath before getting out of the car and circling it, attempting to determine the reason they'd broken down.

"We'll need to push it through," came Charras's groggy solution from the back.

"Through what?" asked Christian. "There's nothing around us."

The sound of two doors closed and Charras joined him at the rear, placing his hands on the boot.

"Take the handbrake off," he said to Charlize who was now in the driver's seat. "Christian, help me push."

"But why?" he said. "The car isn't working. We need to turn it around and go home."

"No, help me push," Charras said with more force.

"It will work if we turn it around. We just need to go home."

"That's just the enchantments talking, fight them and help me."

Christian didn't understand why they couldn't just go home where it was safe. He didn't want to go any further; people didn't go where things stopped working. Everyone knew that it was dangerous to go further. Going further meant never seeing your family again.

But he didn't have a family to go home to...

"Does the enchantment use fear to turn people around?"

Charras nodded. "It knows what you're most afraid of."

"Then it's stupid," Christian said, joining Charras and bracing his knees. "My parents aren't at home." He shoved his weight against the car, tensing his shoulders until it began to roll forward. It picked up momentum quickly, and he found himself soon straightening up and watching as the car moved towards an unknown blockade.

As Charlize passed through the Arx, a deep tug in her stomach signalled she now walked in the territory of the Minae. It lifted almost instantly as a fizz of electric skimmed the length of the car and dispersed. She breathed out and pulled up the handbrake, carefully getting out and standing on the worn and cracked tarmac, noting how even the air tasted differently – almost metallic.

Wondering what was taking Christian and her father so long, she gazed towards the Arx and through the mixture of elements interweaving around the village. They were almost hypnotic up close and she had to concentrate to spot that her father seemed to be struggling. His face contorted, he dragged his weighted leg along the road – a terrified Christian clung to it and refusing to budge. He edged them closer and closer, until one last shuffle managed to force most of him through the barrier – a swift yank by the scruff of his new charges jacket allowing the rest of his leg to join him.

Charras dusted himself down, relieved he managed to get them both through, and then helped a disorientated Christian to his feet, the sheer dread that previously soaked his face turning to horrifying embarrassment as he looked to the space they'd just come from. He desperately searched for a way to justify his misgivings, and upon realising there was nothing there, cleared his throat and got back into the driver's seat without a word.

Charlize grinned at her father and pointed at his trouser leg. In the panic that ensued, a clean rip now exposed his kneecap and two damp handprints slowly faded either side of it.

Charras shot her a withering glare, but when she shrugged and turned to get back in the car, he allowed himself a slight smile.

The rest of the journey was short and they pulled into a small, deserted, and run down car park not ten minutes later. As Christian slowed the car and turned off the engine, his first thought was that they must be lost. The mild day added little credit to the rusted ticket office, which looked as if paint hadn't touched it for years, and it seemed unlikely the station was, or ever had been in use.

A huge part of him wanted to turn back and go home. He didn't know if he travelled with two deranged individuals, or he was truly entering a world he was ignorant to – like an outsider coming home; somewhere he belonged but didn't fit in. Only the words of his mother kept him going, a frail hope that she was still alive pushing him forward.

"What are you thinking?" a gentle voice said beside him.

Christian faced Charlize who was looking at him with concern. He immediately felt guilty. She had her usual long black coat on, buttoned up to her chin, and he wondered if she was cold, even though the temperature in the car was a little under tropical. Her large blue eyes searched his face as she waited for an answer, but he opted to say nothing at all – unsure how to explain his doubts about her sanity. Instead, he shrugged, got out of the car, opened the boot, and heaved the rucksacks onto the gravel.

"Should I bother to lock it?" he asked, addressing no one in particular.

A soft afternoon breeze circled at his feet and Christian sighed. The weather was so calm, surely in the wake of such events, it should at least rain?

He shut the boot and looked up as Charlize and Charras pulled on their packs. "Well?"

Quickly glancing at him, Charras tapped the crimson bonnet. "I can put a protection around it if it will make you feel better?"

Deeming it rude to admit that nothing short of an invisibility cloak would ease his concern, Christian merely nodded. Then, standing back, he watched as Charras held his left hand out to Charlize. She clasped it and in turn reached for his, her fingers stretched towards him indifferently. Christian looked at the offering for a moment before accepting it gently, noting that it was the second time they'd ever touched in such a way. Their fingers seemed to fit like puzzle pieces, and he only half listened as Charras explained how joining hands during a spell 'shared energy' – meaning only those connected would be able to access the protection.

He then called upon fire and held his palm outwards. "*Dicio, Incendiī-Anima, Defendere.*"

A rush of flame surrounded the car, stretching over its entire mass so it was just a shadow within. It burned brightly for a few seconds before folding on its north and south axis to meet in the middle, leaving only a strip of spinning embers. It would do so until either Charras reabsorbed the energy or a stronger spell broke it.

"H… how…?" Christian stammered, his mouth wide open as he watched the flames dance. He took a step towards the protection and touched it with his fingertips, amazed by how it responded to him, parting slightly to allow him entry. He looked back at Charlize, who watched him curiously, and then turned back to the car, startled that the protection was no longer there.

"Where did it go?" he asked.

Charlize frowned. "It's still there Christian, can't you see it?"

He shook his head and folded his arms across his chest. His thoughts were blurry, his head pounding as he tried to digest what he'd just seen. *There was fire right there, just moments before*, he was sure. How could it be there one minute and not the next? Something wasn't right; he must be ill, or worse, hallucinating. It was the stress of his parent's disappearance; it had to be…

"Come Christian," said Charras, steering him towards the station. "You must try to keep an open mind."

The ticket office was beneath an old bridge, long since collapsed, and the three of them entered the rusty shack with caution. It shook with the vibrations, shedding aged dirt off the flimsy roof and covering them all with a layer of dust.

"I was hoping this would be some sort of magic trick too," Christian grumbled.

He wiped his face and shook out his arms, watching as Charras made his way over to an empty counter covered with the same dust they all rubbed from their hair.

A small bell sat atop the fusty wood, its unobvious presence hidden beneath dated brown fastenings. Charras wiped away the cobwebs and pressed down on the button, its trill harsh as it echoed through the tin hovel.

The noise intensified until they were all forced to cover their ears.

"Why is it so loud?" Christian cried, his face scrunched in pain. But no sooner had he asked, the bell granted respite, leaving a quieter resonance.

"It's an enchanted bell only the gifted can hear. It's to prove we're Mages," Charras explained.

"How would a bell know that?"

Charras didn't have time to answer before another noise pierced the quiet. A deep grinding rumbled beneath their feet, and looking towards the source, they saw the counter moving backwards to reveal a hidden opening.

Charlize took the lead and eagerly descended the exposed stairs into blackness. Charras ushered Christian through next so he was safely in the middle, and then they all plunged down the steps quickly, small lights flickering on to guide their way, only to flick back off after they passed. Even though it was pretty, it became apparent as they walked through the makeshift tunnel that decay was a friend in the walls; the damp earth clung to the back of their throats, disturbed in their nostrils.

At the end of the stairs the floor levelled out – trodden and soft, which made walking easy even in the low light. But as they emerged onto a dingy platform as old as the ticket office, there was a loud sigh from Charras.

He sat on a crude concrete bench and rubbed his temples. "You know the Mages at a sorry time Christian. Our facilities have dwindled into disrepair, and as we are stretched thin in this world, very few places remain in order."

Charlize sat next to her father and patted his knee, disregarding Christian's lack of response but acknowledging how he stared at the tracks intently, irrespective of the fact they were barely visible due to a covering of grime.

He said nothing because he felt as if he were almost in a dream, disassociated from his very being. Convinced that he was able to wake up at any moment to find himself warm in his bed, the station was of no concern to him. Even as the tracks rattled against the vibrations of an oncoming train, which then filled the empty space next to the platform, and even as Charras and Charlize pulled him on-board, he simply did not care.

17

Rejection

Made up of compartment cars, the train was busier than Charras expected. He shuffled slowly down the thin corridor and peered into the windows of several polished wooden doors, searching for a vacancy. Some were filled with the excited chatter of Mages on their first pilgrimage, while others were quieter, the inhabitants lost within the pages of a book or newspaper.

It wasn't until they reached the end of the carriage they found an empty booth, and squeezing through the narrow sliding door, Charras lifted the rucksacks onto the overhead slots before making himself comfortable on the worn navy seats. There was little legroom and his shins touched the opposite bench, but the compartment was warm and there was a small sash window to watch the landscape roll past. *It will do nicely*, he thought.

A low rumble signalled the train firing up, which made Charlize lift her head and smile. Excited chatter drifted through the corridor as the train picked up speed, and she listened with interest until the hum of the engine and the pump of the wheel revolutions muffled their conversations.

When their speed regulated, two loud whistles like a teapot declaring its boil on the stove sounded, and she could barely contain herself.

"This is wonderful! I've only seen trains like these in books; I didn't think they made them like this anymore."

"More proof that the Mages are behind the modern times," Charras replied, his enthusiasm less apparent.

"No father, I think it's wonderful," Charlize said, turning to Christian. "Don't you think so too?"

He didn't reply. Gazing silently out of the window, he looked unaware he was there at all. The scenery rushed past, the browns of earth meeting the greens of hedgerows, which met the greys and blues of the sky – as if someone ran those colours in parallel across a canvass, but his eyes seemed to focus on nothing.

"Christian?" Charlize asked softly. "Are you okay?" It took him a while to acknowledge her, but he eventually turned and gave a small nod. She immediately placed a hand on his forehead and frowned.

Her touch warm, it seemed to rouse him from whatever daydream had taken hold. Rubbing his head, he said, "Sorry, I'm not feeling well."

A book landed in his lap seconds later and he looked down to see the gold writing pulsing up at him.

"Keep reading," said Charras.

Charlize grabbed the book from his grasp and fixed her father with a steely glare. "He's rejecting it," she warned, "he needs time."

"Time is something he does not have," Charras replied, tugging the book back from her clutches and replacing it on Christian's lap.

Charlize crossed her arms and sat rigidly against the bench panelling, fixing a glare out of the window. "He is not your son to torment," she muttered.

"Enough," Charras said to the back of her head. Then, addressing Christian: "Keep reading."

A patrol officer sliding the door open interrupted any further argument. Demanding their identities, his palm held ready, he quickly turned white when Charlize obliged. With a low bow, he swiftly shut the doors and continued on his way.

In the resuming uneasy situation, the three Mages listened to the steady chug beneath them, each focused on what was directly in their line of sight. None of them wished to engage in potentially hostile eye contact, but Christian knew the expectation was for him to keep reading. So, moving the ribbon hanging down from the spine, the book fell open at the last page he'd last marked, and as the gold tinged his face, he was soon lost in the secret.

The Firsts: A Tale of Five Warriors

*Let me tell you of the war. Waged hundreds of years ago, when the
need to retaliate became more obvious, five men picked for their strength
of will and truth of heart each received the gift of an element. As the
Firsts, they were readers, the only Mages capable of liaising with the very
Sky itself, to be the messengers of light even in darkness.*

*In those days, they were called exorcists, people that took the dead
from the living and lay them to rest. Superstition surrounded them,
naming them warlocks of dark magic and feared for the elemental powers
they possessed.*

*Nevertheless, the Mages knew the truth and chose to live their lives in
secret, battling in the war against Inferus-Malus – the deepest evil. Their
purpose was to grant the dead their final passing and eradicate them
from an earth they no longer belonged to. Using their destructive gifts of
fire; ice; air; lightning, and water, they fought back with the powerful
energy the Sky provided.*

*As time moved forward and the Mages grew older, each reaching their
thirtieth birthdays, it became clear that they would not live forever. No
earth bound war waged and the Sky could not tell them when it would. So,
in this knowledge, the Mages determined to continue the bloodlines so
their work would carry on even after their demise.*

*In agreement, the Sky explained that they must seek out their other
halves, the person it deemed best suited for them; for in order to keep the
line's undiluted, the Sky had also bestowed the same gifts into five
females, chosen for their purity of spirit and depth of intelligence.*

*To seek them out, the Mages, having never been separated, parted
ways. They called this 'The Divide' and it was during this time the* Book
of Becoming *came into existence, providing a guide for the generations*

to follow. *Each new Mage was to receive one unique to them on their tenth birthday, handed down from the very Sky itself.*

I am your *guide Christian, a gift and friend for as long as you have need of me.*

[NB: Knowledge is merely taught – a lesson to hear and recite. Understanding what I teach is entirely in your hands].

Closing the book with a quick *snap,* Christian put his head in his lap. Every bone in him doubted and denied the story written before him, rejecting the very words that served him nothing but confusion.

When he eventually lifted his head, the compartment was dark, the window having steamed up as rain pattered lightly against it. *That's more like it* he thought, placing his temple on the glass as his brain throbbed and blurred his vision.

The continuous barrage of rain, steel wheels against wet tracks, loose fastenings, and creaking furnishings invaded his thoughts, unhelpful as he tried to refocus. But realising his body wouldn't obey, he gazed about the carriage, looking for a familiar smile of concern or touch of comfort.

Yet he was alone.

The realisation only just dawning on him, he tried not to panic. Instead, he scrambled unsteadily to his feet and pulled apart the small doors. As he took a step, the train juddered and he fell into the gangway, his head hitting the floor, and a renewed pain shot through his skull.

Nausea churned in his stomach, the bile reaching his throat, and he swallowed it down with grim satisfaction. After it settled, he propped himself on his elbows, took a breath, and reached out to the far wall, managing to steady himself enough to twist into a sitting position and stare along the corridor.

The lights dimmed slightly, flickering erratically as he watched them wane. Images of the Minae floated through his mind and he pressed himself further into the shadows. He heard voices calling to him, but his head was swimming so much their words sounded distorted – deep and drawn out.

And then he saw Charlize. She was by his side in moments, holding his hand to her shoulder and pulling him towards her. The lights returned to their full luminescence and his watery eyes cleared, meeting Charlize's concerned expression as she gazed down at him, her beauty masked in shadow from the stark beam above her.

She stroked his hot face and he grabbed her wrist. "I thought you'd left me... the lights," he gasped.

She checked his pulse and temperature, kneeling opposite him as she wiped the sweat from his brow. "It was a tunnel Christian, that's all, we were only next door."

Becoming aware of several unfamiliar faces peering down on him, he let the flush reach his cheeks. He felt foolish and attempted to stand, only realising his failure when Charlize pushed him back against the wall.

"Please, leave us; we will be only a few moments," she reassured the inquisitive crowd.

Her father said nothing as he ushered the spectators away and returned to the compartment he'd emerged from. One by one, the doors all slid shut and the corridor fell into silence.

"Let me look at you," Charlize said, holding Christian's face so she could look into his eyes. Their dilation was normal but his breath remained short. "Come, join us," she coerced softly.

He shied away from her outstretched hand and shook his head. "I read the chapter, about the Firsts."

She nodded her understanding. "It is a lot to take in; it will take time. Try to see it as a story. Use the information when you need to and don't question it too much, otherwise it could cause unknown side effects."

The train rounded a corner, swaying the carriage underfoot, and the motion caused Christian to close his eyes once more. When he opened them, Charlize was holding onto the wall above his head, her tied hair dangling over her shoulder and brushing his arm. He took a breath.

"That bad huh?"

She looked at him, preparing an answer, but stopped when she realised he was smiling. Taking his hands, she pulled him up, and holding onto his waist, guided him into the booth she and her father had befriended hours before.

As the warm light washed over him, coupled with the added reassurance of a company of Mages, Christian felt his body calm. Looking around, he saw Charras in a serious conversation with another man of similar physique. He wore a black suit with a white shirt and grey tie, his face square and jaw set.

"Come, sit," said Charlize, gesturing for him to take a seat in the space opposite her.

He did so without question, proceeding to watch as she continued her conversation with two young men – both dressed in the same clothes as Charras's companion. The obvious youngest of the two stared quite openly at her, which made Christian wonder why; for he did not seem to look with adoration, but instead with fear.

The second eldest of the three – a slender man with a long nose, explained how they'd been to a funeral, and Charlize expressed her pity, wishing their loved one a speedy departure into the Sky.

"He was the eldest of us all. It is a great blow to our family, but he fought bravely." Hunching his shoulders, the man held his fist to his mouth.

Charlize placed a reassuring hand on his elbow. "He will be safe where he is now, you honour his death bravely."

"He knew it would be this way," said the man, wiping his eyes. "He saw it a long time ago." He straightened his back and regained his composure. "Excuse me, I'm tired, I don't mean to burden you with our loss."

"It is no burden," Charlize replied quickly.

"Then you have our thanks," said the man Charras was talking to, turning to face her for the first time. "To have your concern is a comfort.

But to ask any more from you would be imprudent to say the least, wouldn't you agree Niall?"

Bowing his head, heeding the scorn, Niall clasped his hands together. "Of course, of course brother."

"Very well," said Charlize, "but never fear asking for help; we are in this together."

"Indeed, we are, yet I'm sure your concerns will be better placed with matters graver than ours."

Her eyes alight, she replied, "It depends on how you perceive my concern. The matters you deem less important all play their part in making a greater tragedy, one in which we suffer together. To have less concern for one misfortune than another will only dilute the greater tragedy and blind me to what created it in the first place."

Considering her for a moment, Charlize was sure the man would speak again. Instead, he let out a soft grunt and curled his fingers around his beard. If he did have a comeback, she would never hear it, for the train gave a slight jerk, forcing the passengers to brace themselves – the screech of steal a harsh jolt in the equanimity.

Another wave of nausea washed over Christian and he clung to the foam bench. He tried to focus his senses but the effort caused another bout of bile to form in his throat. Once again, he found himself swallowing to keep it down, further clenching his stomach and praying he wouldn't embarrass himself even more. It wasn't long until Charras noticed and pulled him to his feet.

"We're here," he said gruffly, marching him from the compartment and back into their original one.

Charlize followed closely behind, helping to collect their belongings from the rack while her father supported Christian by the arm. They were the first to leave the train, but even so, the whispers of recognition towards 'the Āetis' and the confusion of her ill companion didn't escape her. They were already causing controversy she thought with sadness.

The station platform was a bustling hive of activity, although the busyness meant she went largely unnoticed. Most were too engrossed with admiring the station's wrought iron work, the intricate balustrades resembling a forest of vines and canopies that filtered visitors along the concourse like cattle. It was difficult not to be swept up in the pulse, and many delayed their journeys by looking up to the high glass ceiling, gasping in awe at the chequered dome resting on white polished pillars. Through it, you could see the stars, and Charlize cocked her neck so far back, gravity nearly pulled her pack to the floor, taking her along with it. But her father's voice interrupted her musings, saving her fall, and she refocused on marching behind him, keeping her head low until they found themselves gathered in the square of a quaint market town.

The aura of Mages among the lesser mark of Ungifted stirred in her senses, each thud of life going about their business with purpose. Impressed by how their footing remained steady on the cobbled streets, while hers faltered with every step, she hoped the talent would embrace her quickly.

Fortuitously, they reached the centre of the square where an information booth sat without hazard, and the man within it waved them forward. "Welcome to Miledown!" he boomed.

He was a plump man of medium stature with a friendly smile, which put Charras immediately at ease. "Greetings yourself!" he replied heartily. "Could you tell me where the Millwall hotel is? I heard it was not too far from the station."

The affable information guide passed a leaflet to Charras and pointed out the directions on its map. "Not far at all, see?" he grinned.

Charras nodded. The hotel was a five-minute walk. He faced the man to thank him, but found his attention fixed on something else. Turning to see what held his interest, he saw Christian clutched to Charlize – swaying unsteadily as he tried to compose himself.

"Too much of the old liquor eh?" the man joked.

Charras said nothing as he pulled Christian to his feet. Grunting a quick thanks over his shoulder, he made for the hotel, Charlize following sullenly behind.

"He's rejecting it!" she shouted, angered at his merciless attitude.

"Quiet, you don't want to draw attention."

She didn't listen and threw her hands in the air. "He needs help – a doctor or something!" She watched as Christian slumped further down her father's side.

Rain began to fall as the night air closed in around them and the streets took on a faint glow. Charras propped Christian on a bench before facing his daughter, bending down to clasp her shoulder.

"The choice has been made; there is no going back. He has to accept the truths before him." He loosened his grip. "You need to stop fighting me on this."

"And what if he doesn't, then what, what happens to him?"

Beneath the bench, Christian vomited violently. Reality waned into surrealism as his body rejected what it could not explain, knowing no other way to get rid of unwanted matter.

Charlize faced her father once more, and when their eyes met, her question was answered. "Then this is on your shoulders," she said.

The hotel was a four story building and relatively new. Unlike the other buildings surrounding it, there was smooth brick, not stone masonry on the outside walls. Painted white with black sills and lintels, along with the quoins, wooden shutters thrown open for artistic effect remained fixed against the panels behind them.

Charlize walked up the short-railed stairwell and stood in front of a wide double-leafed door. Painted in the same way as the building, copper studs extended down its length, creating a cross effect, and the door handle was large and tapered at the end. If there were not a sign saying *'Please come in, all are welcome,'* she may have remained standing there for longer. But she needed no further permission and pushed the side closest to her, halving the door as she stepped through into an entrance hall. Rain dripped from her coat onto the walnut and cherry parquet floor and she wiped her face as she decided what to do.

The Mage workers of the hotel tried not to stare at her, each unsure whether they should approach. They'd known the likelihood of a visit from the Āetis, anyone who was anyone knowing she embarked on her pilgrimage – unless they lived under a rock. But they also knew the delicate rules of engagement, and most preferred not to risk offence.

Charlize didn't mind that she was being scrutinised. She knew her namesake would enthral those who'd never seen her up close, and the Hetairia Doman warned her often that her eminence would cause both awe and discomfort. The advice was to remain polite and unflustered in the face of such attentions.

With this in mind, she pretended to be far more interested in gazing around than making eye contact. And the truth was, she didn't know what else to do now she'd stormed from her father's presence. So, walking over the polished squares and suns, she waited next to a water feature, idly admiring the way several dolphins spat water from their snouts into a shell held by a mermaid.

Beyond that, jets of water rose out of a continuous glass basin that ran the entire length of the room, with splash back prevented by a short glass sheet that reflected the water onto the tiles behind it.

"Can I help you miss?"

Turning to the pleasant voice, she faced the owner. He was a tall boy, no older than sixteen, and wore a red suit buttoned down to his hips and a nervous smile. His age cursed him with acne and his composure faltered as she made eye contact.

"I'm just waiting, thank-you," she replied, hoping her current temperament could be sensed.

The boy remained where he stood. "Do you have a room booked?"

With a small frown, Charlize shook her head and looked around for a sign of her father. The boy, seemingly holding no weight to the concept of perception, continued with his questioning. "Would you like to wait in the lounge? We can bring you some refreshments?" he suggested.

The thought appealed to her, but as she began to accept the offer, voices echoed in the large entrance hall. She turned to the familiar sound of her father's deep voice and she saw him stood at the reception desk with a less green Christian by his side. They spoke to a girl with short-cropped hair, straightened flat to her pale pixie-like face.

Charlize thanked the boy for his hospitality and made her way over to her companions, quietly waiting behind them. It took her a little while to notice how the girl behind the counter was actually standing and not sitting as she first thought, her height masking her true age from those who first glimpsed her. The same girl pulled two keys from a desk beneath the counter and handed them to Charras, flashing him a shy smile as he gratefully took them from her.

Then, leaving through two large doors, Charlize followed inconspicuously as they descended into a long thin hallway. Photographs of sepia landscapes lined the walls as they continued into another corridor, and then another, until finally they stopped in front of two metal doors. Her father pressed a button next to them and they parted automatically moments later.

Charlize peered into the small room and squinted before stepping through. "We're not staying in here are we?" she asked, thinking the space limited.

Christian gazed at his school friend for the first time since being sick, unsure if she was joking or not. "Are you being serious?"

Ignoring the evident insult, Charlize waited to hear her answer.

"It's an elevator," said Charras, attempting and failing miserably to hide a smile. "I'm sorry, I should have told you."

The elevator doors shut, securing the occupants in the small space as it rumbled into life and rose until a small bell sounded. Charlize steadied herself against the momentum, but kept silent, not wishing her ignorance of modern technology to amuse Christian further, and seconds later the metal doors reopened, revealing a corridor much the same as the previous ones. They walked through in procession, only stopping when Charras handed Charlize a key with the number '32' engraved on a metal strip attached to it. With a sharp goodnight, she turned on her heels and disappeared into her room.

Charras and Christian exchanged tiresome glances before entering their own quarters, the spherical handle stiff from lack of use. The room was en-suite with two single beds, and a long window occupied one entire wall, framing a view of the village below. The evening glimmer had disappeared, replaced by a dark haze that washed over the town, and the light from the sporadic lampposts almost seemed redundant.

Keen to shower, Charras left Christian to his own devices, although once alone, he merely drew the curtains and lifted the soft linen from its neat confines. He wanted nothing more than to climb beneath the sheets, and curling a plump pillow around his head, he let days of weariness wash over him.

Soon, he was fast asleep.

18

First Steps

Harsh morning light broke Charlize's sleep, deeper than she anticipated. Sitting up in her plush double bed, the warm sheets fell from her shoulders and the coolness of the room took advantage of her bare skin. She rubbed her eyes and shivered slightly, then swung her legs to the floor and darted into the bathroom.

Glad to see it housed a bath, she turned on the taps, inhaling the steam that quickly met her face. Then, undressing, she submerged her cold body and closed her eyes, the gentle thrum of the boiler's vibrations a soothing milieu.

Half an hour later she re-emerged, her damp hair clinging to her upper body. Pulling the towel tightly around her torso, securing it in the folds, she began to search the room, soon discovering it hid no hair-dryer. With a sigh, she walked over to the windows and briskly shut the curtains.

After another survey of her surroundings – not that she expected anyone to be there – she took a breath and cast a quick Anima spell. A warm breeze kicked up around her and she dropped her towel, directing the air through her wet locks and over her skin.

Once dry, she clapped her hands and dressed, deciding on a pair of comfortable black trousers and a grey shirt. Her father had insisted she brought only practical hiking clothes, each Haunt supplying their own form of dress, but it left her with nothing in the way of versatility. Her undergarments were the only items her father allowed flexibility on, and it was strictly her decision what feminine supplies she needed.

Luckily, having a limited wardrobe made it easy to choose an outfit, and pulling out her only choice of footwear, she pushed her feet into black walking boots and tied the laces that rose half way up her shins. Then, tucking her diamond tear into her shirt, its power tingling against her fingertips, she proceeded to pack her belongings into her rucksack and heave it over her shoulder.

Without a backwards glance, she crossed the room, stepped out into the hallway and closed the door behind her. A morning haze suffused the corridor; dappled sunlight sifted through layers of paisley netting, and Charlize listened to the quiet snores of those still asleep. She was marginally envious of the Ungifted that lay unconscious, spared from reality for the duration of their slumber, but she forced the resentment to the back of her mind and knocked on the door she stood in front of.

Charras appeared a few seconds later, smiling as he ushered her inside. The previous night's argument seemingly forgotten, he poured her a cup of tea from the miniature kettle on a tray next to the television. A strange man with a shock of white hair blared out from the contraption, talking about the weather forecast while images flashed behind him, and Charlize couldn't help but laugh, accepting the mug as she sat at the foot of the bed to watch the images on the screen. Even the sight of Christian did nothing to deter her, answering his mumbled greeting with an inaudible response of her own, although she did manage to catch a glimpse of his tousled hair and sleepless eyes before resuming her immediate interest.

In the bathroom, Christian secured the door and held his breath, wary that he may throw up again. Daring a glance in the mirror, he acknowledged the effect fatigue had taken on his features, his expression dull and haunted. Too ashamed to look for long, he began to wash his face.

Meanwhile, Charras sipped his coffee, watching Charlize watch the television with an unnatural ardour. When he could no longer bear it, he turned it off and raised his eyebrows as she broke from her trance.

"Let's hope there's not a television around when you're fighting Minae," he said. She stared at him in annoyance, but he shrugged it off and nodded towards the bathroom. "He's been having nightmares, we must be careful with him today." Shaking his head as she began to protest, he pressed a finger to his lips. "Please Charlize, not now. I need to check out; we've slept longer than we should have. Wait here and I'll be back shortly."

With only a minor pout, she nodded. "Of course father."

The minute he left, Charlize picked up the remote and tapped several buttons until the television blared back into life. Jumping up, she pulled out a chair from beneath the oak desk and sat in it cross-legged. The programme currently airing talked about the situation of endangered animals, concentrating on the Black Rhinoceros that faced extinction. A woman with dark skin was explaining how they were carrying out rehabilitation efforts within the larger Arcēs to ensure the survival of the species, but with little land mass they feared their efforts were in vain. The pictures then changed as the same lady introduced the viewers to Lila and Honko, two mated Rhinos being led into their new home.

"Charlize, what the…"

Almost falling off the chair, she leapt up, her hands ready to strike. Steam surrounded Christian as he fought to keep the towel covering his modesty, and Charlize instantly clapped her hands over her eyes.

"Why didn't you say you were still here?" he said sharply, stepping back into the bathroom.

"I, I didn't think, Honko and Lila were –"

"Huh?"

"It's a Mage channel, I rarely see the news, I'm sorry!"

Christian huffed and slammed the door. "This is why being brought up with no television is bad!" he yelled.

Charlize bit her lip and fanned her cheeks with her hands, which for some reason were extremely hot. Letting out her held breath, she continued to watch the progress of the Rhino's with only half the enthusiasm of before.

Unfortunately, species of animals being re-classed as extinct happened more frequently every year. She heard stories of large cats once roaming savannahs, of gorillas in misty mountains, and of black and white bears in forests of bamboo. They lived until the emphasis to save only beneficial wildlife became a priority, and the world watched helplessly as the beauty of nature faded. Those who fought to maintain the wildlife deemed less essential often failed, and in its wake a hundred books dedicated to its memory would appear – a preservation of historical failure.

Christian re-emerged from the bathroom looking distinctly more awake. He was wearing similar attire to Charlize, and rummaging through his bag for his boots, he realised they were underneath the desk – where he'd left them the night before.

"Could you pass me those?" he asked Charlize.

She looked to where he pointed. "Yes," she said, making no move to pick them up.

The reason dawning on him, Christian sighed. "Please?" he said.

With a smile, Charlize bent down and passed him the boots, their eyes meeting for a few moments before she quickly looked away.

"How are you feeling?" she asked while he tied his laces.

He didn't answer at first. Sitting up, he ran his hands through his towel-dried hair and let the floppy mass fall around his gaunt face. A hint of colour from the showers warmth tinged his complexion, but it also emphasised the dark circles under his eyes.

"I'm fine, I think. I still feel sick, but I figure it will pass."

"And your opinion on our world now?"

Christian stared at his fingers while Charlize waited for an answer. Shrugging again, he faced her. "I have no idea."

She didn't push the issue, knowing her probing would do no good for his mental state. Instead, she let the silence linger between them, happy to wait until her father returned. It wasn't long until he did, a loud knock snapping her senses back into focus. On her feet in seconds, she threw open the door and stood with her rucksack held ready.

Pleased with his daughter's eagerness, Charras entered the room to collect his own belongings. He noted how Christian sat hunched on the bed, his glum face staring at the floor, and stepped towards him. "We're leaving now," he said. "Collect your things."

There was no time for delay, but he watched patiently as Christian pulled on his overcoat, settled his pack on his back, and adjusted the straps accordingly – with a speed not unlike a grazing Rhino…

With the morning routine firmly set into action, the hotel entrance was a clamour of people. Weaving his way through the crowd, Charras led his entourage from the building and into the cool air with ease. Scents of sandalwood hung on the breeze, while an easterly wind carried the subtle aroma of Christmas roses, brought over from the forest beyond the village.

Breathing in the new day, he marched them with purpose through the bustling streets, attempting to avoid the market traders selling their wares. A stout man enticed Charlize with a cinnamon pastry, almost making her stop to buy it, but Charras spurred her forwards before she had the chance. He didn't notice the look of disappointment she shot over her shoulder, or the shrug of the man as he bowed his head and replaced the pastry in its tray.

They were almost at the south exit of the village, where a tended garden sat beneath the eaves of a ruined monument, the ground freshly churned to house an allotment of vegetables, that a passing trader recognised Charlize. He insisted on giving her a freshly baked loaf and pot of honey, refusing payment with an unyielding shake of his head. Charras managed to force two coins into his tray and dart away before they could be thrown back.

"Father, you're being rude," said Charlize, running to keep up with him.

"Acknowledging you in such a manner draws the attention of Ungifted. I am merely saving us the hassle of the Hetairia Doman getting wind of such trivialities."

"They know I'll be recognised, surely they can overlook such minor indiscretions."

Charras stopped and turned to her. "Easy for you to say when you don't have to fill out the paperwork. I won't risk it."

Charlize wanted to say that he cared too much about the Hetairia Doman and their rulebook, especially as they were exempt, but she didn't, knowing to hold her tongue while he remained so cautious. Although she was too powerful to maintain any hex of silence on her lips, her respect for him meant he rarely needed to try.

Nevertheless, she couldn't help but feel cheated. Being the only one whose idea of adventure was stepping beyond the perimeter of the Marsh School, the freedom of travel held an appeal unrivalled by the hardiest of explorers. The bright sun left nothing untouched and Charlize wished she could branch out and explore every inch while she still had time. There was a world outside her sheltered existence and she would discover it as best she could – even at the expense of her father's nerves.

She only wished Christian would perk up and share in her excitement, but the only response they'd managed from him was a couple of mumbled sentences. Looking at him now, she saw apathy written across his face, his denial and rejection of their way of life turned into something else, almost acceptance, but not of this new life. Instead, it appeared that he believed he was dreaming.

"We're walking to the Anima forest," Charras declared, cutting into Charlize's thoughts once again. "It will take us just under five days."

He waited for the complaints, finding himself pleasantly surprised when none were offered; mainly because Charlize already knew, and telling Christian they were flying to the moon would likely be accepted without a hint of protest.

"Let's get going then," he said, setting the pace.

Miledown wasn't large in comparison to the Marsh Village, although it held more cobbled streets than any Charras had experienced, and he led them confidently through the last narrow lane – the south gate in sight.

All the while, Christian trailed behind, unaware of exactly where they were going, only knowing that he had to keep following, thoughts of his parents firmly set in his mind. His dark mood descended on Charlize who paced behind him, making sure he didn't wander off on a tangent, and for the duration of their descent, she resented him.

Their feet touching solid, smooth, easily trodden earth, the cobbles decreasing until there were none, Charras, Charlize, and Christian all stretched out their ankles. A loud horn blow signalled their departure and three guards saluted them as they escaped towards the forest boundary.

"That was all fairly unnecessary," Charlize remarked when they were out of earshot.

She commented on the formality at the gate, where they had to sign release forms and detail their stay. They'd also had to explain Christian, which was tricky considering his status of being a Mage fell into question, challenged by a prudent (and Charlize suspected only recently promoted) guard. That had required further documentation and an SMC: 'Statement of Mage Companionship' form due to Christian's 'unique' status, which meant they had to treat him like an Ungifted, who were usually unaware of their companions abilities during transportation efforts.

Such efforts tended to be rare, so the fact an SMC even existed surprised Charlize, until her father explained that when he and her mother travelled, they would sometimes pay a Mage to sign such forms which allowed them access to more dangerous territory near the Arx borders, if not beyond them. More often than not however, Leanne and Theo were with them, and although their friendship baffled many, to avoid an Ungifted becoming suspicious, an SMC would exchange hands quietly. It took the onus off the Arx's senate and into the hands of the Mages accompanying the 'strange folk' that dared dream of a world beyond the Arcēs.

"It is their custom, we must respect it if nothing else," Charras said, although he quietly agreed.

Charlize shrugged, seeing no logic in understanding any such tradition that required wasted hours of bureaucracy. Then again, she did see the sense in adhering to guidelines from the Hetairia Doman, and their advice was to follow whatever practices the Arcēs' maintained – however seemingly unimportant.

Besides, her mood was calming now the afternoon sun hid behind the trees and the heat on the back of her neck began to cool. Rubbing it, she wished she were able to cast a Glacies spell and create the ice her neck craved for. But of course that was unheard of in the open unprotected radius; so she settled for exposing it by lifting her hair out of the way, grateful that the shadows they headed for would shroud her in cooler air.

They trudged slowly, there being a slight undulation underfoot, and she spent most of her time watching her feet. She only lifted her head when the sweet scent of the Christmas roses piqued her interest – their sheer numbers something she'd never seen in one place. From Miledown, it appeared the forest housed a layer of frost, their delicate white petals creating the illusion, a phenomenon she recognised in the painting that hung above the fireplace in the manor. They called it the 'Trail of Hellebores,' and only the white flowers grew where a Mage had stepped before, sprouting from the essence of magic left in their wake. Conversely, they would wilt if any Minae passed, allowing the Hellebores to act as natures warning system to those travelling to the Anima.

They'd been walking for several hours before Charras decided to bring the progression to a stop, aware they'd hiked without pause. He assumed the lack of communication meant there were no complaints, but now the day was drawing in, he decided to reward their endless pace with a meal, certain that once they began cooking, hunger would rear its head.

The Anima Haunt was a four and a half-day walk from where they currently rest. If they carried on through the night, having a maximum of five hours sleep each day, they could make it in less than three. Although they said nothing, Charras was sure his charges wouldn't agree to his three-day aim, especially when they considered the next few nights sleeping arrangements. In his haste not to delay Charlize's pilgrimage, the two-man tent still lay in its confines. Their new addition would make for a tight squeeze…

Letting his pack drop to the floor, he stretched out his arms. "We'll set up now; night will draw in less than two hours."

Once again, there were no complaints. Christian merely nodded and took off his bag, pulling out his overcoat from its rolled position within a pouch. He flapped it outwards to remove the creases, tugged it on, and sat on the floor. Beside him, Charlize made no movement whatsoever, her attention transfixed on the forest.

Charras came to stand by her side, noting her faraway expression. He knew it well. "Come, the spirits will reveal themselves in time," he said.

A faint hum escaped her lips, although the sound wasn't in answer to him, but to something else. "Charlize, come," he coerced again, pulling her back towards the clearing.

She let him steer her away, although continued to gaze into the forest. It had whispered to her, promising her guidance and truth. It was as if the very air itself was curious to know her path.

"Until tomorrow," she whispered to the breeze.

Charras turned to see Christian staring at them with a deep frown wrinkled across his forehead.

"Who's she talking to?" he asked.

"Ah," Charras replied. "That is a question best saved for another evening. Think no more on it." He would have been honest, but Christian's face was paler than usual and a slight gleam coated his skin. He was worried that his sickness was manifesting itself in ways they hadn't foreseen.

"It's like the forest knows me…" Charlize said pensively, her voice airy. She was sitting with her arms folded around her legs. "It's like we're friends from a forgotten life."

Noticing how the frown deepened on Christian's forehead, Charras tried to change the subject. "Okay. Let's bed down and then eat. Charlize, your bread and honey will accompany a hearty tomato soup from your supplies."

"They're just trees," Christian said.

"Indeed," Charras said. "Now, who would like to help me make a start?"

"You wouldn't understand," Charlize replied, looking into the distance with a thoughtful gaze.

"I understand that trees can't speak."

"Yes, quite right Christian," said Charras, opening his rucksack and pulling out several poles. "Now, the trick with these is –"

"The trees are alive, just like you and I," Charlize interrupted, her stare now matching Christian's. "Perhaps not in the way you see us, but their energy burns as brightly as ours. You will soon discover this."

Taking on an array of expressions before he answered, Christian snorted with mirth. "Oh, forgive my ignorance of talking trees and your popularity with them."

"You're being disrespectful."

"Come now," Charras said, pulling the bedding and tent from the rucksacks and scattering the equipment and materials on the ground. He opened two of the larger folded pieces of material and formed the tent's base shape on the earth.

"Just because I don't believe that you can talk to a trees and they're all your 'friends' doesn't make me rude. It makes me sane."

Charlize's eyes burned with fury. "I will forgive your ignorance and blame it on your lack of respect, but understand that you deeply offend me."

"I don't care about how offended you always seem to be. Perhaps if you were nicer to people you wouldn't have to make up an entire forest of inert friends!"

Charras watched as she stood to her full height, her hand outwards, and he sharply grabbed her wrist and wrenched her to face him. "He is ill. He means no harm. Control yourself." He let the heat in his grip be known and Charlize cast her eyes downwards.

"Go and cool off," he said. "And let that be the last time I ever witness your lack of restraint."

"What was she going to do?" Christian piped up. "Kill me with a fireball?"

Charlize wrapped her arms across her chest, deeply ashamed. "I'm sorry," she murmured, striding from the camp and heading towards a fallen tree. There, she sat with her head in her hands and tried to figure out what had come over her.

"Seriously, is that what she was going to do?" Christian asked.

Charras shook his head. "She was going to warn you, not kill you." He looked into his wide eyes and chose to ignore their strange milky texture, the ebony dulled to a lighter brown. "How about you help me set up the tent and then we can all eat?"

The familiarity of camping a welcome distraction, Christian eagerly helped thread the metal poles through the guide lining, creating a cross, and then bend them so they curved to form a domed roof. It reached the height of Charras's chest, and he slotted the poles into position before hammering the pegs into the ground with a mallet.

Once the main body was secure, Charras threaded another pole through a smaller entrance piece, curved it like the other two, and smiled proudly at the small makeshift entrance hall. To finish, Christian picked up the remaining sheet of material and disappeared into the tent to fasten the flysheet, and while he did that, Charras pulled several pots and pans from his rucksack and placed them next to the clearing he'd brushed aside. Then, closing his eyes, he called on air, reaching outwards with his senses to touch what lay around him. He found sticks for kindling, a few logs hiding a woovle of woodlice, and a cluster of stones once used by other Mages now a home to moss. He compelled them towards him and opened his eyes a moment later.

Everything he called for lay at his feet. With a smirk, he arranged the stones in a circle, placed the logs in a tipi formation, distributed the kindling, and then clicked his fingers to ignite a spark before dropping it into the middle of his creation. A fire flared into existence and he stood back and folded his arms.

"Father!" Charlize exclaimed, charging towards him and standing with her mouth agape. Although her tone suggested shock, he could tell her anger had subsided.

He chuckled. "They had good cause to call me a rebel."

"And you shall never redeem yourself this way!" She laughed in spite of herself.

"You are my redemption," he said softly.

And she was; she knew it. Leanne had told her the story of her parents a long time ago, back when her father smiled with his whole face – the days before her birth. Once a rebel for love, he had to learn to conform once more.

"Besides," Charras continued. "Here there are nothing but nosy insects and a blind wind."

"Not so blind," Charlize mumbled, gesturing towards Christian sat cross-legged in the tent's entrance.

He watched the show with half-thoughtful eyes, having long resigned himself to the fact he was in a very surreal and very long dream, a dream in which he also had to sleep and act as if he was actually awake. He hadn't worked out the finer details, but he hoped that would come in time… For now, he could do nothing but wait.

So when the fire miraculously built itself and ignited with a flame Charras produced from his hand, he observed quietly, trying to process the meaning of something so bizarre.

It wasn't long until it all went black.

Opening his eyes to a night sky full of brilliant stars, Christian wondered how long he'd been dream asleep. A muffled conversation played out nearby and he could just make out the tone above the crackling of a roaring fire. He turned his head slightly, happily noting his dream Charras or Charlize had placed a pillow beneath his head. He was also aware that he was lying on the ground – his buttocks having gone numb.

"Yes, no more spells of any kind in front of him, I think that's for the best. We don't want to push it, he's fragile enough."

It was Charlize's voice he heard, clear and tuneful as always.

Charras answered her. "He's taking it harder than I first thought. It will do no good for him to learn of us yet, or the extent of our abilities." He sighed. "I do wonder how Armmos will endure this."

Understanding nothing, Christian stretched his legs, a groan escaping his dry lips. The conversation ended immediately. "Please, don't stop on my account, go on, talk more of magic and stuff," he said, sitting up and rubbing his neck.

Looking into the faces of his concerned carers, he frowned. "What? I didn't die…"

"How are you feeling?"

Christian looked at Charlize. He liked this dream version. She was far more concerned than the real one would ever be. "I'm fine. But I'd be better if you didn't ask me that every five minutes."

"Five minutes? I think that's an exaggeration."

Huffing, he leaned back on his elbows. "You know what I mean."

By the look on her face, she didn't.

He disregarded her confusion in favour of sniffing the air, the smell of food holding his stomach to ransom, and seconds later Charras shoved a plate of honey on toast under his nose. He received it gratefully and took a moment to think how strange it was that even though he was asleep he still had an appetite. But the thought didn't linger, quickly replaced by rabid hunger, and he devoured his meal down to the last crumb, before crudely wiping his mouth with his sleeve and belching.

"Thanks," he said, passing the plate back to Charras.

"You're welcome," he replied, stacking it on the pile Charlize would wash with her Aquāe element when Christian was out of sight. "Now, I think it's time for rest; we have a great distance to cover tomorrow."

Christian nodded, knowing that sleep was the only thing his dream body craved. Stretching, he crawled into the tent first, followed by Charras and then Charlize a few minutes later. Once settled – Charras firmly in the middle – he soon settled into his dream dreams.

19
Another Burden

Day broke softly. The gentle light filtered through the overhead branches, resting on the lone tent sitting amongst the recently sprouted Hellebores. Christian was the first to wake and wriggle from his sleeping bag, crawl from the tent – careful to avoid the legs of his companions – and gulp in the fresh day. Although he had not slept much, (the snores Charras emitted enough to alert the dead) he still felt wide-awake.

Dimmed slightly from the shade of the trees, the forest that stretched before him seemed like another world. Its dark and foreboding whisper contrasted against the bright backdrop of Miledown, with its quaint town houses and busy streets swarming with ant-like precision. And where he stood, the sun high in the sky but providing little warmth, the bare branches blew in the breeze like ghouls trying to scare children from their beds. *Well, they can't scare me* he thought, puffing out his chest and walking to the edge of the forest.

Squinting in an attempt to see what lay within, he realised that only the nearest trees seemed to fall into focus. No matter how close he got, he could only see three trees deep. Beyond that, it blurred and disappeared into greyness. *Odd* he thought, recalling Charlize's intent fascination the previous day. He wondered who or what she'd been talking to. Whoever or whatever it was, he wanted to find out. It was his dream after all. Perhaps it would be a strange mythical creature, like a unicorn, or a werewolf… and maybe if he found it, it might help him unravel the reasons he was stuck in his dream world.

Resolute in his decision to discover the voices, Christian climbed back into the tent to fetch his overcoat. Charras and Charlize were awake and engaging in logistical conversation, which he promptly disturbed.

"I'm sorry… it's cold," he explained, reaching for his jacket.

Charras considered him with what Christian considered unnecessary intensity. What he didn't know was that his eyes caused the interest, his companions having noticed a film of milky liquid stubbornly clinging to his irises. It seemed to them that they'd been open for a long time without truly seeing anything.

"Christian, if you're cold, I don't expect you to endure it," Charras said finally.

Christian figured the logic in that and shrugged. "Okay. Is there anywhere I can miraculously shower – a magical plumbing device built into the bough of a tree or something?"

Charlize frowned and shot her father a suspicious glance. His face remained composed, although if someone were to look closely, the twitch of a smile brewed at the corners of his mouth.

"I'm afraid not," he said. "Not until we reach the Anima. From now on we'll be using the rivers or springs we come across. You can use water from your flask if you'd like to brush your teeth."

There was no argument as Christian rummaged through his bag and pulled out a fresh undershirt and jumper. Shamelessly stripping down to his underwear – barely acknowledging Charlize as she fled from the tent – he re-dressed.

It was then Charras allowed his smile.

Outside, distinctly flushed, Charlize sat on a smooth rock near the charred remains of the fire. Her stomach stiff, the relief she originally felt towards Christian's perky attitude had dwindled considerably. She feared his behaviour could be the first stages of something more sinister.

Sighing, she grabbed a stick and began to trace patterns in the ash. It was so difficult to know how to handle an unbecome and somehow teach them the ways of a Mage without doing permanent psychological harm. Harder than that was the fear she felt whenever the darker alternative occupied her thoughts.

Pull yourself together, there is no time for such sentiments, she scolded herself, dropping the stick and crossing her arms.

Deciding a walk would ease her jumbled thoughts, she stood up and stretched out her limbs. However, upon her first step, a sharp pain ripped through her chest and she fell to the floor, gasping for air as ice froze the veins in her heart. Waves of pain pulsated in her torso, and opening her mouth, she tried to cry out, quickly finding her lungs held no air. So, clutching her chest, she kicked out with her feet, dislodging the stones and earth beneath her.

It was enough, her father beside her in seconds.

"Hot or cold?" he asked urgently.

"C... col..." Charlize gasped.

Placing his hand over her chest, Charras summoned his Incendiī and directed its warmth into her heart. She gasped in a breath almost immediately, closing her eyes to take in a few more gulps before wiping away the tears on her cheeks.

"I'm sorry, it caught me off guard," she said, sitting up and leaning into her father's embrace.

He merely nodded as his own panic subsided, replaced by the more common emotion of guilt. Reminding himself that his duty was to protect her duty, he eased her forward so she could support herself and stood up. "You must be more cautious."

Charlize grimaced, knowing she'd been foolish not to expect an attack at any moment. She was usually able to sense them, the constant battle within giving subtle clues as to when an element gained the upper hand.

As she'd grown, her control over the attacks had done so too. The episodes were not overly common, but she'd had them since her Awakening – when her power sparked and she began to learn how to use her abilities. The effects of the four circulating powers in her blood meant that every now and then they collided and fought to gain dominance in her body. Such battles from within resulted in dangerous spasms akin to mini heart attacks, and the only way to counteract them was by conjuring the opposite element to the one that caused the attack – administering a personal form of bypass. It redirected the aggressive blood so it flowed peacefully once more.

Of course, the elements didn't always attack her, and considering there were four circulating, they lived quite happily most of the time. To Charlize, it was nothing more than another burden she had to bear as the Āetis. Although she was the strongest Mage alive, it came at a cost.

She looked up to see Christian standing nearby. He kept his distance, but watched her without diffidence, like it didn't matter that he stared because she wasn't real. It put her on edge, and turning away, she clutched her diamond, drawing on the energy within the stone. As its strength filled her, she recalled the story of when its magical properties were first discovered.

Legend said that Lady Aquāe, the female First of the Aquāe clan, had discovered the unique power and properties of a diamond when she fought a battle caught off guard. Several Ghul and Sirenaris outnumbered her when she fell into a village mining pit upon visiting friends. As she scrambled to find her escape, she grasped a diamond protruding from the rocks. It immediately filled her with strength and she abolished the remaining threats, leaving her victorious. Ever since that day, she wore a diamond circlet upon her head, dedicating her life to studying the properties of the precious stone, continuing even in death.

Charlize tucked her own back against her chest, following her father's lead as he began to pack their belongings, already aware that they were falling behind schedule. Christian had moved to loiter beside the tent, some sort of inner turmoil going on in within him as he ran his fingers through his golden hair, his brows creasing and un-creasing in frustration. Then, a decision reached, he made his way towards her, stopping a few paces from where she stood.

"Are you well enough to walk?" he asked, not making eye contact.

"Yes," Charlize said, clearing her throat.

He smirked, clearly satisfied with the answer, and turned to acknowledge her. "I prefer this you. Much more…" He struggled to find the term. "*Amenable…*"

Charlize was unsure whether she should be offended. Instead, she tried a different tactic. "If you think I'm a dream then surely I could be whatever you wanted?"

"I don't think it works like that."

The silence lingered.

"You're not dreaming Christian."

His face twisted into an arrogant smile, as if he pitied her assumption. "Of course not... That's why you just had what looked like a heart attack, but all you needed to cure you was Charras putting his hands on your chest and mumbling to himself."

The rage bubbled again, but Charlize knew its presence now and kept it at bay. "What could be the possible meaning of what you just saw?"

Shrugging, Christian kicked a stone towards the forest. "I haven't worked out the finer details. But probably because you're infuriating and difficult, so seeing you all fragile reminds me that I put up with you for a reason."

"That is ridiculous Christian, are you saying your dream would show you a scene of me in agony, just to remind you that although you dislike me, you don't dislike me *that* much?"

"No, I'm saying that although we're worlds apart, I still wouldn't want to see you hurt. I obviously need reminding of that considering you annoy me more often than not."

Sighing, Charlize threw her hands in the air and attempted to walk away, but Christian stood to block her path. "Tell me, how do you speak to the forest?"

She blinked. Then, after considering her options, decided it was best to ignore him. "Come on, let's help father, he can't do this all by himself."

Christian looked over at Charras working tirelessly to fold, stack, and press their belongings into piles ready for packing. "Looks under control to me," he said, gesturing with his eyebrows that he still expected an answer.

She huffed. "Why ask me a question you won't believe the answer to?"

"I'm curious."

Eyeing him with doubt, she was about to refuse him again when a soft breeze swept through the campsite.

She took the hint.

"Fine," she said, sitting on a large rock, Christian eagerly joining her. "There are spirits – I can talk to you about this, so I assume you've read the chapter?" Christian nodded. "Well, then you know about the Firsts who sacrificed themselves. The last nine left to create the Haunts in their visions, their children helping to build what we're about to visit. Their spirits have lingered in life ever since, watching the generations come and go, witnessing every pilgrimage. The leaders of each Haunt are descendants of the original leaders, the children of the Firsts."

Christian's eyes glazed as he listened. Although his attentions had not turned, Charlize could see the difference in them. His dark irises, once so full of passion, dimmed to an even milkier shade of brown.

"Aren't spirits that walk the earth bad?" he asked, refocusing Charlize's observations.

"Well, these were the First Mages. They sacrificed themselves to create the pilgrimage. Inferus-Malus has not interfered with their deaths so their spirits remain whole. They wanted to prepare every Mage for the ultimate war and in doing so find a way to end it."

Her explanation clearly enthralled Christian as he shuffled closer, his eyes not once leaving her face. He was sitting ever so close…

Charlize cleared her throat and continued. "However, if they were no longer of this world they couldn't do that. So instead they prepared an Orbis, each putting their separate powers into it, binding their unique, unsoiled power to the earth and Sky. But of course, the opposite elements reacted violently, so they could not reside at any length inside their new home.

Choosing to protect the Haunts and keep watch, they left the raw essence of their magic inside the Orbis, separating themselves from the Sky. It was a huge sacrifice. Yet the Orbis could now act as an interpreter, a way to communicate with the Sky through a simple touch." Charlize stopped to pull her hair behind her ears, unsure if Christian was aware of his close proximity, and she edged back a little. He didn't seem to notice, not once averting his gaze, so she surmised quickly: "As a result, without them we wouldn't have the Orbis, and without the Orbis we couldn't see the future."

Still unaware of the uncomfortable atmosphere, Christian had one more question. "So how do we end it?"

Charras cleared his throat and Charlize felt his warning beat against her chest. Turning away, she looked into the forest. "With many sacrifices," she murmured.

The reaction from Christian was unexpected as he snorted a cruel laugh. "That's too bad then isn't it?!"

Scowling towards his heartlessness, Charlize kept her temper in check, reminding herself that his ignorance was the problem, not his morals.

He held up his hands and smiled. "Come on, you don't seriously expect me to believe all this?"

"I expect little from you," she replied calmly, getting to her feet.

Christian stopped smiling and shrugged his shoulders. He stared after her as she finished helping Charras complete the packing, (he didn't see why he should help in his dream) and watched with amusement as they both attempted to light another fire. It took longer than before, but soon there was progress and he clapped his encouragement.

Charras lowered his brow. "Grab me a pan from your rucksack please Christian."

He obliged, heaving himself from where he sat and ignoring the glare Charlize fixed on him as he sauntered off. He returned with the rustier of the two pans minutes later and bowed low as he passed it to Charras.

"Thank-you," he said, taking it and placing it on the makeshift grill. "This will keep us going until lunch."

Christian looked down at the breakfast of tinned food with a suspected age of over four years. "No eggs?" he said, staring at his meal of corned beef and baked beans with distaste.

He didn't see the twitch of Charras's wrist as he restrained himself from striking him across the head.

It was late morning and the light was bright and welcoming on the border of the forest. Ready to go, leaving only a small imprint of their presence in the campsite, the air was a buzz of electricity. Charlize's excitement radiated outwards, her expectancy causing her to break into a nervous smile. They all stood side by side as they prepared for the moment of crossing.

"Remember, aim for the first tree and push through," Charras advised.

Charlize took a deep breath and stepped towards the first branch beyond the border. A resistance tugged in her stomach as a thousand warnings coursed through her body, urging her to turn back. Her heart responded by beating faster, but she pressed onwards. She could hear her father fighting with Christian, blind fear gripping him as he refused to enter the forest, and she rolled her eyes, reached outwards to grab onto a waiting branch, and pulled. Her head screamed with refusal with each small step, but after one last heave, the resistance faltered and she fell forwards into the Hellebores.

They greeted her instantly, twisting towards her touch and gently curling around her fingers. She pushed herself into a kneeling position and sat among them, fascinated. When she stroked their pale petals with her fingertips, their stamens flicked back and forth as if ticklish.

She would have stayed there all day, but a low growl tearing from her father's lips made her jump, and she turned to see him shove Christian through the boundary, his face one of irritation as his charge refused to fight the enchantment. And yet, the minute they broke through, he calmed, and the atmosphere changed immediately. It was as if the forest suddenly awoke from a slumber, but instead of setting her on edge, Charlize warmed. Although they were no longer protected so far away from the village, the territory signposted as extremely dangerous, it also offered freedom. The constant tug of magic dissipated beyond the boundary, offering light relief – but it came at a cost; for now they walked in the territory of the Minae.

Christian looked around, bemused by the eerily deceiving forest. It promised beauty, but whether it was merely his paranoia, it seemed hidden from him, dulled somehow. Watching the bare branches sway in the breeze, silver frost glistening on the bark, he'd never felt more unsafe. It seemed as if the entire forest caused some sort of enchanted coma, losing one's senses to the surreal scene laid before them.

Charlize seemed to be the most affected, her quiet gasps of adoration heightened within the silence of the trees. She looked almost manic, her eyes shining with intrigue that seemed to reflect off objects that emitted light, even though Christian saw nothing but endless clusters of brown bark.

Charras stood beside his daughter and wrapped a protective arm around her shoulder. "The effects will wear after time," he whispered.

Charlize didn't want them to. She'd never felt more alive than she did in that very moment. Every rock, every whisper of air, every flutter of leaves all seemed in tune to her senses, alighting them with frenzied awe. It promised more beauty than the painted landscapes she'd long admired in the manor. In this world, the intricate brush strokes came to life, surrounding her as if she'd stepped through their frames.

And yet, to Christian, the silence between them was strange and unnerving. He had clearly entered another stage of his dream, although it seemed so tangible that it was hard to maintain his faltering certainty. His companions had taken in every detail of the forest, every tree, bush, plant, and texture. Yet to him it looked like nothing more than a dingy forest… A strange one indeed, but it still had tall trees with green leaves on evergreens and naked branches on deciduous trees. Nothing seemed out of the ordinary.

The sun was breaking through the mess of branches above, casting rays of sunlight on the brown earth – plain brown earth with nothing of notable difference – and he followed his companions blindly, hoping whatever they waited for shortly appeared.

After walking for several hours, he soon realised that no threat or danger was imminent, and in fact, the silence was an appreciation of what was around them… oddly. This settled him only slightly, attempting to work out the factors that made a forest so interesting. Charlize had seen plenty of forests before; he'd been there for most of those experiences. The family camping trips his parents forced him to endure generally included the killjoys Charras and Charlize.

"How long before we rest?" he asked, his voice louder than he intended.

Zoning back to reality, Charras ushered Christian forwards. "We'll rest tonight," he replied, picking up the pace.

Christian accepted this inevitability, although the pack on his back seemed to get heavier as the prospect dawned on him. It wouldn't be so bad – he didn't mind walking, but it was difficult to maintain a sense of calm when Charlize mumbled to herself every few minutes, an action which naturally put him on edge. More and more, his previous assumption that he followed two deranged individuals into a world of their own seemed less unlikely…

The forest soon grew dark as they strode ever forwards, keeping their pace to a brisk walk. Charlize disappeared into her own quiet ramblings, maintaining a respectable distance from Christian as she spoke with the spirits of the Anima. Intriguing her with their interest in who she was, she answered their questions about her life, passing their tests of knowledge and laughing at the subtle humour they seemed to possess. Yet all the time they stayed hidden from her, merely nothing more than excited whispers. At times, she was sure she could pin point where the voices came from, but with her father walking so fast, following the Trail of Hellebores, most of her concentration focused on making sure she didn't trip over. The forest was dense and the roots of trees and brushwood threatened her safety constantly. So much so, it was with relief she found herself stepping into an open clearing. The trees were sparse but stood close enough to provide adequate cover.

Happy to stretch his neck, Christian looked up and breathed in the fresh air, mildly charmed by the bright half moon and mass of brilliant stars. A presence of someone joined him and he turned to watch Charlize stare up at the Sky too, broken, even for a short while, from her deep reverie.

It was Christian who lost interest first, walking away from his childhood companion and her newfound obsession. He felt as if the tables had turned, his dream friends becoming what they saw him as. But there was nothing to be alarmed of; for now it was a waiting game. Nothing could hurt him in his dreams, and he'd soon wake up from the nightmare he found himself trapped in.

Making his way towards Charras setting up the tent, he joined in the assembly, glad to help and share in the familiar monotony. The chore of idly constructing their sleeping quarters meant he could pass the time with his dream friends without actually talking to them. He was completely oblivious to the frown Charras wore every time they made eye contact. In fact, he was oblivious to most things. He'd even started to forget what his parents looked like.

20

Encountered

The days that followed seemed tireless and long. Christian wasn't sure how deep the forest reached, but the further they delved, the more he wondered if it actually ended. His dream had become nothing more than an endless succession of trees and strange pallid flowers, broken only by the lightly falling snow. Every night the tent nestled on a blanket of white, and every night a layer of powdery flakes camouflaged it.

He didn't mind; he enjoyed the pleasant crunching of footsteps, providing sound on an otherwise mute hike. It also cooled the closeness of air beneath the treetops, for the forest had become increasingly crowded, resulting in darker days and slower progression. Random spots of luminescent bark and some remaining leaves seemed the only source of light in parts, and it confused him greatly – especially how Charras and Charlize appeared consistently awed by them.

When he grew bored enough to ask, they told him a story.

In another legend (there seemed to be several), the First Glacies and the First Fulgor placed lightning inside domes of ice, giving them as a gift to the forest. It represented the peace between clans, thus avoiding undue animosity erupting between the two opposites. The forest used the gift to light the path to the Anima Haunt, maintaining that only the Evalesco, the ones with power, could look upon the dewdrops. So delighted with the gesture, the forest also allowed the Haunt to be built within its heart, providing sustenance for the strongest and most reliable trees.

A nice story, although probably more impressive when read at bedtime, Christian gathered that their destination was a gigantic tree house – something generally unassuming in a forest, which was why he reckoned his dream wouldn't fail to surprise him, and he absently wondered if he would meet any Ewokees. Upon sharing his sentiments, and further explaining what Ewokees were (a popular cartoon of hairy, humanoid creatures that lived nomadically among trees), Charlize choked on her tongue before scolding his ignorance. In light of this, he decided it was best not to voice his thoughts anymore.

It was becoming a game of sorts, Charras listening to Christian and Charlize relaying constant insults, and him trying different tactics to ease the tension, their bickering tiresome and petty. Any fears he had towards their potential growing affections was something he worried much less about now. They seemed unable to converse for more than a few minutes before one of them huffed: usually Charlize.

They currently discussed the merits of the prefects at the Marsh School, a conversation marred by the fact Christian wasn't chosen and remained bitter about it. Their voices became a drone of dissent that wound through the trees, absorbed by the Hellebores and acknowledged only by the worms and beetles nestled beneath the earth. Charras was sure that if they had hands to cover their ears, they would certainly have done so. And he felt marginally jealous upon thinking how the soil must muffle the conflict, sparing them the brunt of the arduous noise.

"Well I'm not so sure Helenea would have made the ideal choice, considering her interests lay in vanity and not productivity."

"We weren't interested in her productivity Charlize... She had other assets far more appealing."

Charras sidestepped a log, his foot falling into a muddy puddle that squelched beneath his boot.

"What assets were they Christian? Her unwavering ability to flick her hair and blink until she got her way?"

The puddles had grown in size, their prevalence increasing, and the Hellebores seemed to thin as they followed their trail. Charras felt uneasy, but knew they were getting close to the Anima and didn't want to stop when no Minae seemed obvious. There were still enough of the flowers to denote that merely Achak or Akuji had disturbed them recently, which meant if they did encounter the lesser Minae, their numbers shouldn't be too hard to eradicate. And besides, the closer they got to the Haunt, the more there would be anyway. It would do no good to be overly cautious when only a day and a half stood between them.

"...you do sound jealous! I'm merely pointing out a fact."

"Why on earth would I be jealous of a girl with no intellectual skill and quite frankly, weak morals?! It makes absolutely no sense Christian, listen to yourself."

"I wish I had a tape recorder so you could hear yourself *and how obviously jealous you are..."*

There was a snap underfoot and Charras looked down to see what he'd trodden on. Lifting his leg, he saw several large bone fragments. They poked out from the boggy mire just a fraction, the one he trod on looking big enough to be a femur.

"I won't engage in much more of this ridiculous talk, you are utterly impossible to reason with."

"Just because you're not hearing what you want doesn't mean I'm impossible."

"I could say the same for you!"

The forest fell silent and Charras pressed down on the bones beneath him until the mud reabsorbed them.

"See? You can't take criticism, you always turn it around."

A short sucking sound made audible by the silence found its way to Charras, who knew it was Charlize holding her tongue, and he compelled his face into a picture of calm before turning to his charges.

"If you two are quite done, we need to pick up the pace a little."

"I am more than done father, I've had enough."

"Me too," said Christian.

It was only then Charlize noticed the mist surrounding them, the forest floor grey as the Christmas roses wilted. She found herself absently walking to her father's side and watching as he carefully lifted his foot. He took a few steps and his footfalls revealed flashes of white, the ivory of dirtied bones protruding from the mud – mud that hadn't formed part of the frosted forest before that moment. She immediately realised what they'd stumbled upon.

Giving her father a subtle nod, she turned to Christian. "I've always wanted to ask you about Geraldine Tilderberry," she said, striding away from the grave and forcing a smirk into the corners of her mouth. "I hear she and you were quite the item."

Christian raised his eyebrows. "Since when did you listen to gossip?"

"I couldn't help but hear that rumour. Didn't she write a note and put it in your desk? Something along the lines of how much she admired you?"

He shrugged and walked towards where Charlize waited, her feet amongst half formed Hellebores, their state conflicted. "She was a nice girl, but I'll tell you what I told everyone else: it's none of your business."

Crossing her arms, Charlize flicked her hair back and began to pace backwards, leading Christian to follow subconsciously and put distance between him and the bones her father was stamping down. "Aha! So it was true?!"

"I honestly don't understand your interest. You have never ever asked me anything about anyone we went to school with before."

"I'm curious, that's all. I mean, you never had any problems parading your conquests around like trophies on a shelf. But Geraldine was always someone you never talked about."

Christian mimicked Charlize's crossed arms. "That's because she was different. It wasn't like that. She was troubled."

His face seemed unsure of what expression to take, his eyes drifting into the forest and then back to Charlize's face. It was only when Charras's heavy bulk stood to block his view, he decided on a nonchalant shrug and a set jaw.

"Well, I didn't know her that well. Shall we keep going?" Charlize said, whipping around to lead them confidently from the bog.

More than a little confused, Christian looked to Charras who gestured for him to go first. He nodded his acquiescence and hurried to keep up with his – now more than ever – obvious dream friend.

"It was a nest."

They sat in a small clearing that, upon their arrival, had a fire stacked and waiting, which apparently meant they were within a day of the Anima. The flames burned brightly, the heat a welcome solace in the deepening snow. It was so deep in parts that sometimes the Hellebores were barely visible, and they had to stop and clear away the flakes to find them and make sure they remained on the right path.

"My worry is that it was relatively fresh," Charras replied, his face sombre. "A party before us didn't make it."

A shiver brushed Charlize's spine. She looked to the tent where Christian slept soundly and thought how close he'd come to seeing the remains of a Ghul's catch. It was almost lucky that his oblivion was so prominent, his eyes appearing blind as the milky texture covered his entire cornea and most of his pupil. It didn't seem to hinder his vision, although those who saw him would assume otherwise. And she could only conclude that what he stared at wasn't actually there.

The spirits of the Anima sympathised with how she felt, although they could offer no cure. Therefore, it seemed she was doomed to watch her friend slip deeper and deeper into his own world, until he walked in a place of nothing but his own imaginings.

Sparks crackled greedily from the fire as they licked the pans and warmed the food Charras cooked. He'd managed to find a few tins of soup in his rucksack, and after remembering Charlize's own supplies, pulled out a large malt loaf and their pudding of tinned pineapples.

Once ready, he served it all up on the red plastic plates and instantly satisfied their growling stomachs.

"I think it's best we let him sleep. We can always make sure he eats more tomorrow," said Charras, when the odour of tomato and basil did nothing to rouse Christian from his slumber.

Charlize nodded and volunteered to wash-up, happy to disappear into the forest for a while as nature called to her.

Returning later than expected, she softly laughed towards her father's constant sentry duty. "I couldn't wait any longer; I had to at least wash myself," she explained, guilty as she noticed how exhausted he looked.

He wasn't angry; he'd known her decision when she snuck a bar of soap and some shampoo from her toiletry bag before dinner. Her change of clothes also offered a subtle clue. "There is no harm done, I only fear our proximity…" He rest his arms on his knees. "I don't know what would happen if Christian saw –"

"I know," said Charlize. "We should aim to get there before nightfall tomorrow; the sooner the better."

Charras's face darkened. "I'm hoping Armmos will have an insight into these things. I've never before known the risks to be this great, he's on the verge of slipping away completely."

"The Anima are neutral. Surely they will help us…" The doubt in her voice was evident.

Dropping his head, Charras nodded slowly. Unsure what help there could be, he could only hope that Christian's unique situation gained him sympathy. No one had ever taken a pilgrimage unbecome, let alone attempted to make the transition from a dormant Mage to an active one at the age of eighteen. If it were not for his protection while he travelled with Charlize, her exemption from the laws of Mages providing him safety, his fate would be one of exile or death.

Christian awoke at an unknown hour and couldn't get back to sleep. He tossed and turned in his sleeping bag, trying and failing to get comfortable before he gave up and turned on his side. Charras's shoulder squashed against his nose and his repugnant body odour soon became too much to endure. So, sitting up in the cramped space, suddenly aware of his own personal hygiene, he decided that he would wash the minute the sun came up. He just hoped that wouldn't be too long.

The moon currently bathed the tent in a faint light, and he caught Charlize's silhouette in the far corner, her soft breathing just audible above the muffled snores of Charras. It was only when she slept her features softened, making her appear the age she really was, an innocence present that rarely materialised when she was awake.

He stared at her for a while, soon realising that any notion of sleep was futile, a strange feeling unsettling him that quickly turned to claustrophobia. Needing to breathe in fresh air, he quietly heaved himself from his sleeping bag and gently unzipped the tent. Charlize murmured something and he froze, a heartbeat lapsing before he realised she was dreaming, and then he disappeared through the coarse material and into the cold night.

He inhaled deeply, feeling more awake than he had in weeks. Wrapping his arms across his chest, he stood oblivious to how exposed and vulnerable he was. The virgin snow beneath his feet swirled gently as soft sensations whipped around him, teasing his ankles, and suddenly calm, he became aware of air pushing lightly on his legs, guiding him as he moved happily with it, an urge to crawl back into his sleeping bag invading him.

A noise snapped behind him and he turned slightly to see where it came from. As he did, logic assured him that it was nothing but an animal and he shortly forgot his grievance. He remembered his safe bed awaiting him and knew to return to it. But then another thought broke through, bursting in his mind like a warning sign:

No animals lived in the wood, at least not on the path they'd taken. The last four days had been devoid of life but for the three of them.

Christian sat back and jumped up, every sense on alert, angry that his thoughts hadn't been his own – the only claim he had in his bizarre dream. The fire still burned, not quite raging, but high enough to give sufficient heat. It melted the snow that lay around it, but didn't affect the rest of the heavily quilted clearing.

He wondered if it ever burnt out, knowing no one had touched it since their arrival, and curious, he took a few tentative steps towards it and peered into the darkness.

The area was clear, dreary almost; save for one tree that grabbed his attention – a single speck of light wedged between its trunk and one of its branches. He remembered the story of the dewdrops and gingerly walked towards it, reaching out and hovering his hand over the strange droplet for a few seconds, unsure if it would cause harm. Then, swallowing, he grabbed it from its home and tensed, happy to note that it merely caused a light tingling sensation. It was about the size of the ball of his thumb, cold to the touch, and with a strange yellow haze that emanated from it.

"Enchanting aren't they?" said a sweet voice, piercing the night.

Christian's heart jumped into his throat. With deliberate effort he tore his gaze away from his discovery and stared out across the campsite.

There was nothing there, everything as eerily still as it had been before. He took a breath and turned to replace the dewdrop, gasping in fright as a huge force lifted him off his feet and launched him through the air. He landed heavily beside the fire, the wind knocked out of him, and he gasped for breath, wheezing as his lungs impulsively tried to fill with air. They managed to draw enough for him to stagger to his feet and look to identify his attacker.

A beautiful woman stood before him. Long blonde hair wrapped around her smooth silky skin, highlighting her naked form, and her glassy eyes peered through thick lashes seductively, incredibly blue – clear even from the distance between them.

Christian took a sharp intake of breath and stood stunned, her radiant beauty one of perfection. He felt a familiar stirring within him as he stared shamelessly, mesmerised by her prowess.

Clearly delighted by his reaction, she sauntered towards him, smooth muscles flexing in her thighs as she came to a standstill inches away. There, she forced him to his knees and bent down to face her victim.

"Curiosity killed the cat," she laughed prettily, tilting his chin upwards with a sharp fingernail – too sharp. It scratched at his neck and drew blood.

Christian flinched and cupped the wound. Looking down at himself, unsure why his other arm still beckoned for the woman to come closer, he forced it back, bewildered by the strange turn of events.

Nothing made any sense, his dream of before turning into something far more sinister. He pressed down on his cut as it began to ache, then inspected the blood in his palm – blood he shouldn't bleed in a dream; pain he shouldn't feel; the sensation of burning as his neck bubbled; a searing fire his cool hand couldn't reduce…

A slight shift in the air brought his attention to an object lying in front of him. It was buried beneath a layer of soot, and picking it up, he turned the item over in his hand, revealing the unharmed dewdrop. He brought it close to his face, glad of its survival, and studied the complexity. A small lightning bolt darted within an ice capsule, producing the faint glow that illuminated his skin in daisy yellow.

You're real he thought, instinctively knowing that the dewdrop needed returning.

"Handsome young man," the woman complimented.

Surprised that he'd forgotten her presence, Christian turned his attentions back to his mystery assailant. But as he looked upon the previously glorious form, he stifled his shock and clambered backwards, pushing her icy hand from his face in an attempt to escape her.

She was hideous. Deep welts lacerated her entire body, her skin sallow and decrepit, no longer fitting her bones. He wanted to look away, but he couldn't take his eyes off her as he moved to put the fire between them. She smiled hollowly at him, the heat distorting her features – blurred and unnatural. She seemed in no hurry to reach him, but he stood ready, the tent not far from where he held himself poised.

His eyes shifted to where Charlize and Charras slept, and then back to the deformity opposite him. Her eyes also shifted, but quickly, too quickly to be human as she figured what he planned. She let out a shriek that sent his spine into spasm, and he lumbered towards the tent, his heart drumming in his throat as he yelled nonsensical words and covered his ears against the vocal onslaught.

He wasn't fast enough, only acknowledging this fact when he found himself airborne again. This time he landed with a definite *crack* as his shoulder slid out of joint.

Writhing in the snow, disorientated and in agony, he tried to crawl away, his right arm hanging limp and useless as he dragged himself towards the trees surrounding him, their luminosity suddenly brighter than he'd ever noticed before.

The Sirenari let out another shriek and closed the distance between them with impossible speed. Christian kicked out with his feet, connecting a blow with her knee and jarring the bone so it protruded the wrong way, an action she corrected by simply bending her leg until the joint forced it to snap back into place.

Christian held his rising bile at bay as he scrambled towards the fire to kick hot ash towards the relentless Minae. He managed to singe her skin, but barely slowed her as she continued to give chase. Nothing seemed to tire her, no matter how many pirouettes, exaggerated strides, jumps or rolls she performed. It was a game to her. She would continue until he gave up, exhausted.

And that was exactly what happened. The pain in his shoulder soon unbearable, Christian fell to his knees. He angrily wondered why Charlize and Charras hadn't woken to help him, and then he realised that he could still be asleep.

It was his last hope as he tightly shut his eyes, hoping his nightmare would soon be over; he would finally wake up, shaken but alive.

As if the Sirenari could hear his thoughts, she let out a laugh, although this time it wasn't the soft voice of before, it was deep, the bass note reverberating off the trees as if it came from another being entirely.

The horror had no time to register before the demon switched to a scream, the high pitch ringing shrilly in his ears. This time it didn't stop, and as Christian covered one ear with his mobile hand, he let the rising nausea wash over him until there was nothing but darkness.

Screeching rattled in her head as Charlize awoke from what she assumed was a nightmare. Groggily searching the tent, she rubbed her eyes, unsure why the commotion hadn't stopped. Startled to see her father also sitting up, she was even more startled to see two others had joined them.

Doubtful she was dreaming anymore, Charlize stared at the figure perched neatly on the end of her sleeping bag, head bowed. The Lady of the Anima was a grand looking spirit. Sat with her knees tucked beneath her, she wore the green of her clan; vines wrapped delicately around her body, hiding her modesty beneath a dress made from silver birch and field maple leaves. They matched only two of the species Charlize had encountered while walking through the forest.

Turning to her father, she saw that he appeared deep in thought, the Lord of the Anima sitting calmly beside him, his regal appearance donning a crown of oak leaves. The spirits of the forest had come to them, their expressions grim, sorrow written in their bright emerald eyes. She couldn't find words to describe their beauty, their pale and milky skin radiant even in the dim moonlight of the tent.

"Your friend needs you," Lady Anima warned. "He is ready to be rescued now."

Her voice was like a breeze on a hot day, airy and light, a refreshing whisper. Charlize could have listened to her all night if it were not for the warning in her words. "Ready to be rescued?" she murmured.

The fact Christian was absent suddenly occurred to her. Breaking from her reverie, concern replacing all other senses, she looked to her father for action. He remained sitting upright, although she soon realised he was still asleep – some sort of trance keeping him unconscious.

Ignoring him, she threw herself from the tent.

Her eyes didn't need to adjust to the bright fire as she stood from the earth and scanned the campsite. Beyond the flames, she spotted Christian lying face down, motionless in the dirtied snow.

The lone Sirenari circled him predatorily. Having stunned him with her scream, she would then feed on his life force, preferring the blood to remain warm. The Sirenaris were vampires of the Minae world, the blood of their victims providing sustenance and strength. Inferus-Malus claimed the remaining spirit if a Mage could not reach it in time.

Busy celebrating her catch, the creature danced in her sadistic form, unaware her victim travelled with two other Mages. She must have been certain to leave her pack, promising to return to them with dinner.

The thought gave Charlize hope. If the Sirenari's pack were near, then she wouldn't have delivered the final strike. Instead, she would preserve the blood for as long as she could to keep it fresh and warm. They must have picked up the scent of what they thought was a troupe of Ungifted, Christian's unbecome scent distinctive due to the light and purity in his blood. They wouldn't have risked coming alone if they knew fully fledged Mages accompanied him, and as only one Sirenari had followed, the pack must be starving and desperate.

Good, thought Charlize, *you're weak.*

Taking a breath, she edged towards the Minae, never once taking her eyes off her target. She knew she had one chance to save Christian. Sirenaris could move quickly, and if she missed and the demon fled with her prey, she wouldn't get another chance.

Slowly and deliberately, she took another step closer, her heart thumping against her ribs, every sense on alert as she prepared for the moment of attack. The flames distorted her view, and using their camouflage, she spread her fingers and released her breath slowly.

A cool wind blew through the clearing, the fire flickering against the breeze, but it was enough. Crouched low, the Sirenari flicked her head upwards and sniffed the air.

Charlize's fingers twitched and the demon turned. She hissed through her teeth and scuttled over to Christian, preparing her flight away, and Charlize didn't waste any time raising her hands and screaming the words of power: *"Dicio Āetis, Deresco, durescere, durui!"*

As the words flew from her mouth, a silver line of light escaped through her outstretched fingers and into the stomach of the demon, sending her careering into the forest. Charlize didn't wait to see where she landed, already running the short distance to Christian and wrenching him onto his back. His eyes closed and body still, she frantically checked his vital signs, relief washing through her as the familiar drumming of a pulse greeted her fingers.

"Christian?" she said, shaking him slightly.

He didn't respond. But just as she was going to try again, the hairs on the back of her neck stood on end. She snapped her head up as the recovered Sirenari charged from the undergrowth, and Charlize stood, stepping astride Christian with her palms held ready.

Half of the Minae's stomach was missing, enabling Charlize to see through it and into the woodland behind. She felt oddly satisfied, knowing the damage would take weeks to regenerate. The Sirenari on the other hand was angry and snarling, and she closed the gap between them in seconds, leaving Charlize little chance to defend herself as icy claws dug into her shoulder, tearing the flesh. Another attack caught in her hair as she dodged the talons, but she climbed to her feet in seconds and resumed her defensive stance.

At an impasse, the Sirenari began to pace a semi-circle, weighing up her assailant. She would know the Mage she fought now, her blood revealing her status, but what worried Charlize was how the revelation hadn't perturbed her – she wanted her prize and was prepared to combat anyone who tried to stop her getting it.

Within a heartbeat, the Sirenari rushed towards her and Charlize stooped, missed the sharp claws by inches, her footsteps faltering, and then immediately staggered up to protect Christian again. She turned in time to see the demon crouch in the snow and kick it up in preparation of another charge – unaware of the large figure standing behind her. Her serrated jaws opened to emit another screech and Charlize covered her ears, although still managed to smile at her father through the demon's stomach.

A growing bolide formed between Charras's palms before his deep voice boomed through the clearing: *"Dicio, Incendiī-Anima, Deflagro."*

The word of command incinerated the remainder of the Minae in an impressive flash of heat, the fire enveloping the mock body until it became nothing more than a pile of ash. It was loud, which made Charlize glad she covered her ears, but the pang of death dissipated as the Sirenari's spirit disbanded and the strain lifted.

A hand grasping her face made her jump and she almost broke the wrist attached to it, until she realised it was Christian's. Surprised that she was currently arched over him, her nightclothes hanging dirtied and torn, her shoulder a bloodied mess, she looked into his eyes, glad that a deep recognition stared back. It was as if he was seeing her for the first time, his irises and pupils almost black again, the milky appearance gone without a trace.

Charlize breathed a sigh of relief and slumped to the floor crossed-legged. He'd finally accepted the truth.

"Everything is so beautiful," Christian croaked, attempting to lift his head. "I feel like I've just woken up." There was a pain in his body he couldn't describe. "Everything seems real Charlize; tell me I'm not dreaming anymore."

"You're not dreaming, I promise," she said.

The days of before seemed a blurry memory, and as Christian looked around the forest, he did so with fresh eyes. There were millions of dewdrops scattered among the trees, varying in size and brilliance. The majority were gold and yellow, although some were blue and purple, and their ethereal beauty set the forest alive with magical luminance.

He tried to sit up, but his shoulder and head throbbed so much he merely groaned and fell onto Charlize's lap. She immediately fussed, checking him over and pressing her hands on each of his limbs, asking him where it hurt. Within seconds she'd established that his shoulder was dislocated, and with a quick jerk and a scorching pain that ripped through his arm, she set it back into place.

The ache subsided swiftly and Christian finally managed to sit upright. His head remained fragile, but he was aware of Charlize staring at him and tried to maintain his balance, resisting the desire to lie down again. However, leaning forward caused his head to swirl and he swayed towards her steadying arms anyway.

Pull it together; she thinks you're an invalid he told himself, wishing the trees would stop dancing behind her.

Thoughtful as she watched him, Charlize grinned, rediscovering something she'd long forgotten. "Your skin sort of glows in the dark," she said, reaching out to touch it.

Although his face was familiar, she had never really looked at it before, their eye contact limited. She traced his lips, soft and pink, the bottom slightly larger than the top, then followed the curve of his oval face, which squared off into a defined jaw. Stubble clung in random patches along his cheeks and chin, and his pale skin tone seemed emphasised against the snow, prominent due to his lack of sleep and food.

He screwed up his nose as she ran her finger across its gentle bridge, and she pulled her hand away an inch before returning her gaze to his eyes. They were large, framed by long lashes as dark as his irises, and his golden hair had grown, waving only slightly as it hung around his ears.

"Erm, Charlize," he said, when it seemed unlikely her probing would end.

A memory flashed of when they were children, back in the manor on her tenth birthday. She had studied him the same way, with fascination and uncomfortable scrutiny... Christian reached up and gently took her finger away from his eyebrow, wondering why she seemed constantly fascinated by other human beings.

His touch seemed to break the trance and Charlize dropped her hand, looking away in embarrassment.

"I'm so sorry." She blushed, propped herself on her heels, and wrapped her arms around her legs. "I keep forgetting to ask."

Christian shook his head, attempting to reassure her, but stopped as a clear whistle rang through the air, almost otherworldly in serenity. Both turning their attentions to Charras, they watched as his whistle ended the Mittere.

Seconds later, a ball of flame holding the spirit captive rose from the ashes of the Sirenari. It twisted and turned as it darted upwards, disappearing into the night to meet whatever fate lay before it.

21

Purpose

Mittere: A Mages Purpose

The Mittere is a ritual each Mage must perform upon the destruction of Minae. The ritual allows the malevolent energy to join its benevolent counterpart. None know the fate of the spirit thereof, but it is widely considered that upon reconciliation, the 'whole' spirit can pass into a true death, without further interference from Inferus-Malus.

Many believe Inferus-Malus can only take hold of the darkness; that the light within a spirit is beyond his reach. A recent theory, cited by 'Sir Matthew Winslow the third, of Norfolk', proposed that the level of darkness within a spirit determined the Minae it became once earth bound. He went so far as to quote:

'The greater the evil, the higher their status on earth. Let us consider the Sirenaris, female spirits that hunt in packs of three, or a Ghul, male spirits known for their might and bulk. They are the highest forms, the most human. With that in mind, it would not be a gross misjudgement to assume that they had dark spirits in life, equal to that in death.' Ref: 1298, paragraph 20. 'Guide to defeating the Dead.'

Widely accepted amongst most scholars and preachers, the origins of each Minae cause little debate. The only contested theory lies with Wraithart's, their very nature a source of constant dispute. Although the animal spirits are not useful to Inferus-Malus, they are an unfortunate by-product of his prison, unable to enter the Sky into death. Therefore, they wander the earth freely, some malevolent, others benevolent, but all capable of walking through the material world.

When a person or Minae dies, they leave behind an energy that only a Mage can see. The matter is relative to the power they held when alive, and it is what the Mages send into the Sky. No Mage knows where the spirits wait, although most believe they linger between the planes of this world – the æther – between the spirit world and the veil into death. It is here Inferus-Malus resides, prohibiting the spirits their final passing, tearing them from their humanity to know of nothing but anger and hate.

A Mage's Mittere grants that spirit a true and fair death, and beyond the veil, Inferus-Malus holds no power. This is the reason the balance has shifted. The dead should not defy death. It is against the natural order of life and outside the limits of this earth. We must fight, for we must return things to how they should be.

Christian placed his book in his rucksack, calming his breathing as he did so. The night of before seemed a distant memory, faded against the realisation his nightmare was real. There was no way he'd wake up to find himself soaked through and stuck to the bed, fear clutching at his heart as he jolted from a night terror. He'd give anything for that to be the case, but he knew, somewhere, deep down, that the path he walked was right.

Looking upon everything with newfound clarity, the world became a beautiful backdrop to his bleak mood. It wasn't hard to understand why he'd fallen so easily into denial. Even the trees looked surreal, like elegant ballerinas decorated with drops of light as they watched from above.

He couldn't remember the days of before, the memories fading further by the second. The only recollection he still nurtured was the moment he placed his hand on his book. It was the only decision he'd made that seemed to hold meaning.

Charlize's gaze halted his contemplation. He gave her a lop-sided smile, picked up his book again and held it above his head. "I've just finished. Good to know our purpose."

Although she returned his smile before continuing to pack, she didn't look overly convinced. He sighed. She always seemed concerned; worried he'd suddenly fall off the edge again. It made him anxious, as if every one of his actions deserved scrutiny.

Further still, amidst all of their polite exchanges, a darker fact remained: His mother and father were missing, their attack the reason he'd ended up learning about his heritage. Although he daren't ask for confirmation, he knew, without a question of doubt, his parents were alive.

It seemed a long time since he last considered their whereabouts and the thought brought an abundance of guilt. He was following his mother's wishes and joining Charras, yet there was so much to learn he felt it would overcome him – it almost had.

Glancing back towards Charlize, Christian grimaced as Charras currently busied himself by tying a fresh bandage across her shoulder. It had looked messy the night before, the bleeding only stopping once the deep cuts had been cauterised. She had been brave, not once crying out, although the pain must have been incredible.

What surprised him the most were his thoughts towards the crazed blood-sucking monster, or Sirenari as he now knew it to be. On the one hand, he hated it for the hurt it caused, while on the other, he was grateful for the part it played in 'waking' him. He only wished there were better ways to suffer an introduction…

Charlize watched Christian's expression, wary he'd lose his grip again. His eyes remained dark, much to her relief, but he seemed unsure of himself, guarded. They were due to arrive at the Anima Haunt later that day, their first stop on her pilgrimage, and she hoped the sight of the village wouldn't cause him to relapse. She needed him to appear healthy, even to those who would know him as unbecome. His presence would not be a welcome one, but she hoped that the compassionate nature of the Anima would hear his story and understand that, although he remained dormant, he was learning, and his unfortunate circumstances were not of his own choosing.

Zipping up her rucksack, she placed it over her left shoulder. After her attack, her father had been more receptive to the idea of lightening it, and it now sat happily on a larger vacuum of air, causing no extra strain to her already tender muscles.

She looked to her father sat talking to Christian and decided to take the opportunity to gather her thoughts. "I'll be back shortly," she said, walking into the cluster of trees to her left.

Her father looked up but didn't try to stop her, much to her relief. He'd become almost unbearably protective since their encounter and she needed him to relax before their arrival in the Anima.

The forest was cool, the snow thickening the further away from the fire she strode. Rubbing her arms, Charlize leaned against one of the ash boughs to catch her breath. Privacy seemed a luxury she couldn't possess, and as she sat amongst the Hellebores, their stems twisting to greet her, she closed her eyes.

When she opened them, the Spirits stood before her.

Stood weightlessly atop the snow, their majesty even grander than the night before, their presence caused the Christmas flowers to sway, the petals all pointing towards them, even the ones near Charlize. Although briefly lost for words, she soon felt anger swell within her stomach.

"Do not be angry Āetis."

She said nothing, accustomed to the Spirits knowing her mood. Instead, she watched as Lady Anima drifted closer, her arms open and elegant as her dress of leaves billowed behind her. The vines wrapped around her slender body matched her emerald eyes – the same sad stare imprinted in them, as if they had been that way for many years.

She stopped so the distance between them was close enough to touch, then delicately twisted her head to look behind her, meeting the poised expression of her husband. Lord Anima bent his head in response, an unspoken agreement passing between them, and she turned back to Charlize.

"You are angry that we did not wake your father as soon as we woke you." It wasn't a question. She raised her hands inches from Charlize's face and tilted her head. "One day, you must learn to lead without his guidance."

Diluted by the airy resonance of her voice, the truth in her words failed
to produce the desired effect. Instead, Charlize angered further. "Your
interference could have cost lives, Christian's life for that matter."

With deliberate effort, Lady Anima lowered her hands. "I assure you
Āetis, it was not our intention to cause harm. We attempted to coax him
back to his bed." She furrowed her silky brow and her blonde hair
tumbled over her face. "He was not receptive."

Charlize noted that both of the Spirits seemed agitated by that fact, but
she ignored it as a breath of air confirmed Lord Anima's decision to join
his wife. He placed a hand across her shoulders and cast his gaze towards
Charlize. "We shall no longer test you."

Unlike the voice of his wife, Lord Anima's was rich, earthy, and deep,
as if the very ground would answer to his call if he asked.

Charlize nodded. "It is not the harm you caused me that causes my
anger; it is the harm you caused my father. His guard has strengthened
even further after last night."

"We needed to know," Lady Anima whispered. "Please forgive us
Āetis."

Before Charlize could react, a cold sensation ran through her temples,
as if a winter's kiss penetrated her skull. Sinking to the floor, she held her
hands over her face as visions swirled in her mind. They came so fast she
could barely register them before they passed. Nausea stirred, threatening
to consume her, but just as she thought it would, the images slowed,
permitting her to draw shapes and textures from the blurs.

Hundreds, no, thousands of trees raced past, some that grew and
flourished, other's that wilted and died. Constantly, the seasons changed,
from the buds of spring, to the bloom of summer, to the vibrant reds of
autumn, and then back to the naked winter. She saw Mages of different
eras flashing past, full of jubilant smiles and hearty laughter. The forest
grew before her as the Haunt expanded, and a constant stream of new
Mages walked in and out of the imagery. Previous Āetis', the same faces

she recognised from books, glared out at her, their appearance strong and resolved. They wore the same expression she saw whenever she looked in the mirror: determination; fearlessness – forever hiding any sign of weakness. Charlize wanted to speak with them, but as she reached out, they melted into the endless stream of memories – and they were memories, she was sure.

Soon the images changed, the years drawing out endlessly. The Mages grew darker, the laughter and smiles lessening, and the Minae rose in numbers, devastating the lands outside the boundaries. She saw the destruction they caused, the pain they inflicted, and the number of people who fell beneath their onslaught. Yet still there remained light, the fascination the dewdrops held shining upon the faces of those who came and went, working towards an end that seemed everlasting.

Eventually, the scenes faded until Charlize saw nothing but the back of her eyelids. Groggy, she took her hands away from her face and opened her eyes. The world still spun, so she steadied herself against the trunk of the tree behind her and gave herself a moment.

When she peered back up, her view remained fixed. Grateful, she looked around in an attempt to see where the Spirit's had gone.

They stood at a respectable distance, their concerned faces focused on her attempts to stand. And not wanting to seem weak, she balanced away from the hidden tree roots, dug her feet in the snow, and then brushed herself down, mildly peeved that her trousers were damp. Then, folding her arms across her chest, she sighed.

"I understand. You didn't need to show me."

"We have been waiting so long," Lady Anima expressed. "We need to know it is you."

In no mood for riddles, Charlize found her footing and walked towards the Spirits. "What am I supposed to be? I am already the Āetis."

With a fleeting look at her husband, Lady Anima flicked her wrist. Beneath her spectral feet, one of the Hellebores stretched upwards, its stem breaking as it snapped from the earth. She guided it towards

Charlize's hand, smiling as her gift was accepted. "Strong enough," she replied.

Charlize looked down at the flower, surprised that it still twisted towards her. "For what?" she asked.

There was nothing but silence in answer, and when she raised her head, the forest was empty.

Stepping back into the campsite, Charlize tucked the flower into her trouser pocket. Protected by an enchantment, the like she had never witnessed, the delicate Christmas rose was no longer frail. Instead, it had taken on an elastic quality, allowing it to bend into the fold of her pocket.

Charras rushed to meet her and quickly patted her down. "What happened?"

She held out her arms and allowed him to fuss. When he was satisfied she'd endured no harm, he stood aside, although continued to eye her suspiciously. Meeting his stare, Charlize knew he wouldn't rest until he had some sort of explanation.

She touched her temple and shivered as the decades she'd witnessed came flooding back. It was a lonely fate for the Spirits, roaming the earth until the end, helplessly watching all those years of devastation. Yet the moments Lady Anima revealed were private, wordless, raw… She wasn't sure how to explain what she'd seen anyway.

So, looking into her father's expectant eyes, weighing up how much she should divulge, she composed her face into a smile. "The Spirits apologise for their interference. It won't happen again."

Charras raised his eyebrows. He knew there was more his daughter wasn't telling him. "Did they give an explanation as to why they did?"

Careful to keep her face blank, she nodded. "I must one day learn to lead without your guidance."

He scrutinised her expression. There was no sign of wavering, and content, he looked away. "Be sure to relay my thanks and acceptance of their apology."

"Of course."

Charras wasn't about to dwell. The day was full of promise, the morning sun an omen of good fortune. He was glad the Sky beamed down on them with grace, for he knew the days that followed would be less kind. They could only take each moment in their stride and prey for providence. And with that thought, he beckoned for his charges to follow as he led them from the clearing.

"We need to be on full alert; the Minae are attracted to the haunts; the closer we get, the more likely we'll have another encounter," he said, clarifying the earlier two times he'd warned them.

Rolling her eyes, Charlize held a branch out of the way for Christian. "Watch your step."

He nodded and ducked slightly, missing the tree root but still stumbling forwards. He splayed his hands, ready for the impact, but was surprised when he remained suspended. Twisting his head, he saw Charlize stretching her hand towards him.

"I meant the second, less obvious root," she smirked, pulling the air towards her so he was able to regain his footing.

"Wow…" Christian gasped. "That was cool."

"There's nothing cool about it," Charlize snapped, sending another gust towards him. He fell backwards and landed on a patch of broken earth, and letting the branch snap back, she climbed over the hazard and stood above him. "Our gifts are deadly, there's nothing 'cool' about being deadly." She held out her hand.

"You clearly don't get men do you?"

With a grunt of indignation, she heaved him to his feet. "If being a man means taking pleasure in killing, then I'd rather not." She whipped around, flicking her hair with purpose, and followed her father into the forest.

For the first time, Christian was left with the choice of whether to join them or not.

Inhaling deeply, he took a step forward.

22

The Anima Haunt

Hours passed, time an anomaly lost to the consistent pounding of feet that seemed to count the seconds themselves. The trees had taken on a new texture and the bark shone with frost – an artistic milieu to the dewdrops. Tall beech trees lined the path they followed, housing many of the gifts; along with grand oaks, seemingly older than time with their knotted bark and rich brown textures – patches of ash and silver birch interspersed between them. Holly trees still bloomed, adding a tinge of red against the yellow and white backdrop, and Christian was certain that when winter was over, the array of colours would be quite dazzling. But for now, his attentions focused on navigating the forest floor, which was a challenge in itself. The natural obstacle course was a constant threat and he had stumbled several more times.

Not that anyone noticed. There seemed to be an abundance of excited energy between Charras and Charlize, and their steady pace had gradually developed into a brisk walk he could barely keep.

Even lunch was hurried, the remainder of the malt loaf being gulped down with nothing more than an inhalation before they were on their feet again and ready to go.

Barely satiated, Christian quickly dusted himself down, letting the crumbs on his lap fall to the floor. He blinked twice as they flew further away than he anticipated. They darted into the trees, pulled by an unknown force, and their escape drew the hard won attention of Charlize and Charras.

The former slowly got up to inspect, making her way to a thicket of birch trees that grew so a small V shape opened between the trunks. It was big enough to step through, but before she did, she twisted her ankle in the invisible but moderate force, noting how the forest floor beyond the beeches was worn smooth in its slope downwards. She couldn't see where the force led but she had a pretty good idea.

"We're here."

Charras looked up to see his daughter disappear through the warty bark of the dainty trees. A broad smile swept across his face as he felt the Anima's call, its whispered melody carried on the breeze. Without knowing what possessed him, he followed Charlize and took off into a run.

"Hey, wait up!" Christian called, grabbing his pack and chasing after his companions.

The route was fairly easy to follow once he cleared the initial hurdle, the earth seemingly swept aside to allow for easy passage. Bent strangely, the trees twisted towards the unknown force, as if drawn to what lay at its heart. Christian darted downwards in panicked pursuit, picking up speed until the shape of Charras became more distinct. He stood on the edge of what seemed to slip into nothingness, and with a sudden jolt, Christian realised he was running too fast to safely stop himself.

Unsure what else to do, he took a nosedive, landing on his chest as he came to a skidding halt at the base of Charras's foot. He said a silent thank-you to the earth mounded around his shoulders, wiped his eyes to clear the dirt, and got to his feet, seeing that Charlize also stood nearby. Annoyed no one had noticed his dramatic arrival, or tried to help him before he plunged off the edge to his death, he folded his arms across his chest.

"It's okay, I'm fine," he grunted.

There was no response, and following the stares of his oblivious companions, it wasn't long before he realised why.

With a gasp, he took a step back, taking in the scene that captured his fellow travellers so completely. It was like something out of a faerie-tale, what he imagined Never-Never Land to look like, minus the clouds…

A stream gathered at the foot of a huge ravine, circling like a moat and splitting off to the north and south – the waters flowing to the south in a steady run. Yet it was the island they protected that held the real spectacle.

About sixty giant trees gathered together, the type Christian had never seen before, their huge trunks giving the base for what had to be the world's largest tree house.

"Now, this is cool..." he murmured.

Charlize admired the Haunt, her knowledge allowing her to distinguish the trees as giant sequoias. She'd never known a forest to allow so many to grow together so happily, for they *were* happy, each tree having to be over seventy metres high and eight metres in diameter, and that was at a guess. From their perspective, the sequoias stood out even against the enchanted forest surrounding them, their grandeur marking them as the kings of trees.

Christian shielded his eyes to try and get a better look, certain he could see small dots moving among the branches. Then, as it dawned on him, his mouth fell open. Amongst the giant gathering of the mutant trees, there were *people*, real live *people* living and breathing as they made their way along the branches, which, as he stared, suddenly became bridges too. He could even make out different levels, and there were *houses*, little green and white things of different sized boxes all placed randomly, as if they'd been shoved wherever they'd fit. There were bulbous lanterns floating around, covered in transparent material to provide light in the tree village, and from his perspective, they looked like Christmas baubles. As he watched, more and more came alive until they masked the twilight in a soft haze.

A small grunt escaped Charras's lips as he tore his nostalgic longing from the Haunt. He nodded towards Charlize and casually shut Christian's mouth. And then, without speaking, led them to the edge of the ravine. He took the lead, and soon, they were all carefully descending the slope, climbing backwards in the smooth earth on their hands and knees.

Muddied and sweaty, they reached the bottom half an hour later, the drop further than they expected. It would have taken them longer, but

Charlize grew bored and glided them all down on a gust of wind – much to Charras's dismay.

"You must not be seen to rely solely on your gifts to get around; your strength must be witnessed without the aid of magic."

"It's dusk, and I don't want my remaining energy to be wasted fighting the Ghul trailing us."

Darkening his brow, Charras looked to the summit of the ravine. "How did you know?"

"I didn't," said Charlize. "I just knew you were wary. Is he close?"

"Let me check," he mumbled, closing his eyes and reaching outwards with his senses to touch everything that lay around them.

There was the constant energy of nearby water, the brusque breeze of the twilight hour, the deadened crisp of the fallen leaves – he expanded further afield; the rush of energy in the dewdrops an electric pulse; the sleepy hollows of resting trees; Hellebores wilting in the progressing darkness; the cold touch of resistance as the Ghul stamped its way closer; a tug of oblivion plucking at Charras's nerves – the same way a spider felt vibrations along its web.

He opened his eyes. "Close enough to outrun, but we must go now."

Staring up at the Haunt just beyond the calm river, he was able to pick out more settlements in the wide spaces between the sequoias. There were huge platforms built into the soft bark and hundreds of bridges varying in size and shape granted access between them.

Beneath the village on the forest bed, large machinery rumbled quietly, and Charras guessed modern installations had been fitted since his last visit. He gestured for Charlize and Christian to stay close and they cleared the short expanse between where they stood and the riverbank in minutes.

A large bridge awaited them as they reached the edge. It rose high over the river, the bottom cord arched and decorated with painted leaves and rosettes, while the top chord and interlocking posts were polished smooth. It stood on the inside edge of the Arx, which Charras promptly held his hand against. The responding shimmer rippled along its extensive breadth, repelling with only a mild resistance, and he stood back and folded his arms across his chest. He knew what happened next.

Charlize was impatient however. Wanting to find a way across the river, she paced slightly, knowing the Ghul would be upon them within the hour. "How long do we have to wait?" she demanded.

Before Charras had the chance to answer, three figures materialised and stood on the peak of the bridge. The man in the middle wore an olive green robe, while his two companions wore loose shirts and brown slacks. They each held a branch of some description, using them as makeshift staffs, and they talked amongst themselves as they weighed up the newcomers, in no hurry to invite them in.

Charlize was about to protest when the man wearing the robe stood forward.

"I am Armmos, leader of the Anima. Please identify yourself," he said, his staff the only one decorated with a crystal.

It was Charras who answered. "Armmos, please, that kind of language is not suited for a friend as old as I am."

Looking at the stranger with sleepy eyes, annoyed that he'd been a source of humour, the leader of the Anima pointed his staff at the ravine summit. "Times are troubled," he said.

As if to prove a point, a distant growl tore from the pursuing Ghul. Standing to his full height, the moon cast the demons silhouette on the ravine slope. Although still far away, his mass looked no less frightening, and without thinking, Christian held onto Charlize's pack.

Unperturbed, Charras opened his arms and gestured towards himself. "*I* am troubled that you do not remember me old friend."

Armmos considered Charras sceptically, before turning his attentions to his comrades, and then back to the humorous stranger. After a few moments, recognition flooded his expression.

"You've grown," he said finally, although the lightening in his voice was clear.

"And you," said Charras.

"You are welcome. Please walk through the barrier."

Ushering Charlize forward and freeing Christian's hold, Charras pushed her out towards the stream. It was then the bridge lost half of itself, the drop inches from Armmos's feet. Christian spluttered a protest but cut himself short as Charlize disappeared momentarily, only to reappear on the other side of the river, unharmed and dry. He had no time to react before Charras clutched his arm and carried them both through at the same time.

An alien feeling of weightlessness plunged to his stomach before his feet touched solid ground, and looking up, he found himself standing in front of Armmos and his companions.

Raising an eyebrow only marginally, the leader eyed Christian with a hint of confusion. "You bring another Charras?"

"There were unforeseen circumstances."

Armmos promptly held his palm out to Christian, his fingers splayed slightly, and waited for the courtesy. When it was clear none would be offered, his eyebrows rose in unison.

Jumping forward to offer her own palm instead, Charlize did so with such vigour it made a clapping sound. If the leader seemed perturbed, he didn't show it, kindly bowing his head as he acknowledged her status.

"Your reputation precedes you, it is an honour. I apologise for our first introduction, I could not see your face beyond the Arx."

Charlize took a deep breath and bowed low – more to compose her blushing than any real need. It was one thing knowing the Mage community had known her since her tenth birthday, pictures of her growth and training splattered in newspapers and books only Mages could see, but it was quite another meeting the people who'd grown alongside her. Their faces were strangers to her, while her face was imprinted in the minds of all those who were able to see it.

Her inner turmoil went unnoticed however, Armmos already turned to embrace Charras, their exchange one of genuine affection as they patted each other's backs.

"It is good to have you home; I feared you were lost to us for good," said the former.

"It was never my decision to leave old friend."

Although it was said with warmth, Charlize couldn't help but detect a hint of bitterness in her father's tone. Growing up, it didn't escape her that her father resented the Mages. Their rules and regulations, the same ones she was taught to abide by, were always relayed to her with the utmost of importance. It was only the monotony of his voice and the dullness in his eyes that told her his words were rehearsed.

Every year an assessor sent from the Hetairia Doman would come and take photos and write notes and test her on almost everything she'd ever learned. When they left, she would often find her father sulking in the kitchen or slumped in the library with an empty whiskey glass. Up until her thirteenth birthday she would beam at him and tell him how well she'd done. Then, that year, everything changed, and she also learned to dread the yearly visits...

Throughout her musings, Armmos had decided to try again, his palm held up to Christian who now knew what to do. The stout leader's reaction as their palms touched was far more animated than before, his expression incredulous as his short beard twitched and his face took on a red tinge. He dropped his hand as if he'd been the brunt of a sick joke and glared at Charras. "I hope your explanation is sound, this is unheard of."

"He is unbecome, he travels with us as a precaution, let me explain all this to you in the privacy of your quarters. I do not know who may hear us while we stand here."

Armmos said nothing as he continued to stare at Christian. Then, after a few moments, his shoulders drooped in defeat, his decision made. "You are lucky young man," he addressed him. "Soon, you will understand why."

Grasping Christian's shoulder, Charras said, "You have my assurances; neither I nor Charlize would ever do this unless we thought it absolutely necessary. We have only respect for our laws, exempt or otherwise."

"Indeed," Charlize said. "Christian was in great danger."

Grunting, Armmos leaned on his staff. "With all due respect, there is no greater danger than what he faces now. His fate is on your shoulders, I will not be a part of this."

"It was my decision."

All eyes turned to Christian, who faltered, wondering if his outburst was wise. "I mean, they gave me the choice. I chose to come."

"And you were warned of the dangers?"

Christian nodded and Armmos scratched his beard. "Then I can't blame your ignorance. But I can blame your stupidity."

Turning his back, the leader addressed the two men standing behind him, their expressions amused as he whispered a private joke in their ears. Then, a decision made, Armmos beckoned his guests over to him. "These are my guards, Hugo and Glen," he said, gesturing towards them.

Greeting them traditionally, Charlize stood back as her father and Christian did the same. Confusion crossed their faces the same way their leader's had when they realised Christian was unbecome, but they said nothing as Armmos led the assembly towards the village.

As they walked down the real, solid, and corporeal part the bridge, Christian stared up at the Haunt. The lanterns had grown in size and luminosity, countering the dark that fell quickly. Music drifted through the village, a fusion of pan pipes and bass drums managing to weave a melody his feet longed to dance to, and the closer they got, the more he could hear the muffled chatter of the village residents.

Soon, one of the enormous trees stood within his reach, and forgetting himself, he ran ahead and began to circle it. When he reached the other side everyone was waiting for him, some amused and some annoyed by his obvious fascination.

"They're quite impressive aren't they?" said Armmos.

Christian nodded eagerly, stroking the flaky bark with his fingertips. "What are they?"

"They are Giant Sequoias," Armmos replied proudly. "Or Wawona if you name them after the Native Americans we acquired the seeds from."

"You *grew* these?"

Armmos chuckled. "You have much to learn. We are the Anima clan; we are the wind, the air, and breath itself. We give life to what surrounds us; we are connected more closely with the earth than all other clans. Give us the means and we will grow a forest in a desert." Armmos sighed. "Of course, only those native to the land, such as those we acquired the seeds from, understand this completely. Although we can grow such things, we rarely have the means to maintain them. A tree such as this needs to be near a stream, but also relies on fire to maintain its health. We provide the balance and in return our village remains intact."

Christian's brow furrowed. "Surely fire isn't good for a tree…"

This time everyone but Charlize laughed. Armmos shook his head and led them to the base of another tree, a few metres from the last where a staircase spiralled up the trunk.

"You will see soon enough. Fear not young man, the Giant Sequoia is fire proof." Armmos winked at Charras and promptly waved his guests upwards, the forest floor soon lying abandoned as they disappeared into the treetops.

Lost in his complete involvement with the proceedings, it was easy for all around Christian to forget his status of unbecome (as good as saying he was faulty). He positioned himself next to Armmos as they tackled the stairs, wide enough for two people to climb side by side, and soon had the leader laughing from his belly, the wonder attributed to his unbecome ignorance contagious. So much so, it took them twice the time it normally would to reach the first gate.

When they got there, a bored looking guard asked for a password, but soon stood to attention as Armmos pushed through and held up his palm.

"Hurry now Demetrius, let us pass," he commanded, shooing him with his hand.

The guard didn't seem to take offence as he opened the steel bars to allow passage, his head bowed slightly – which was lucky, as it enabled him to hide his shock when he saw the Āetis sweep past.

The group shortly found themselves in front of a hollow log as wide and tall as a healthy man. Their animated voices echoed as they passed through, coming to stand on a platform surrounded by more guards at the other end. It was here Armmos gave Christian a hearty laugh and patted his shoulder – their congeniality apparent for all to witness.

Then, throwing his arms wide open, he turned his attentions to his other guests. "Welcome to the Anima!"

Stood in a rounded area about the size of a discus cage, six guards occupied the circumference, their right palms facing the centre. In between them, and spaced evenly, were totem poles, carved and sculpted to reflect images of Native American tribes, each painted in bright autumnal colours. All held a plaque, the inscriptions detailing directions to various sections of the Haunt.

During her observations, Charlize also noticed that there were carvings in the tree bark, along with patterns and decorations, mainly painted in varying shades of green. Every now and then, a huge lantern would intersperse, its soft gleam casting an almost tranquil luminance, and on closer inspection, the transparent material revealed a dewdrop at its heart, much larger than the ones she saw in the forest.

Armmos stood in the centre of the platform, his arms still open as he gazed proudly around him. Glen and Hugo stood either side of their leader, their loyalty evident by the patience they exuded, even though they must have heard the same speech several times.

For Christian however, it was the first, and he listened eagerly, entranced by the powerful aura Armmos radiated. Clearly in love with his Haunt, and just as clearly loved by those who dwelled in it, it wasn't hard to see why he was the chosen leader. Authority oozed from his countenance, but it was with kindness he spoke, gaining the respect and attention of all who listened.

"We have a far larger trade aiding our income from the days you remember it Charras," Armmos said pointedly, beaming at his old friend. "The fish in our rivers are of the finest quality, as is our fertiliser, and of course we specialise in wood. This influx of trade means we are blessed with our own mini market, here in our very own village." He gave a slight chuckle. "Of course we receive our funding from the Hetairia proprietors of the Mage's trust." He looked towards Christian. "For those who don't know what that is, it is a rather substantial amount of money that holds five separate accounts for each Haunt. It is sufficient to live on and maintain a way of life. Yet the extra inflow of money via our own means allows us to upgrade as and when we see fit." Walking over to a small contraption that resembled a roofless lion cage with the letters A.A.E marked on the brim, Armmos held his hand over it. "Air Assisted Elevator's. They are for the elderly of our village, or the incapacitated. Those not fitting that description use the more traditional means of ladders. There are many of them on each platform, but the Haunt only has three levels so it's no great effort."

Beckoning his companions to join him on the contraption, just big enough to hold five well-proportioned adults, Armmos closed the gate and tapped the letters twice. Vines spiralled up the bars and a rush of air beneath the elevator pushed it upwards.

"Welcome to the first floor," Armmos introduced, allowing them to climb out onto the platform.

Here, there were many more Mages, all pre-occupied with their own thoughts as they went about their business. Some still managed to peer at Charlize through half curious eyes, yet most ignored her in favour of discretion: Armmos had obviously warned them not to stare...

Looking around her once again, Charlize gasped with appreciation. The Haunt was as intricate as it was fascinating. Everything looked so oddly positioned that if they were not in the trees she would have wondered why there was no order to it. Shadows striped across the first floor from overhead bridges and platforms, yet the long pathways that made up the first floor were still bright due to the many lanterns that bobbed softly along them. It was so vast that she couldn't see where anything ended. Market stalls, shops, restaurants, cafes, and a manor of other novelties jutted out sporadically in every direction – the lowest level seemingly providing the perfect cover for the busiest.

"…we even have a brewery now, and a bank!"

Charlize returned her attention to Armmos, listening mutely as his enthusiasm threatened to spill over. If that happened, she was almost certain Christian would lap it up, his eyes brighter than she'd ever seen them.

"…the second floor holds all of our village events. We have a huge decking area where four of the Sequoia trees grew apart from each other, and there are also the infamous gardens." Armmos nodded pointedly at Charlize. "Did you know it was your mother who caused all of the trouble?" he said, oblivious to the look Charras shot him.

Charlize was intrigued, the stories of her mother so rare she relished the opportunity to hear more about her. Shaking her head, she couldn't help but smile as Armmos prepared the tale.

"She was quite the wild one," he said. "I was just twenty when this sprightly, viciously spirited young woman demanded my help one evening." He chuckled. "And how could I refuse such a beauty? Even if Riccto, the leader at the time, and my father, had forbidden any meddling or destruction of his experimental gardens…"

Charras crossed his arms, his jaw tight. The memories of his wife spoken aloud for all to hear were almost as unbearable to listen to as they were to relive… He had tried to stop her, but she had such a hold over him that it was impossible to refuse her. He was deeply in love and would have followed her anywhere.

It was a balmy evening when they'd sprung Armmos from his private quarters. Sneaking into the gardens using the key he'd stolen from his father, the three of them were high on adrenaline and mischief. Isalize was convinced she knew how to make the plants grow and thrive, and her magnetism was such that no one argued.

When they reached the centre of the plot – Armmos and Charras on the lookout – she'd tucked her long blonde hair behind her ears, whispering commandments of moisture and warmth. She then directed it into the wood and air, but the spell was too powerful and she ended up soaking them all, stinging Charras in the process. Realising the damage they'd caused to any chance of growth, they fled, a disappointed Isalize trailing behind, her notorious sulks that had so endeared her to him forcing Charras to turn around. She'd smiled that beautiful smile as she realised he was going to help, and he took her hand as they returned to the scene of the crime.

It had only taken a minor spell to counter the dampening effects – a simple casting of wind that parted and thinned the water particles in the air. But the delight on Isalize's face was worth the risk, and their kiss in that moment was one they often talked about.

"…so your heritage has a mark even now," Armmos finished, cutting sharply through Charras's memory.

A dark mood now resting on his shoulders, he clenched his stomach, attempting to ease the ache. He tried not to be angry with Armmos, for he wasn't to know that the demon Vrealâ was his dead wife's spirit, that she wandered the earth inflicting more devastation on the living than any of them knew. It was enough to bear that his beautiful wife was the right hand of Inferus-Malus in death, but to hear her spoken of as she once was felt far too surreal. She was a powerful Mage in life, too powerful some said, but he refused to accept that she had been so evil, so twisted, that she became the monster she was in death. No, there was more, and he intended to find out what.

Christian held his hand up which made Armmos laugh.

"Yes Christian, please, have your say."

"Er, it's more of a question… I just wanted to know what wood this was?" He stamped his foot on the flooring beneath him.

"Ah, well that is not such a wonderful story. We use Hickory, known for its durability, strength, and character. The reddish-brown colour changes with the seasons, yet it fits well with all of them, the most vibrant in the autumn when the leaves turn. It is a shame you first saw the Haunt in winter… yet spring is just around the corner and that is a sight to behold…"

Satisfied with the answer, his zeal for learning still dominant within him, Christian followed Armmos as he led the party through a series of walkways, ever smiling at the Mages he passed who waved eagerly back at him. He stopped in front of a shopkeeper who bowed frantically, but Armmos held his palm up to greet him. The man emerged from his stall beneath a branch he'd used to create the point in his canopy. He looked to Charlize, blushed, and then shyly held his palm to his leaders'. Armmos nodded kindly and went to move on, but was quickly stopped by several bags of nuts being squashed into his hands.

"Pistachio," the shopkeeper said with an accent.

Receiving a bag, Charlize frowned as she studied the little open seeds, and then watched as Armmos handed over three coins, insisting the trader take payment even against his wishes.

"I love these," Christian grinned, tearing off the shell and putting the nut in his mouth.

Not wanting to seem ignorant, Charlize did the same, pleasantly surprised that she found the taste to her liking. Unfortunately, there wasn't much time to enjoy them, for Armmos soon led them into another small clearing. This time there were six ladders positioned between the trees that led up to the second floor. They each picked one and climbed, emerging out onto yet another platform. They walked through an archway built between two trunks, twigs and bare branches wrapped across its structure, and as they passed beneath, Charlize found herself wondering what it looked like when its flowers came into bloom.

They emerged out into the largest section of the Haunt, which stood true to Armmos's explanation; the spacious deck curved into the trees quite spectacularly. Tables and chairs dotted prettily across the flooring and lanterns hung in ordered sequences, each stood upright on poles that overlooked their separate tables. Potted plants adorned the periphery, positioned in front of thick three-tiered ropes that protected those who strayed too close from falling to the earth below.

To the east, a small building stood deserted, its camouflaged roof dark as it lay shut for the night. Refreshment and food carts sat statically outside, their bright green parasols collapsed for the evening, while a signboard indicating the earlier dishes from the hot kitchen now stood redundant.

Out of curiosity, Christian walked to the nearest edge and held onto the top rope to steady himself. Leaning over, he looked down.

They were a long way up. If the fall didn't kill him, then the metal poles jagging outwards certainly would. He ran back to his companions and waited for Armmos to finish explaining that the second floor was the place of dwelling, with sporadic houses built wherever they'd fit. Then, holding up his hand, he asked his question without waiting for permission.

"I was just wondering how on earth the platforms stay up, or have done for so long? I guess partly maintenance… but after almost nine hundred years, doesn't it start to decay? The wood I mean… I just wonder how safe it all is, doesn't it start to weaken?"

Armmos chuckled, torn between scolding Christian's ignorance and praising his thirst for learning. "The Anima is air dear boy. We do not put any unnecessary strain on this forest. The poles that keep everything upright are merely a precaution, for there is air beneath every surface you walk upon.

As for the decay – that is solved by an extremely high concentration of wood preservative, and yes, every year maintenance is performed which keeps the Haunt in top condition. So fear not, you are perfectly safe in these trees."

With a nod of his head, signalling the end of further interruptions, Armmos turned and continued to lead the group further into the Haunt. Crossing a rope bridge, which swayed slightly underfoot, they reached the other side and came to a halt in front of another Native American sculpture, this one of a girl with a wolf by her knees.

"You will be staying in the Amber Glade," Armmos informed his guests, pointing towards another rope bridge. "It is the only house down there. I hope you find it comfortable; please just follow the signs. I would show you myself and share a drink, but there are other matters to deal with." He handed a key to Charras before addressing him. "We will meet tomorrow so you can explain everything to me, old friend."

And with a final bow of his head, he bid them farewell.

Glen and Hugo said their goodbyes in turn and left to follow their leader. They didn't get far before Armmos hurried back. "One more thing," he said breathlessly. "The third floor is where everything important lives." He pointed upwards. "The school you will be attending Charlize, the library, the bank, the hospital, the brewery, and the Tower of the Sky watcher. The forest floor holds the water tower, water plant and the waste disposal and recycling units. Nothing to worry about, but during your visit you will be expected to learn and volunteer for the smooth operation of these things."

Charlize was taken aback. She knew she had to partake in the running of each Haunt – it was good politics, but no one told her about dealing with waste…

She forced a smile nonetheless and nodded dutifully, before watching Armmos finally scurry off to attend whatever matters required his attention.

"That sounds fun," Christian said, laughing loudly as he followed his ashen-faced companion to the Amber Glade. "Can I come and watch?" He slapped his knees between further bouts of laughter.

They were crossing the last bridge, and with a huff, Charlize stormed ahead and turned as Christian reached the middle plank. With a swoop of her hand, she forced the bridge to sway, and the smirk soon disappeared from her foolish friends face.

"Okay, I'm sorry, I'm sorry!" he said, holding onto the ropes with a white knuckled grip.

Charlize smiled, but before she could really have fun, Christian was pulled by a force behind her, glided to safety, and set down on static ground.

She turned to her father. "Spoil sport."

23

First Impressions

Waking to the familiar sounds of snoring, Charlize opened her eyes. The cottage still clung to the sweet scent of orange blossom and the earthy aroma of cinnamon, but it was the warmth that truly pleased her. For days they'd woken cold to the bone, groggy, and distinctly odorous. But today she woke feeling more human than she had in weeks. The bath from the night before and the homely meal left in the oven ignited her memories of what it felt to be clean and wholesome, and the deep sleep brightened the shadows beneath her eyes. Even so, she couldn't shake the heaviness in her bones as she crept from the bedroom, careful to tie her emerald robe tightly around her.

The cottage was cosy and housed every amenity they needed. The kitchen and lounge occupied the same room, and open beams throughout disguised its small size. Wildflower and more orange blossom decorated the surfaces of the kitchen, and several herbs grew in potted plants along the cooking counter beside the oven.

Green was the common theme, the walls painted with faint forest landscapes, while sofas of mint and cream surrounded a wooden coffee table facing the kitchen. There was no fireplace, but the heat of the cottage confirmed that the air was enchanted, as well as the thatched roof, which seemed to direct any sort of rainfall away.

Opening the front door, Charlize peered out across the platform. All was as it had been the night before. The cottage still sat perfectly on its circular frame with three small steps leading up to it just beyond the rope bridge, and the granite post with the name '**AMBER GLADE**' still sat to the left. She hadn't been dreaming, it was all real…

She took a seat on the doorstep, ignoring the chill of the morning, and idly fingered one of the bulbous evergreen shrubs placed either side of the entrance. Then, looking up, she touched the number '**1**' written on the olive door.

"Home," she mumbled.

And it was, even if it was for a matter of months. Strangely, for she wasn't used to feeling that way, the simplicity of the amber glade soothed her. Here it seemed as if nothing could harm her, although she was wiser than that to truly believe it was the case.

She thought of how far they'd come in only a few short weeks. It already seemed a lifetime ago that she stood in her back garden and said goodbye to the Marsh Village – and not once had she looked back. Life had taken her on a journey, and for now, she was exactly where she should be.

Occupied with her thoughts, Charlize idled the time away, unsure how long she stared into the distance, but certain it was at least an hour. So when Christian joined her, she accepted his presence gratefully and turned to smile at him.

"Morning," he said, looking quite ridiculous in his own green robe.

"Good morning," she replied.

Unsure where to put himself, he sat on the floor beside her and put his back to the wall. "I keep waking up expecting to be at home."

She didn't answer, but Christian knew she understood.

They sat in silence and enjoyed the company of one another, both waiting for Charras to rouse. In that time, Christian allowed his mind to wander, the calm of the cottage reminding him of a day at home in the Marsh Village, a day his mother had been baking. She'd made cinnamon swirls, his favourite treat, and she'd picked lavender from their garden. She always loved the way they smelled, saying the scent picked up her mood on even the dreariest of days… She'd been so happy too, something about her glowing, and she sang to him as he entered, spinning him in a circle as she danced. He'd thought her mad, and had told her the same, but she just smiled the same way she always did.

Christian's heart pounded, rousing him from his memories, and he clutched his chest.

"Are you okay?" asked Charlize, her eyes fixed on his face.

Shrugging, he cleared his throat. "Yeah... yeah I'm fine."

With a slight frown, she shuffled to sit in front of him. Looking into his eyes, she saw such sadness that her stomach turned and she reached out to touch his arm.

"Don't..." Christian said, brushing her away, although not unkindly.

Slumping back, a different flip in her stomach replacing the last, Charlize looked at her knees. "I miss them too," she said. "But if they're out there, we'll find them."

Christian shrugged and smoothed the hair from his face, and then clasped his neck, and then crossed his arms, and then sighed again. All signs that told Charlize a conversation wouldn't be taking place. So, standing up, she stepped into the cottage, walked to the kitchen, and began rummaging through several cupboards. If he wouldn't talk, then he would most certainly eat...

The sound of food being prepared seemed to lure her father from his coma, and after a breakfast of cured ham and scrambled eggs, courtesy of their stocked fridge, Charlize's mood had lifted considerably.

Pouring out three fresh mugs of steaming coffee, she handed one to Christian sprawled on the sofa before she settled into one of the chairs.

"Thanks," he said, sitting up so Charras could take a seat.

"You're welcome," Charlize replied, before turning to the sight of her father scratching his head and chin stubble, which she had never seen clean-shaven in her life.

The sight of him made her laugh, his mannerisms reminding her of a long extinct species called 'ape' she'd once seen pictures of in a book. With his broad chest proudly on display, the curly hair that adorned it added to the visual.

"What?" Charras asked when he caught her expression, looking around in confusion.

"I just don't understand it father."

Folding his arms, his face turned serious. "Why, what have you heard?"

"I hear you're quite the talk of the village, the woman keep trying to glimpse you as they pass the glade… and I just don't understand it."

Charras chuckled and shook his head, feigning mock hurt as he grabbed his heart. "I see, well perhaps they see something in my appearance my own daughter can't."

"Do you think so?"

"I think you're goading me," he said pointedly, standing up and taking a step towards her. There was mischief in his eyes.

Quickly glancing at the door, Charlize stood and backed towards it. "Christian, duck!"

Suddenly, commotion burst into the cottage like a freak storm. Ducking just in time as a potted plant flew over his head, Christian watched as Charras caught it in a vacuum of air and gently placed it on the floor. Then, within a second, the door swung open as Charlize disappeared through it, Charras immediately following – his departure so fast it sounded like the crack of a whip.

Suspended in mid-air, Charlize revolved around to face her pursuer, although his onslaught wasn't forthcoming. Twisting her head and securing her footing on the air beneath her, she squinted against the winter sun. He was no-where to be seen.

She dived downwards, as graceful as a swan, and hovered above Christian leaning against the door pane, amusement written on his face.

"Did you see where he flew?" she asked quickly.

He shrugged theatrically and grinned.

She didn't have time to consider it before a huge force sent her catapulting towards a tree, leaving her barely enough time to steady her collision. Casting a quick spell that landed her against a cushion of air, she jumped upwards and flew above the opening between the platforms.

There, she caught her father sat behind a shrub, peering at her through the foliage. She watched his lips move and dodged a concentrated gust, ignoring it in its trajectory through the overhead canopy of branches. And whipping around, hands open wide, she pointed towards him.

"*Dicio, Āetis, Flabra.*"

A blast of air punched Charras in the stomach, sending him careering to the platform below, and a now horrified looking Christian. Charlize found her feet on solid ground and caught her breath, just as her father darted upwards again, apparently unharmed. She shielded her eyes and looked up, waiting for him to reappear. A flurry propelled towards her and she sidestepped it, laughing as she tried to find him in the atmosphere.

After a quick scan, she managed to pick out a small dot in the clouds, and bending her knees, launched into the air once more. She collided with her father seconds later and they continued their invisible battle.

Meanwhile, a gathering began to form outside the cottage, the spectators chatting animatedly between themselves as they pointed upwards. Christian said nothing, watching with interest himself, although he didn't escape the curious glances of a group of girls no older than himself, all giggling and whispering in their tight huddle. After a moment's deliberation, he chose to ignore them.

"Is that you-know-who?"

Startled, Christian looked to the person who spoke. Stood in front of him, having left her group of friends, a short blonde girl peered up at him, her deep green eyes waiting for a response. More giggles emanated towards them, but he didn't care, strangely unable to take his eyes off the girl before him.

"I don't know, who are they meant to be?" he said, sure it sounded more confident in his head.

"You know… *her*?"

He didn't know, but before he managed to ask what she meant, Charras and Charlize landed metres from where they stood, their impact against the platform vibrating the wood around them. They were both red faced and energetic, laughing and scoring each other's performance as they walked towards the cottage.

"I win again old man," Charlize boasted, pushing her father's shoulder to no avail.

He shook his head. "You have an unfair advantage."

She put her hands on her hips. "And what's that?"

"You have no fear of hurting me, while I have every fear of hurting you!"

"Ha! That is no excuse father; I am hardier than even you!"

About to make a witty retort, Charras stopped as loud cheers rang out behind them. Turning to face the crowd of spectators, both he and Charlize blushed, before smiling widely and bowing dramatically, causing more excited chatter to erupt. It was only then Charras remembered he wore nothing but his jogging bottoms.

"One way to make an impression," Christian said, snorting with mirth as his mentor backed into the cottage.

"Indeed," said Charlize breathlessly, spinning on her heels to follow her father. She stopped as she spotted the blonde girl standing mouth agape.

"Hello there," she said, holding up her palm.

The girl bowed her head and mirrored her palm tentatively. "It's an honour," she whispered.

Charlize smiled politely, and with half curious eyes, addressed Christian. "Will you not introduce me?"

"We've just met," he said, puzzled by the change in the girl's attitude. She seemed so confident only seconds ago.

"Amy. My name is Amy," she said.

"Ah, Amy. It is nice to meet you too; I hope Christian isn't causing trouble already?"

With a frown, Christian pursed his lips, wondering when he regressed and became nothing more than a nuisance child. Unfolding his arms, he stepped down from the entrance and stood next to Amy. "Actually, we were just talking about exploring." He held out his hand and his new friend grasped it happily. "I'll try not to go too wild without you."

And with nothing more than a tilt of his head, he disappeared across the bridge and out into the Haunt, Amy firmly clutched beside him.

The rest of the morning passed quietly. Charlize sat in the sitting room, wondering where Christian and Amy had got to, only hoping that he didn't cause any offence to those who realised he was unbecome. She also found herself wondering if they were laughing with each other, the way she often saw him doing at the Marsh Village School. For some reason, Christian always seemed the popular choice with the girls – most likely because he was loud and the first to cause trouble. Oddly, that impressed people...

She shook her head, mentally swiping away the distracting thoughts, and returned her gaze to the book Armmos delivered only minutes after their exhibition. Apparently not as impressed as everyone else, her pack explained the rules of the Haunt and her expected duties while she resided there. One of the rules was not to cause any unnecessary danger to themselves or others. It pointed out that the Mage community was forbidden to use their powers unless necessary. To keep their skills fresh in their minds, they all attended an hour of secure practise daily, in a hall on the third floor, situated under the tower of the Sky Watcher. It then explained that the Sky Watcher was the person who kept a look out for any threats: Minae, Ungifted, or even other rogue Mages. There were also historical reports of rare machines that could fly crossing the Haunt, and it was the tower guard's job to alert the villagers. Known as 'code blacks,' in the case of such an event, a bell would chime and the Mages of the Anima were expected to stop any activity and stay still and silent until the second alarm sounded, signalling they could return to their activities. It was a precaution to keep the Haunt a secret. Although the Arcēs protected them from Ungifted eyes, who would see nothing but a thicket of trees, larger than usual but nothing of importance, it was wise to remain cautious. A break in the air or flicker of magic could easily alert their presence.

On the ground, it was easier to ward off threats. If any strayed too close, the guard towers would instantly be alerted. Luckily, it was rare any Ungifted made it to the Haunt, let alone alive. Their fortitude in crossing the barrier from the protected villages in the first place was one scarcely documented. There was only one such case recorded – a wanderer named Frederick Brown. He was being chased by a Wraithart in a common bear form, and managing to reach the river, had to stop when the barrier coaxed him to turn back. But taking pity, the Mages of the Anima rushed to help him, greeted by a look of pure joy as Frederick repeated over and over that he 'knew it, he just knew it.' In return for his safety, he promised his silence, and his tongue was sealed so he could never speak of his encounter again.

Not three months later, Frederick repaid the kindness, starting a rumour that grew like wildfire within the surrounding villages. With two scars as proof, he said the Anima was a forest of trapped spirits doomed to walk the earth, and only danger awaited those who tried to find it. To confirm the rumours, the Haunt began to play music every day, so on certain nights when the wind blew south, the noises could be heard, eventually donning Frederick the bravest man alive.

Turning as the door opened, Charlize eagerly looked up, her smile lessening when it was her father who walked in.

"I purchased a few extra supplies on the way back. They also sold fruit," he said, placing a book on the table next to her.

Charlize watched as he started to unpack. "Well," she said, "is she nice?"

Shrugging as he closed the fridge, Charras poured himself a glass of water. He'd been to meet the Anima teachers – Mrs Arno in particular.

She would be the one tutoring Charlize's class, along with the rest of the pilgrimage visitors during their stay. He'd asked if Christian could join the lessons, but she'd refused once he divulged that he was unbecome. 'When he's finished his book, we'll discuss it again, but until then I cannot allow it,' was her final answer.

"She's very pleasant," he decided, throwing Charlize a red apple.

"I see, well that's good," she said, taking a bite. "I should introduce myself."

Lost in her thoughts, faint chatter drifted through the single window in the cottage, and she perked up slightly when the distinct voices of Amy and Christian could be heard. She listened closely as their conversation drew to a close.

"You're so brave, not knowing what danger you'll be in, or who you even are. I admire you Christian."

Even from where Charlize sat, she could almost see the hair falling over Amy's face as she coyly looked up from beneath her lashes.

"Thanks, I'm not sure if it can be blamed on bravery, or merely stupidity, but I want to learn, and my eyes are truly open now."

Amy gave a small giggle and Charlize rolled her eyes and took another bite of her apple.

"Will I see you again?"

A slight shuffling could be heard, and then with a voice laced with velvet, Christian replied, "I hope so."

That was all Charlize heard before the world began to spin. Dropping the apple core to the floor, she found herself falling. Dark surrounded her, seeming to offer warmth, although at the same time threatening oblivion. All thoughts of fighting it seemed to melt away, peace encompassing her like a cotton blanket, refusing anything but the heaviness of sleep to penetrate her fortress.

Somewhere, her father's muffled voice called to her to fight, and she vaguely felt arms wrap themselves around her shoulders. But she merely wished they'd leave her to rest and tried to ignore them. Everything was almost peaceful – how cruel it was to deny her that freedom. Did they not know the bliss that was about to be hers?

And then suddenly, something stopped her. It was the slightest touch against her thigh, but it stung her consciousness like a wasp to her flesh. With sharp rapidity, the dark melted away and she felt herself pulled upwards, back from the warmth and promise of freedom, back to the cold light and harsh colours of life.

Opening her eyes, Charlize found herself on her father's lap; Christian knelt beside her, his eyes full of fear. Her head still muffled, she sat up and rubbed her eyes.

"What happened?" asked Christian.

"Nothing, I just felt queasy…" Her voice trailed off.

Charras handed her a glass of water and disappeared from the room, his lips tight.

"Are you two ever going to tell me what's up?"

The silence that lingered answered his question, and Christian wished he hadn't dismissed Amy so brashly when he heard Charras's cry of alarm. She was the only person he'd met besides Armmos that seemed to take any interest when he spoke. She had answers for all his questions, and she seemed happy to provide them – not irritated she had to.

"It's coming back to me you know. All those memories I thought were dreams, they're starting to make sense now."

He could have sworn he saw Charlize's sapphire eyes flash, but when he looked again, the cold stare that he recognised so fondly was still there. He threw his hands in the air and laughed. "I'll figure it out, trust me."

What he didn't know, and what Charlize hoped he'd never know, was that she said nothing because if she spoke, her beating heart might betray her.

24
Memories

Armmos had been kind to make sure whiskey and rum found their way into the cupboards. What had not been so kind was the lack of glass with which to drink them. Instead, Charras had to make do with a garish tumbler striped with black and lime.

He didn't like to admit he sulked, but seeing Charlize almost fall into a coma was cause enough to sustain anger and pity; the feelings all sloshed together much like his stomach contents, and he could not ignore them any more than he could ignore his desire for the liquor's trajectory through his body.

It made for no easy cure – no matter how far he delved into a bottle. It surrounded him; the scent; the air; the memory of *her*. No matter where he went, she haunted him, her face as clear to him now as it was the day she died…

Charras groaned and fell backwards, his head landing heavily on the back of the settee. This time, when she came to him, he didn't fight it.

Dawn seemed to creep from the shadow of night with nothing more than a whisper. Even so, the soft light still pierced his closed lids as if the sun were above them. Grunting, Charras turned over, knowing the precious moments of sleep were lost to him.

Months had passed since Isalize's departure, and still he could not bring himself to store her belongings, their presence a painful reminder of what he'd lost. Her perfume still lingered on the bed sheets, marred only by his repugnant body odour, but he would not wash them until all trace of her disappeared.

Heaving himself from the confines of his quilt, he trudged downstairs, knowing his stomach wouldn't allow him another day void of food. He only managed a breakfast of toast and jam, gulping it down slowly, every bite an effort more for self-preservation than for pleasure.

Then, once satiated, he entered the bathroom and avoided his reflection in the mirror, although noted his beard had started to curl. He let out a sigh and ran the taps, proceeding to wash several days of sleep from his weary body.

A few hours later he emerged from the bathroom, a towel wrapped around his midriff, and slumped into the lobby. He'd replaced the door, but looking at it still sent waves of nausea through his stomach. So, turning away, he began to ascend the stairs.

A sharp knock stopped him in his tracks and he listened carefully, wondering if he'd imagined it. The manor remained static, save for the unmistakable tapping coming from somewhere in the living room.

"Who's there?!" he growled.

There was no reply, nothing but the constant patter that quickly infuriated him. Tearing through the lobby, his hand at the ready, Charras threw open the living room door and stormed inside.

Sat in the rocking chair, Isalize stared up at him, tears falling silently down her face. She instantly stopped the left rocker knocking against the hearth and stood shakily to her feet. "I couldn't do it," she said, wiping her face. "I couldn't leave you. I'd rather bare a thousand knives in my stomach than spend another day without you."

Charras breathed in deeply, his head cloudy as he concentrated on his footing. He'd imagined the same scenario a thousand times in a thousand different ways.

"Please forgive me, please tell me you'll have me," Isalize pleaded, folding her arms across her chest.

His head swirling, wondering if he was still asleep, Charras held out his hand. "Why... No. *How* could you leave, after everything?"

Looking to the ceiling, Isalize blinked back more tears. "We're supposed to have a baby."

"But we'd never…"

"We don't have a choice. She's going to be the next Āetis."

"*She?*"

Isalize nodded.

"But that means that you…"

She looked away, the room suddenly cold. "It seems only fair after what we've done. We couldn't be happy forever, not living like we do, against the Hetairia Doman, living as outcasts…"

"But, we don't have to… we can not –"

"Live without touching? What life would that be?"

Turning away, Charras felt for the nearest wall. "You can't expect me to just go along with this," he said. "You've had months to come to terms with it."

"Think of the consequences Charras, think of what will happen if we don't do this. We're already seen as monsters. Do we really need to prove them right?"

"I won't, I won't do that to you. I won't put a child in your belly knowing that's what kills you."

And then he felt it, her intoxicating scent, her sensual touch on the back of his neck, her breath in his ear. "You won't… or you can't?" she purred.

Falling, the nights of loneliness and despair coming to drag him into her open arms, Charras found her face, her lips, the small of her back, and he wanted her, more than he'd wanted anyone ever. She wrapped herself around him and he could feel her sadness, her desire… and her desperation.

Gasping, he pushed her from him. "Don't. I can't."

"Charras…"

His vision blurred. All he knew was that he had to refuse her, to somehow get away. He forced himself to stumble from the sitting room, and as he reached the lobby, exhaustion overcame him and he fell to his knees, the floor cold against his legs. He staggered back up, only to fall again as a bracing darkness took hold and he gave into the collapse.

When he re-awoke, he was back in his bed and Isalize was not there. Sure he'd been dreaming, Charras let the wave of despair consume him once more. Clutching his head where a slight swelling had curiously appeared, he wished sleep would swallow him completely, only for the sun to wake him once everything stopped hurting.

"Morning."

His stomach turned. Facing Isalize as she glided towards him brandishing a tray piled high with food, he watched silently as she placed it on the bed. Then, perching neatly in the burgundy chair next to the bedside table, she crossed her legs. "You've not been eating."

Without answering, Charras sat up and rubbed his face. The smell of eggs too strong to ignore, he polished off the offering within minutes, unabashed as crumbs and yolk dirtied his beard. He wiped it with the back of his hand and accepted the napkin Isalize offered, continuing to watch in silence as she picked up the tray and placed it on the chest of drawers.

She then sat back on the bed and cupped his face in her hands. "I've missed you."

Swiping her away, Charras clambered out of bed and stormed towards the door. A field of energy stopped him from getting further and he span around. "Let me out Isalize," he said, a warning in his tone.

"You can't ignore me forever."

Charras cleared the space between them, grabbed her shoulders, and threw her onto the bed. "Clap," he demanded.

"Please, just talk to me, that's all I want."

"CLAP!" he roared.

Unable to control his shaking, he drove his gaze into Isalize's watery eyes. "You left me. You punished me for a crime I didn't even know I committed. I spent weeks asking myself what you saw, why you left me here alone. And then you come back, expecting me to put some reject in your stomach without a hint of protest."

"Please, please just listen…"

"You want to talk? Well I don't. So now you can see how it feels." He clenched his fists. "Last chance Isalize. Let me go."

"We have a responsibility Charras."

He knew he shouldn't have, but he couldn't help it. Dragging her from the bed by her foot, he hauled her towards the force field and knelt her in front of it, taking a hold of her neck and squeezing so tightly she yelped. She quickly clapped her hands and he released her.

"Stay away from me," he snarled.

She shied away from him as he passed, her face full of fear and sorrow. But he couldn't see it and he left her there sobbing for hours; unaware at that very moment it would be one of his darkest regrets.

25

Introduction

Looking up, Charlize could see a cloudless sky harbouring a faint glow. The bare branches that rose up on each side of her were motionless, the early morning static and crisp.

She settled herself into a casual walk as she wandered from the Amber Glade and out towards the heart of the Haunt. She tilted her head to the Mages she passed, each of them bowing back, while some – she was happy to note – also managed a warm smile.

Not bad for her first outing alone she thought. And how nervous her father had been when he made sure she ate breakfast – flittering around her like a bee to a flower. But here she was, taking her first day of school in her stride, doing as she was told and following the signs that would lead her to the building where she would finally meet Mrs Arno.

She stopped in front of a wooden plaque and tried to make out the inscriptions. An arrow pointed upwards, while another pointed straight ahead. Both arrows had the symbol of a book and a scroll beneath them, which she assumed meant 'Library' and 'School' respectively. She gazed up and saw that one of the platforms jutted out slightly, an obvious landing square for those who chose to lift themselves with air. Of course, she wasn't to know it was only for emergencies; she definitely 'missed' that entire page in the rulebook...

With mischief in her heart, Charlize checked around her, seeing that very few people milled about. So, decision made, she bent her knees and prepared her casting.

"Dicio, Āetis, Aura."

A light wind kicked up beneath her feet and she directed the force so it steadied her on each side. Then, lifting herself onto the awaiting square, she placed her feet with ease and clapped to release the energy.

Unable to help a smug smile, she turned to face the third level.

What greeted her first were the bright smiles of two girls, obviously twins, and each with a shock of red hair and piercing emerald eyes. Faint murmurs grew around her, quickly hushing as she tried to pinpoint the origins, and she suddenly felt nervous.

She stepped from the platform and cleared her throat. "Hello," she said, annoyed there was a slight wobble to her voice.

Only the twins seemed to acknowledge her, while the rest of the Mages all bowed quickly and dispersed, leaving Charlize with no choice but to engage with the girls before her.

"You know, you totally look like your photos."

Open mouthed, while gasps from passers-by made the twin who didn't speak turn and scowl, Charlize composed her face. "Did you expect someone different?" she replied, folding her arms.

Never had she seen girls who looked so odd before, their freckles and startled looking eyes as fascinating to her as she clearly was to them.

"Nah, I just reckoned you'd be taller."

Bursting into raucous laughter, the twins slapped each other on the back, but swiftly composed themselves when Charlize's expression remained stony.

The one with cropped hair held out her palm. "I'm Jess."

Charlize touched her palm tentatively, the sensation of pure Anima swirling between her fingers, and she knew Jess felt the five elements of Incendiī, Anima, Aquāe, Glacies, and the weaker gift of Fulgor sting along her hand.

The suddenly serious Mage lowered her gaze and nudged her sister, who had longer hair and fuller lips. "Go on, you do it," she whispered sharply.

"Alright, alright." Copying her sister, she said, "I'm Jade."

Charlize repeated the same action and received the same result. She nodded her head. "It's nice to meet you both, and to feel such strong Anima within you."

Jess shrugged and flicked the hair from her face. "Perks to being pure."

Having never been spoken to so bluntly before, Charlize couldn't fathom the shock needed to be offended, somehow finding Jess and Jade more refreshing than any Mage she'd ever encountered.

"You know, if anyone knew the way you spoke to me…"

"Oh, it's just her way Charlize, don't take offence, honestly," said Jade, wide-eyed.

Her tone was so sincere that it made Charlize laugh. "I can truly say that I don't. Between you and me, it's nice to meet Mages my own age who don't recoil the minute I speak."

Jade beamed, her lips spreading wide as they revealed rows of large white teeth. In spite of herself, Jess also smiled, scratching the back of her neck. "Yeah, well, we don't have those graces folk talk about."

"Even so, it was a pleasure to meet you both," said Charlize, walking past them and out onto the platform. She stopped as they called out:

"You like coffee?"

She nodded.

"Well, the school won't open for half an hour. Wanna get some?"

Contemplating the request for a few moments, it being the first time she was invited anywhere without her father, she nodded again.

Having run along several bridges until they reached a small decking area, alive with people casually sitting wherever they chose, the chill of the day seemed non-existent as Charlize settled into her wicker chair. The part of the Haunt she found herself in was decorated moderately, with fewer lanterns, sculptures, and paintings, but the buildings were larger and covered in camouflage netting that hung down like a blanket. She knew it was a disguise, another precaution in case any machines happened to fly over the village, but it was calmer high up, the air fresher and the scent of the ashen red bark earthy and rich. When she looked to the sky, she could see the tops of branches as they stretched towards the sun, while the rays enriched her with nutrients, even as her skin prickled with goose bumps.

The café they sat in was adjacent to a red brick building with the large words 'MUESUEM' written across a heavy wooden door studded with metal bolts. It was currently closed, although this did nothing to perturb the gathering of people enjoying the steps that led up to it.

What she noticed – more than the cake and biscuits on display – were the smiles. Whether it was the euphoria of being so high in the trees, or the fact that any sign of Minae seemed many miles away, she wasn't sure… But she did consider that it could be the other more unfamiliar scent in the air – the sweet smell of fermenting alcohol that sat atop the breeze and wafted seductively past them.

"You look tense."

Bringing her attentions back to her companions, Charlize looked at Jess, blinking to moisten her eyes. "My apologies, I was just admiring."

"It's cool if you're tense, makes sense that you are – ouch!"

Jess rubbed her ribs where Jade elbowed them and frowned.

Unable to hide her smile, Charlize picked up what was described to her as a vanilla latte. Taking a sip, the comforting sweetness tickled the back of her throat and warmed her to the core.

"Good right?" Jess piped up, forgetting her bruised rib. "We always come here to Summer Café. We'd go to Amanda's but it's overpriced."

"So, you both live here?"

"Born and bred," said Jess proudly.

"I see," Charlize replied, "and my schooling will be in your class?"

Jade nodded vigorously. "We've been so excited to meet you, everyone else has been dead nervous, but me and Jess knew you'd be cool."

Charlize laughed loudly, causing the other customers to peer up from their newspapers, and she put her hand over her mouth. "You two are quite something!" she whispered.

Before they could respond, three loud bells chimed and the twins suddenly launched into a flurry of action. They threw their coats and scarves on as they tugged Charlize from the café, who stared longingly after her half-drank latte as it disappeared from her grasp.

"Come on!" shrieked Jess as she tore through the crowds.

Market sellers with baskets around their necks, filled with various foods and trinkets, danced away as the three of them ran past – Jade now pulling Charlize by the hand.

They passed several platforms and bridges until they reached the library set back in a covert of branches. Stone steps led up to the entrance and the open doors looked welcoming as people came and went, some with books in their baskets, others with their nose already buried between the pages.

Here they slowed their pace to a brisk walk. A couple left the building hand in hand, laughing between themselves, and Charlize found herself staring after them, admiring the way they touched with ease, as if nothing in the world existed but their admiration for one another.

"Keep up!" shouted Jess, her arms gesticulating frantically.

"Of course!" Charlize called back, ignoring the odd sensation in her stomach as she caught up with the twins.

They passed another building; a stately looking manor stood proudly between two out-of-place evergreen ferns. Creepers ran the length of its brick surface, coming to a rest on the ledge of the windows and doorframe. It was a pretty house, although didn't quite fit with the surrounding forest décor.

"That," sounded Jade matter-of-factly, "is where Armmos and his wife live. It's also where *the* restaurant of the village is too, best grub going so they say."

"Very posh," said Jess in the best English accent she could muster, before swinging her hips and sauntering up the path towards the front door. She held her head in one hand and placed the other on her hip before continuing: "You make a reservation at the door." She mimicked the action. "You are settled in the highest quality chairs and served with

the highest quality wine and food; all paid for of course by your fair self."
Jade stifled a giggle. "Real money only *daaarling*, no trade," she said
drolly, sighing dramatically. "Then once you have your three course meal,
you can do…" For this she gave a dirty smile. "Whatever tickles your
fancy…"

Charlize knew there was a hidden meaning, but she couldn't place
exactly what. Instead, she applauded.

"Nice accent hey? Not all of us speak so good," Jess said pointedly.

"Well, not all of us need to," Charlize replied.

Jess eyed her for a moment, seemingly deciding something, and then
nodded towards Jade. "She's alright. You were right."

Beaming, Jade hooked her arm through Charlize's – an action she
found alien and awkward. But she didn't pull away in case she
accidentally caused offence, and was pleasantly surprised that she soon
found herself relaxing, the three of them falling into step as they chatted
spiritedly – right up until the moment they reached the end of the
platform. Just beyond it, the school loomed in front, its green gates open
wide as several Mages lounged in and around the grounds.

"Eurgh," grunted Jess.

And although Charlize hated to admit it, that sentiment reflected her
thoughts exactly.

26
Facts and Fiction

Walking into the small and airy classroom where paintings of oceans and marine life adorned the walls, the intricacy was breath taking. Each brush stroke seemed to tell a story and Charlize admired the skill greatly.

The carpet was light seaweed green and the entire room appeared to be underwater, something the painters captured completely, even with small details such as light refractions and dust particles.

Three wooden tables stood at the back of the classroom, each decorated with various sized jars of water housing creatures and plants. Charlize recognised some as tadpoles, triggering a memory of a family outing she and Christian had when they'd been around eleven years old.

The day was warm as they fished in the local park pond, squealing with delight as the baby frogs squirmed around their ankles, which they collected in glass jars. Charlize remembered the look on Theo's face when Christian innocently handed him a jar of dead ones, asking why they didn't swim like hers. Her father had smirked and hushed her attempts to explain, his finger tight to his lips.

Not that she could say anything anyway; her words were sealed, doomed never to repeat how a bolt shooting from Christian's eyes had killed them, his untamed power sparking in his excitement. They explained away his tendency to spark as minor electric shocks. It was rare, and when it happened, nothing more than amusing, although sometimes deadly for unassuming pond life…

Charlize felt the smile on her lips and readjusted her focus so she could examine the rest of the classroom. Jess and Jade were both sat on large cushions placed around a drawing board, each slouched casually as they waited for Mrs Arno to arrive.

They weren't waiting long before a voluptuous woman entered the room. Her long brown hair was braided into two plaits that touched her expanding waistline. They disappeared beneath her armpits as she flurried over to the wildlife and started humming, a flat tune made worse by the trills attempting to bolster it. She checked the thermometers on the tanks and flicked her braids behind her shoulders before huffing.

"You are getting far too big darlings," she said to the spawning frogs.

Charlize wasn't sure if the sniggers coming from Jess made her turn, or because she finally sensed their presence, but even so, her startled cry was so loud she found herself tensing.

"You scared me sweet hearts!" Mrs Arno exclaimed. "Nearly died on the spot I did!"

Forming an apology, Charlize stopped as she found herself smothered between two large breasts. Luckily, after only a few seconds, she was granted air, which she gratefully took a gulp of.

Mrs Arno then turned to the twins and frowned. "We knew this would happen; have they all run scared?"

"Dunno." Jess shrugged.

"Right," said Mrs Arno, clapping her hands and rubbing them together. "Well, we'll just have to make do." She waddled to the drawing board.

Without putting words to her thoughts, Charlize knew the people running scared were her other classmates, her legacy more illustrious in the haunts than anywhere else. She couldn't help but feel disappointed, and sitting on one of the cushions, put her chin in her hands.

Mrs Arno made to shut the door, but no sooner had she done so, she called out: "Ah, here we are – more arrivals!" She tutted and shook her head at several sheepish Mages walking in, their heads down as they flopped onto the remaining cushions.

Aware that all eyes stubbornly avoided looking at her, Charlize felt the same way she had at thirteen going to school with Christian for the first time. He'd told her off the entire day, coaxing her to make friends and stop being rude. But of course he didn't know why she couldn't, and when he found her at the end of the day, sitting alone on a patch of grass, he'd sighed. 'You don't help yourself you know.' She'd shrugged as he helped her up, but how she'd wished more than anything in that moment that she could have told him the truth.

"She don't bite," Jess snapped at a blonde girl who immediately went red.

Remembering where she was, Charlize warmed towards Jess even further. Jade giggled, although stopped as a withering look from Mrs Arno was sent her way.

"Perhaps we could introduce ourselves?" said a boy with the darkest skin Charlize had ever seen. His irises were bright white against the black of his pupils, framed by a thick set of lashes matching his coarse hair.

"That's an excellent idea Tunde, let's start with you."

The newly introduced Tunde revealed a dazzling smile as he faced Charlize. "I'm on my pilgrimage too; it's an honour to meet you."

Unable to form words, or take her eyes from his face, she smiled back, resisting the urge to reach out and touch him. Wearing a robe of the Anima, Tunde also wore a red wristband – symbolic of the Incendiī clan he belonged to.

A gentle jab of an elbow brought her back to reality and Charlize composed some words. "It is an honour too," she said.

Tunde bowed his head as further introductions were made, but Charlize barely listened. A raw strength emanated from him, his power touching her even as he sat several cushions away.

It was only when the lesson began her attentions finally turned.

Charlize left the classroom mesmerised. The words and way in which Mrs Arno spoke quickly earned her first place on the short list of Charlize's favourite teachers. She grinned from ear to ear as she stopped at the school gates and turned to the twins.

"I would never have thought to use a memory prism to reflect onto walls and then paint on top. I honestly think that kind of creativity is genius."

"Yeah, pretty niffy hey?!" replied Jade, opening the side gate.

Walking through, Charlize followed the twins towards a bench where the three of them sat down.

"Not sure how I feel being volunteered to help you volunteer mind you… if you know what I mean…" Jess's face looked sour as she kicked a stone towards the opposite tree.

Mrs Arno had earlier informed them how, as they seemed to get on so well, they made the perfect company to aid Charlize with her work while she resided in the Haunt.

"It's not so bad," said Jade. "It'll be fun, and we'll look important."

Jess snorted and rolled her eyes.

"Please, don't feel obliged; I am happy to go alone," said Charlize.

"I don't feel like that!" Jade cried.

There was something in her tone that made Charlize think she didn't know what 'obliged' meant. "No, I mean, you don't have to, it's okay if you don't want to."

Replacing her smile, Jade shrugged. "Oh, I don't mind!"

"Well, then your company would be most welcome."

Although Jess didn't confirm, Charlize knew she'd join them too. If there was one thing she was quickly learning about twins, it was they rarely separated.

A swift breeze blew through the deck, rousing the dust into a frenzy. Charlize shivered and pulled her coat tighter, noting how the twins did the same. And suddenly, a stirring in her gut caught her unawares and she stiffened.

"What's up?" asked Jess, peering inconspicuously through her hood.

Standing, Charlize took a step away from the bench, knees bent slightly. She squinted into the grey, noting how the deck was deserted, and turned back to the twins. "I think we need to leave."

"Who's that?"

Snapping her head towards what Jess pointed at, Charlize held up her hand to cast.

Stood several metres away and blurred by a soft mist, a man stood silently. There was such a stillness about him that if she didn't know any better, she'd assume he was a statue.

Behind her, she could feel the twins' presence on either side of her, their adrenaline pumping the magic through their potent blood.

"Can I help you?" Charlize called.

A slight shift in the man's demeanour made her steady her footing as he walked towards them. Hands tense, she held up her chin.

"Āetis," the man whispered, his voice somehow carrying on the wind.

"That's rude you know!" shouted Jess, quickly hushed by Jade.

Moments later, he came to a stop, his bulk formidable as he locked his gaze on Charlize. A mutilating scar across his jaw made his face seem uneven, but his dark eyes spoke of torment. He put his palm up and Charlize instinctively touched it, although snatched it away just as quickly, as if she'd been burnt.

"Incendiī-Anima; although strong, you insult me," she said, shaking her wrist to ease the stinging.

"Not as much as you insult *us* Āetis."

His voice was gravelly, the tone controlled as he composed his face. Something about it stirred a memory, but she didn't know why. Even so, as he leaned towards her, so close she could hear the smack of his lips as they opened, Charlize found herself unable to move.

"I had to make sure it was true," he whispered.

His breath was nauseating – and confusing; for within the proximity, she could smell death. Its cloying stench clung to him, as if he'd recently hugged a Ghul. But that was ridiculous. No one could get close to the Minae; not long enough for their essence to penetrate so deeply…

"Do you find me a lie?" she replied quietly.

A low growl tore from his throat and Charlize prepared a casting in her head.

"You're alive, and you're *female*." He spat the words as if they were a disease.

"And that angers you?"

Laughing, a wild and deep sound, he shook his head. "Not just me. Much has been sacrificed to stop you. You walk when you should not."

The words snapped Charlize into action and she sent a torrent of water flowing through her hand and into the man's stomach. He recoiled, yelping in pain, and darted into the air to be lost almost immediately.

"Let's go," Jade urged, pulling Charlize back towards the school.

The day, once holding such promise, seemed to darken as they returned to the classroom they previously vacated. Bursting into the room, they met Mrs Arno straight away. She stood with her arms folded across her chest.

"Has he gone?" she asked.

Charlize nodded. "How did you know?"

"I could feel him, a skill you'll soon learn."

"How did he get in?"

Mrs Arno shrugged. "That remains a mystery sweetheart. What did he want?"

Trying to find the words and fathom the reasons, Charlize shook her head. "He wanted me dead."

"That makes no sense," Jade snapped. "Why would any Mage want you dead, you're what we live for?"

"No, there was something wrong with him, he was weird," Jess replied, who had remained strangely silent.

Nothing more was said as Mrs Arno left the room.

Beyond the walls, a muffled conversation could be heard, followed by the shuffling of papers and a huge sigh. Reappearing a few minutes later, she held a clipboard in her hands.

"Right, I've called your parents. They'll be waiting for us at my house shortly. Come, we have matters to discuss."

27
Revelations

Charras was worried as Charlize and her new friends gathered in the sitting room of Armmos's large house. He hardly paid attention as he altered between looking out of the window while perched on the arm of the settee, to pacing a semi circle with his head bowed.

At some point, the new arrivals were offered tea, and they quietly drank from their quaint mugs, replacing the floral china on the saucer after each sip.

Charras, now sat on the window ledge, peered at Charlize and her friends lined up on the worn brown settees. Once again, he felt as if they'd invaded a school library. Literature lined the walls: leather bound; paperback; hardback; folders; binders – there seemed no style that wasn't present. Even a quintessential aged globe sat on a mahogany desk in the middle of the room.

Interspersed with the educational décor were several specimens of stuffed animals, and it quickly became apparent that Armmos's love of antiques and his wife's love of taxidermy contrasted dramatically, the random mix working more for them than it did for those who witnessed it.

Refusing the shortbread currently being wafted under his nose, Charras ignored the disappointment on Armmos's face as he replaced the dish back on a silver tray and stood to pour himself another tea. He then sat on the armchair Charras now perched on and took a breath.

"Gwen has told me the gist of things, but let me hear your account."

"It's as we explained. It all happened very quickly," Charlize replied.

"You didn't see where he went?" Charras grunted, clenching his fists as he stared at his daughter. The fury emanating from him made the twins avert their gaze.

Charlize shook her head. "He left the minute I cast."

Charras stood up and ran his hands through his hair, before gritting his teeth and resuming his pacing.

"It's a good job no one got hurt," said Jess and Jade's mother, putting her arms around her daughters.

She had exactly the same shock of red hair and green eyes, although her hair grew more wildly with the curls branched out from her scalp like she'd been electrocuted.

Mrs Arno nodded in agreement and took another biscuit. "His essence was corrupt, that was for sure."

Halting his pace, Charras sat back on the arm of the chair and adamantly stared at the coffee table. There was something in Armmos's curious glance towards him that caught Charlize's attention.

"What is it father; what do you know?" she asked.

Without looking at her, Charras instead looked to Armmos, his eyes almost pleading. The leader gave a slight nod of his head, followed by a short sigh as he put his cup and saucer on the coffee table, granting whatever request was silently begged of him.

With a deep breath, he addressed Charlize. "There are Mages out there who wish you harm."

Dumbstruck, and happy to see the twins reflected the same sentiment, she frowned. "But why?"

He gave another sigh and sat back. "You must understand young Āetis, that you are the first of your kind."

At first Charlize didn't understand. Then, as it slowly dawned on her, she looked towards her father.

"You knew didn't you?" she accused.

He shook his head. "I did not know the extent of some people's prejudices," he said bitterly.

Fire crackled through the atmosphere between them, forcing Armmos to once again break the tension. "You are as prepared as any before you Charlize. Yet change is difficult at best for some who have followed the ways for so long. They only need to see your spirit and strength for themselves before you will be accepted."

"What of those who can't?"

Armmos sighed for a third time. "There are those who conspire against you. They do not believe that you will win this war and they doubt your ability in completing your purpose."

"I am no coward!" Charlize burst, standing in outrage. "I know my purpose as well as I know the fate if I fail. There is no question of that."

Armmos held his hands up in defence. "It is not the opinion the majority of us share. We trust in the Sky's selection of you," he assured, offering her the space on the seat again.

The words still stinging however, Charlize defiantly crossed her arms.

"Have respect," her father warned, his tone low. "Unlike some, you have been brought up to honour those who fight for you. Armmos is not the enemy."

"How far does it go? I have been threatened with an earlier death than I already have. Why would any Mage do that, whether they believe in me or not? Surely conspiring to kill me would certify the doom they foretell?" Another wave of fire washed over her as her father's anger radiated. "How far?" she repeated when no answer was forthcoming.

As if the room was empty, Charras focused solely on his daughter. Reaching within, he found the courage to speak the words he could barely believe himself.

"They have a leader," he said, his words heavy. "The demon Vrealâ."

Although Charlize defied her emotions, her body would not as her knees buckled and she found herself sitting back on the settee.

"Vrealâ?" she mumbled, rolling her tongue around the word. "She's behind this?"

Charras nodded.

"And Mages are *following* her?" she confirmed, the idea implausible.

"To what extent we are not certain," Armmos added.

Jess and Jade looked at each other, until that moment completely silent. It was Jess who spoke.

"So what you're saying is that Vrealâ, the new demon no one has actually seen before, has suddenly come out of hiding to get loads of people on side, and is now going about trying to find a way to kill Charlie?" Holding up her finger as Armmos tried to interject, she continued. "And the only way she's managing all this is because some traitors out there don't believe a *girl* can win a war, or that she's too cowardly to even fight it?"

"Yes, put simply," said Armmos.

Whistling, Jess slapped her legs. "That's madness."

"We are doing all we can to rectify this. You must not let it dishearten you Charlize, it is a minority."

The kindness in Armmos's words evident, Charras patted his back and Mrs Arno squeezed his knee. In a small way, this lightened Charlize's mood.

"Thank-you for your support," she said, before standing once again. "I don't mean to be rude, but I think I need some time alone."

"I don't think it's safe," said Charras, picking up his coat.

"Does this mean we're all in danger?" Jade asked, her eyes wide as she looked towards Armmos.

Touching her temples, Charlize nodded. "Of course, how silly of me. You both have been so kind, but it's best you –"

"Bring it," said Jess. "You're safer with us than on your own. We'll make sure nothing hurts you."

"Girls, I don't think that's the best idea," said Mrs Arno quietly, to the thankful smile of the twins' mother.

"I think the three of us would be safe, we're all strong," replied Jade, confronting the adults. "If our Āetis, (and she whispered the word Āetis) is in danger, then we should help protect her. And as we're the only ones who aren't scared of her, then we're the best for the job."

After a few moments pause, the twins' mother dropped her shoulders, her chest deflated. "Let's not decide this now; we can talk more with your pa later tonight."

Jess and Jade beamed, which Charlize took as a sign that they knew their mother had been defeated.

A quick clap of hands broke the silence and all eyes turned to Mrs Arno. "You're all staying for tea I hope? I've shut the restaurant in favour of my guests tonight."

Polite murmurs all confirmed their attendance and Charlize began to take off her coat. It was only as a sudden thought hit her she twisted and ran for the door.

28
Alone

... *Lessons are never something to be taught. A true lesson is something you experience at the beginning, which then changes you at the end."* Quote: Lady Gamnel of Hertfordshire.

And so your journey has begun young Strike, a lesson unique to you. You must find your own path, for self-discovery is not about being told how to do something; it's about deciding what feels right to you.

So what is different about this lesson? Well, it is part of a puzzle. That puzzle helps discover and hopefully steer for good the fate of the world. A heavy burden indeed, yet not one you will carry alone. To explain, Diana II of Hammersmithe, Londres put it most eloquently in 1950.

"Years have passed, time changing with each modernisation, and yet the Mages stay the same, adapting as best we can. It is no secret we are growing tired and restless as a race, the Ungifted developing within their confines as fast as bacteria in a petri dish. Soon, they will discover what we protect them from. And who can blame them, living how they do? Is it right to cage an animal that deserves to be free? Even for its own good? Is freedom not a basic human right? Is it not what we fight for every day?

So, where's the progress? It's been nine hundred years, nine hundred years and generations and generations of sacrifice for an uncertain end. Why do we fight, why must we continue to stand against the darkness in the face of such challenges and uncertainty?

Because we are light. We are charged with power and hope, and a promise that this earth and its inhabitants will not suffer at the hands of evil. We are weapons against that evil, Mages with the power to give freedom in death, the power to grant final rest, and the power to restore balance, as is the true nature of the universe. We are not alone, the Sky and the representation of its light in our Orbis will guide us until the end comes, until we can finally rest. We must not give up hope. We are at war and we are light. We must put an end to the defiance of death, and an end to our secret."

'When the war is waged and won,
when good or evil is overcome.
Then begins a future new,
of love or hate through and through.'

"Always makes light reading," Christian said aloud.

Not that anyone was there to hear him. Charras had left hours ago, his short grunted warning to stay inside confining him to the cottage – which had turned curiously cold.

Placing his book on the cushion he hugged to his stomach, Christian lowered them both to the floor and stood to stretch his legs. He cracked his knuckles and then cupped his hands to his mouth, heaving air from his lungs in an attempt to warm them. Then, mumbling a short curse, he looked to the window and the source that disturbed him from his reading.

Rain hammered outside, its heavy onslaught quickly turning the wood into a gleaming surface of damp. It didn't touch the cottage he sought shelter beneath, whatever enchantment worked into the roof directing the flood away. Grateful, he stood, watching and wondering – not for the first time, where Charlize and Charras were.

It wasn't long before he saw a large figure cross the bridge, a heavy coat wrapped tightly around his shoulders, and he breathed a sigh of relief. *Finally* he thought.

Making his way to the door, something in his gut stopped him. It was the slightest sensation, yet it immediately put him on guard, and without knowing why, he dipped into the shadows and pressed his back against the wall closest to the door, just out of sight of the windows.

Held there, as if a primal instinct sensed the danger, he waited. The shadows that loomed in front suddenly seemed foreboding and he found himself afraid of the close proximity. Another shadow streaked across the floor, growing in bulk as the window silhouetted its existence to

Christian's left, and he pressed further into the wall.

Time passed slowly, his breath held, and just when he thought he would pass out, the shadow receded and he slowly emptied his lungs, light headed from the effort. Beads of sweat fell down his face, the cottage warmer now adrenaline pumped through his blood, but he still didn't dare move.

"I know you're there."

Frozen, as if space and time fragmented, Christian felt his heart reach his throat. Facing the door as the handle slowly turned, he realised the only option left to him. Two short knocks – one harder than the other – spurred him into action as he relinquished his station from the wall and ran at full speed towards the bedroom. The window was open and he darted towards it, clambering over the beds that blocked his way, but before he reached it, he was yanked backwards, a force on his ankle that sent him careering into the far wall. Although winded, he wasted no time trying to assess his attacker, instead using his energy to dart back into the sitting room and make for the door.

He slammed into it, surprised that it remained locked as before. *What the…*

"There you go again, running as before."

Fear and recognition flooded Christian's being as if he'd just faced the darkest recess of his soul, and it rendered him useless as his knees buckled. With hope of escape lost, he turned to face his tormentor, the man who helped capture his parents standing merciless and massive before him.

"That's better," he snarled.

Crossing the distance between them, his attacker heaved him to his feet, bringing his disfigured face so they were inches apart. "You've caused quite the commotion."

"Where are my parents?!" Christian demanded, his voice tenuous with his throat constricted.

The man merely laughed and threw him against the kitchen island.

Christian hit his head and slumped to the floor, disorientated. He shook himself, refusing to give in, and clambered to his feet, holding the counter for support as he scowled at his attacker. "Where are they?" he said again, somewhat more coherently.

Outside, a thunderclap sounded and the rain seemed to highlight the choking atmosphere within the cottage. The silence that followed allowed Christian to find his nerve.

In a calmer tone, he said, "What do you want with me?"

The man clenched his fists, took a step closer, and mumbled something beneath his breath. Seconds later, his hands were alight and a strange expression crossed his face. He took three deep breaths, the inhalation and exhalation reminding Christian of the meditation he saw Charlize perform most evenings. Then the fire went out and he looked distinctly worn, the hunger that once burned brightly dimmed beneath his stare.

It was in that moment Christian decided to run. Shouting a quick curse, he hunched his shoulders and lunged forwards using a tackle stance he often performed at Rugby matches.

He wasn't the strongest, he knew that, but he was still surprised when his shoulder struck just below the ribcage of his parent's kidnapper and he didn't move an inch.

As if he were nothing more than a nuisance fly, he found himself swatted to the floor, before just as quickly being suspended between the grasp of thickset fingers, unable to do more than stare back at the man smiling menacingly at him.

"First a coward and now a hero. There's still some fight in you."

Christian struggled against the unyielding grip: kicking out; flailing his arms and legs, only to make little to no impact; trying to shout, although quickly stopping as he managed nothing but a hoarse whisper, and finally giving in when his air supply was barely permissible.

It soon dawned on him that there was no rescue shortcoming, and with nothing left to lose, he tried a different tactic.

Conserving his last breath, he rolled his eyes into the back of his head and let his body slowly relax until he went limp. It wasn't difficult; the world about him started to wane and his previous adrenaline merely thudded dully in his ears, there to remind him of his weakness. But it seemed to work, and his assailant dropped him to the floor where he crumpled convincingly.

Keeping his eyes closed as the man stepped towards the door, he felt his presence withdraw. A soft *click* of a lock seemed louder in the quiet, and then Christian felt hands grasp his underarms. He concentrated on not responding as he was heaved roughly over a large shoulder.

"All this for an unbecome…" the man muttered.

Christian dared to open his eyes, dismayed how the floor was still a fair distance away, the man easily standing at nearly seven foot. His plan would require further mathematics… He would have to act fast too. There was a small window where the element of surprise would work in his favour, but when that was gone, he could only rely on his hurdles record from the Marsh Village fete to aid his escape.

He was just reminiscing about his trophy on the mantelpiece at home when the sound of voices in the distance piqued his interest. Sharp shouts fired off one after the other as faint footsteps thudded against wood, and a screech of hinges followed by more footsteps gave Christian a twinge in his stomach. It was his only hope…

Seeming to hear it too, the man perked up, his shoulders flexed as he secured Christian by his arm and ankle. He let out a short growl as he prepared his sharp exit.

Two things happened then. Firstly, the kidnapper kicked open the door, sending it flying off its hinges onto the deck below. Secondly, Christian wrenched his body from the momentarily slack grasps around his wrist and ankle and swung himself down his attackers back. His surprise was evident as he whipped around and tried to re-affirm his hold, his cumbrous mass hindering him in the open space, and it gave Christian enough time to dart away and make for the voices he hoped he hadn't imagined.

The rain had eased but the wood remained soaked, the sheen a warning to tread lightly, even as his body screamed to run no matter the consequences. Around him the air seemed close, while the clouds above doused the Haunt in a bleak greyness that offered no relief.

He reached the glade's bridge where he slowed and stepped onto the first board, catching himself on the railings as his foot slipped. Red faced as his heart thrummed in his ears, he stood once again, and with a quick glance behind him, noticed that the platform was empty. Turning back, he let out a cry of alarm as his attacker stepped from the air and blocked his escape.

"How?!" he shouted, retreating slightly.

How, and why? They were questions that burned in him.

Christian backed up until his feet found the platform once again, and spinning around, he forced his tired limbs to carry him to safety.

His pursuer had other ideas however, managing to block his every move, using his air trickery at every turn to send him running back and forth, like a cat and mouse chase, him being the mouse with nowhere to hide. And when it was clear his efforts were futile, Christian dropped to his hands and knees.

The wood beneath him cool, he let his chest heave in the air he sorely needed. He didn't need to look up to know he wasn't alone, the bulk warm and imposing as it closed in on its catch.

"Why?" Christian asked again.

Hot breath brushed against his ear as he was dragged to his feet. "Because we need you."

With a hopeless laugh, Christian looked up. "For what? You got some big guys you need me to take care of?"

The man leaned in close so his face was level with Christian's. He could see the crease in the man's skin where the scar gouged its home, his inane smile further deforming his features.

"Your parent's didn't say you were funny."

Without thinking, Christian swung his fist towards his tormentor's smug face, every piece of anger and confusion concentrated into his attack.

It was no use though. With a reaction twice as fast, his target caught his wrist and bent it backwards with such a force that he heard his bone snap before he felt it.

All colour drained from his face as he cradled his wrist, fighting the urge to throw up and scream at the same time. Hate and anger coursed through him as the nauseating pain seared along his arm, and he knew he was nothing more than a minor nuisance to his attacker, a mere flea to a horse. There was nothing more he could offer in the way of resistance; it was over.

So it was with minor confusion he saw Charlize race towards them.

Hands splayed and face taut, she looked every bit the warrior charging into war. Behind her, two bright haired girls kept pace, their faces contorted in the same way. *So he hadn't imagined it.* The thought gave him reassurance.

"How dare you come here!" screeched Charlize, sending a firebolt into the stomach of the man she reproached. He stumbled backwards, tripped over Christian, and landed on his back.

The three girls circled him. "What brings you here?!" said Charlize, her eyes alight as she demanded an answer, standing so assuredly Christian wondered if she was the same person.

He knew there would be no answer, and closing his eyes as the throbbing in his wrist intensified, the world began to spin. A brief scuffle ensued, followed by a cry as someone hit the deck, but Christian no longer had the energy to pull himself away. Instead, he rest his head on the wood beneath him, the cool moisture a welcome relief. He could fight no longer. And just as he accepted his fate, a voice full of the fury of a storm echoed through the glade.

"Tiron!"

Suddenly, with that one word, it all came back to him. The name Charras spoke with such venom released Christian's memory with the force of a bolt to the head, and the fateful night of his parents capture flooded through his consciousness.

There had been three, the other brawn named Bahmut, and the third, a female, cloaked in black with eyes of blue blazing beneath her hood. Her face was whiter than snow but for a slit where a mouth should be, blood dripping and congealing like a sinister lipstick.

The three of them spoke about a purpose, about the one they sought being connected with him. Concentrating, he tried to remember, his mind piecing together the jumbled sentences as he listened to his painful memories.

He watched them torture his parents as he sat shaking on the stairs, too cowardly to confront the people that bruised his mother and held his father by the throat. They demanded to know his connection, to know the reasons his fate was unknown. They asked why he didn't know of his heritage; they called them traitors and spat in their faces.

Then they spoke his name and he fled, his mother's screams echoing in his ears as he fought his way past to collect her. Together they could escape, he'd been so sure…

There had been colours, lights, and noises he couldn't determine – but then he was free and the night air enclosed him, his legs taking on a life of their own as he ran to his car and drove away.

It wasn't until he reached Charras's house, until he was certain of his safety that he became aware of where he was. And blocking out the truth, about how his parents lay dying to save him, he collapsed by the gates, knowing, one day, he'd remember how he betrayed them.

29

Snow White Syndrome

Stirring from broken sleep, Christian groaned. His wrist still throbbed, the skin strangely reddened where the fingers of Tiron left their mark, but no matter the pain, he knew he deserved worse.

Trauma had a way of blocking out painful memories. He'd heard the tales of men and women turned to madness because of denial, false recollections and lies they eventually believed. But he would not let that be him. He knew his cowardice well. The weakness of his fear stung him every time he remembered how he'd fled, run from the suffering his parents endured because he was too feeble to help them.

He shifted his weight onto his side and stared at the white curtains surrounding him. Instruments of steel and plastic lined shelves and trolleys, their purpose to detect injury and aid healing lying inert and unassuming before him. How he envied their disassociation from their purpose, oblivious of the good or bad they inflicted – free from guilt. If a patient died at the hands of unskilled scissor wielders, or lived because of a tightened bandage, they would know nothing of it.

With a bitter laugh, Christian rubbed his face. To be envious of inanimate objects… now that was a new low…

He lay there for some time, aware of the aching in his limbs and the pulsing of his wrist, but caring little about it. The hospital bed was warm, although the sheets were thin and quickly tangled between his legs, and they smelled of paint stripper, only marginally better than the underlying scent of bleach everywhere else.

It was no matter though. He had nowhere to be… and he didn't want to face anyone just yet anyway.

With that thought, a sense of calm washed over him and he began to daydream, recreating every eventuality of the night his parents were taken.

In one fantasy, he would become inhumanly strong and destroy the three intruders with nothing more than a swipe of his almighty fists – while in another, he would fight valiantly by his parent's side and prevail in the face of certain death.

There were many ways he achieved victory, some more fanciful than the other, and he smiled with smugness each time he overthrew his enemies, clenching and unclenching his stomach with every fatal blow.

It was only when he tired of fighting he succumbed to the truth: there was no way he could have saved them, but he still chose to abandon them.

The curtain pulling aside startled Christian from his maudlin thoughts. Grateful for it, he attempted to sit up as a nurse perched next to his bandaged wrist. She smiled kindly and propped the bed so he was upright, before returning to her place by his side and continuing to redress his wound. There was no eye contact while she worked, although the small talk was a welcome exchange after a day of quiet. She explained how the infection had begun to respond to the salve, and gently cleaned the exposed wounds, pointing out the progress. It took a while, and Christian winced several times, especially when she applied tincture of iodine, but he was grateful, and as she replaced the salve and wrapped his hand and wrist in fresh cotton gauzes, he thanked her sincerely.

Nodding once, she handed him several painkillers and pulled back the curtain to leave.

"Wait!" he said.

The nurse turned to face him, her round eyes meeting his gaze for the first time. She seemed agitated, but allowed his question nonetheless.

"Is there any change?" he asked.

The nurse shook her head and withdrew. She had no intention of staying for long. A nice boy, no doubt – but she'd heard the rumours before confirming them herself. An unknown entity within their midst, brazenly walking around… who would have thought it?! It appeared *this* Āetis had a habit of breaking rules…

As the curtain swung back into place, Christian sighed and pressed himself into the pillow. Although the hospital staff were kind, each politely ignoring the fact he was unbecome and therefore illegal in the Haunt, he sensed their guarded approach every time they touched him. It was a minor annoyance, and one paled against the growing concern he had for Charlize.

Charras and the nurses he'd managed to engage in conversation assured him she was fine and stable, but surely if that were true she'd be awake by now? Instead, she seemed to be in some sort of coma with no indication of when she might re-join the waking world. What frustrated him further was that every attempt he'd made to see her resulted in him being marched back to his bed for more rest.

All he could do was wait.

Christian wasn't sure what time he drifted off, but the ward seemed darker and the cries and murmurs of patients and visitors fewer when he awoke.

Stretching out his arms and legs, noting the strain on his limbs was less painful, an idea struck him. He'd have to act fast though; the nurses were diligent in their rounds.

He felt galvanised as he swung his legs to the floor, his body twisting in response, and he slipped off the bed, his excitement driving his wooden limbs to regain control. Bending and extending his knees, feeling the blood rush to aid him, he took two tentative steps. A smile of resolve spread across his face when his body responded normally, and he carefully parted the curtains to peer into the ward.

He was in the last cubicle, as far away from the other Mages as they could place him – obviously put there as a precaution in the event of any mishap involving the other patients. The thought amused him, how being unbecome was seen as dangerous, and yet all any Mage had to do was cast and he'd be at their mercy.

The magical globular lights overhead, dimmed for the evening, cast a soft reflection on the strangely empty, although pristine floor. As he continued to stare, his smile soon turned into a frown.

Something didn't seem right.

Before he considered it further, the nurse from earlier crossed the ward, a man clearly her superior walking alongside. Engaged in an intense whispered conversation, they kept their heads together before passing the corridor and disappearing into another section of the hospital.

Waiting until their footsteps sufficiently withdrew, Christian made his move and crept from his synthetic prison, tiptoeing towards the nurse's office situated opposite him. Unusually, the door was open, the filing cabinets, an ancient looking computer, and several spare medical supplies all exposed to potential snoops. If he had more time, his curiosity may have gotten the better of him. Instead, and lucky for whichever staff member had made the faux pas, his mission was of a different kind that hour.

He reached the cross section, grateful his bare feet padded quietly on the tiles beneath them, and quickly peered out to the left and right. Once again, there was no sign of life.

With an intake of breath, he darted across the intersection and bounded through the singular curtained partition next to the office. Drawing them shut, while silently congratulating himself on the success of his mission, Christian turned around.

Peering up at him, a picture of calm, was one of the red haired girls he'd seen trailing Charlize during his attack.

"Wow, you look like –"

"I know."

"How's your hand?"

Looking down at his bandages, Christian shrugged. "Pretty painful," he admitted.

"Does it burn?"

He nodded.

Lying whatever book she'd been reading on the floor, the girl stood up. "Bet you're glad you aren't Aquāe then huh?"

Unsure why that would matter, Christian shrugged.

The girl took a step towards him and narrowed her eyes. "I'm Jess," she said, holding up her palm.

Considering her for a few seconds, sceptical of her motive, Christian placed his palm against hers, as he'd seen Charras and Charlize do with countless other Mages. He waited for the familiar look of shock and fear to cross her face, but was surprised when she merely tilted her head, smiled, and then dropped her hand to her side.

"Take it you didn't feel a thing?" she asked.

"No," Christian confirmed.

"Weird…"

Jess sat back in her chair and crossed her legs. She picked up her book, and then just as quickly replaced it, looked at him, and sighed. "So, you don't even know what you are?"

"I'm a Mage."

Jess laughed, a grainy sound that seemed at odds with her slender body. "I am pure Anima," she explained, tapping her chest as if she were talking to a child. "What clan are you?"

Until then, Christian had never thought to ask. Both Charlize and Charras surely knew, but guarding information from him was a habit they only broke if he asked – lest his brain suddenly explode.

"I don't know."

"Well you aint Aquāe or Glacies, or that wrist of yours would probably have to be amputated."

Christian looked horrified, so Jess continued. "We all have opposites: Incendiī and Aquāe; Fulgor and Glacies; Incendiī and Glacies; Fulgor and Aquāe – you see? Aquāe and Glacies are the closest related elements and Anima's the only neutral element. It can hurt any other element, yet also *be* hurt by any other element."

"So when will I know what I am?"

Jess's eyes flashed as he asked the question, and she seemed guarded when she replied. "When you become it. Haven't you ever figured it out yourself? I think I knew the day of my Awakening, before they even told me. I could *feel* it, you know?"

"I've never thought about it. There's been so much," he waved his hand around, "stuff. It's kept my thoughts elsewhere."

"Weird…"

"You like that word," Christian mumbled, offended, although not sure why. "Is that why most of the Mages here avoid me? I'm some sort of freak?"

Her face softening, Jess leaned forward, narrowing her eyes once more. "Nah, they're all just scared of you. Until you're a fully-fledged member of the Mage community, we aren't gonna know much about you. Fear of the unknown and all that… your magic isn't connected yet, you need to 'become' before you can cast freely, and all that takes about four years, unless you're the –"

Clutching her throat, Jess coughed, her face red as she felt the full weight of the binding in her throat. For the first time, she looked scared. Then, as if a realisation just dawned on her, she looked to the bed and then back at Christian. "Shit," she said.

"You can't tell me?" Christian assumed.

She shook her head, and in a softer voice said, "You need to finish your book. Then we can chat."

Unsurprised, but disappointed at the same, Christian resolved to read with added fervour the minute he returned to the cottage. All these secrets he didn't or couldn't know… how was he to ever understand the world he was a part of if no one could tell him about it?

"You come to check on her then?" Jess asked.

Almost forgetting why he'd made the perilous journey, risking the wrath of the matron nurse to attend Charlize's bedside, Christian nodded and walked over to where she lay.

Her face calm, as it always was when she slept, he smoothed a strand of ebony from her cheek, re-joining it with the mass of hair that fanned her pillow. She wore the same garb as he did – and it was only at that moment he realised he'd been talking to Jess in nothing but an open backed mint gown. Blushing, glad of the underpants he insisted on wearing, he pushed the thought aside and returned his attention to Charlize.

There was something final about the way her hands lay clasped across her chest; the mint seemed to pale her and there was a heaviness to her lids. He didn't like it, and something in his stomach stirred. Reaching out, he placed his hands on hers, shaking them gently as he murmured her name.

"She isn't gonna wake up Christian, go back to your bed so the docs don't hear you," said Jess.

"Why, what's wrong with her?" he asked.

With the same soft tone as before, she replied, "Read your book; that'll explain it."

Christian didn't want to leave. He wasn't sure what he expected to happen, but he knew that Jess wouldn't allow him to stay much longer, certain she hadn't turned a page in her book since his arrival.

Deflated, he gave Charlize one last glance before forcing himself to walk to the gap where the curtains met. Poking his head out, he assessed his return, still mildly concerned how the corridors seemed empty.

"Where is everyone?" he said aloud, not really expecting an answer.

"Beats me," Jess replied, her voice coming from over his shoulder. "We're just making sure sleeping beauty doesn't get disturbed."

Peering round to face her, noticing for the first time how green her eyes were, Christian smiled. "You know, I didn't thank you for what happened, about how you saved my life and all. I owe you."

Jess snorted. "You owe me nothing, it doesn't work like that."

"Even so," Christian said. "Thanks."

The look he received confirmed he'd outstayed his welcome and he made to open the curtains.

"Wait!" Jess warned, grabbing his shoulder. "Someone's coming."

"What?!" whispered Christian, darting back into the cubicle.

"Under the bed!" Jess said, pointing sharply at the floor.

Christian wasted no time in doing what she asked. Dashing over, he dropped to his front and slid himself so his feet hit the wall and his head faced the foot of Jess's chair. Luckily, the space beneath the bed was shallow – all he had to do was stay quiet and hope the unoriginality of it was effective.

True to her word, the footsteps Jess foretold quickly echoed through the hospital. Hurried chatter sounded throughout as instructions were given and more footsteps sounded off in different directions.

Seconds later, the curtains were thrust open, the screech of hooks against the track opening a gap big enough for three sets of legs to walk though.

"Any change?" one of the sets of legs asked.

"None," Jess replied, placing her book on the chair and standing at the foot of the bed.

Christian resisted the urge to reach out and clasp her ankle, although the thought made him smile.

"We need to move her," the same voice explained.

"Why?"

He could almost see the frown on Jess's face.

"Her father and Armmos wish it."

To clarify the point, a wheelchair was hastily rolled through by another set of legs before the rest of them surrounded the bed. With a quick countdown from four, they heaved Charlize into the chair.

"Go and tell them she's on her way," a different, obviously senior set of legs said.

"No, I'm staying with her," Jess shot back, an edge in her voice that said she wouldn't back down.

"Very well."

The legs all shuffled to depart the cubicle, following the squeak of rusted wheels. They'd not walked far before Christian heard his name. It was so quiet; at first he thought he'd imagined it.

Then, slightly louder, he heard it again.

It was weak and lethargic, as if she spoke from another dimension, but to him it sounded like the ringing of harmony bells and he almost left his hiding place to embrace her.

"It's alright Charlie, he's alright. We're just gonna take you home."

Joy flooded him where he remained hidden, waiting for the moment he could return to his own bed. She was okay and she asked for him, that was the best part. The first name she spoke was his – he just *knew* the doctors didn't know what they were talking about – all their arrogance and fancy medical words trying to confuse him and all she needed was a little nudge.

Lost within his own smug musings, Christian barely registered another set of footsteps. It was only as the ward grew silent and they remained heavy and cautious, he realised they weren't supposed to be there.

30

Escape

Christian felt the all-too-familiar feeling of his heart rise in his throat, the cold surface of the polished floor knowing its every beat. His whole body tingled with fear, and as the steps got closer and louder, he knew it was a matter of minutes before they discovered him.

A shift of material revealed two large leather boots, worn and dirtied as they entered the cubicle. Bizarrely, Christian found himself slightly peeved that they sullied the cleanliness surrounding them, but remained fixated as they moved to the end of the bed. He swore he heard several intakes of air, as if someone was *sniffing* out his location, and for the first time, he was grateful for the overpowering stench of bleach.

Sweeping from one side of the cubicle to the other, the boots suddenly stopped at the edge of the bed to Christian's right. Not moving a muscle, even as the throbbing in his wrist seemed noticeably more concentrated, he waited, certain he'd soon come face to face with the man intent on capturing him.

A loud crash made him jump as something fell to the floor further down the ward. It rolled for several seconds before hitting an obstacle and stopping. The silence that lingered seemed to stretch on for hours before the boots slowly moved away, disappearing back through the curtains.

Christian listened as the footsteps made their way around the ward. Further sounds of disturbed material could be heard, quickly descending into frantic scraping as partitions were swept aside with less and less caution.

Frightened whispers began to grow in urgency, and then a brave man cried out: "Who's there?!"

Faced with whoever was there, the man's cry was cut short and Christian sucked in his breath, fearing the worst.

"Where is the unbecome?" he heard the cold voice of Tiron demand.

Small whimpers resonated, followed by the scuffle of several patients attempting to escape. The sound of short thumps and more cries made Christian guess they hadn't got far.

"The... the last cubicle... that's where they kept him," said a young girl.

A soft thud sounded where Tiron obviously dropped her, and she broke into retching sobs, quickly consoled by someone Christian assumed was her mother. They were also promptly silenced.

Next, the ripping of another curtain echoed through the ward – presumably the one that used to conceal him, and Christian winced as Tiron roared upon finding the bed empty. He tried to think of a plan, acutely aware that he could do little in his current useless state. But he reminded himself that he'd escaped Tiron once before, so surely he could do it again...

Sliding to the right, Christian pulled himself towards the far side of the bed, ready to prove his worth in the form of a personal best sprint. Yet, before he even got close to escaping, a strong gust circled the ward.

It was as if a hurricane chose to invade. Instruments began clattering to the floor; trolleys and tables upturned in the sudden offensive, and every curtain billowed violently before lifting above their tracks to reveal the occupants of each cubicle.

From beneath the bed, which was luckily bolted to the floor, Christian could see a huddle of bodies behind Tiron, each clung to one another as they hid their heads in their hands. He tried to spot any sign of injury, but he was too far away to see. But what he did notice was their apparent inability to move, and keeping his eyes on them as the winds grew louder and stronger, he watched as they began to slide across the floor, remaining rigid in their group.

Christian soon felt his own legs sliding out beneath him, and turning himself onto his back, he grabbed the bed slats with his good hand and dug his toes into the underside. Above him, the sheets on the mattress flew into the far wall, sticking there as if glued, and in response, he tightened his grip. He wasn't sure how long he could hold on for. Tiron was relentless; he wouldn't give up until he had what he wanted.

A sharp pain on his scalp made Christian yelp, and he turned to see a large metal instrument hurtle past the bed, having ricocheted off his head to join the upturned chair in the far corner. He yearned to rub the violent throbbing, but tried his best to ignore it by sucking in a breath and closing his eyes.

The world seemed to wane slightly. He could hear the air thrashing around him, throwing people and objects into whatever wall was available, no care or emotion; just raw, arrogant, merciless power. It was the apex predator, intent to play with its prey before finally finishing it off.

Christian knew it was no use. Whatever had hit him weakened his grip, and one by one, his fingers came loose, until all he held on with was his thumb. He pressed his toes further into the bed slats and managed to reinstate his index finger as another bout of wind poured beneath the bed. He clenched his jaw as the sound of wood splitting dropped to his stomach. *No no no!* He heard himself screaming.

But it was too late. The crack and groan of the slats beneath his feet quickly buckled, sending him careering into the far wall with the mattress and remains of the broken bed.

The winds stopped then, and everything airborne began to rain down in a collusion of abolition. Finding himself under the mattress, Christian pressed his body as close to the ground as he could, glad of his protection from the potential injuries clattering around him.

When all fell quiet, he wasted no time pulling himself from the rubble, breathing in the calm air that greeted him. Certain that Tiron had spotted him, he stood to his full height and assessed his surroundings. The curtains of the cubicle were back in their natural position, although they hung dirtied and askew. An opening between them revealed the extent of Tiron's rampage, the floors littered and broken, and clearing a patch of floor with his toes, Christian readied himself, shaking out his limbs and carefully touching the bruise on his head. There was a slight protrusion, but he was glad to note it wasn't bleeding.

Then, with prudently placed footing, he tiptoed across the cubicle and parted the curtains, before slipping out into the ward. He was just about to run when he spotted the huddle of patients in the same position as before. Some of them were hurt, he could see from the bruises and scratches on their arms and faces, but as far as he could tell, they'd all survived. With no sign of Tiron, and the ward eerily still, Christian made his way towards them. A little girl, no older than ten – and the one who he guessed revealed his whereabouts – began to struggle when she saw him approach.

He held up his hands and knelt beside her. "I'm not going to hurt you," he said. Her eyes were alight and he could both sense and see her fear.

He reached out, his hand meeting the resistance trapping the group: a stream of air that weaved its way around them like a knot. A memory flashed of the protection spell that wound around Charras and Charlize's manor, and a hit of nostalgia plunged to his stomach.

"How do I help?" he asked a man with a cut above his eyebrow.

The man shook his head and opened his mouth so Christian could see another spell that bound his tongue.

"I'll get help," he said, standing back up and looking for an escape.

He spotted a window at the far end of the cross section, opened just a smidgen, and made towards it. Dubious about leaving the remaining patients to their fate, but knowing he was of no use, he pushed open the window as far as it would go and climbed out, dropping down and landing heavily on a couple of shrubs and petunia plants.

"Shit," he cursed, dusting himself down.

The air was cool as he stepped off the flowerbed and looked up at the eight-foot drop he'd just fallen from, higher than he first thought. Painted with greens and browns and covered in camouflage netting, the hospital looked more like a war bunker than a place of healing, the large words hanging on gold plaques over the main entrance the only giveaway.

As a soft breeze tugged at his ankles, Christian refocused on his mission. With no idea of where he was going – only certain he had to be away from the hospital and in the company of someone who could help him, he searched the half-light surrounding him. Deserted and deathly quiet, the third floor seemed like a ghost town.

He began his search, keeping to the shade of the trees as he walked, maintaining an alertness while he tried to spot somewhere that led down to the second floor. The sequoias spread patches of shade across the walkways, and every time he stepped into a darkened area, he released his breath, grasping the various trunks for support. The third floor was a vast empty shell, seemingly forgotten to the Mages dwelling below. And where were they? Was he the only Mage who walked there?

The thought bothered him as he crouched by the foot of a bridge. He didn't want to be alone. Maybe he should've stayed in the relative security of the hospital, where doctors and nurses patrolled, Mages with powers beyond what he was capable… But they hadn't been there during the attack had they? Tiron could have wiped them all out without a single defence against him. And why hadn't the patients, Mages with powers of their own not fight back? Was it the seals on their tongues?

Christian didn't know, none of it made sense, nothing the entire time since his parents' attack had made sense. All he knew was that he needed to accept it, learn quickly before the cloying disbelief that almost consumed him daily actually succeeded in driving him completely insane. Unless he was already…

Walking from the shadow of one of the twin posts securing the bridge, he collected himself. He had to find Charras and ultimately find out what was happening, where Charlize had gone, and why there were no Mages around when one was sorely needed.

He crossed the bridge, which swayed slightly underfoot, the gentle creak thunderous to him in the silence. But when he reached the two bordering trunks and climbed onto a small clearing, he noticed steps leading down to a larger deck.

He cautiously descended onto it and stood amidst the desolate café's and stalls, each locked tightly for the evening. The air chilled his exposed back and he held his cast tightly to his waist.

Upon reaching the farthermost border, he sat on one of the five benches facing the outer edges of the deck. Dimmed for the evening, the soft glow of the floating orbs allowed the naked eye to see all the way to the horizon, to the peaks of a hundred sequoias each interspersed with various sized orbs. The sight was invisible to the Ungifted eye, and to Christian before the Sirenari helped lift his blindness.

And how grateful he was to the demon in that moment. If he'd never felt the pain of her sharp claws, he wouldn't be able to see what he saw now. He wouldn't see the canopies littered with a luminescence of warmth, he wouldn't know of magic – an idea implausible and unimaginable, yet surrounding him and forcing him to accept the truths his heart sought to deny each day. What life would he have led in ignorance?

He would have stayed there forever, contemplating his potential future, if it were not for the chattering of his teeth that stirred him... and the voices.

Christian jerked his head towards the direction he thought they came from. Through the gap between a café and a lantern, he saw the shadows of two figures as they made their way towards the deck. They hadn't spotted him yet, deep in conversation as they marched along the bridge.

Ducking behind the bench, dismayed at the puny coverage it offered, Christian peered through the slats, praying that the figures would somehow walk on by without noticing him there. They seemed distracted, bickering amongst themselves as they edged closer, and a flash of orange beneath a lantern caught his attention.

He breathed a sigh of relief. It was Jess with another almost identical Jess next to her.

Christian stood to reveal himself. "Hey!" he called.

Turning to face him, the twin that wasn't Jess stretched out her hand

and the bench in front of him shot into the air above his head.

"Jade, stop, it's Christian!" Jess scolded.

To his relief, the bench landed inches in front of him and the twins ran over to greet him.

"I'm so sorry!" Jade yelled, blushing. "I'm all nervous."

Christian shook his head. "It's fine. I'm getting used to flying furniture. Did you ring Armmos just then? I need his help."

"There's no answer, these phones are as old as forgotten magic," Jess replied.

Throughout their exchange, the twins didn't take their eyes off Christian, which he found odd as they spoke without looking at each other.

"Keep trying Jade. You okay?"

It took him a moment to realise she meant him. "Yes… sort of, but Tiron attacked the hospital a minute ago. He's got the patients under some sort of spell."

"Yeah, we had the call, thought we better come find you," Jess explained. "Armmos and Charras got a hunt going on for Tiron – whole Haunt's on alert."

"He's here," said Christian, his face suddenly white.

"Yeah, we know, let's get you somewhere safe."

"No, he's here, behind you."

There was no time to consider their predicament as Jade's phone flew from her hand, disappearing far into sky. Jess tilted her chin up, steadied her footing, and immediately stood in front of Christian, hands held ready. Jade followed suit but put her back to his so he was wedged between them.

In nothing more than a breath of wind, Tiron's silhouette disappeared from the deck and reappeared in front of Jade. "Clever," he snarled, before clutching her neck and flinging her to one side.

He then lunged at Jess, who released several blasts of air into his stomach. He staggered after her as she led him away from Christian, swiping at her with his fist. But Jess ducked beneath it before twirling to return a blow – a sharp jab to the jaw that unbalanced him. Christian was impressed that she managed to hurt him, figuring the twins had tricks when it came to using their magic.

Jess was quick as Tiron spun in another attempt to connect a punch, and was once again able to dodge it and return a jab, each hitting expertly, although lacking the force needed to move him with any real impact.

Meanwhile, back on her feet, Jade joined the fray, flinging herself around Tiron's neck and sinking her teeth into his shoulder. He grunted loudly, his face turning red with rage as he blocked a kick from Jess and reached up to pluck Jade from his back. He flung her towards Christian, who watched as she landed with a sickening *thud*. And in that moment, Jess's attention shifted to her sister, giving Tiron the opportunity to deliver a substantial blow to her stomach. She doubled over and cried out as Tiron sent her flying into one of the benches.

Christian made towards her, but was stopped by Jade who clambered up and tugged him by his good hand. "We need to run," she said, "come on!"

He shook his head and pointed to Jess crumpled against the bench, her neck twisted at an unnatural angle. Jade let out a choked scream and darted to her sister's aid, anguish pouring from her cries as she left Christian at the mercy of Tiron.

"Finally," he said, smiling his familiar distorted smile.

Without knowing where it came from, Christian found himself pulled towards his attacker, the weight of air constricting him and pushing him from behind. Powerless, he could do nothing more than wait as he was dragged along the deck. He scowled at Tiron, his face becoming more distinct, and acknowledged a dark hatred within him – unlike anything he thought he was capable of feeling. And with nothing but inches between them, he prepared to tell him so.

Yet, before he formed the words, something sliced through the space between them and the binds lifted.

It was Jades doing, a fury in her eyes that charged the night as she ran towards the mercenary. Christian watched her approach, and as if in slow motion, saw Tiron cast her into the air and catch her upside down. His hands squeezed around her neck like a clamp and she clawed at his arm, helpless against the steel hold Christian knew far too well.

His heart raced. He looked over at Jess now lying on the ground, and then back to Jade squirming in the unyielding grip. *He's going to kill us all,* he thought, the realisation thumping him in the stomach.

Finding himself reliving the night of his parents capture once again, familiar guilt rippled up his spine – the same guilt he felt then as he did now; the same cowardice that caused him to flee and leave his parents; the same desire to run and escape the doom they each had coming; the same pathetic fear that drenched him.

"Stop!" he shouted.

Tiron snorted with mirth; the same mirth that mocked his weakness time and time again.

Christian took a step forward, just as Jade's pleading eyes began to dull. Adrenaline burned within him, the fight response decided as a rage he hadn't known before erupted in his veins. He clenched his fists and bore his stare into Tiron's disfigured face.

"I said, STOP!"

This time, Tiron faced him, his smile faltering as he saw the power in the unbecome's eyes, the same eyes that changed to black, completely black – like night had set within them, and from all of his experience, he knew what was coming. There was no time to get out of the way as a bolt of energy struck him squarely between the eyes.

The force jolted Christian backwards and he skid along the deck until his back hit a bench. Rubbing his eyes as if acid burned them, his heart fluttered rapidly, each part of his anatomy stinging with the shock of a thousand volts.

He had failed, he was sure; he'd fainted before he'd even touched the monster. Now he would suffer the consequences, and he deserved far worse than that. Perhaps Tiron would be merciful and keep him locked somewhere comfortable. He may even see his parents again. That would be the only redeeming feature to his future as a prisoner, assuming they were alive... Maybe it was all a dream anyway and it would finally be over?

"Christian?"

At first thinking his ears played tricks on him, and then glad he hadn't fainted, he used his remaining strength to lift his head.

Jade sat staring at him, her hands clutched to her throat as she gulped in air gratefully. "Thank-you," she mouthed.

Tiron lay at her feet, sprawled awkwardly where he'd fallen, but Jade paid him no attention, a sudden light in her eyes as she grinned widely. She received Jess who hobbled over and slumped down to embrace her, and they both began to sob into each other's hair.

Christian didn't know what he'd done, or how. He wasn't even sure he wanted to. All he knew in that moment was that they were okay. It was enough.

And with that grace, he slowly sat up and hugged his knees to his chest, breathing in a sigh of relief. He caught Jess's gaze over Jade's shoulder and nodded his head. She smiled back, saying nothing for a while, although her eyes portrayed the thanks she felt.

When she did finally speak, her voice was hoarse. "Well, I think we know what Mage you are."

31

Pieces that fit

The Hellebore between her fingers gave off slight warmth, its friendly presence a comfort as Charlize clutched it beneath the bed sheets.

"Four days?"

Her father nodded, his face sombre as he leaned forward, elbows on knees and hands clasped.

Disconcerted with the discovery, Charlize found herself clutching the rose harder. *Four days?* That was a long time to be asleep, and with so much disruption and danger surrounding her… She couldn't bear to think of the consequences should she have fainted in the face of her enemies alone.

What a strange twist of events, and such luck! If Christian hadn't sparked at the moment he did, he and her new friends would have died. And yet… they should have never been in that position to begin with.

Unable to recall the events leading to her slumber, her thoughts blurry and confused, Charlize only knew that the fight against Tiron didn't go in her favour. The next thing she remembered was waking up in bed surrounded by flowers and get-well cards, an insatiable hunger barely quelled with strawberry jam on toast.

"I misjudged the effects the Anima would have on my episodes… I should have better control."

Charras shook his head and placed his hand on hers. "Enough, you are still learning. If anything, this shows why lessons with Gwen will do you good. She can teach you more than I can about control over the Anima."

"You always have been more Incendiī," Charlize said with a smirk.

"To fuel a fire, you first need air, remember that."

A shadow at the door shifted Charlize's attention and she called for the owner to enter. She smiled as Christian walked through and stood with his hands in his pockets.

"I'll leave you to it," Charras said. "Armmos and I have matters to deal with." Placing a hand on Charlize's shoulder and squeezing it gently, he patted Christian's back as he left the room.

Alone, the two teenagers smiled shyly at one another.

"So, you know your clan," Charlize said, motioning for him to sit.

Nodding, Christian shrugged. "Seems silly I didn't. It makes sense now. I don't know how, I just get it. When Jess told me I was Fulgor, it's like a light went off in my head."

"We should have told you before; I'm sorry, we just –"

"I get it," said Christian, holding up his hand. "It's okay."

Charlize smiled. "You know, Leanne and Theo were very strong. I'm not surprised you managed what you did."

"Are," he corrected. "My parents are alive."

"We don't know that for sure."

"I do."

Pressing her lips together, Charlize shuffled backwards, her pillows propped against the headboard sagging slightly. She turned to plump them, but stopped as Christian helped her by beating them with his good hand.

"You're still weak," he murmured, easing her back and perching next to her.

"I'm fine," Charlize assured him. "But thank-you."

Through the open window, a ray of sun streaked across the bedroom and along the chest of drawers, highlighting numerous bunches of flowers, all squeezed together in every gap available.

Amongst them, an orchid stood.

An odd flower, with its singular beauty unique and very nature hard to fathom and maintain, it seemed the perfect fit to Christian.

"You said my name," he murmured.

His eyes averted, he looked at his bandaged wrist and fiddled with the tape peeling away at the edges. He could feel Charlize's gaze, but he didn't immediately look into her eyes, a silence passing between them he didn't find uncomfortable. "When they took you from the ward, before everything happened... you said my name."

Finding herself unable to speak, Charlize continued to stare, a slight crease on her brow. Why had she said his name? And out loud? Was it the coma? Did they give her drugs?

Clearing her throat, she asked, "How did you hear me, where were you?"

Christian blushed and met her gaze. "Well, I was worried, so I came to see you." She raised her eyebrows and he shook his head. "No, no not like that. Jess was there. When I tried to leave she heard footsteps and I hid under your bed."

"You hid under my bed?"

"Yes, but it's not how it sounds." He rubbed his neck, sighed, took a breath, and then tilted his face to look at hers, watching how her eyes blazed with blue as she tried to fathom what she made of it.

He couldn't help but smirk. "You said my name."

"I wouldn't know why."

"I do."

And with that, he kissed her. It was firm but brief, leaving Charlize stunned as she spluttered an indistinguishable retort. Her chest rising and falling rapidly, she touched her lips, her expression one of contempt and fear.

"Don't be angry," Christian said, standing. "I know what you think of me. I'm weak; a burden; ignorant; rude..."

"I do not think any of that," Charlize uttered, still touching her lips.

"Yes you do, and you're right. I'm all of those and more... I'm a coward." Walking towards the window, he stared into the Haunt. "But I will get stronger, and I will find my parents."

"You're not ready Christian, you need to become, you need to have full control of your powers before you can even consider –"

"And I will. I will learn faster than any Mage. My scars show my weakness Charlize, but they also remind me of why I'm here. I'm going to get stronger and I'm going to learn what I can, as fast as I can, so that when I find the people who took my parents, I can kill them."

Turning from the window, Christian stared straight at her, his resolve so strong it ignited a fire between them Charlize couldn't break. The argument she held ready in her mind disintegrated. She lost her nerve and forced herself to look away – an effort requiring greater self-control than she first imagined.

The Hellebore against her palm grew hotter, and realising it mimicked her emotions, she eased her grip. She sensed Christian's presence draw close but didn't dare look until she felt his hand brush against her cheek.

"Please don't," she said quietly.

Feeling him tense, and knowing that hurt flashed in his eyes, she reached up and grasped his hand. "I am sorry Christian, I am so sorry I said your name. But there are things you don't know, things I should have told you before…"

The sound of voices stopped her saying more, the cheery chatter filling the cottage and breaking the moment between them.

Christian dropped his hand from her face, disappointment flooding his expression. He took a deep breath, turned from the sapphire stare, and left to greet the twins.

Alone, Charlize closed her eyes and squeezed them tightly. Sinking back into the bed sheets, she realised she would have to act fast before Christian's affection grew deeper. How foolish she'd been to keep it from him, and now his hurt would be greater than before…

No. Better to hurt now than to suffer the tragedy later; it was just a matter of timing. The revelation would not be an easy one. But it was necessary; now more than ever.

32

The Anima Winds

One week had passed. Spring pervaded the Anima as buds opened and leaves adorned previously bare branches. Sunlight trickled from the breaks above and the once grey skies turned to baby blue.

Not that Charlize saw the change. Each dawn she left for her lessons, returning to the cottage after dusk, her private tutorage with Mrs Arno drawing out longer and longer each day. Exhausted, sleep would be welcomed the moment her head hit the pillow, and when the sun roused her, she'd leave before her father or Christian awoke.

So it was they became ships in the night, passing by one another with only requisite exchanges. But she was learning, her control over her Anima element increasing with each passing day. And today would be the day of her ultimate test.

She crossed the bridge to the cottage, her lesson suspended for the afternoon, and allowed herself to admire the purpling creepers running along the archway to the deck. Where lonely wood once stood, it now teemed with colour and life.

As the cottage came into view, she heard voices, soft giggles that wafted through the glade as if the world were free from trouble. Her stomach clenching, she composed her face so that when she saw Amy and Christian sat on the porch steps, currently entwined as some sort of hilarity possessed them, she looked entirely indifferent.

Amy was the first to spot Charlize's determined approach, her head bowed, while Christian merely nodded and shuffled to the side to let her pass.

"Thank-you," she said with spiky courtesy, stepping through into the cottage and shutting the door firmly behind her.

Beyond it she heard another giggle dislodge from Amy's throat, followed by a comment about Christian's clear and obvious wit. She gritted her teeth and bit back the urge to kick the door.

"You seem agitated," Charras said, standing with his hands splayed on the kitchen island.

"Hmm? No… no, just apprehensive about later."

She managed a half smile, but it soon disappeared when the door opened and hit her on the heels. She turned as Christian waltzed through.

"Are you ready?" Charras asked him.

He nodded. "Almost."

As he walked towards the bedroom, he caught Charlize's glance before quickly looking away and disappearing inside.

"Have you two fallen out?" asked Charras, straightening up and crossing his arms.

Rubbing her temples, Charlize shook her head. "Not as such. It's been more of a misunderstanding."

"I see…"

"Don't look too far into it father, he'll be over it soon enough."

"And you?"

Taken aback, Charlize shrugged her shoulders. "There is nothing for me to be over."

Charras nodded. "Make sure it stays that way. There is enough complication."

Again, the bugs disturbed her stomach, crawling around and making all sorts of nuisance she didn't appreciate. Swallowing, she kept her face stony.

"Of course father. Soon, none of it will matter anyway."

"What won't matter?" Christian asked, appearing in kitchen with a fresh shirt in his hands. He tugged it over his bare chest and Charlize saw the scar beneath his right pectoral, a grim reminder of the night she found him huddled by the manor gates.

"Our tiresome quarrel," she replied, spinning on her heels and opening the cottage door.

Surprised that Amy was still sitting on the step, Charlize nearly tripped over her, barely managing to sidestep and land unharmed on the platform.

"So sorry!" Amy exclaimed, scrambling up and making towards her.

"It's fine," she replied, holding up her hand to stop a suspected brush down.

Face to face, the girls studied each other, a silence neither felt the need to fill.

Luckily, Christian and Charras joined them moments later, dispelling the gauche manner Charlize adopted each time she and Amy were forced to communicate. It's not that she didn't like her, she was pleasant enough, if not somewhat young – it was the constant mouse like fear her face embodied if eye contact between them lasted more than a few seconds. It was disconcerting...

They were half way to their destination – moments after Charlize heard Amy whisper 'she hates me' to Christian – when the twins appeared from the deck above, landing in their path with huge smiles.

"I have to say, this is gonna be fun," said Jess, falling into step with Charlize.

"I wouldn't be quite so excited young Mage, the business we're dealing with today is grave."

Rolling her eyes at Charras, Jess jabbed him in the rib. "You always so cheery?"

Unable to help a small smirk, Charlize peered behind her, catching the grin on Christian's face too. Hand in hand with Amy, he didn't notice her glance, so she quickly turned back.

Her father had gotten used to Jess's brash manner, although she suspected he preferred Jade's softer approach. Nevertheless, he tolerated their presence, grateful for the protection they provided, even if he deemed their mannerisms less than decorous.

"You would do well to take these sorts of matters more seriously."

Jess said nothing, shrugging instead and opting to turn and chat with Christian and Amy, leaving Jade and Charlize to take the lead.

"You worried?" Jade whispered.

"More apprehensive. We don't know what we're dealing with," Charlize replied.

"Whatever he is, he's a monster." Her tone held venom.

A cool wind fluttered onto the deck, freeing a couple of cherry blossoms from above. They fell gracefully, but were soon swept aside as Tunde bounded towards them and stopped in front of Charras.

Robed in green, but with the same red band around his wrist, the young Incendiī straightened up. "Armmos sent me to hurry you. Tiron stirred an hour ago and there is something you must witness."

Bowing to Charlize, who once again felt raw power radiating from him, he swivelled on his heels and disappeared back the way he came.

Charras's brow darkened. Tunde had been a great aid with several incidents over the past few days. The clan he belonged to was old and wise, his strength dating back to an ancestry as old as the First's. Before his pilgrimage, his father died a peaceful death, but Tunde chose to continue his journey alone. And how fortunate that turned out to be...

"Let us make haste; I don't like the sound of this."

Tall and stately iron railings reared along the periphery of the elevated deck, tiered above the third floor so it stood over the heads of those who gathered below. Within its guard, another red-bricked building lay, large and dominant. Spelled above the main entrance, comprised of a thick oak brace door, was the word '**BREWERY**.'

Looking up and shielding her eyes, Charlize saw a large netted cover draped over the roof, secured on the tips of each iron spike. Leaves and flowers adorned the interwoven gaps, but it did nothing to detract from the sheer ugliness of it. As if the building was some sort of captive, there seemed no way in or out.

"Behold our factory, it is quite impressive, no?" said Armmos, shouting over the heads of the large gathering of Mages.

Parting to allow Charlize and her companions through, the crowd silenced, eyes focused on their progression towards Armmos – who stood waiting in a dazzling emerald robe.

"Charras, what do you make of it?"

"It is a sight to behold old friend."

Jess sniggered. "That's for sure…"

Even Charras couldn't help the grin that swept across his lips. Luckily, Armmos paid no attention, his obvious pride towards the garish building something only he could hope to understand.

He wet his lips and clapped his hands before addressing the crowd. "Fellow Mages, friends, and family members; we are here today to witness the bravery of these four young people, four young people who have been the target of such poignant hate." Sighs and murmurs of agreement reverberated through the deck.

"Indeed it is sad," Armmos continued. "Which is why we have called them here today, allowing them to witness the very abomination put to rest, preventing any further harm he may try to cause. Once the Hetairia Doman arrive he will be dealt with severely, and then we can continue with our duty free from fear of attack within our ranks, as we did before these past unfortunate hours."

Cheers rang out and Armmos bowed low, his face a picture of delight. He knew how to rile a crowd…

When the cheers died down, he marched to the foot of the platform and tapped twice on the rounded wood. Seconds later, a protection revealed itself, tracing the outline of a door. It opened outwards to reveal a larger than usual A.A.E within its depths.

He motioned for his companions to follow, with Charlize going first, followed by Jess, Jade, Charras, and lastly Christian – Amy not permitted (much to Charlize's relief).

When the door resealed, blocking out the faces of an adoring crowd, she took a breath. A small dewdrop lit the A.A.E as it ascended into the brewery, and she was grateful for the slight reprieve.

"Be prepared, for what you're about to see won't sit easily," Armmos said.

Glancing at her father, Charlize caught his gaze, their minds connecting almost instantly.

Before they had a chance to voice their thoughts, light ensconced them, the A.A.E emerging into a small chamber.

Stone surrounded them, the smooth surface offering no escape. But once again Armmos bounded to the far side, tapped twice, and a door was revealed.

As they passed through, the smell of hops and malt hit them almost instantly. Charlize held her nose, the alcoholic realm something she was unaccustomed to. She followed Armmos's lead, only marginally paying attention as they walked through a storage room where caskets upon caskets rose either side of them, stacked atop each other and reaching high into the ceiling. The room dim and cold, she could make out various labels on the wooden barrels, marking them with age and type.

Twice they saw trap doors leading into cellars Armmos explained hid wine and mixers, and when Charlize questioned what mixers were, she soon discovered flavoured carbonated liquids were popular with the Ungifted. Fascinated, she pressed further, only to stop herself when Christian's laugh followed her into an open factory workspace.

"Fruitfizz, Limepop?!"

"Water is quite sufficient."

"That's enough Christian," said Charras. "Remember, our worlds co-exist, but they are far more separated than you realise."

"Precisely, we have a duty; unhealthy distractions such as television and teeth corroders do not concern or interest us, and nor should they you, now."

"That's enough too Charlize. Besides, a vice or two befalls the most of us."

"Not me, I have no vice."

With that, an uneasy silence fell on the party. On all but Christian, whose smile hadn't faltered. "No, but not all of us can hope to be worthy of your perfection."

"Easy Christian, it isn't like that," said Jess quietly.

Clearing his throat, Armmos pointed out a lavish tapestry on the far wall of the workspace, which the twins showed an exaggerated interest in, leaving Charras to stare down his charges.

"There will be no more of this. Tonight you will show him," he told a reddened Charlize.

She nodded.

"Show me what?"

"The truth," Charlize replied. "Perhaps then we can hope to be friends again."

Bowing her head, she walked over to Jade and Jess, who still stared at the vulgar wall hanging with a look of slight shock. A picture of a fishmonger displaying a Sirenari attached to a hook by her mouth was embroidered into the textile, with clearly no sense of caution taken when considering its audience.

"It's... er... a bit graphic," said Jade.

"Yes, well, certain fine arts aren't to everyone's taste," Armmos mumbled, ushering them away and gesturing for Charras and Christian to hurry.

They continued to make their way through the factory, passing three cylindrical containers with warnings attached to them. A plastic sheet separated two from the other, the tanks labelled 'copper tun,' 'mash tun,' and the separated 'hot liquor tank.' Standing as large centrepieces, each connected to several wires and machinery emitting low hums.

Charlize decided to ask their purpose another time, fearful of Christian's mirth. And not long after, they stopped at the foot of a metal staircase where she half listened to Armmos explain how below them was the Fermenter room, and opposite them, behind one of the several closed doors, was the cold storage area.

"And why is Tiron here, and not in a prison?" she interrupted, having no interest in listening to Armmos's tiresome boastings.

Blinking once, his sleepy eyes attempting to convey offence, he still answered her question without dispute. "We have never had need of a prison, and until the Hetairia Doman arrives, this is the most secure place in the Haunt."

"Indeed," Charras interjected. "If a Mage chooses to betray us, there is little we can do but contain them and inform the proper authorities – as you well know."

Charlize felt the scorn in his tone, nodded, and fell silent. It would do her no good to argue the point. The Anima had no enemy, the element neutral. Of course Armmos felt little need to introduce a prison… the brewery was enough of an eyesore alone…

Mrs Arno appeared at the top of the stairs, her cheeks rosy, and called to them: "About time too! I've had to turn the lights off. I couldn't face staring at him any longer."

"My apologies Gwen, we let our mouths distract us," said Armmos, ascending the stairs.

With a knowing nod, she flipped her long braid over her shoulder and held open the door she'd just emerged from.

For a short few moments the stairs chimed with footsteps until they all reached the top and bundled into an office. The room was small. A cluttered desk with papers strewn across it sat centrally, while a dated phone, the handset musky grey, acted as a paperweight. Beneath the desk, a bin brimmed and a shredder sitting to the left had a newspaper jammed in its teeth. Tilted at an angle, Charlize could make out the headline: 'VREALÂ SPOTTED. For the full story please turn to…'

Shuddering slightly, she widened her gaze. Across the walls, pictures and photos detailed the construction of the brewery, the landscape of the Haunt before its newest construction appearing bleak and barren.

No mementos adorned the back wall. Instead, a glass sheet halved it horizontally, and although dark, she knew Tiron lay trapped behind it.

"He's been silent for days now. It is time for you to put him to rest,"

Mrs Arno said softly as Charlize edged her way closer.

Suddenly, a switch was flicked and light flooded the room beyond the glass.

Pressed against it, Tiron's fingers traced the seals around his prison, his hands stretched high as he sniffed the air and tried to find an escape. Manic, his façade of composure completely diminished, he bared his teeth and let out a scream, although no noise could be heard from the other side of the window.

"Can he see me?" Charlize asked, watching as he began to throw himself against the wall and glass, hitting his head over and over again – ignoring the blood gushing from his nose and knuckles.

Mrs Arno shook her head. Then, taking her by the hand and leading her closer to the window, she placed her palm against it, a little way from Tiron's face. He immediately stopped hitting out, instead grasping and scratching at the place Charlize's hand now rest.

"He can smell you though."

Jerking her hand away, disgusted, Charlize didn't let her gaze leave his face. His eyes were white, his irises milky, but not in the same way Christian's had been. Tiron's held an insatiable hunger, desperation to feed not unlike a Ghul's burning within them.

"What has he become?" she murmured, turning her head to hear the answer.

It was Armmos who spoke.

"We have been studying him. He is all but human; he still feeds with food and water, but he does not seem to taste it. It is almost a necessity for him, not a pleasure. What he truly hungers for is flesh, as a Ghul would... yet he is not of that kind." His gaze shifted to watch Tiron resume his inhuman ferocity as he thrashed and tore about his prison. "We don't know for sure."

"Perhaps he is both human *and* Minae," Charlize suggested.

"A hybrid," Charras mumbled in answer to his daughter. "That kind of power... it is old magic, destructive in its very nature, unknown by Mages for its peril danger should it fall into the wrong hands."

"Then who?"

"One that speaks with Inferus-Malus himself," Armmos replied, his voice strained.

No one needed to speak the name aloud as the shredder kicked back into life and the words of the demon disappeared into nothing but strips of paper.

The atmosphere in the room changed as the horror of such a contingency befell them. Spells of old, the evil magick's long since banned and destroyed, only known by Inferus-Malus himself, being brought forward once again.

"No one else must know," Charlize whispered. "If this gets out..."

She didn't finish her sentence, the prospect too daunting to say out loud. Yet all in the room knew her meaning, save for Christian.

If the Mage world discovered the dead had new tricks up their sleeves, almighty powers that Inferus-Malus himself was granting, there would be a rebellion, an uproar, an outcry... and Charlize, the Āetis, would be side-lined, or worse, more would turn from her and to the darkness. Those such as Tiron would roam the earth and in its entirety, she would fail before she had the chance to succeed.

"Who would do that to themselves?"

It was Jess who spoke, standing close to her sister, their bright eyes holding genuine intrigue.

"Fear causes us to do many things we otherwise wouldn't," Armmos replied, his tone sombre.

"As does stubborn blindness, or pride," Charras added darkly.

"Yeah, but selling your soul to Inferus?!" Jess exclaimed, "You've gotta be pretty desperate, or pretty sure you've got no other option!"

Armmos shook his head. "Fear isn't so black and white. Many live with the burden of their actions because their fear caused them to behave uncharacteristically. We have all reacted in ways we hoped we wouldn't because of it."

Christian lifted his head and stared at the monster behind the glass. He felt as if the leader he greatly admired spoke only to him, his past indiscretions explained away with understanding, not judgment. No matter his fear, he'd never become what Tiron was, and that thought eased his guilty conscience a little.

"Maybe he didn't know what he would become," he suggested.

Armmos let out a soft laugh. "He is as aware as you or I. He holds power greater than before; he is the very essence of air and fire with the eternal life of a Minae and the body of a human. All he has to do is keep that part of him alive."

"That comes at some price though!" Jess argued. "He's given up his humanity so he can be nothing more than a monster with an IQ."

The squeak of a chair made everyone turn to the source. Standing up, Tunde faced Jess, his intelligent eyes kind.

"Not every Mage holds honour as valuably as you do Jess. In my tribe, there were stories of a sacrificial passage, old magicks performed before their dangers were properly understood. It was told to warn us of the risks our gifts could potentially cause.

A long time ago, a man named Arron the Mighty, from the tribe of Garâtaroo went forth into the forest to search for game. A sure hunter, keen sighted with a strong spear arm, he kept the village in plenty.

That evening, when dusk fell, Arron returned home, wherein he collapsed to the ground in a fit of trembles. Foam poured from his mouth and the village elder called for aid to heal him, for he was a great warrior and she feared their fate should he die.

A young village Lamia, a Mage of unique energy, came forward with a rite of passage. She told of a passage within her book that spoke of demonic sacrifice. In their death, their energy can pass to the dying.

And so it was a Ghul was brought forward and sacrificed, his energy transferring into the dying Arron.

None believed it would work, but several days later, Arron revived, new and improved. His first hunt brought much joy and food to the village, although it was noted he rarely dined himself, his hunger lessened than before. Nevertheless, he married the young Lamia and the village rejoiced.

But that night, during their consummation, tragedy struck. The spirit within became monstrous, taking over Arron's mind and body and killing his wife, leaving nothing but her bones the next morning.

When the village found her, alongside the dead body of Arron, his own hunting spear through his heart, they destroyed the magicks and never revealed its source. Instead, this tale stands to warn us."

As Tunde finishing his recounting, Jess folded her arms across her chest, her face a picture of disgust. "You got told messed up bedtime stories."

Revealing his white teeth, Tunde shrugged. "Perhaps if Tiron heard the same, we wouldn't be here now."

"But someone did tell him, and they found the spell to go along with it," said Charlize, shaking out her arms and facing the hybrid before her. "Let this be a warning to *them*."

Releasing a ball of flame into the glass, shattering it, she raised her arms above her head. She couldn't kill him, she knew that – not while a part of him remained human. But she could put him into a deep sleep, the winds affecting him the same way they affected her.

Stunned, Tiron spun into a crouch, and in those moments, Charlize recalled the winds, bringing the needed words to mind – words of power, warmth, and of the west wind.

"Dicio, Āetis, Zephyrus."

Lost in the fearsome roar as Tiron recovered his senses, she held her ground as the warmth of the wind encircled her, its soothing monotone humming in her ears.

"Can you feel the power?" Mrs Arno asked, her voice carrying above the noise. "Can you feel the element?"

She sounded far away.

The weight of the warm air crushed Charlize's body, the heaviness of sleep entrapping her in her own spell as it coiled around her limbs.

"Don't lose yourself."

The sweet voice of Mrs Arno was desperate, although the words were drawled out, distorted.

"Remember the properties of each wind."

What a silly question... The Anima winds were each unique, why must she remember them?

A force pulled at her arm and she heard Mrs Arno cry out, "The winds Charlize!"

She was incredibly impatient... Even so, she did as she was told and recounted her lessons.

So, there was the North Wind, the strongest yet hardest to control, having a will of its own. Then there was the South wind, the easy friendly wind, mainly used to propel objects or whoever cast it.

Another weight barged against her shoulder, more forceful this time...

Ah, the East Wind, the boisterous and loud wind. It was the weakest, although good for a distraction or scare. And lastly there was the West Wind, silent and powerful, almost deceitful...

Yes of course, the West Wind... now she remembered.

"Circumplico!"

The command snapped Charlize back to her senses as she regained control, causing the air to fold and twist together. Realising she was horizontal, she pushed the spell outwards from her body, the transparent mass quickly engulfing Tiron who lay on top of her. Although he fought it, his eyes bulging and jaw snapping, they soon unhinged and fell open inches from her face.

She shoved him off and watched as his limp body gradually fell to sleep. Then, sealing the spell with a binding, she allowed her father to help her upright.

The room was destroyed. Paper littered the floor; the phone dangled from its wire; the bin and shredder lay upturned, and every picture was either smashed or hanging askew.

Charlize smiled towards her three friends backed against the front wall, their relieved expressions confirming her suspicion that Tiron almost escaped. Clearly his hunger had been too much of a temptation.

"We will clear up from here Charlize, go home and rest."

Without protest, she thanked Armmos and left with the twins and a quiet Christian following closely behind. Her head spun as she fought the urge to give in to fatigue, sure the temptation of her bed was worse than Tiron's hunger.

So as they left the brewery, the door sealing behind them, the shouts and cries that immediately hit them startled her. She'd forgotten about her unwanted entourage...

"Shall we get coffee?" Jade suggested.

"Is it safe?" Christian murmured, watching the adoring Mages struggle to get closer, although somehow maintain a respectful distance.

"You doing that Charlie?" Jess asked, a smile fixed on her face as they nodded to all who called their names.

She shrugged, in no mood for the attentions of those she hardly knew. Her mind otherwise occupied with the revelations of Tiron's hybrid status, she knew the faces staring at her now with awe and respect could turn instantly if his power was revealed. If they knew the origins of whence it came, faith could be lost to the darkness once more.

A tug on her arm pulled her from her thoughts and she span to face Christian. His eyes dark and brow heavy, he brought her closer.

"Who are you?"

33
The Truth

... After The Divide, and upon finding their other halves, The Firsts scattered to five separate corners of the earth and built their settlements, to later be known as 'Haunts.'

Many years passed, the Firsts bearing many children, yet time soon revealed those children could never bring themselves to touch. For their bond was not one of lust, but one of kinship.

And so it was the Firsts beseeched the Sky for an answer, reading it's complexities of love, yet finding it knew little of the heart, nor the bond that bound their strange race. They met with refusal each time they asked for links to be made between every being on the planet, as it had done for them, for the Sky refused to meddle further in matters it didn't fully understand. As warriors of light, little freedom was left to them, their sacrifice and duty binding them to a cause with no certain end. It would not take away the only freedoms they had left, lest it be no better than the darkness they fought.

In desperation, the Firsts came together once more, the dangers in their proximity one they all feared. They called this: 'The Joining.'

Upon meeting, their debate lasted for many nights, although their bond as old friends and new strengthened with each day. Then finally, with heavy hearts, the answer became clear.

In agreement, the Sky granted their request, giving their children the gift of choice. And yet, with all things, having a choice came at a cost.

Now, whenever their children chose to love another, they would sacrifice half of themselves: half of their power and half of their life. On their eighteenth birthday, they would venture into the surrounding villages and settlements to find their partner in all things, and upon doing so, they would live as one, sharing the joys of the world together, fighting the darkness together, and bearing more children together, before finally dying together. And it was that way for many, many years.

Back in their Haunts, The Firsts grew older, their bodies aging – both a gift of their humanity and their curse. Upon meditation, the First Mage of Fulgor suffered a heart attack. His wife fled to his side and heard her husband whisper his final words, a prophecy that spoke of an Āetis – to be born whenever the need arose. They would be able to create and control all of the elements.

Although it was an outrageous concept to weaken the blood lines through cross-kin, Lady Fulgor listened to her dying husbands words. The Āetis would be born dangerously, but nevertheless lead them into war, sacrificing their life to defeat the surging numbers of Minae. It would bring a period of calm throughout the world, prolonging the light and holding off the dark until the end.

The only problem lay within their bloodlines, which needed to stay pure and strong for as long as they could. The Sky promised to choose the Āetis's, granting them strength beyond the physics of their blood.

Old, and with mere years left to them, the remaining nine First's came together once more, for what became their 'Sacrificial Joining.'

To prepare every Mage that followed, and remain the only pure connection to the Sky, they sacrificed themselves. Cutting their own throats and draining their gifted blood in a room protected with each of their elements, they bound their life force, their essence, and their energy into a crystal Orbis, unable to enter death until the binds were broken by the ending of the war, where the Sky would finally free them.

Now, with one touch, the Orbis could see the destinies of each bound Mage. Their souls could wander the earth, walking a plane of existence not in between, nor nowhere, but somewhere their powers equalled an Akuji, although remained ensconced in light. And so, it knew each time an Āetis was needed, and it knew exactly who would bear the sacrifices needed to create them.

Dropping his book on the bed, Christian put his head in his hands, his stomach churning so hard he thought he was going to throw up. He rubbed his face and stared up at the 'Get Well' cards adorning the chest of drawers, their presence now full of mockery, their well wishing words cold, the pastel coloured papers splashed with fake sympathy.

Slowly, he reached for them one by one and threw them into the top drawer until only the orchid remained. Reaching out to touch it, he allowed himself a rueful smile. How right he'd been...

The sun hid from Charlize at least an hour ago, and it was that entire time exactly that Christian remained in the bedroom, reading his *Book of Becoming* as she read Jayne Eyre until the moment she realised it was upside-down.

So it was, when she heard the creak of footsteps edge their way towards her, she continued pretending Edward Rochester was the sort of man she understood.

"I read the chapter, about the Āetis," Christian said softly, coming to stand opposite where she sat.

With the dreaded words spoken, Charlize froze. Allowing her heart to resume its beat, she placed her now upright book on the floor and curled her arms around her knees. When she looked up, she immediately met Christian's sad stare.

"Is it true?" he said quietly.

She didn't say anything, knowing her silence would answer his question.

"Shit." He spun to face the opposite wall and slammed his fists against it, squeezing his eyes as he let the news sink to his stomach.

After a few seconds, he took a breath, cleared his throat, and straightened up. "So, that's it then. You just die at the end of all this?"

Hearing it out loud, Charlize winced. She stood from the settee and walked over to where Christian held onto the wall, and reaching out, placed her hand on his shoulder. "It's who I am."

"No, it's not right."

She tilted her head to his level and waited until he met her gaze. "It's who I am," she repeated.

Christian brushed her arm from his shoulder and walked towards the kitchen. He placed his elbows on the first surface he saw and put his head in his hands. There, he tried to calm himself.

"I know it doesn't make sense," Charlize said softly in his ear.

He tried to move away again, but she stood to block his exit, her arms folded across her chest.

"I know –"

"No, it makes sense; it answers every question I've ever had about you. It's just not right."

"Christian…"

"Don't, don't speak to me like that, I'm not a child."

"I didn't –"

"You did." He bore his stare into her, watching how her usually defiant gaze faltered. "I don't know how to deal with this."

"I know, I'm sorry, I wish there was another way you could have found out."

"It doesn't matter Charlize! Whatever way you tell me, the end is the same. You're still going to die."

She winced again and broke their eye contact. "Don't say it like that."

"Why? It's the truth isn't it?"

"Yes, but, it's not spoken of like that. You make it sound so cold."

"It is."

The words hitting her like shards of ice, she choked back her retort, too shocked to know how to reply. Stepping back, she found the settee and sat down.

Seconds later, Christian joined her. Tentatively, he reached out and placed a hand on her knee, and although she still turned from him, she didn't attempt to move it.

"When did you find out?" he asked.

Charlize leaned back into the cushions and stared at her lap. "It was my thirteenth birthday. My father and a man called Jenkins from the Hetairia Doman told me. They made me read a chapter similar to the one you've just read."

"What did you say?"

"Not much, I tried to run out of the room, but Jenkins stopped me. I threw up on his shoes."

Smiling despite himself, Christian twisted his body to face her. "Then what happened?"

"Father punched him. They had a huge fight and there was lots of swearing."

"But Charras won right?"

Charlize shook her head and sighed. "He broke Jenkins' glasses, but Jenkins wouldn't leave until he'd spoken to me."

"Persistent huh?"

"His intentions were good. Father just has a temper; he's never gotten along with the Hetairia Doman."

"So, Jenkins explained it all to you?"

Charlize nodded and clasped her hands together. "He tried. I refused to listen for a long time. Father couldn't get me out of my room for several weeks."

Shivering, she recalled those bleak days. The memory of her father's empty expression every time she begged for his help remained a permanent scar. He would simply hush her tears and return her to the library to study.

One night, at a particular low, she'd attempted to run away. She'd reached the lobby, bag in hand, when her father stepped from the archway of the kitchen, his eyes red ringed and beard shaggy. He watched her leave without attempting to stop her, his face so torn it almost broke her resolve. She ran straight to Leanne and Theo's, and when she looked through the window, saw them curled up with Christian on the settee. There was something so innocent and pure in that moment that she realised if she didn't fight and fulfil her purpose, all good, and all joy in the world would vanish.

"So what made you?"

"Huh?"

"What made you decide to fight?" Christian repeated.

Shaking the chill, Charlize shrugged, wanting to keep the truth a secret. "For him; for everyone. I guess I realised that my purpose wasn't something I could ignore or take lightly. Better to die for the greater good than to die selfishly."

"And what about you?"

She lowered her gaze and gently removed Christian's hand from her knee. "Everything I've seen and continue to see only makes me more determined to end the suffering. I am honoured."

"Did Jenkins teach you that?"

She rolled her eyes and stood up. "Life taught me that. You'll soon see it too."

Returning to the kitchen and running the tap, she proceeded to pour herself a glass of water.

"So why you? Aren't you an abomination?" Christian asked.

He jumped as Charlize slammed the glass on the surface and whirled around to face him. He was now perched on the back of the settee.

"I could have been, yes, if the Sky didn't choose me. But that's a very rude thing to ask."

Christian shrugged. "So why you?"

"That is something you need to ask my mother and father."

"You're the first female Āetis aren't you?"

"Do your questions have a point?"

"I'm just trying to understand," he said, gesturing to all of her.

Sighing, Charlize drank the entire contents of her glass before returning to the settee and patting the available space. When Christian rejoined her, she tucked her hair behind her ears.

"What else do you want to know?"

He smirked. "How long have you got?"

"A year or two – give or take."

"No Charlize, I didn't mean…" His heart thumped and his stomach dropped. *A year or two…? But that would make her…?*

"Would you like some water?"

He shook his head. "No… no… I just need to… a year, wow, that's not long…" He swallowed. "So, I guess this whole time you've been a cold, unemotional machine was because that's exactly who you are – who you have to be?"

Hurt spread across Charlize's face, her gaze fixed on Christian's clenched cheek.

He let out a grunt of mirth and slapped his legs. "Of course, of course. That's why you go around as if you're better than everyone – because you're the divine princess! How didn't I see it before? It all suddenly makes sense!"

"Christian, please…"

"No wonder you didn't make friends. People were scared of you weren't they?" His glare bore into her.

Tears sprung in her eyes, unshed as she felt anger radiate from him. He gripped her wrists, bringing his face close to hers. "You're a stranger to me. I have tried to know you my entire life. And now, when we have that chance, you tell me you're going to die. What the hell am I supposed to do with that?"

"I'm sorry," she whispered.

"Why you?"

"Please Christian…"

He was shouting now, demanding for her to explain: "*Why you*?!"

"I don't know!" Charlize shouted back, frantic. "I don't know, it just is! Please try to understand!"

He released his grip, leaving her to stare at him wide-eyed. All he could recognise was the anger and betrayal somersaulting through his body. "How can I understand if you don't even know?" he said, watching Charlize's chest heave as she tried to compose herself.

There was something about seeing her squirm – a rare moment of vulnerability – that he almost enjoyed. But no sooner had the cruel thought crossed his mind, he automatically reached out and hovered his hand over her shoulder. She dropped her head to watch his inaction, and he suddenly realised he couldn't do it. He couldn't provide the comfort she needed. He couldn't be the friend she deserved.

And with that revelation, he stood up; bounded towards the door; yanked it open; slammed it behind him, and ran head first into Charras.

"Whoa there, what's happened?" he said.

Finding his anger, Christian shoved him backwards. "She *dies*?!"

His face white, Charras held his hands up in defence. "It is not that simple."

"No, but it was simple enough to bring her into this world, to be used as some sick sacrifice, thrown to the wolves as if her life has no meaning!"

"You're out of line Christian."

"Am I really though? I think I'm the only one thinking *in* line!"

"Try to calm down, this is a great shock."

"Her life has meaning, it has meaning Charras! It means more than this; she means more than *all* of this."

The moon cast Christian's face in a swathe of silver, highlighting his anguish.

"You love her," Charras murmured, the realisation dawning on him with serene clarity.

Clasping his hands behind his neck and staring at the sky, Christian let out a breath. He shut his eyes to stem the welling in his throat and bit down on his lip. And then, slowly, his expression changed and he shrugged. "I don't *love* her. What would it matter anyway? It's all for nothing."

"No…" Charras stepped closer and placed a hand on his shoulder. "Love is never for nothing."

His expression cold, Christian set his jaw. "Then let's be thankful she means nothing to me."

"You don't mean that."

"I do. At least I do now. And at least I know now, you know, before –"

"Christian…"

But it was too late, there was nothing more Charras could do than watch as Christian wiped his face, straightened his shoulders, and disappeared into the Haunt.

34
Memories

A fierce wind whipped the sides of the quiet cottage, its rowdy tongue searching for a way in. It only managed to enter through a gap beneath the door, satisfied to cause a slight chill within the small rooms – as was its aim.

Noting how alike he was to that vicious wind, Charras swallowed another dram of whiskey.

Unaccustomed to Charlize's emotions, finding her in tears brought out a side of him that he wished he didn't possess. Most fathers would console and aim to help heal the pain of their children. But not him… His duty was about teaching her to be strong. So, sitting her up, demanding she pull herself together before sending her away to calm down was the best he could do. He had to ignore the look in her eyes as they silently begged for comfort, it long becoming a brutal habit. And when she stormed from him, another bond broken, another comfort denied, he knew she hated him – which of course she should; he was a terrible father. To be honoured with that title, you had to protect your offspring with every fibre you possessed. But not him; he couldn't do that, not without being selfish. They were chosen to sacrifice, to bear the burden for whatever reason the Sky decided.

And why them? He would never understand it… Only Isalize had ever truly accepted it.

Although the winter was cold, it was nothing compared to the atmosphere within the manor, and Charras was grateful when he could light the fires, bringing anew warmth.

It had been months since he and Isalize shared a bed, and if it wasn't for her soft presence, he would barely notice she lived there. Somehow, they managed to avoid each other for the most part, and when they did cross paths, polite and mumbled exchanges were commonplace and always short lived.

But then, one night, a knock came at the door.

Looking up from his book, marginally annoyed his knowledge about, 'THE IMPORTANCE OF MEDIA IN A MINAE INFESTED WORLD' had been disturbed, Charras left the library. He met Isalize in the lobby and she bowed her head politely before opening the door and greeting their visitors.

Leanne and Theo stepped through into the warmth, each wearing hearty smiles as they embraced Isalize. When it was Leanne's turn, she held her at arm's length and wiped the hair from her cheek. "You're sad."

Shooting Charras a quick look, Isalize shrugged. "Let me get you some tea."

"Tea?" Leanne laughed, holding out a bottle of brandy. "No, my darling, tonight is cause for celebration."

With a marginal rise of her eyebrows, Isalize took the offering from her friend's grasp and disappeared into the kitchen, leaving her guests to greet Charras in the same manner as they had her.

"It's good to see you," said Charras.

And it was. It seemed as if the last two months had been drawn and stretched out for as long as they possibly could be. The distraction of their closest friends was more welcome than the brandy they promised.

After a few hearty hello's, Leanne and Theo allowed themselves to be ushered into the sitting room.

"She's back then, for good?" asked Leanne when they were settled.

Charras shrugged.

Opening her mouth to say something, she stopped as Isalize entered with several glasses of brandy on the rocks and a bowl of crisps. She handed them around before contenting herself in the rocking chair, smiling as her guests enjoyed the company of one another.

It was always so easy to do so, their bond one that almost seemed effortless, each ignoring the fact that their friendship was considered outrageous. It was quietly known that if Leanne and Theo were not lucky enough to have found each other, they would also be outcasts. And in that knowledge, their loyalty and support lay firmly with the love and bond between the four of them.

Charras let out a hearty laugh and pointed his brandy at Theo so it swilled and almost escaped the glass. "But you weren't to know, I wouldn't be so hard on yourself!"

His eyes wide, Theo stretched out his arms. "She could barely fit in my car, let alone explain to me why she failed to mention the several whales she'd devoured over the summer!"

"Don't be cruel Theo," Leanne scolded. "Mildred was a lovely person. Charras here could at least see her potential."

"Yes, yes I did. She had huge potential."

Snorting with laughter, Charras and Theo ignored the scornful expressions of their other halves.

"I will never forgive you for that you dog."

"Come now Theo, I introduced you to your wife, which has to count for something!"

Twisting his head to smile at Leanne, Theo caressed her stomach. "It counts for everything."

It was then Isalize pointed at Leanne's brandy, which had not been touched. As they all followed her finger, Leanne held the glass above her head. "You've got me," she beamed.

Unsure how to behave, Charras watched his friend's mouths move as they explained how they would soon become proud parents – gushing as they revealed how they conceived a boy only two nights ago.

He put his glass down. "Excuse me," he said, getting up and leaving the room.

Walking through the lobby and into the kitchen, he threw open the door and breathed in the frosty evening, the slap of cold a sobering hand. Sooner than he cared for, a gentle touch clasped his shoulder.

"Is everything alright?"

Charras closed his eyes and reached for Leanne's fingers. "Forgive me, it is wonderful news. You'll be amazing parents."

"Hmmm, I'm not so sure the Hetairia Doman will agree, but we want you and Isalize to be godparents."

Clenching his fists, Charras tried to stop the welling in his stomach.

"Come now, what's wrong?"

He forced a smile and turned to put his arm across Leanne's shoulders. "Nothing, we'd be honoured."

"Do not think I'm ignorant. I can see how you and Isalize ignore each other. There's ice between you."

Charras stopped smiling and shook his head. Then, pulling two chairs from the table, he sat on one and coaxed Leanne onto the other.

With a deep breath, he spoke to her lap. "She came back to tell me we need to conceive."

Confusion crossed Leanne's face as she struggled to find an expression. "But neither of you wanted…"

"We don't, we don't want to."

"Then why?"

Putting his head in his hands, Charras sighed. "We conceive the next Āetis."

"Oh my," Leanne gasped, fanning her face as hot tears sprang down her cheeks. "But that means…"

Charras nodded.

In the silence, they both took in the revelation. Then, sitting upright, Leanne held onto Charras's arm. "So, you won't touch her now?" His tortured eyes answered her question. "And what of Isalize, how does she feel about it?"

"Well, first she ran away, and then she came back and dropped it on me. She wants to go ahead with it."

"Oh my…"

Wishing his brandy was within reach, Charras waited as Leanne collected herself.

"Okay, so you've talked about this?"

He shook his head.

"Well, surely that's a good start?!"

"I can't Leanne, it's too…"

"Painful?"

Nodding, Charras looked into his friends face and saw compassion. "You think I should don't you?"

Leanne reached for his hand and grasped it tightly. "Have you considered both possibilities?" She put her finger to his lips as he tried to say something. "If you don't do this, you risk more than just your own happiness, although by the state you're both in tonight, that happiness doesn't seem to be forthcoming."

"So you think I should do something that I know will kill her?"

With more tears springing down her face, Leanne squeezed his hand. "I think you should trust her. What's the alternative? Could you live years the way you are now, or spend your last month's together as fully as you can?"

Charras stood from the table, flinching as the chair scraped across the tiles. He span to find an escape but only saw the wall clock – its endless job to mark time mocking him. He slapped his hand next to its face. "You sound just like her."

Leanne joined him and pulled him into an embrace. "It is not for me to say my darling," she whispered. "But just know we'll be here whatever you decide."

Unashamedly burying his head in her hair, Charras clutched Leanne so tightly he wasn't sure he'd let go. It was only when she coughed he released her.

"Got a grip on you there," she smirked, shaking out her arms.

"Is everything okay?" came Isalize's concerned voice from the lobby arch.

Appearing in the kitchen moments later, she looked accusingly at the both of them.

Leanne immediately broke into retching sobs and ran over to throw her arms around her friend's neck.

"Hey…" Isalize hushed, stroking her hair. "It's alright, I'm here." From over her friend's shoulder, she caught Charras's eye and shot him a look that would cut a Sirenari's talon.

He knew he was in trouble.

It was a while before Leanne and Theo left, the night having turned sombre quicker than any of them hoped. Explanations were made, tears were shed, and promises of support declared… but it was only when the door shut and Isalize stormed past him, Charras realised just how angry she was.

"She knew something wasn't right," he tried.

"So you devastate her? Rain on her parade?"

Face to face and locked in eye contact for one of the first times in months, Isalize waited for him to answer, her hands firmly on her hips.

"I needed to talk to someone."

"You could have talked to me! I have waited and waited for you to stop sulking!"

"Sulking? After what you did, I think I'm entitled!"

"No Charras, no you're not, because there are things bigger than us, bigger than the world we've built around ourselves so we can be together." She let out a sigh of exasperation and dropped her hands to her sides. "When did you get so selfish?"

Spluttering as Isalize walked into the bathroom and slammed the door behind her, Charras called after her: "If not wanting to lose you is selfish then I'm guilty, and if it means you hate me for the rest of my life then so be it. But I love you, and I will never do something that's going to hurt you, let alone kill you!"

The door was thrown open, Isalize appearing in its frame as she pointed at him. He found himself airborne as a gush of water slammed him into the opposite wall. His skin prickled and burned as she stood over him, fury in her eyes.

"That pain you're feeling? That's not even close to the pain I feel because of *you* right now."

Charras sent a rush of air to dry himself, scowling at Isalize as she disappeared into the bathroom once more. When he was sure she wouldn't come back, he got to his feet and escaped into the library, slamming the door behind him. Then, picking up his earlier whiskey glass, he threw it against the nearest bookshelf.

An hour later, after he licked his wounds, Charras lay back in his favourite leather chair, deciding to sleep in the library that night. He listened as Isalize wandered about the manor, making no effort to be quiet anymore as she cleared the mess she made. He would wait for her to go to bed before he dared close his eyes, but that eventuality wasn't shortcoming, the shower she previously wanted soon running at full power.

He closed his eyes and tried not to think of her naked body; tried to ignore the memory of soapsuds running down her porcelain skin, her hands massaging the scent over her slender form. He knew how she looked, how the water would turn her light blonde hair to gold; how her lashes would flutter as he admired her...

Luckily, before the heat intensified, he was cut short from his daydreams by the sudden silence. A minute passed before he heard Isalize leave the bathroom and disappear into the sitting room.

He wondered if she was enjoying the fire he made, spitefully hoping it wasn't as glorious as earlier. But even as he tried to hold onto the anger, it slowly ebbed away, leaving him with nothing but the empty understanding that he was desperately alone, a hollowness made deeper by the library's vastness.

Tentatively, he stood up and left the haven of his favourite chair. He crossed the lobby and stood outside the living room, listening, waiting for some sort of sign... But nothing came, only the growing wave of loneliness, arms that offered solace in mutual despair; a life he didn't want...

Taking a deep breath, he quietly opened the door.

Sat in front of the hearth, Isalize hugged her knees to her chest. For a moment she looked so fragile that Charras nearly retreated, but as she picked her head up and faced him, he saw the strength emanate from her sapphire eyes. Golden flames danced within them, so that when she stared they almost looked otherworldly.

He shut the door behind him and slowly made his way over, crouching beside her so their faces were inches apart. "Aren't you scared?"

Isalize nodded and stroked his cheek. "I'm terrified."

He touched his forehead to hers and kissed the tip of her nose. "I'm so sorry," he murmured.

Entwining her fingers in his hair, Isalize rubbed her cheek against his. "So am I. But I love you Charras; there's nothing you can do to stop that."

And somehow, the months of despair fell away, forgotten and clouded by the truth in those words. It was all that mattered to them; all that had ever mattered.

Charras took Isalize in his arms and laid her on the rug, kissing everywhere he could find, rediscovering what he vowed never to touch again.

They refused to think about the consequences, safe in the knowledge that if a thousand years passed, the moments between them that night would be remembered. And as he brought himself into her, fitting as if they were made for each other, he knew: that night would be his greatest memory.

"Charras?"

Reality hit him like a ton of bricks, snapping him from his reverie as he faced Christian. He sat on the chair adjacent to the settee, his pale face somehow shining in the gloom.

"When did you get in?" he asked, sitting up and rubbing his stubble.

Christian shrugged. "About ten minutes ago. You were just staring. It's like you didn't even see me."

Nodding, Charras picked up the whiskey bottle and poured himself another measure. "Where did you go?"

"Amy's."

"I see."

"It's not like that."

A sharp gust rustled the plants outside the window, followed by two short raps against the door.

Instinctively pulling his jumper tighter, Christian spoke softly. "I didn't mean to act like that. I just didn't –"

"I know."

He nodded and walked to the kitchen, proceeding to open several cupboards before he found what he sought and returned with his own tumbler. He shoved it towards Charras and watched as an obliging and generous measure was poured. Then, taking a sip, he let it burn the back of his throat, deciding that his taste for whiskey seemed greatly improved.

"I just hate that it's her. With everything else – my parents, this life... I hate how it's her."

Charras nodded.

"I guess she's pretty mad at me?"

He shook his head. "Not so much at you. We both expected a less than favourable reaction."

Allowing another swig to sear his throat, Christian leaned forward, gripping his tumbler in both hands. "Does it get easier?"

Taken aback, Charras took a while to answer, exhaling slowly as he fathomed an explanation. "The pain lessens, scars somewhat… But scars don't stop the pain, they just remind you that you've survived it before and can therefore survive it again."

"How do you do it?"

"Because there are things bigger than my desire for Charlize to live a full and healthy life, bigger than everything I want for her. Better her live to the fullest now, to die for the greater good and be honoured and proud, than to die selfishly, outcast, and alone."

"But she doesn't live, does she? She hides herself away."

"She always has."

"But why?"

"I don't know Christian." Shifting his gaze to the bedroom where Charlize slept, Charras sighed. "I suppose its easier for her, I suppose she sees me doing the same. But if you carried her burden, what would you do?"

Christian put his glass on the coffee table and clasped his hands. "I would live. How can you die for a cause you know nothing about?"

"You don't know what she feels."

He snorted. "Neither do you, neither does *she*. Isn't that dangerous, doesn't that worry you? She's so tightly wound up, aren't you scared that one day she'll snap?"

"She's strong."

"Do you hear yourself? Is this what you convince yourself every night? Strength isn't about how much you can quietly carry. Strength comes from experience and expression, knowing yourself and your values. If my parents taught me anything, they taught me that living and loving are the greatest tests of a person's strength."

"And look where that got them Christian," said Charras, standing as he clenched his whiskey glass. "All love has ever done is create suffering. Do not come in here and act as if you know me, or my daughter, or what you think is right or wrong. You are an unbecome."

Also standing, Christian crossed his arms. "I don't need to be a Mage to see you falling apart. Walking in to see you sitting around staring at walls tells me that. None of this is fair, none of this is right, whatever you might tell yourself."

Placing his glass firmly on the table, Charras turned his back. "You'll understand soon enough. Your intuition and good intentions are much like your mothers, but even she grew weary. Why do you think she hid you from all this?"

"So I didn't become bitter and twisted like you?"

Peering over his shoulder, Charras smirked. "Precisely."

35

Spring

$\mathcal{W}$hen Armmos explained how spring was a remarkable sight, he did the Haunt an injustice. In all his eighteen years, Christian had never encountered such a beautiful habitat. The entire Haunt had come alive, a botanical oasis born beneath the warming season, and everything it touched seemed to burst with vitality, injecting the trees with life previously hidden through the winter.

Sequoias, once fully grown, were not known for their dense foliage, yet the leaves they did produce were saved for the third level, creating a spectacular montage to the rich depths the forest possessed. Potted plants of varying colours and species filled the previously unoccupied spaces, with intertwining plants such as emerald and trumpet creepers crawling their way along the once bare archways and bridges, the contrasting blues and reds bursting with vibrancy. Some hung down from the decks above, creating natural curtains where Mages could hide for play or privacy, and it was in one such section Christian sat, his eyes half closed as a hue of soft light beamed from above, kissing the sequoia's bark with patches of light.

It was here, as he sat among the dewdrops, watching butterfly's dance with blood red tulips and pale yellow witch-hazel, here where he laughed at the odd looking Hummingbirds drinking the nectar of their favoured trumpet creepers, and here where tame forest animals dwelled and made noises, the likes he barely recognised; it was here where magic happened. He believed that now.

And it was a relatively recent change of heart, a moment he wouldn't forget as he stepped from the amber glade that day and out into the glorious sunshine. Through appreciating the majesty of what he beheld, it gave him the ability to mask the darkness of the previous nights, his estrangement from Charlize, and the constant ache inside his stomach as he grieved and yearned for his parents. It was as if his eyes were opened once again and the clarity of thought bestowed him with a faith that somehow, in some way, everything was going to be okay.

Charras would comment his Fulgor nature was mostly to blame, but to be positive, even against such odds seemed a gift to him, and so he paid no heed to his sullen, drunken mentor.

"There you are!"

Snapping his eyes open, Christian shielded his face as he peered up at Jess who stood with her hands on her hips.

"You haven't got long."

"I'm not going."

"Yeah, you are."

Christian scowled.

"Come on, it's not like she bites." She put her hand out.

With a shake of his head, Christian dismissed her offering. Then, folding his arms across his chest, he sighed as Jess sat on the bench next to him.

"You can't just ignore her."

He grunted in response, a sign that his intentions were precisely that, but soon yelped as Jess flicked his ear.

"Now, you listen to me Christian Strike. She's got enough people staring and judging and fearing her, the sorts of people who can't even have a conversation with the person who's gonna save us at the end of all this. Don't be the kind of arse who joins 'em. Us lot is all she's got at a shot of being normal." She stood up and grabbed his good wrist, pulling him to his feet. "Don't be selfish, be a reason for her to fight."

"She'll fight whether I speak to her or ignore her. Speaking to her just makes me angry," he said, rubbing his ear.

"She isn't a robot! Yeah, she'll fight, because she's got honour and the weight of millions of lives on her shoulders, but don't you wanna make her last moments on earth happy ones?"

"It's not that simple…"

"Sure it is. Just get your head outta your –"

"Okay," Christian said, interjecting before she could fire another insult. "But it's not that easy either."

Rolling her eyes, Jess prodded a finger towards him. "And you think it's easy for her?"

He said nothing, a short stab of shame hitting him in the same place Jess's finger pointed.

"We're her best friends, probably her only friends," she said. "Start acting like it. It might be painful to lose her, but at least when you do, you can say you made things less crappy while she was here."

With shame now searing through every part of his body, Christian reached out and hugged Jess to him. Two short and tense pats on his back confirmed his bout of affection was misplaced, so he let he go, smiling in response to her flushed cheeks. "When did you get so wise Jessica Gale?"

"Dunno," she said, grimacing slightly. "Just go and be nice."

"Aren't you coming?"

"Nah, I lost Jade in the frock section of Foila, gotta go find her."

Nodding once, detached from the trials of dress fittings, Christian parted the vines.

"Oh, and by the way!" Jess called after him. "Don't ever call me Jessica again. Not unless you want your other ear to match!"

Three newly placed lilac trees stood outside the cottage, swaying languorously as they soaked up the afternoon rays. Sitting cross-legged on a garish lime blanket beneath the shade of one, Charlize read what looked like a manual of sorts.

She seemed frustrated, her brow creased and hair tucked behind her ears as she furiously traced the words with her fingers, her lips moving as she tried to digest the meaning of the small and complicated text.

Christian couldn't help but feel a pang of guilt as he walked towards her, and bending low, swooped the manual from her grasp. He held it above his head as she squinted up at him, anger flashing in her expression. She didn't say a word, which made him feel foolish, so he handed it back, smiling apologetically as she took it gently and hugged it to her chest.

Then they stared at each other, neither speaking, a tension Charlize refused to break after her week of silent treatment. So when Christian sat next to her, she hid her annoyance by re-opening her guide and continuing to read the instructions for the upcoming traditions – of which she was to play an integral part. Unfortunately, it didn't seem to have been updated for several decades and the language used drawled out for longer than necessary.

"You're not going to make this easy for me are you?"

Meeting his gaze, Charlize sighed. "There is nothing to make easy or hard Christian. It is what it is. I expected nothing less."

The words stung, but Christian knew he deserved worse. He leaned back on his elbows and considered his next move.

Overhead, a bird chirped, its song attracting another just like it. Entrapped in some sort of dance, they hopped from branch to branch, chirping and dancing over and over before flying away onto another tree in the distance.

How simple that mating ritual seemed to be, Christian thought, stealing another glance at Charlize and noting how her irritation brought a stubborn flush to her cheeks.

"So," he started. "I was thinking about this whole cross-kin stuff. Pretty crazy how that's bad right?"

Charlize snapped her guide shut, resigning herself to conversation as she pondered a response. "I suppose it depends what angle you look at it from," she said. "Most would agree everything we do is *pretty crazy*."

Christian ignored her tone and pushed on. "I guess Mages need to go at it like rabbits too, especially back in the days of the Firsts."

Coughing, her cheeks flushing for a different reason, Charlize composed her face. "If what you mean is Mages bore many pure blooded children, then yes. It kept the bloodlines strong and omitted the risk of cross-kin, or worse, diluting, which is when an Ungifted and Mage procreate."

"I see. Guess you have to have some perks."

Stunned, although curiously unable to hide a smirk, Charlize rubbed her neck. "I wouldn't know," she said quietly.

"What, aren't you allowed? –"

"I don't want to talk about it Christian."

"But you're missing –"

"Is your every question meant to offend me?" she barked, getting to her feet.

"No, I'm genuinely interested!" Christian said, his hands held up in defence.

Charlize scowled, although stayed where she was and folded her arms across her chest. "It's not that I can't, it's just too high a risk."

"Risk...?"

Looking at him pointedly, she rubbed her stomach.

It was his turn to blush. "Ah, yes, I see why that would be a problem."

"It would be a catastrophe."

With a sigh, Christian lay back on the rug and stared up at the Sky, the deep blue limitless and perfect. Not for the first time, he wondered what lay beyond it, where it ended – if it ended – and if he would ever discover the secrets within the stars.

"I don't understand you," he said quietly.

Charlize hugged her arms tighter, not sure she understood her either, and knelt back down. "Well, what do you want to know?"

"Do you believe in love?"

"Hmmm," she murmured, pondering how to answer. She joined Christian and lay on the blanket, gently placing her head so it just touched his shoulder. "I think so."

"Changed your tune?"

She laughed. "Perhaps, but I can see what people class as love all around me. I can't deny its existence, but I do question its value. The phenomenon seems to cause more hurt than good. It makes people *pretty crazy.*"

"Don't you love Charras?"

"He's my father."

"That's not what I asked."

Frowning, Charlize thought about it for a second. Then, finding her answer, she replied, "We have a blood tie, a bond, and everything I am, I owe to him. If I were to believe in love between family and friends, then he is the closest I have to that."

Christian turned his head and saw the confusion on her face. "You still didn't answer me."

With his breath on her cheek, Charlize turned so their eyes locked. His dark eyes searched hers, flecks of lighter brown around his pupils almost pin pointing the holes in her unfaltering certainty about her purpose, as if they symbolised truth and the fact it wasn't absolute.

He cleared his throat and returned his gaze to the sky, and it was only at that moment Charlize became aware of the friction between them.

"So, sacrifices…" he said.

She swallowed. "Yes, there are many."

"I mean the old ones; the ones between Ungifted and Mages – when love wasn't so taboo. Couldn't a Mage just sacrifice half of themselves now? I mean, instead of diluting?"

"Oh they do, there are rare cases of the blood ritual continuing if a Mage can find an Ungifted who believes them, and without driving them to madness. Unless you can fall in love at ten of course, which is quite implausible. Also, it is a huge sacrifice to half your life for each other, especially now there are plenty of options within each clan."

"Hence why love is such a faerie-tale notion huh?"

"No, it's just a lucky phenomenon. But that's why dual kin's became more accepted. Inbreeding has never been something favourable."

"But didn't the villagers or nomads go mad hundreds of years ago when Mages turned up searching for their love and showed them a fireball or something?"

Laughing, Charlize shook her head. "Magic was not such a faerie-tale back then, or in the farthest reaches of the earth. It is only now the tale seems far-fetched – something you should understand well! Besides, Mages weren't always so dramatic and bitter, most would have assumed it exciting and romantic."

Christian raised an eyebrow and propped himself on an elbow. "Really, how was it done?"

His head blocked the sun, casting a shadow across Charlize's face and shielding her from its rays. She admired the contour of light emanating behind him, making it appear he had a lion's mane.

"It takes a personal sacrifice – one of great bravery," she replied. "In the case of lovers, a blood sacrifice will do, a ritual where they drink a vial of the other's under the spell of a full moon."

"That's disgusting."

"I hear it is an impressive feat, although rarely performed nowadays."

"I can see why."

Smiling despite herself, regardless of Christian's disrespectful tone, Charlize generally agreed. There was something almost primitive about drinking another's blood, saved generally for the more eccentric of Mages, or Mages steeped in tradition, such as the Aquāe or Glacies. She dreaded to think of the impact Christian's presence would have in those Haunts – how they would treat him once his blood status became known. Not all clans were as gracious as the Anima...

Disturbed by the sounds of several pairs of feet joining them in the glade, Charlize and Christian sat up as two flames darted into the air, followed by the sounds of laughter.

"Jade, Jess, enough!" came Armmos's scolding as he bustled up behind them. "It is not yet secure!"

Having never heard Armmos angry, Christian found it amusing how his sleepy eyes wobbled and his voice broke slightly.

"Come Armmos, they are excited, and the Haunt is almost ready," said Charras, releasing another flame that Jess and Jade blasted upwards to prove the point.

Scowling so his lids fell to his lashes, Armmos grumbled a profanity but said nothing more on the matter, instead watching as Jess and Jade pulled Charlize and Christian to their feet.

"You ready then?" Jade asked, picking up and passing Charlize the aged manual.

She shrugged. "As I'll ever be."

"Oh I am so excited! Charlie, you *have* to see my dress."

Jess rolled her eyes. "Took her long enough to pick it."

"I'm sure it's beautiful."

Beaming with pride, Jade turned to Christian and playfully hit his arm. "I saw Amy there too. She can't wait to dance with you."

Christian turned pink, unsure what to say. He shot Charlize a quick glance, noting how she seemed perfectly composed.

"Great!" he said with more enthusiasm than intended.

No one seemed to notice however, the twin's simply high fiving him before running up to Charras – who dutifully released another flame. They blasted it high, their cheers and laughter quickly spreading throughout the glade. And when it seemed their excitement couldn't reach more dizzying heights, a bell tolled.

Its bass note deep, the reverberation shook the Haunt beneath their feet. On the third chime, it rang out for a second longer and then stopped, granting a few seconds of quiet before a drum sounded, followed by a trumpet, a trombone, and then several saxophones.

"I see everything is prepared," Armmos said, a smile finally adorning his face. "For three days we will be shielded from eyes, ears, and even smells."

Charlize nodded her understanding. Any longer and the resources needed to maintain the protection would drain the energies of all the

Anima Mages, for it was they who offered their magic to sustain the powerful protection.

With several high-pitched squeals, Jade and Jess took flight, leaving the others to stare after them as they disappeared towards the music.

"Well," said Armmos, clapping his hands, "let the festivities begin!"

36
Festivities

ᐯanilla and must hung on the breeze, the warm scents mildly disguised by the citrus plants lining the walkways. But the mix of conflicting aromas was not the reason Charlize held her breath.

The vines wrapped around her head itched and the poorly inspired dress of foliage had a train which lagged behind, threatening broken ankles with every step as it gathered various needles and un-swept debris along its journey. Although terrified, she managed to smile dutifully as she made her way towards the podium, through the lines of Mages standing either side of her, and into the hands of Armmos as he helped her up to join him.

Standing above the sea of Mages, she could better admire their decorative handiwork, their pride and skill poured into their home to mark the Spring Festival. Bunting of greens and gold adorned the fringes of the spacious deck, the barriers decorated with matching crepe streamers and tied like bows along each rope tier, while the familiar lanterns of dewdrops bobbed gently in the cooling breeze.

"Welcome," Armmos beamed to the crowd. "Today marks the first day of our traditional festivities, although this is no ordinary spring; for this spring we have our Āetis, and this spring brave warriors can challenge her might."

Although her title of Āetis could be spoken in formal circumstances, Charlize still hated the sound of it, what the connotations stood for: unique, deity, saviour, all-powerful… and what it really stood for: sacrifice. She wondered who first banned the word outside of formality, who first explained the turmoil it caused to those it applied to. Whoever they were, she thanked them silently.

"…so to those who feel they are worthy opponents, I ask you to step forward."

Staring at the faces looking up at her, Charlize resisted the urge to itch her scalp. Instead, she jutted out her chin and squared her shoulders in an attempt to look formidable.

A bass drum started beating a rhythm and a ripple soon parted the crowd as two bright haired Mages climbed onto the podium. They bowed to Armmos before turning to Charlize and repeating the action.

"Would be rude not to!" said Jess.

Hiding her smile, Charlize simply bowed back, as her manual instructed, and stood to let the twins stand to her right.

As she took her place, Jess eyed her curiously. "You look stupid," she said, just loud enough for Charlize to hear above the resuming drumbeat.

"Not as much as I feel," she shot back.

Another ripple started further back, although one with no intention of making haste. Almost in slow motion, it took what seemed like an age before the face of the next challenger appeared at the foot of the podium. His shoulders back and face determined, Tunde climbed the three short stairs and bowed towards Charlize, who mirrored his action.

Worthy opponents indeed she thought, glad her skills would be challenged.

But it was the next opponent who shocked her the most. A petite blonde, releasing her permanent grasp from Christian's arm in the front row, stepped forward; levitated herself up; landed light footed, and then bent straight into an elegant curtsey. So stunned, Charlize nearly forgot to acknowledge her challenge, hastily doing so before she caused insult.

With a smile, Amy twirled around and took her place next to Tunde. She smiled into the crowd, catching Christian's stare, and Charlize was happy to note she wasn't the only one who found the turn of events surprising, his face a mixture of shock and admiration.

"Very well," Armmos boomed, holding his hand up for silence. "As the final challenger, I will also step forward, an act seeped in history that dates back to the time of the Firsts – my direct lineage."

He turned and bowed, Charlize doing the same, lower than before, so the tips of the vines around her head clattered against the wood beneath her feet.

Roars and cheers rang out then, the big band kicking back in as the Mages all began to dance. They hooked their arms through their neighbours to swing them around, interweaving in random patterns and finding a new partner at each turn.

It was easy to get swept up in the lively jig, the violins fast and joyful, and soon Charlize found herself lifted on a pocket of air – the challengers balancing her above their heads. She had to force herself not to retaliate, her defensive reactions almost innate. But after she was bounced from Mage to Mage a couple of times, the music slowed and she was lowered to the floor. Glad of it, she tried to find her balance, stepping forward and tripping on what she later decided was the maple leaf layer. She splayed out her hands, although her knees took the impact first, the vines following to whip her arms and fingers as she steadied her landing. Crimson, an arm closed around her waist and pulled her up – to the alarm of those who watched.

"Are you okay?" Christian asked, supporting her weight.

"Christian, you can't touch me," Charlize scolded, straightening up. "It is rude in formal circumstances."

She didn't mean to sound spiteful, and the hurt that flashed in his eyes made her stomach feel strange, but she couldn't let him act so brashly at a formal event while everyone watched.

"Please forgive him," she addressed the crowds. "He is still new to our world, but I'd like to thank you all for your kindness towards him while he learns."

Receiving various forms of smile back, some vacuous, others genuine, Charlize felt shame sink to her stomach. She knew the whispers that followed her and Christian, the fear of her blatant disregard for the laws binding their race. But she also knew how the Anima saw light in dark, kindness in malevolence, and hope when all seemed lost. Although Christian was unbecome, he was still a Mage, and hope, light, and kindness would help him reach his potential.

"Come Christian," Armmos boomed through the parting crowds. "I will teach you a thing or two about how to handle a powerful woman!"

Laughter erupted, lightening the mood, and the band began to play a song that pulsed in Charlize's heart, both soothing and distracting while she watched Christian follow Armmos to the bar. She refused to meet his fleeting gaze, turning away abruptly, but she wasn't angry, she was deeply sorry for the embarrassment she'd caused him – even if he could never know it. *And just when we were starting to be friends,* she thought.

Two... no, three... or maybe four... perhaps more, Christian wasn't sure. All he knew was whiskey and ale made a fantastic concoction. So fantastic, earlier that night he danced with Amy, Jess, Jade, and other Mages he didn't know on the decking area, the same area Armmos first explained existed because four trees grew away from each other. To him, it seemed the sequoias knew the Anima liked to party...

Spinning around, his eyes slightly blurry, he half listened to the conversation Charras and Armmos participated heartily in, their cheeks red and foreheads glistening. They talked about their own mishaps with women after explaining to Christian all the rules and regulations regarding Charlize. He felt quite enlightened.

According to the big invisible rulebook, he could not touch her unless she allowed it or initiated it first, for to the eyes of those watching she was higher-than-high with a big red throne in the Sky waiting for her and must be treated with respect. After all, she would be the one walking onto a battlefield to sacrifice herself for the rest of them; it was only fair to allow her a superiority complex.

Searching for her face for what seemed like the fiftieth time, he saw she now engaged in conversation with two men of who must have been a combined age of one hundred and eighty.

She sat prettily on a golden chair at the back of the podium – the dress of decaying leaves lying across the deck – where she listened and laughed to whatever she heard, regardless of whether it was actually amusing, he was sure…

A decision made, he slammed his drink on the bar and stood from the stool. "Back soon," he said to his oblivious companions.

With a slight wobble, he made his way through the dancers and reached the foot of the podium unharmed. He clutched the side of the deck before leaning his elbow on it, and then casually stared out towards the crowds – most of whom swooned in each other's arms.

The lanterns now seemed to bob in time with the music, their soft ambiance casting patches of light beneath their trail, and squinting slightly, Christian swore he saw Jess embracing Tunde. Fist pumping the air, he pointed at her and winked.

Not that she saw any of it.

"Christian?"

Twisting around, he looked up at Charlize who was crouching so her face was just above his.

"Oh hey!" he said, and then holding up his hands in defence: "I'm not touching you."

Her eyebrows rose and she shot an accusatory glance at her father and Armmos still by the bar. Then, returning her gaze to her inebriated friend, she said, "I think you should go to bed."

"I think *you* should go to bed. All that talking… exhausting. You haven't even danced!"

Charlize studied him for a moment before replying, "You're right, I haven't danced."

She stood up and bid the elderly gentlemen goodnight, then hitched up her dress and climbed down from the podium. Once at the bottom, she faced Christian directly and dipped her head.

"Do the same," she whispered.

He did as he was told, although soon found that balancing was a skill requiring more effort than usual.

"Of course I will dance with you!" she said, louder than needed.

A few glances came their way, but most people carried on with whatever previously held their attention, something Charlize was glad of. She held up her hand, which Christian touched immediately.

She smiled. "You're learning fast."

"I have good teachers."

With his bandaged wrist against her waist, they kept their right hands together and began to step backwards and forwards, then side to side, Christian surprisingly able to lead.

"When did you learn to dance?" Charlize asked.

He shrugged. "Mum used to dance with me and Dad all the time. She'd always spin us in circles until we got so dizzy we'd fall over."

Thinking it sounded exactly like Leanne, Charlize laughed. "That sounds fun, but this dress isn't very flexible."

Christian considered her before nodding. "You look like a plant."

"It was not my choice to wear it, I assure you!" she protested, open-mouthed. "Besides, this outfit looks better on the spirit it's based on."

Christian stopped their stride and looked aghast. "You mean the Firsts are talking trees?"

"Talking trees? What on earth? No, of course not!"

He smirked and shook his head, noting how Charlize's face brimmed with intrigue. "You really didn't get out much did you?"

"You know I didn't."

Resuming their dancing, he said, "That was something we Ungifted call a joke."

"Oh…" she turned her face downwards. "My apologies."

He shrugged. "You know, I would have shown you all the delights of Marsh if you'd let me. It may have socialised you a little."

"You barely spoke to me."

"No, you barely spoke to anyone else, other than Elliott."

Accepting that was probably true, Charlize concentrated on the new steps Christian added to their dance. He pulled her close and then bent her towards the floor before snapping her back up to face him.

"Ah! So he's a Mage too!" he declared, only just piecing together the obvious.

"Indeed," Charlize confirmed. "And a dedicated one. He aided my studies greatly."

"That's because he worshipped you. We used to call him your little pet."

A flash of annoyance crossed her face. She locked eyes with him, ready to snap back a retort, but instead, inches away, her heart raced and she faltered. Entirely confused by the effect Christian's nearness had on her, Charlize stopped their dancing, although remained in the same position.

"Well then; there's the reason I didn't speak to you. We were ignorant to each other," she said quietly.

"But we're not now, are we?" he said. "I can still remember walking in and seeing you with him, how I felt even back then."

With a strange surge in her stomach, Charlize tried to loosen his hold.

"Wait," he said, tightening his grip. "I've had more than a few drinks, I know that. I'm under the influence of whatever Charras and Armmos gave me. But I have to tell you –"

"Don't."

"I have to," he said, staring into her frightened eyes. "I need to get it out."

"Christian, whatever it is, it can wait. Tell me when your mind isn't clouded and you have more control over your thoughts."

"That's just it, my mind isn't clouded, my mind has never been clearer than it has been standing here, with you, now."

"Please…"

His eyes were dark and serious. "Nothing is more real to me than you Charlize."

Wrenching herself away, she bowed her head. "Thank-you for the dance."

Then, hurriedly gathering her dress, ignoring the curious glances cast her way, she made towards the exit of the deck, the need for space almost overwhelming. She was dizzy, her thoughts cloudy, and in absolutely no mood to see three men in suits marching towards her, armed and stern looking.

She instinctively held up her hands to cast.

"There will be no need for that Āetis," said one of the men curtly, "we're here for Tiron."

Charlize was unconvinced. Nevertheless, she slowly dropped her arms and waited for them to approach. The music was cut as all present noticed the new arrivals, save for a drawn out note from a trumpeter, which quickly trailed off when his fellow band member elbowed him.

Grunts of indignation sounded from the bar – before Glen and Hugo rushed over to point out what caused the disturbance. They then passed their leader his staff and followed him as he stormed over to Charlize and the intruders.

"You were not due for several days," said Armmos, bristling.

"We came early," the same curt man replied.

"How did you get in?" Charlize asked, stepping towards them.

They immediately all bowed their heads and she returned the formality, although still expected an answer.

"They are part of the protection," Armmos answered for them. "Only the highest security clearance within their ranks allows such an honour. They join us every five years to replace the barrier."

The way Armmos spoke seemed to suggest the decision was not one he agreed with.

"So, you can come and go as you please?" Charlize asked, raising an eyebrow. "Who decided to undermine the leadership of each Haunt?"

"Please Charlize, we can discuss this later," said Armmos, although he said it lightly, a hint of gratification in his voice.

"I would be glad to hear the answers," she replied tersely. "In the meantime, let me show the Hetairia Doman where Tiron sleeps."

"Of course," he replied, extending his arm towards the direction of the brewery.

Behind him, Charras joined the gathering cautiously, holding Christian by the arm. His brow darkened as the Hetairia Doman members eyed him with suspicion.

"You are embraced back into the world you shunned, and yet you still find ways to disobey?" the same abrupt man addressed him, looking pointedly at Christian. "Is there no end to your temper towards us?"

With the grip tightening on his arm, Christian noticed how Charras shook where he stood, the tremors violent as he fought whatever war waged within. Pulling his arm away, it seemed to snap him back to reality, and with controlled calm, Charras replied, "You know well the cause of my temper, Jenkins."

And then Christian saw it: the slender physique, an ill-fitting suit, the slicked back hair, black rimmed glasses perched on a scarred hooked nose, the animosity exuding from him… it all fit.

Lifting his chin, Jenkins squared his shoulders. "We all play our parts. Sky knows why you have yours, but we obey as we must. At least you have that saving grace… now."

"Come, I will hear none of this in my Haunt," said Armmos, holding his staff outwards so it hung between the quarrel. "Please gentlemen, do your bidding. We wouldn't wish to keep you longer than needed."

"Thank-you," a man who wasn't Jenkins replied. "Apologies for any intrusion, we were informed this was urgent. Continue with your celebrations and think of us no more, save until we have use of your hospitality."

Nodding his head, Armmos waved off the comments as if they were unnecessary, although Christian could see they eased his hostility.

"Please, come with me," said Charlize, leading the suited company from the dance floor. "It shouldn't take long."

As she left, disappearing into the depths of the Haunt, Armmos placed a coercing hand on Charras's shoulder. "Come old friend; do not let them anger you. Their place is not here."

Sighing, he unclenched his fists. "Coming home was never going to be easy, especially with the likes of those bureaucrats," he growled.

"They have a part to play like the rest of us."

"The part they played caused the death of Isalize and the doom of my daughter. Whatever part they play, I could never forgive it."

Armmos nodded his understanding and led Charras back to the bar, leaving Christian to stare after Charlize.

He couldn't be certain, but there was something familiar about Jenkins.

"Who gave the authority Armmos? Are you not to be trusted? Is the Sky not to be trusted anymore?"

Aggravated, Charlize paced up and down the corridor of the school, her footsteps echoing against the cold floor.

His hands cupped over the crystal on his staff, Armmos shook his head. "We debated for many months, but ultimately, we need their protection and funding. They straddle both worlds, the Ungifted and our own. They know how best to protect us from all threats. Do not forget the weaponry you saw on them. If the Ungifted were to learn of our existence, war could break out in more worlds than ours."

"But why Armmos?! What kind of earth is this if those we fight to save could be the very ones who turn against us?"

He let out a rueful laugh and straightened his shoulders. "Power, young one. It is all to do with power."

"But what is power if there is only darkness in which to use it?"

Taking his staff and tapping it on the floor, Armmos gestured for Charlize to take it. She reached out and clasped the neck, a rush of energy within the wood immediately greeting her.

Enriched with enchantments to aid strength should the wielder have use of it, the staff knew years of leaders, each a relative and each a provider of power to those it passed down to.

She handed it back to Armmos who took it gently, as if reunited with a fragile friend.

"Do you feel enriched?"

Charlize nodded.

"Do you feel able to conquer the world with a single swipe of your hand?"

She didn't respond.

Armmos smiled. He knew the answer. "You, who have more power than any who walk the earth, you could never know what it is to feel at the mercy of those stronger than you. I cannot answer why those without it yearn for power beyond them, for to do so I'd have to think like them, but I can speculate the reasons. They are the same reasons you *don't* yearn for it."

Frowning, Charlize crossed her arms, a chill setting within her chest. "Why would anyone yearn for something that will kill them?"

His eyes twinkling, Armmos leaned towards her. "Because it is only on the brink of death we truly feel alive."

Leader and Āetis stared at each other, ignorant to the intense silence as they each acknowledged the others truth sadly.

"Do you fear me Armmos?"

Atop his staff, the crystal clouded. Looking down at it, he chuckled. "My staff knew my lie before I uttered it. She has a way with my moods…" He took a breath, thought for a moment, sighed, and then looked into Charlize's eyes. "I do not fear your soul or your spirit. Those I trust the Sky chose wisely. But in all honesty, I fear your heart and those who could corrupt it. You are so young, with so much resting on your shoulders, and so full of questions…" His face downcast, Armmos composed himself, and then in a softer tone said, "You will face your demons like the rest of us. Remember to always follow the light young one. You will know its guidance."

A door opened in the long corridor, spilling faint light onto the surfaces. From the room, two shadows expanded until the forms of Christian and Charras emerged, both looking worn.

"You are to face your challengers in less than six hours, please go and rest," said Charras to Charlize, his face drawn.

"Is everything alright?" she asked, making no effort to move.

"For now." Then turning to Christian, he said, "You impressed them with what you already know, you impressed me, but we have much more to teach you in such little time."

"I know," Christian replied, the hours of questioning still fresh in his mind, and the knowledge that his ignorance hindered him more so.

From the classroom behind where they stood, two of the Hetairia Doman, neither of whom were Jenkins, poked their heads into the corridor.

"Stand back please," one demanded.

All obliging, a bulky form bound at the hands and feet and wrapped in a sheer black sheet floated into the corridor. Followed by the remaining Hetairia Doman member guiding him, an unconscious Tiron drifted towards the doors at the end. They swung open, allowing the faction to disappear into the schoolyard and leave those remaining to trail after.

With dawn rising only an hour before, an auburn glow bathed the Haunt. Birdsong trilled amongst the trees and a squirrel foraged eagerly undisturbed. It was gathering nuts, until it noticed the oncoming procession and darted away in alarm, chattering its annoyance as it dropped an acorn that clattered against the deck. Picking it up, Charlize used air to propel it towards the drey the squirrel poked its head from. It clasped it between its claws, immediately burying it amongst its already vast collection, and then returned a lookout for any other floating titbit.

"Cute," Christian mumbled, holding his head as it throbbed against his skull. "Do the birds answer to your call too?"

Her retort cut short by the incantation of the Hetairia Doman members, Charlize watched as the space between the two suits developed a sizeable cuboid of ice, which then moulded into the shape of a canoe, before levitating up to hip height. One of the members, who Charlize now realised was a Glacies Mage and the polite one from the night before, pulled out a similar but thicker sheet to the one wrapped around Tiron. He placed it in the canoe and then propped his prisoner at the end, making sure he was secure before joining him and seating himself comfortably in the front. The other member then climbed aboard, settled in, and prepared for their journey.

"Have you far to go?" Armmos asked as their combined spell rose into the air.

"Far enough, but not far enough our energy will dwindle," the newly identified Anima Mage replied. "Thank-you for your hospitality."

All bowing their heads in farewell, the Mages watched as the Hetairia Doman disappeared far into the atmosphere, remaining transfixed until they were nothing more than a lingering jet stream.

With the still air on their faces, it was Christian who first broke the calm.

"I need water," he said.

"Me too," Charras and Armmos agreed in unison.

With a slight smirk, Charlize held her palm towards them and accommodated.

37

Challenges

Parrying another blow as cheers erupted from below, Charlize darted upwards, hitting the roof of the dome barrier and catching her breath. Luckily, her challengers were easy to spot.

Before the match, several rules were put in place. She could not use the North Wind – the strongest and hardest to control; she could only use her Anima element, (otherwise this put her at an unfair advantage), and she had to face all of her challengers one by one, without rest.

"*Dicio, Āetis, Aduro,*" she commanded, sending Jess in the opposite direction of Jade as they attempted a joint spell.

"Owww!" Jess yelped, rubbing her shoulder as she re-balanced her footing several yards away.

Another bout of cheering roared through the dome, making Charlize look towards the spectators beneath. Around the edges, within an outer dome, they watched avidly while the battles played out. Once again, the Anima villagers all supplied their energy to form the impressive creation, which sat several feet above the Haunt and remained invisible to the outer world. But due to the complexity, along with the maintenance required to shield the Haunt, it could only last a few hours before the energy began to drain the magic, along with the life force of the Mages too.

"*Dicio, Anima, Equito!*"

Her attention immediately drawn to the twins, Charlize countered their attack, meeting them in the middle of the arena and returning her own blast of air. But their retaliation was fast, circling her with increasing speeds as they launched blow after blow.

Trapped between them, Charlize covered herself with a simple protection, which refracted the concentrated gusts and enabled her to clap her hands and release a previous elevation spell.

With nothing keeping her airborne, she plummeted several feet to the ground, her stomach turning as she bent her knees to withstand the shock, knowing the protection would absorb most of it.

And it did. She landed in a low crouch, straightened up, and with no time to lose, closed her eyes and concentrated.

Quieting her senses so the roar of the crowds dulled and the earth seemed to slow, she reached out with her mind, touching the newly laid grass beneath her feet, the young seeds forced to grow quicker than they liked. Then she touched the particles above, the spores and organisms, oxygen breathing life into lungs filled with energy. She stretched further, the resistance stronger as she touched and tasted the world about her, connected to the Anima, the air, the breath of life, and all of the ecosystems sustaining it.

Pushing even further, as Mrs Arno taught her, as her father taught her, she extended and expanded until she finally found them.

Bright, ferocious energy – the youthful zealousness that made up the personality of the twins burst against her mental touch. Encircling them, she wrapped them tightly with her mind and took two deep breaths.

"*Dicio, Āetis, Auster, Concido,*" she whispered gently.

And then the energy she bound dulled, its greedy excitement diminished to nothing more than a soft hum, the south wind friendly and welcoming, the binding unequivocal.

Charlize opened her eyes. Jess and Jade lay safely at her feet, curled together as they slept soundly. She grinned and gradually let her senses recover, although the cheers of the crowd still threatened to deafen her. Then, arms wide, she brought them together to clap twice; first to release the wind, and the second to undo the binding.

The twins awoke suddenly and peered upwards, dazed and confused. Charlize helped them to their feet, bowed low, and then held out her palm. "You fought well!"

With a small smile, Jess tried to line her palm against hers, failing as her arm seemed to weigh several more kilos than usual.

"What did you do?" she demanded, although her words slurred

slightly.

Jade, who seemed less affected, clutched her scowling twin. "It will wear off soon. Do you *never* pay attention in class?"

The wind caused somatic drowsiness, so helping her sister bow, Jade touched palms with Charlize before walking herself and Jess towards the edge of the dome, smiling and waving at those within the separate outer layer. Greeted by Armmos – and to Charlize's constant dismay – Jenkins, they each received a blanket and took their seats in the exclusive balcony among their fellow challengers.

Charras and Christian sat at the very back of the box, their faces concerned and shoulders rigid. Knowing Jenkins' presence was partly to blame, Charlize narrowed her eyes towards him.

Clipboard and pen in hand, his pinched face stared back at her, and she thought how obviously he revelled in the discomfort he caused her father. No amount of time seemed to quell the enmity between them. But the Hetairia Doman were not all the same, her father able to retain civility with other members who crossed his path. For some reason, Jenkins was the exception.

Charlize cut off their stubborn eye contact and walked to the middle of the arena. There, she shook out her hands and clicked her neck, ready for the next battle.

And it wasn't long until the dome shimmered and the ever-unhurried gait of Tunde stepped onto the battlefield.

"Greetings!" he said, his smile dazzling as he took a bow, before striding with poise to stand in front of her.

Curtly nodding in response, Charlize held out her palm, which Tunde calmly received. Their powers collided instantly, flaring through their fingers and sparking the others adrenaline.

Strong, stout, and fierce energy flowed in Tunde's veins, an Incendiī force to be reckoned with, and Charlize found herself excited. *This* was going to be a good match.

"Ready when you are," she said, taking a pace back.

"*Dicio, Incendiī, Caminus!*" cried Tunde.

A rope of fire whipped through the air. It crackled and flared, licking the ground it lay across, and flicking it up, he snapped it at Charlize's heels so she had to jump out of the way.

Thinking fast, she remembered she could only use the elements of her opponents; so, shifting through various counter spells, diving to her left as the whip smacked against her heels a second time, she cried out, "*Dicio, Āetis, Scutum!*"

She held out her arm as the air around it ignited to form a shield. Using it almost instantly, she blocked another crack of the fire whip, and then another, before running nearer to Tunde, rendering his attack useless at close range.

"Clever!" he said, darting backwards and re-casting the fire along the ground.

Watching as it singed a semi-circle in the grass, Charlize waited until it reached her, and then lifted her foot at the right moment to stamp on the tail.

Happy that she caught it beneath her boot, she swung her leg around and brought her other foot down on the rope – so hard that Tunde surged forward, enabling her to place a careful elbow and push him to the floor. But before she could disable him further, he rolled out of reach; wrenched the whip from under her feet; flogged it so it curled about her waist and stopped her fall; pulled it taut, and smiled as he entrapped her within the fiery constraints.

As he tugged her towards him, his face determined, Charlize used her shield to slash at the rope, sparks and flares flicking violently in every direction.

It was no use however; he finally had her where he wanted.

Inches apart, he bowed his head and Charlize begrudgingly accepted the challenge, relinquishing her shield and preparing for physical combat – her greatest weakness. It required reliance on survival instincts, instincts she was least practised in. Being all-powerful meant she rarely had need of them, which Tunde knew.

"Clever," she said.

He showed his teeth and Charlize dodged the first swing of his fist, the force behind his punch perforating the air next to her head. Closer, she could smell the adrenaline radiating from his skin, his desire to prove himself and gain notoriety, the overwhelming sense of loss his isolation brought him...

She closed off her Anima senses, the aid a form of cheating, and became figuratively blind. But she couldn't bear the thought of a dishonest fight. There was something sinister in a victory won through deceit.

She took a small breath and focused on Tunde's face, the sweat on his brow matching her own forehead that glistened with exertion.

And then they began. Arms swung and deflected as feet sidestepped and parried; limbs stretched and extended as each fought to gain the upper hand, circling like lions protecting their territory, caught in a dance of aggression as they attacked and evaded, each blow more powerful and intricate than the last.

Her jaw taut, Charlize creased her brow as Tunde attempted another rush, like a bull to a rag, his arms wide as he tried to tackle her. But ducking low, she brought her fist into his stomach – the first she'd connected, and twisted from his grasp.

When she span back around, she saw him bent double, and in her haste to finish the fight, failed to notice the smile on his lips. Grabbing his shoulders, she yelped as he pulled her ankles from under her, her back hitting the ground so hard the air was knocked from her lungs.

She lay gasping for breath as Tunde stood to deliver the final blow. He was wary though, his own trick making him paranoid, and she took the chance to bring both of her legs to her chest.

Air flooded her lungs, just as Tunde stepped within reach, and she used the last of her energy to drive her feet into his shins.

He stumbled forward and fell heavily onto her. She could just make out his surprise before his head cracked off her temple and they both lay stunned – Tunde more so on account of his limp bearing.

Charlize allowed him to lie on her for a few seconds. From beneath him she was able to catch her breath, the moments precious considering her inability to breathe only minutes ago.

It couldn't last though, and with mild regret, she pushed him onto the grass beside her and sat up. Then, waving her arms and smiling, while resisting the urge to vomit, she shakily got to her feet – the roar of the crowd drowning out the thudding in her head.

The dome shimmered and two men wearing green and white robes ran into the arena. Charlize limped past them, waving off their help and demanding they tend to Tunde while she headed towards the only person she accepted aid from.

He wasn't hard to reach, storming to meet her half way with supplies ready, Christian loyally at his heels. She caught Jenkins' eye for the second time, the distaste on his face as her father aided her something he made no attempt to hide. Thinking it odd, she wondered if he had any children of his own, (sincerely hoping he didn't).

"You're fighting well," Charras said, avoiding eye contact as he checked her for wounds.

Along with her head, a footprint on her thigh marked the place Tunde connected a kick. But otherwise, she felt unharmed. "He was a worthy opponent," she said, wincing as a cold compress pressed against her temple.

"He looked like he was going to kill you," Christian said, an edge to his voice that suggested he was angry.

"Then my victory is greater than I first hoped."

Opening his mouth to protest, he closed it again as a bell tolled, marking the beginning of the next fight.

With a quick nod to her father, Charlize passed him back the compress and returned to the middle of the arena. Once there, she felt knots tighten in her stomach. For some reason, this was the fight she dreaded most.

Allowing her Anima senses to rush back, their sensitivity initially heightened, she waited for them to settle, the smell of charred grass and sweat making her head throb with a vengeance. She steadied her feet and watched impatiently as the familiar shimmer of the dome marked someone's entry.

The challenger approached confidently, garbed in a fitted green catsuit, the sight of which made Charlize instinctively tilt her chin up, her spine curiously tingling as she felt the presence of excitable anger – emotional contradictions.

Reaching her, Amy held out her palm, to which Charlize tentatively pressed her own against, searching her face for any sign of foul play.

Blank, Amy's green eyes stared innocently, blinking once as their elements collided.

Hot, pure, and passionate air marked her strengths, but as Charlize let go, she felt it again, the same surge of anger, excitable and eager, almost holding back its full potential.

She dropped her hand and bowed her head. "Let us begin."

Making no effort to cast, Amy simply rose upwards, rising to the summit of the dome before dropping her chin and murmuring an incantation.

All around her, a wind kicked up the dirt and debris left over from the previous battles, sending masses of rubble to circle her as she drew moisture from the earth to add cloud cover and hide the spectators from view.

Far below, marginally confused about what was happening, Charlize stared upwards, waiting for Amy's game plan to reveal itself. Instead, she merely remained airborne, cocooned in a steady flow of cloud and dirt.

With little choice, she mumbled her own incantation and rose to meet her, Amy's face a picture of calm as she broke through the concealment and joined her in the cocoon. She floated cross-legged, smiling prettily, her blonde hair slicked away from her face and tied in a bun.

"Welcome," she said.

Charlize didn't immediately answer, distrustful, and instead decided to search for her spirit. She attempted to clear her mind, took a deep breath, and reached out – immediately stopped by a sharp slap across her cheek.

Her mind recoiled and she found her anger. "How dare you! If you want to physically combat me, you do so with etiquette!"

"Etiquette? For you? Ha!" Unfurling her legs, Amy bore her stare into Charlize's furious face. "You've treated me with nothing but scorn; I owe you no such honour."

"You have caused inconceivable insult by striking me Amy. This fight is over, you will be disqualified."

Charlize did her best to control her breathing, refusing to soothe the sting on her cheek, and waited for Amy to end the battle and return to the ground. She avoided eye contact for the sake of her indignation. For, having never been in such a position before, the awkwardness intensifying with each second that passed, she felt utterly ridiculous, like a schoolchild confronting a bully after years of torment.

When it seemed obvious no end would be forthcoming, Charlize ventured another glance. Amy's face was a picture of malice, her arms folded across her chest – whatever bitterness surging within revealing itself quite visibly.

"It's over, now end this," said Charlize sharply.

"It's your word against mine," Amy replied darkly.

"Then *I* will end it."

Deeply disturbed and shaking almost uncontrollably, Charlize promptly clapped her hands to release her spell and let herself drop. Her stomach turned and briefly lightened her mood – before she landed with a jolt much sooner than expected and her legs gave out from under her.

She clambered up from her fallen position, seeing that she stood atop the cloud and debris, the cocoon having hardened. She was trapped inside, along with – and she acknowledged this bitterly – a deranged Mage holding a grudge.

Snapping her eyes upwards as Amy floated down to stand in front of her, Charlize tensed her jaw and lowered her voice. "Let me out, this fight is over."

"It's over when I say so."

The urge to strike her in the same manner she'd received was almost overwhelming, but Charlize controlled herself. "I'll ask you one more time…"

Cut off by another slap across her cheek, she offered no more resistance as she threw a right hook and united it with Amy's nose. Upon hearing the crack – Amy's frail body no match for the continuous training Charlize underwent – she immediately felt guilty.

"End this; I don't want to hurt you again."

Amy shook her head, sending droplets of blood in each direction as she clenched her fists, her emerald eyes alight with rage as she focused on a space near Charlize's feet.

"What is the meaning of keeping me here? You won't have the strength to hold this for long!"

"To punish you," she said scathingly.

"Why Amy, what harm have I caused you?!"

Her face contorted, she lifted an arm and wiped the blood from her nose. "He looks at you differently to the way the rest of us look at you. He looks at you as if you are pure, wholesome, and worthy of him."

Open mouthed, Charlize couldn't find any words to reply, caught between wondering what Amy meant by *the way he looked at her* and why she believed she – the Āetis – could be any threat to her future with Christian.

Watching her eyes grow wilder, emphasised by pacing as Amy persistently stared at the floor, she continued her ramblings.

"You, you're an abomination. You're sacrificed because you are lower than the rest of us. You have five elements when Mages are outcast for more than two. But because we expect you to die, you somehow get to be all-powerful and worshipped for it. You are shunned by those around you, feared, loathed, but still you remain superior. But you can't win," and with 'win' she looked up, "you'll never win against us."

And then Charlize saw it, a flicker in her eyes that twitched too quickly, a jagged arm that didn't quite know how to behave...

"You're dying in her Achak, give her back to me."

Knowing the game was up, the Minae smiled. "Almost fooled you," the voice of Amy said.

"You know as well as I do that you can't last long in there."

As if to prove her point, the cocoon shook slightly and Amy's nose dripped a little more blood, the swelling along her bridge already bulbous.

Charlize steadied her footing and waited, watching intently as the Achak took a few steps backwards. Above, the ceiling of the cocoon caved in and a rush of air drove the broken debris down so fast it crashed through the bottom to leave two symmetrical gaps, flooding the remaining shell with light and dust.

Cut off from Amy, Charlize could barely make her out, her silhouette indistinct. She seemed to stagger forward somewhat awkwardly, and by squinting, Charlize saw a flash of green step dangerously close to the ever-collapsing floor, a vortex materialising as the rotating air thrust downwards.

"Stop!" she cried, preparing to jump across before realising she'd be sucked downwards immediately.

"Her death will be on your hands," said the demon, convulsing once before lunging Amy's body towards the gap.

With a final push, the Achak left her body, allowing the downward drag to pull Amy from the cocoon and plummet towards the ground. There was just enough time to see the fear in her eyes before Charlize dived after her.

She was instantly forced against the spin of the cyclone, the world blurred and spinning about her, debris and cloud all morphing into a wash of grey matter. Knowing there was nothing more she could do than close her eyes and pray to the Sky that her spell worked, she raised her arms above her head and released it outwards from her body.

"Dicio, Āetis, Concipere, Munimen."

Charlize tucked her arms across her chest in preparation for impact. Torturous seconds passed, moments that felt longer than any era gone by, the world seeming to crawl on its hands and knees in a sick attempt to extend the finality and reveal the ending.

And then she landed on the reassuring cushion of warm air, only to bounce several times before landing in a pile of limbs several metres away.

Scared she'd failed, she scrambled up, ignoring her dislocated shoulder as she searched for Amy. Spotting her sprawled over a pile of rubble, face down and arms hugged either side of the mound, Charlize ran to her side and turned her over, holding her breath as she searched for a pulse.

She almost cried when the reassuring throb beat against her fingers, and overcome with relief, slumped back and lay in the mud, exhausted.

At one point she acknowledged a flicker near her face where the energy of the Achak now rested. Upon wondering if she had anything left to send it with, any further contemplation of her wavering energy source was cut short by a commotion emerging from the dome. A cacophony of voices increased in volume as they neared, her father amongst them, his face red with fury – even more ferocious upside down, as was her view. Demanding to know how a possessed Mage bypassed all security, for once Jenkins seemed quiet, standing back as Charras barked orders and exchanged insults with Armmos.

Charlize turned her head as a warmer presence neared. She saw Christian tend to Amy, helping her sit up and leaning her against him while medics checked her for injury.

"It was an Achak Christian," she said, tears running down her face. "I've been forgetting things all week."

Hushing her, he hugged her to his chest and stroked her hair, his touch so warm that Charlize could see exactly why Amy would be so protective of him. There was something about his way, the softness with which he soothed her tears that intrigued Charlize, and sensing the attention he drew, he twisted his neck to catch her eye. But instead of the smile she hoped he'd offer, his face was one of mild disgust.

He immediately shifted his attention back to Amy and continued to rock her in his arms, his back colder than the shoulder he turned from her.

For the first time, Charlize acknowledged her jealousy.

38
Flawed

A strange ambience rested, the buzz of an evening almost underway as Mages hurried to finalise preparations for the finale of the celebrations. Not that any particularly wanted to continue, the dramatic events a drain on any party spirit they once had. But of course they would, not least for morale and respect, but for a moment of respite.

And Charlize watched it all playing out, sat high in the Haunt, her feet dangled over the edge of a platform as she stared down at the swarm of Mages dashing to and fro, some weary, others slightly more motivated. Wishing she could avoid the evening at all costs, she knew she had little choice, the threat of her father's wilting look if she refused banishing any thought of rebellion – that side of her personality long crushed beneath the weight of duty. Instead, she chose to disappear into her daydreams, the freedom of her own thoughts a solace none could penetrate. Often, she would imagine a world without Mages and Minae, a world void of magic and duty. It would be much like the Ungifted world, an individual bound only by the choices they willingly made, but each able to walk freely from village to village where lands were lush and plentiful. In that world, she was sure the people would respect it, for they would know what a rich life they had on offer and be grateful. In that world, there would be no war.

A cool breeze swept through the Haunt and Charlize shook slightly, the goosebumps along her arms stirring her from her thoughts. Pulling her cardigan tighter, she turned around, startled that Christian stood watching her, his face slightly contorted, an expression she'd never seen him wear before.

"Are you angry?" she said quietly. "I'm sorry; I tried not to hurt her."

"You broke her nose."

Charlize nodded, unable to hide the flush in her cheeks.

"Luckily she doesn't remember much, only that you saved her life."

Strangely comforted by that, Charlize nodded again. "I'm sorry I hurt her," she said, making to stand.

Putting his hand out to halt her, Christian shook his head. "And what about you?"

"Thank-you for your concern, but I'm fine."

"But one day you might not be. You might get really hurt, or worse… and then what? What happens if you die?"

"I don't understand…"

"What if you die Charlize, before you're meant to? What then? What happens to the world?"

"I don't know. It has never happened before."

"So every Āetis conveniently manages to end their own life before any part of this dangerous world does it for them?"

"We are strong."

His chest rising and falling as he calmed himself, Christian put his hands behind his head and looked to the sky. "No one is unbreakable, least of all you," he said quietly.

"You continue to find new ways to insult me."

With a slight smirk, he dropped his hands. "You choose to be insulted because you see it as an insult. And *that* is the real difference between us."

Without another word, he turned on his heels and walked away, leaving Charlize to frown after him and anger at her traitorous heartbeat.

Fortunately, there was little time for consideration when only minutes passed before her father replaced the quiet of Christian's departure.

"You're expected to give a speech, have you prepared?" he said, marching to where she sat and offering a hand.

She swiped it away and gathered her simple mint gown about her waist. Then, heaving herself to her feet, she let the layers drop back to the floor, dusted herself down, made a minor adjustment to her spaghetti straps, quickly slipped her feet back into a pair of white pointed shoes, and then patted the diamond circlet on her head with a forced smile.

"Mostly."

Charras nodded, gesturing for her to walk first and falling into step at her side. Together, they made their way towards the music, the steady beat a gentle reminder of the evening's processions. As far as Charlize knew, there would be entertainment, speeches, and offerings of unity, all ending with the lighting of a fire on the forest floor.

Glad it was the last night, she endeavoured to enjoy it, especially in the wake of earlier events. Coupled with having a mere three hours of sleep, her body longed for rest, such a luxury only earned with the finalisation of each tradition.

"Christian says Amy is well," she said, attempting to make conversation.

Reaching an A.A.E, Charras opened the gate and ushered her through. "Yes, she can't tell us much though, the Achak was a stronger force than we've previously known and her memory is very patchy."

"How did it get in?"

With a sharp sigh, Charras shrugged. "That is something we would all like to know. Armmos is embarrassed to say the least, but can shed no light either way. Why Amy was targeted is a mystery too."

Charlize had her own guesses but kept them to herself, unsure her father would understand any more than she did.

"She's close to Christian and therefore close to us. It was a targeted attack. A Mage is behind this," she offered instead.

Wincing as his darker thoughts were voiced, Charras looked grave as the A.A.E reached the lower deck. "That is what I'm afraid of," he said. "But let us dwell more on this tomorrow."

"Indeed," Charlize acquiesced, opening the gate and continuing towards the rowdier beat of a drum, mentally preparing herself for the barrage to come.

A gentle hand on her shoulder surprised her and she glanced at the large fingers attempting to offer some sort of reassurance.

"You fought well today," said Charras quietly, almost under his breath. "I was very proud."

In a state of shock, Charlize could only return an affectionate pat on the back of his hand, the rare display a moment she knew she'd never forget. Although it lasted a matter of seconds, it confirmed a long held theory of hers; her father was once capable of love.

39

A Song of Fire

"You must go and enjoy yourself; I am tired and far too boring to be good company right now."

Christian heard the words and understood them, but he was in no mood for celebration, choosing instead to sit in a rocking chair next to Amy's bed and read her a story about a caterpillar that ate through a book painted with food. Hungry as he may have been, and as beautiful a butterfly as he was to become, he couldn't help but feel the food was wasted, the small indent the caterpillar made through each morsel almost selfish. He said as much to Amy, who agreed whole-heartedly, before ordering him from her room to enjoy another fun filled Charlize-worshipping evening.

"Honestly, I'd rather be here with you," he said.

"It's important Christian, you can't stay mad at her forever, the swelling is already improving, don't you think?"

Looking at her and nodding against his better judgement, Christian agreed that the swelling had indeed gone down, only for two dark bruises to spring up under her eyes, leaving her left one bloodshot.

"She did what she had to. I would be dead otherwise," Amy justified.

Grunting his protest, Christian refused to believe the violence used to cause the damage to Amy's nose was necessary. But then, he didn't have to face a possessed Mage in the sky in a stupid cocoon and deal with everything else that caused the near death of his friends.

"She feels bad, that's something I guess," he offered as way of agreement.

"Of course she does! She wouldn't have meant to hurt me, why can't you see that?"

"Why are you sticking up for her all of a sudden? You aren't exactly friends."

Amy rolled her eyes, sank back into her pillow, and looked up at him beneath her lashes. "You don't make friends with the Āetis, it's not the done thing remember?"

"Jess and Jade have."

The twins' notoriety established through their unconventional mannerisms, Amy nodded. "Yes, well, I doubt she had much choice there. And besides, she saved my life. I think I owe her some gratitude."

Eyeing her with doubt, Christian pointed at her face. "I'd say you're even."

Amy frowned, an action she immediately regretted. Gently touching the bridge of her nose, a tenderness that made any extreme facial expression painful, she shrugged her shoulders and pulled her quilt to her neck.

"Go Christian, you'll miss the celebrations and I am getting too tired to argue more about it."

"It's fine, you sleep and I'll read another book, maybe with a protagonist who's less greedy."

"Please go. We both know what this is really about."

"Yes, it's about me not wanting to join the mighty praise brigade and pretend the system isn't completely flawed."

Huffing, Amy rolled her eyes a second time. "If you say so."

"What's got into you? You think it's cruel too. You sat with me and said so when I first found out."

"I do. I think it's awful how we have to sacrifice an Āetis, and I think it's even worse that no one is allowed to talk about it in case we offend someone's sensitivity. But that's not why you don't want to go to the finale."

"Yes it is."

"No it's not, and you know it. We both know it. Heck Christian – everyone knows it. So stop denying it and pretending otherwise. It's tragic and it's doomed, but it is what it is."

"Fine, well I'll go and prove to you it's not whatever you think it is!"

"Good, go, have fun, and say hi to everyone for me."

"I will!"

And with that, Christian stood from the rocking chair, pulled on his suit jacket, kissed Amy's forehead, and left – making sure the door didn't slam behind him. *I'll show her* he promised himself as he stormed down the crooked stairs of the triangular shaped cottage and out into the Haunt, his mission to sit through the charade of traditions and drink whiskey until his throat seized up so he couldn't speak – all to prove that whatever he felt he didn't really feel; although of course he didn't know what he was supposed to feel that he denied. Either way, he would prove some sort of point, and that was what mattered.

With the sun setting behind him, Christian climbed three steps leading to the west entrance of the deck and scanned the crowds for someone he recognised. A few people eyed him strangely, glints of emotion in their eyes he couldn't place, but for the most part, they ignored him in favour of discretion, a Mage trait he quickly realised was habitual.

Taking a deep breath, he began to sweep through the deck in search of Charras, his guardianship a familiarity he loathed to give up among the company of so many people who could kill him.

It was a while before he found him sitting offset to the podium adorned with Charlize and Armmos, their conversation obviously serious as her forehead creased slightly and his tired eyes were wider than usual.

Picking up a chair, Christian walked over to Charras and placed it next to him. "How long do we have before the bar opens?"

Charras managed a slight smirk as he beckoned for his charge to sit. "I fear my bad influence has grown beyond my control."

"Nah," said Christian, sitting down and putting his hands behind his head. "I just like your style."

The bang of several drums disguised the responding snort of mirth and their attentions quickly drew to the podium where five men dressed as Native American warriors all lined up and bowed to Charlize and Armmos, before turning and bowing to their greater audience.

Rows of white chairs tied with green ribbons packed the deck, each seat occupied, and two flashes of red caught Christian's attention about four rows from the front. He waved at Jess and Jade who saw him looking, and they grinned with their usual excitement, signing something with their hands that he took to mean 'catch-up later.'

Deciding the night wouldn't be so bad after all, he allowed himself to relax and enjoy the entertainment.

And what a show it turned out to be. After the Native American troupe finished their warrior dance, coupled with bright tassels, jingling bells, strange shouts, and synchronised drumbeats pounding against his chest with every blow, a moment of relief prepared them for the next spectacle.

Led onto the podium by its handler, a huge animal Christian thought resembled a cross between a wolf and a bear, with pointed ears, a long snout, and covered in white fur on its underbelly and dark fur on top, sat down and began panting.

"Hullo. I am Jackson, and this is Priscilla," said the owner, patting the head of the beast. "Can anyone tell me what she is?"

Nervous laughter rippled through the crowd and a few hands rose.

"Yes, you," said Jackson, pointing at a boy around Christian's age, but with decidedly more spots and a pair of glasses.

"Beowulf?"

A few chuckles from those who knew the legend sounded through the night air, before Jackson shook his head and pointed at a woman with a silk scarf tied around her neck.

"She's a type of wolf of course!"

Nodding, Jackson smiled. "Almost. She is a Malamute, a type of domestic dog our friends in the Glacies Haunt breed to help them with their lifestyle. She is very rare."

If a pin was dropped at that very second, it could have been heard. Jackson had everyone's full attention as he patted his chest and Priscilla jumped up to wrap her paws around his waist, causing him to steady his footing as her height almost matched his own.

"She came with me after my wife and I came back from taking my daughter on her pilgrimage. The leader of the Glacies Haunt, Iken, decided it so when as a runt, Priscilla suffered bullying in her pack and had little access to food. Taking a shine to me as a puppy, Iken told us how a Malamute chooses *you* as its owner, a pact that is almost unbreakable."

He clicked his fingers and Priscilla jumped down and sat at his heels once again. Smiling ruefully, Jackson scratched her behind her ears. "We didn't know exactly what we would be taking on until she became fully grown."

In awe, Christian watched the Malamute as everyone else did. Animals were heavily protected by the law, with owners having to be trained, licensed and registered for the specific animal they wanted to keep, and then screened yearly to make sure they still met all the requirements. Qualifying for a dog was particularly difficult, Christian always believing they were wily, strong, and hard to tame – or so his parents always argued whenever he begged for one. Of course, now he knew the real reason. Walking dogs after hours could put an Ungifted in danger, a stray dog or rogue horse perhaps crossing the protections with their owner in tow, only to be fed to what waited outside.

"So," he whispered to Charras. "When Mum said dogs were dangerous, she wasn't talking about their teeth was she?"

Charras shook his head. "I always said a cat would suit you better as they're more independent, but after an incident with Charlize, they decided against it."

"Wraithart?"

"Indeed."

The years of bitter pouting over his animal-less childhood melted away, and Christian smiled despite himself, watching as Charlize knelt next to Priscilla and stroked her long fur, avidly asking Jackson questions about her age, temperament, and appetite. Her face glowing with adoration, she took on the aura of a girl who'd just discovered the first joys of chocolate.

As other Mages took up the rare invitation to pet a dog, she stood up and backed off slightly, only to laugh as Priscilla licked the hand of a seven-year-old boy who earlier that evening spilled vanilla ice-cream down his shorts. His small eyes unsure what to make of it, he began to cry and was swiftly carried away by his mother.

Once the initial excitement subsided, Armmos called for quiet by clearing his throat, pleased that within seconds, the racket died down to a low frequency hum. Leaning on his staff, he ushered Charlize to stand next to him while he implored the crowd of hungry and thirsty Mages.

"You have been so gracious, and we hope you are enjoying the night we have painstakingly put on for you in honour of our highest of guests. We ask for your patience and attention for only a few more moments."

Armmos turned to Charlize and held his hand outwards. From about him, several species of leaves danced onto the stage and began spinning above his palm, cascading like a water feature – to the admiration of all.

In a low voice somehow carrying on the breeze, he said, "We are the Anima. We are the air and the breath of life. We must follow the winds of change as they guide us to our future, and we must honour the Sky, which has bestowed such foresight upon us." With a small nod, he handed his creation to Charlize, who took it gently. "We are passing our foresight, our insight, and our knowledge onto you, so you may use your gift wisely in the days ahead. Let us guide you Charlize, let us always be by your side, and let us aid you whenever you have need."

She bowed her head in respect and then halved the creation so two smaller piles of leaves spun atop her palms. Handing one to Armmos, he held it high and blew it out towards the crowd.

"I promise," Charlize said, following suit and sending her own pile out onto the laps of several Mages, who all secretly swore to hold onto them as keepsakes.

One landed on Christian's lap, and holding it up, he couldn't help but taste the irony as a sycamore leaf – the badge of his Marsh School uniform – fluttered slightly on the gentle draft. *How far we've come,* he thought to himself.

"And so, before we adjourn for sustenance, let us hear a song several of our choir members have been rehearsing endlessly for the last few weeks."

Although his stomach rumbled and he hoped the song was short, Christian liked listening to music and looked forward to hearing the number written in tribute, although guessed it consisted of lots of words roughly meaning 'thank-you-great-wonderful-amazing-saviour-of-us-all.'

Three girls ranging in age from eight to fourteen all shyly made their way to the podium. Identical in styling with their hair plaited down their back and each wearing a green tunic emblazed with emblems symbolising peace, love, and respect, they stepped onto the podium and quickly curtsied to Charlize and Armmos before clearing their throats simultaneously, procuring several laughs.

It was only when they began to sing they hushed the pity on each Mages lips. Sweet, soft, and pure, they harmonised a melody with such power for their size that mouths sat agape. Lifted on the sincerity of those who felt the sadness and hope in every word sung, taken to a place where they united in their pain and yearned for the freedom from darkness, tears soon flowed.

Surprised to see Charlize was one whose eyes glistened, her stare so intense she looked physically in pain, Christian's heart went out to her; so much so, he could almost feel her anguish, her desire to be strong enough, her determination to succeed, and the pressure every face put on her shoulders. Next to him, he could feel Charras tense and he knew Jenkins had finally joined them, but he didn't care, choosing to ignore them as he felt himself stand and walk towards the podium, ready to wipe away all the fear and doubt, erase all of the worry.

So when Charlize turned and stared back at him, her deep eyes aflame, he suddenly realised what Amy meant by saying everyone knew. It was transparent, his soul naked, bare to the eyes of those who saw him long after the one woman on earth he could never have.

Ashamed, he shrank back and fled from the deck, barging past Jenkins and Charras in his urgency to escape his fruitless denial.

Watching Christian leave sent another wave of emotion plummet to her stomach, and Charlize swallowed to avoid any tears spilling onto her cheeks. The melody drawing out a final note, she forced a smile and clapped along with the rest of the audience as the three girls beamed gratefully.

She held her palm to theirs as they each shyly greeted her, and she gently complimented their performance, warmed by how their faces grew awash with pride. She waved as they departed, running back into the arms of their awaiting families.

Seconds later, Armmos called for silence and declared the long awaited time to satiate with food and wine. Almost able to hear the collective sighs of elation as the Mages dispersed to satisfy their thirsty gullets and hungry bellies, she took a moment to gather herself, shaken by the effect the song had on her.

"It is almost over Charlize," came the soft tone of Armmos's reassurance. "We have your speech and the fire to light and then we can rest."

He sat next to her in his chair, his voice full of weariness, his weathered face worn from the last few days. But Charlize was reminded of an oak tree. To her, the leader was wise and old, yet sturdy and strong. And she was about to air those sentiments when a ruffle of commotion to her left caught her attention instead.

She sighed. "Will they ever stop arguing?" she asked, nodding towards the heated discussion her father and Jenkins were currently absorbed in.

Armmos shook his head and heaved himself from his chair. "That is an ideal I wouldn't put too many hopes on." He walked towards the fray with his arms open wide and promptly led Charras to the bar.

The scowl on Jenkins' face as he watched them leave made Charlize stand, worried that a fight would break out. His hostility was so penetrating that she could almost see his fingers twitching. But whatever reaction he might have had, he quickly decided against it and put his back to his fancied targets, wiping his face with his hands and then shaking them out.

"Goodnight Charlize," he said, making sure she knew he could see her staring.

"You seem troubled," she replied.

With a small laugh, he dabbed his forehead with the back of his sleeve. "No, no more than usual. You take care now."

She didn't reply as Jenkins hurriedly walked away, his demeanour careful and almost nervous as he sort of skip-hopped past the deck boundaries to be enveloped by the subsequent darkness and lost to the naked eye. Intending to discover the source of his discomfort from her father the next day, she pushed it aside and tried to relax.

The celebrations were a more intimate affair that evening, the string quartet favouring softer melodies opposed to the former blaring instrumental numbers, the gentle strokes of their horsehair bows along their viols encouraging calm. It was odd then that even this, coupled with the balmy evening offering a rare sense of tranquillity, she still felt uneasy. She didn't know where it came from or why she felt it, but in the consequent lull, where Mages spoke softly or danced closely, each huddled together and appreciating each other's company without diffidence, she felt an unexpected pull, an urge to find solace.

In short, she wanted to be alone.

Careful not to be noticed, she climbed down from the podium and swept along the periphery and out into the depths of the Haunt, quickly finding herself running, her legs dancing lightly along the walkways and bridges, quick and agile, her mint dress accommodating as she delved further and further onwards. She didn't feel the burning of her muscles or the beating of her heart, she couldn't care less that the bridges rocked violently underfoot or her now bare feet dirtied and ached. She only delighted in the freedom, the ecstasy of being infused with magic; the way her body sang its own tune and drummed its own beat; the way the world about her answered to her call and she could touch it, feel what lived and breathed and sang about her.

And then she stopped, her chest rising and falling rapidly as she caught her breath. Spinning around to look about her, she saw she stood upon a patch of grass that led up to a gate. Strong polished pikes loomed in front, extending – as far as she could tell – around the entire enclosure, as if warning her the area lay guarded.

A fragrant smell wafted from within, an earthy sweetness to it that promised beauty and nourishment. And then she realised, they were the gardens, the very gardens Armmos and her father spoke about – the gardens that caused such controversy when her father first undertook his pilgrimage with her mother.

She made them she found herself thinking, somehow feeling close to the mother she'd never met, embraced in her memory, as if she'd wanted her to find them, to experience a part of her legacy.

Wiggling her toes on the lush blanket beneath, making sure they worked, Charlize took a step towards the gate. The full moon above cast a silver glow on the lonesome deck, the warm night waiting as curiosity consumed every nerve within her body. But before she took another step, something strange happened.

From the gardens, several petals drifted upwards, each holding a drop of light carried by bugs that also emitted a light of their own. The vibrations of their wings sounded like a propeller fan and she watched in awe as hundreds of them flew towards her, dropping petal after petal at her feet.

Fireflies she realised, holding out her hands as they circled her. Some landed, while others chose to orbit just above her head, although more seemed to come, displaying their green and yellow behinds and depositing various offerings in what she figured was some sort of ritual.

"Charlize?"

Startled, she jumped, not realising she'd been followed, and the fireflies on her hands flew upwards to join the swarm.

"Christian?" she uttered, watching as he carefully walked towards her.

A breeze seemed to push him from behind, a breeze the night hadn't offered until that moment, and Charlize watched in amazement as the fireflies began to douse him with petals of light too, flying above his head as the gifts cascaded on him.

"What's happening?" he asked.

Speechless, she merely stared open mouthed as Christian flicked off a rose and daisy petal from his shoulder. She grasped his hands and pulled him towards her, shaking her head and softly scolding him.

Eyes locked, Christian felt his heart pound, the beating in his chest so loud he could have sworn Charlize heard it. Neither said a thing, the closeness an attraction stronger than a magnetic pull, stronger than mere lust – a connection that absorbed them. Every touch, every smile, every glance brought them a step closer, every step leading up to that moment; that single moment in time where nothing seemed to matter but everything counted.

The earlier breeze made another appearance and kicked up the petals around them, sending them swirling in a flurry of fragrant light. They span faster and pushed them closer until the moment Christian couldn't stand it any longer. He took his hand from Charlize's grasp and swept his fingers along her cheek before closing the tortuous gap between them. He hesitated once and then brushed his lips against hers – tentatively, exploratory, the action proving its worth as fire erupted between them, desire and longing coursing through every nerve, confusion flooding every instinct as denial and pain, unspoken truths and realisations all stood to break them. But none of that mattered yet, for Charlize responded, her resolve broken, her yearning realised, and she reached up to clasp his neck, returning the kiss and pushing against him as they embraced.

Mouths warm and breath short, their lips locked over and over again, murmurs and grunts escaping into the night as they fell into each other, lost and desperate, refusal to acknowledge the contravene turning their frustration to urgency.

So caught up in the moment, they barely noticed how the fireflies spun wildly about them, the breeze so strong it lifted them into the air and over the gated area, gently placing them on the earth beneath. And it was only then, as their feet touched the ground, they broke apart, whatever bewitchment that had taken hold returning their senses.

Panting, they stared at each other, both confused and both shaken. Above, the fireflies dispersed and the breeze departed.

"What just happened?" said Christian breathlessly.

Charlize shook her head and wrapped her arms across her chest. "I don't know."

"I wanted you, I wanted you more than anything, I, I don't know why I…" He shivered slightly and let his words fall away.

Ashamed, Charlize turned from his gaze and looked around her. It suddenly dawning on her where they were, she let out a gasp, the coincidence too surreal to digest. Bright arrays of flowers brimmed from assorted plant and vegetable plots, the borders lined symmetrically to create several walkways and enable ease of access, while trellises with similar vegetation were scattered along the borders, stood against the gates in whatever space a bush or tree didn't occupy. Gnomes also made a home among the gardens, littering the ground with various tools in their hands, some sitting in hanging baskets that swung from overhead branches.

Taking a breath, the intoxicating scent of Christian still alive in her consciousness, Charlize let it out slowly and faced him. "It was some sort of ritual; you must have been caught up in it."

"I'm sorry, I know you can't, you know… I shouldn't have…"

"Please, don't apologise, these are the gardens my mother made. I know it sounds insane, but I feel like she wanted me to see them."

Opening and closing his mouth, as if just realising they were somewhere different from moments ago, Christian frowned.

"Yes, she did."

The voice that answered wasn't his.

40
Burning

"Charras! Come come," Armmos beckoned him.

Putting his – what he considered – poor malt on an empty table with derision, Charras pondered the time it would take to dash back to the cottage and pick up the finer malt from his collection. He only discarded the thought upon considering his friend gearing himself up by the podium, the tall leader chatting animatedly to a firebrand wielding youth. He knew Armmos would care more for his sober state than his inebriated one.

"It is as if you are twelve again!" he commented lightly, his friend's expression reminding him of a child who'd first stepped into a sweet shop.

Armmos ignored the comment as he gestured, pointed, and then patted the young boy's shoulder, his innocent face lapping up every word as the gravity of the task soon dawned on him, his leader's reliance on his success thoroughly spelled out, no details spared of the consequences should he fail.

Amusement rattled in Charras's throat, although he kept his face serious, nodding and grunting his agreement in all the right places, and almost feeling regret as a well-established fear grew in the eyes of the poor boy.

When the tortuous charade ended, Armmos dismissed him and acknowledged Charras with an arm across his shoulder, nostalgia written in his expression.

"It was not so long ago we stood here side by side – a pair of bare-faced youths. Surely you have not given into old age so easily?"

"Speak for yourself old man, we are not yet forty! Although not as sure of limb as we once were, what we lack in pliancy we make up for in experience."

With a chuckle, Armmos patted his arm. "Quite, quite." Then, leading him to the edge of the podium so they both stared into the abyss, he lowered his voice. "I want you to count down with me, like old times."

Warmly patting him back, Charras nodded and leaned on the boundary rope until it became taut and supported his weight. Of course, Armmos referred to a time when he, Isalize, and two other Mages earned the honour to light the fire, an honour relayed to him as vehemently back then as it was to the now terrified boy shivering in the corner with a white knuckled grip on his firebrand.

Just as he thought to ease the boys nerves with his reminiscence, three more bearers emerged from somewhere beyond his peripheral vision and stood next to their fellow, each with faces to match that confirmed they'd all received the same severe direction.

"Honestly, they'll barely be able to throw them the nerves you've given them," said Charras to Armmos, knowing how the initial excitement to be chosen would have long vanished.

With a shrug, Armmos squared his shoulders. "Yes, well, they'll be grateful looking back."

He stepped to the front of the podium and suddenly looked around him in confusion before settling his gaze on Charras. "Where is Charlize? She must give her speech," he said with mild urgency.

His brow dark, Charras scanned the crowd for a sign of her, picking out the twins huddled together alone. Then, darting his search over the heads of all others, he noted how Christian also seemed to be missing.

Anger rose in his chest. "I'll find her," he said.

Fearing the worst, the connection his charges had seeming to grow stronger the longer they spent together, he hoped the unthinkable hadn't happened. With Christian confusing his feelings for love, and Charlize's constant look of discomfort and puzzlement whenever he got too close, he prayed to the Sky that the young entrapment of lust hadn't won.

"Wait," said Armmos with a hand on his chest. "Let us finish the tradition and find them afterwards. Their escapade can wait, but I doubt the children can hold onto fire for much longer."

Knowing that was probably true, Charras conceded, promising himself that when he got his hands on them, strong words would be had.

He stood back while Armmos addressed the mingling Mages, his pointed finger a signal to the band for a drum roll as he swiftly garnered all attention. "Friends, it is time," he said proudly.

Cheers and excited chatter erupted across the deck as everyone edged their way to the outer boundaries and peered down. A few dew lanterns drifted across the void, but the light gave very little measure of depth.

"Every year, as is our tradition, we set the forest on fire," Armmos continued, holding his hands up to silence the shock of those who didn't understand. "Fear not, for the sequoias are fireproof. This act is an act of kindness, not malice. It will enrich the soil and clear the forest floor of any rival to the proud kings that protect this Haunt. For this island is theirs alone."

Whispers interspersed with curious and impatient murmurs swept through the masses as Armmos beckoned for the firebrand bearers to come forward.

"So, to mark the end of the Spring Festival, I ask these three young men and young lady to take up their positions and stand before the forest depths."

The youths held their flames high, which flickered in the breeze as they marched to each corner of the deck. There they stood ready – chests puffed and grips tight.

"From ten," Armmos prompted Charras.

Although angering further by the second, he composed himself for his friend's sake.

"Ten," he boomed.

"Nine... eight..." Armmos joined, "...seven... six... five..."

All joined in for the last counts of, "four...three... two... one..."

As 'one' left their lips, the firebrands were dropped from the steal grips securing them and into the forest below. The deck exploded with clapping and everyone rushed forward in an attempt to see the ignition.

Charras joined Armmos at the boundary on the podium and looked down to see the forest floor engulfed in hungry flames, incredible waves of heat and light rushing to greet him. Almost able to feel the sequoias breathe a sigh of relief, as if the fire soothed a backache that had hindered them for months, he vaguely acknowledged the band kicking back into life.

After a time, Mages slowly siphoned off and returned to their previous engagements. Charras didn't however, continuing to stare at the flames – something very much a part of him. It coursed through his blood and awakened him from the inside. His nerves tingled with the satisfactory sensations rippling across his skin, and he soon realised that other Incendiī Mages such as Tunde remained fixated too.

"It's a hungry one this year," Armmos commented, an edge of concern to his voice.

Charras nodded. Watching the yellow and orange flames lap up the undergrowth and some smaller trees attempts to grow that year, he was mesmerised, as if an old lover hugged him, the strength of his element bursting within his chest, powerful even though only half of him held claim to Incendiī.

Other Mages who were pure felt the effects even more, sat cross-legged as they stared downwards, their element calling to them as it surrounded the Haunt, licking further up the sequoias, almost holding out its torrent arms for an embrace.

A subtle change in the winds pricked against Charras's concentration, loosening the fires hold on him, and he shook himself back to reality. His mood serious, he tasted the air, an unfamiliar scent on it, almost unnatural… Then, staring back down at the fire, he was mildly surprised to see it so close to the first floor, its reach spreading further than usual.

Something was wrong.

Armmos knew it too. His face, moments ago so proud and full of joy, now held worry, the creases in his forehead pulling his eyebrows together.

They exchanged looks, each knowing the fire should not be so high, and spurred into action.

"We need to get to higher ground," Armmos called over the sound of the crackling flames.

Charras nodded, knowing that panic would shortly ensue.

The villagers, blissfully unaware that there was danger, still danced to the band, basking in the moonlight and soft lighting of the lanterns. It was only when those nearest their leader heard the command they began to stir from their trance.

"Why sir?" one Mage asked, a small plump boy with wide eyes.

Laying a hand on his shoulder, Armmos told him to re-join his parents, which the boy did obligingly, not daring to argue with authority.

"The bells," Charras said, allowing Armmos to speak the spell.

Soon, a deep toll began to reverberate throughout the Haunt, but not one of 'code black', this bell at odds with the sounds they usually made. This one rang of danger.

"To the third floor!" Armmos commanded. "All those who are Aquāe or Glacies, come with me, we must put out the fire."

"Let me help," Charras demanded, holding his hands open in a gesture of goodwill, knowing that air would only fuel the fire, but his Incendiī half could endure the heat.

Armmos studied his friend. "It is too dangerous; you must help the women and children to safety. We will cast ice blockades to keep the fire away, but it won't hold for long. There is darker magic here."

Charras nodded gravely, the thought inescapable as it crept up his spine. *Could it be her? What would she want here?*

The villagers scattered as they fled towards the airlifts, some Anima choosing not to bother as they lifted themselves up into the trees and safely onto the third floor. Charras watched them leave, waiting to see a glimpse of Charlize, knowing she would come to their aid once she heard the bells, her Aquāe and Glacies elements of great use.

He darted into the crowd and found Jess huddled in a corner around several groups of visiting or pilgrimage Mages. She was attempting to explain what had happened.

Above her, Jade floated down to land by her side and swiftly gather another Mage onto her back before launching upwards again.

"Jess," Charras barked, "have you seen them?"

Her face hard, her dark freckles and whitened skin the only giveaway of her fear, she shook her head. "They left after the song, both of them looked miserable, dunno where they are now."

Jade landed for the second time, her face pallid and clammy, and stood breathless. "Your turn," she said to Jess. Then, turning to Charras, she pointed to the east. "They both ran that way. Charras, she's not back. Why isn't she back?"

The thought choked him for a second as panic rose in his throat. He backed away as the prospect dawned on him, but he didn't answer the question; he couldn't, because it couldn't be...

Yet even as he denied it, the thought grew.

Vrealâ... She had come for them.

41

As I lay here

The gardens, once so glorious moments before, suddenly took on a more sinister tone. The voice that spoke froze everything in its place. Nothing moved, nothing breathed, as if death itself inhaled time, keeping everything in motionless suspense.

Charlize and Christian clasped each other's hands instinctively, an unspoken refusal to release their holds. They clung onto life as their hearts beat and their pulses' drummed through their fingers, reminding them that power and heat lay within their blood.

"So it is true," Charlize whispered, refusing to turn and face her enemy.

A crackling sounded underfoot, the shift of dirt along the garden path, a promise of something creeping closer, slowly. There was no doubt that power moved towards them.

The smell of sulphur hit them first, like a wave rushing to pollute the air. It brought bile to Charlize's throat and she felt the icy touch of death close in around her.

"I am many truths," the voice spoke again.

It rang like the sound of harmony bells, the tone familiar and sweet, and a half lodged memory attempted to resurface as Charlize listened. It seemed to come from far away, as if it did not belong to the bearer of the words, having no place in life. She felt Christian tighten his grip on her hand and she knew he heard it too.

Without turning, their backs still to the stranger approaching them, Charlize summoned words to her head, powerful enchantments that would protect them. Sensing fire below, rising rapidly, she used that to release the spell.

"Dicio, Āetis, Contego…"

It surrounded them in a dusty haze, and quickly checking for weaknesses, she found none.

"Ever cautious Charlize," the voice sung again.

Although she expected the demon to know her name, it was still a shock to hear it escape into the night, the same melodious tone confirming her fears... an attack was imminent.

Looking over her shoulder, she scanned the gloom. At first, there was nothing out of the ordinary; the gnomes still smiled, the flowers still bloomed, and besides a surreal stillness, everything had its place... So carefully turning a half circle, coaxing Christian to do the same, they faced their fate.

But nothing greeted them, nothing but a gentle breeze that washed through the gardens and disturbed the quiet as it kicked up a few fallen leaves.

"Show yourself," Charlize demanded, although her voice held tension. "Do not hide in the shadows like the lesser Minae."

A low growl rumbled, causing Christian to jump with fright. Then, inches from their protection, a whipping motion sounded through the air and the demon revealed itself. Christian immediately shrank back, causing Charlize to stumble and almost lose her footing.

She pulled them both upright. "The minute you step from this protection, you are helpless," she snapped.

His reaction went unnoticed as a shift in the air carried the scent of more death. She struggled to shut it out, using more of her strength than first intended to reinforce the boundary and regain composure.

A spell Mrs Arno taught her about how to close off the effects of Minae echoed in her head, but she decided against using it, reluctant to waste any more energy unless necessary. Her mind was better occupied thinking of a plan...

On the contrary, Christian was stumped, immobile even though his muscles surged with adrenaline. The nausea afflicting Charlize didn't have the same effect on him. He could only stare into the limited face of Vrealâ, her features clearer up close, but no less terrifying.

She stood at over seven foot tall and wore the same hooded cloak he remembered in each nightmare, although he now saw it was not black, but midnight blue. Strange symbols adorned the heavy material, the several layers cascading down her slight form – the shape of a woman, what once may have been beautiful in life, but twisted so it mocked every form of human physics.

An elongated neck accompanied a long face, the colour of pure white standing as a poor replacement of flesh, while the only humanity lay within her eyes – pools of blue that disappeared into limitless oceans of azure and turquoise, ringed with a brown and red hue. The red matched a mouth of badly drawn lips, retaining a measure of vanity even in death, as striking as it was terrifying.

"You walk where you should not," Charlize warned the demon.

The form of Vrealâ tilted her head, watching them curiously, waiting…Then letting out a screech of mirth, the like no Sirenari could ever accomplish, Charlize fell to her knees and covered her ears.

And still Christian stood, staring dumbfounded, watching as Vealâ's mouth fell open, unhinging so it spread wider and wider until the depths of the newly formed hole revealed blood bubbling, disturbed in her throat.

With a sickening jolt, he realised the lips were not drawn, but stained, and what stirred in her distorted form fed her, the blood her strength. He imagined his parent's blood inside her, but before he could think more on it, Vealâ snapped her jaws shut without a drop spilled and growled, the bass note resonating in his stomach.

"What are you?" she demanded, reaching out with her sharp nail-less finger to touch the protection.

She recoiled instantly.

Christian didn't answer. The arrival of more Minae turned his attention, their forms formidable as they filed into the garden, the once beautiful oasis wilting beneath their weight.

"You are not affected by the same things as other Mages of your kind, yet you cower before us like the wretched Ungifted," Vealâ continued.

Any response he may have had was cut off by the desperate toll of a bell. While glad the Anima knew there was danger, he still wondered how anyone would find them in time to help, the gardens hugely secluded. He imagined their discovery the next morning, nothing left of them but dusted bones, and he prayed that if death came to him that night, it would come quickly.

Charlize lifted her head to the emerging onslaught as their separate identities coursed around her. Doing her best to ignore the several tugs of darkness vying for her senses, instead using most of her strength to keep the protection reinforced, she wished she'd chosen a weaker spell – one that didn't require so much of her energy to maintain.

There was nothing she could do about it now though, and forcing herself to her feet, her control stronger, she counted out the Ghul's, of which there were seven; the six Sirenaris, which came in their traditional packs of three, and the Shadowlan's, of which there were many. No lesser Minae were present, at least none that she could sense.

Betrayal soon manifested in her gut, it quickly dawning on her that in order for the demons to infiltrate the Haunt they must have had help. It also meant the unnatural fire below, which she assumed the bell warned against, was not the fault of a careless Mage. Its intention was to incinerate the Anima, leaving nothing but ash and embers.

She silently cursed the traitors.

Then, brushing her anger aside with a practised hand, she stood to her full height, closed her eyes, and reached out with her mind. Next to her, she felt Christian, his life force warm, warmer still as adrenaline pumped frantically through his body. Wishing to embrace it, she denied the comfort of life and pushed further outwards, careful as the oblivion of Vrealâ drew her closer. She felt her way to the edge of the demons energy and bypassed it, any Mage worth their namesake aware of the danger to those who strayed too close. Greater Minae teetered on the edge of death, able to come and go as they pleased, and Vrealâ was stronger than most. If Charlize was careless, she could accidentally fall in and be lost forever.

The concentration she used to avoid that fate meant she briefly suffered the force of the accompanying horde, all ferocious and hungry for the life that beat inside of her and Christian, and quickly withdrawing, she cast her gaze back to Vrealâ.

"What are your intentions, *exanimis?*" she said with venom.

Vrealâ stood forward, outraged, and the Minae behind all barred their teeth, snarling and angry.

"What did you say to her?" whispered Christian.

Crouched low, the Greater Minae fixed Charlize with a murderous glare.

"I called her lifeless, dead; I named her for what she is, but naming anyone lower than their status is an insult."

"But she is…" Christian replied, not understanding.

More growls erupted around them, the night suddenly animated with bloodlust and rage, fusing the sentient evils together in their mutual cravings.

"Oh…" Christian murmured.

Charlize knew she had to act fast, her lack of action providing the Minae with more confidence in their ability to defeat her. But outnumbered, she had two options. She could run and get help, although it was a risk that could leave the Anima divided when the Minae gave chase, or she could try to fight, the odds stacked against her.

Eying them now, each stood in regimented lines of various malevolent forms, the stench of decay hung heavily in the cracked icy air, as if she'd stumbled upon a pile of dead bodies left for weeks to waste away. There were so many of them, and there was only one spell she could think of that would be effective enough. Able to channel it outwards from her body, it would cause damage to everything within a short radius of her, although that included Christian…

She turned to him now. His face was full of fear, his ignorance and limited knowledge providing him with no tools to withstand the small army surrounding them.

"Christian," she whispered. He tilted his head towards her and tightened his grip on her hand. "If you leave this protection, you will be killed." No answer came as one of the Ghul flexed his putrid arm, lending evidence to her grim warning. "You must stay within this circle until help comes, no matter what happens or what you see. While you are in here, they cannot hurt you."

Not unless I die, she thought bitterly, although she didn't admit that.

It suddenly dawning on him what she was about to do, Christian tried to stop her – tried to keep his grip on her hand.

But it was too late; she ripped herself from his grasp and stepped from the protection. There was nothing more he could do but shout after her, his voice soon swallowed in the thunderous bellows of the Minae, their cries of exultation roaring through the gardens.

"Stay in there!" Charlize screeched before turning her back to him.

Then, standing ready and with poise – even as the screeches and growls of approaching darkness closed in on her, she raised her hands above her head.

"Dicio, Āetis, Concido!"

The command, lost in the noise, produced several knifes of magical property to sprout around her body. She bore a striking resemblance to a war-mongering porcupine, the dim blades infused with sharp cutting power. They could not only slice through the flesh of the dead, but the essence also, meaning the Minae would instantly disintegrate.

An eager Sirenari was the first to test her spell, reaching through the blades to her flesh and accidentally cutting herself. She immediately dissolved into a pile of energy and Charlize smiled.

But then more Minae came, surrounding her with their sulphur-ridden corpses, their jerking, decomposing, and mutilated limbs circling her like lions.

When it was clear none would attempt to touch her again, Charlize released the spell.

"Adfor!" she screeched – a farewell to the dead – and clapped her

hands above her head.

The art form perfect, the quick peal of her clap sent the blades darting in all directions about her body.

Where they connected with a target, she felt the lessening of their influence upon her senses, although it only helped marginally, her own strength considerably weaker. There was no time to recover however, a dull thump beating in her chest that warned her an attempt to reach Christian was underway. She forced herself into alertness and looked towards him, seeing that two Ghul's relentlessly pounded on the protection.

Each time their fists connected, she felt it, and even though the threats would hurt themselves far more than they ever would her, the tactic of distraction was effective. The type of barrier she'd conjured was too strong to release, so the maintenance served as a drain on her energy.

For the second time that night, she wished she'd been less hasty and cast a lesser spell, but she knew if faced with the same scenario again, she would never take a risk with any life but her own.

"Dicio, Āetis, Concido!"

Repeating the spell, it took greater effort than before to exact, but she managed it, raising her hands and clapping once. Again, the blades shot in several directions, one – she was happy to note – shooting through the skull of an incessant Ghul. As it dropped to the floor and dissolved into a pile of angry embers, she could almost hear Christian let out a sigh of relief.

The destruction of several more Minae aided Charlize's strength, although she knew it wouldn't last much longer. She needed to return to the protection so she could cast another and destroy the first. The reabsorbed energy would sustain her so she could finish off the remaining threats.

Focusing on Christian's face, she made her way back to him.

Christian watched as Charlize cut across the once plentiful potato patch, now ground into nothing but wilted leaves and black ash. His relief that she was alive and returning to him was more than he expected. He felt like a supporting role in a horror film, except his body stood rigid and his vision waned, which made it very real. Only the comforting sight of Charlize's nearing footsteps kept him from panicking, and watching as they brought her closer was all he could do to maintain his calm.

She was weakened; he could see that. Every step seemed an exaggerated effort that further whitened her face. *Hurry,* he thought, doing his best to ignore the remaining Ghul beating down on the resistance above his head. Wanting to sweep her into his arms and bring her to safety, he felt utterly useless that the most he could offer was encouragement.

She was meters away when she reached towards him, his own arms held out wide, ready and desperate for her to dive into them. But suddenly, quicker than his eyes believed, Vrealâ stepped from the shadow of a tree and clasped a bony grip around Charlize's hair, slamming her to the ground.

Christian yelled as loud as his lungs would allow. He willed Charlize to get up and fight back, wishing with everything he had that he wasn't a helpless victim, that he could somehow retaliate…

Instead, he was condemned to be the only audience to the gory scenes unfolding. He wanted to look away, but knew he couldn't. He watched as Charlize regained herself, whipped away from Vrealâ's grasp just in time, and then lifted herself onto her feet with Anima.

And it was at that moment he realised the remaining Minae had abandoned their relentless attacks in favour of aiding their leader, forming a circle around Charlize and blocking her escape. Able to make her out through the gap between a Ghul and Sirenari, he could see that she was scared – a look he'd never witnessed before. But he knew her fear didn't come from impending death, but from being unable to obliterate the threats, what that meant, and who would suffer if she failed…

Fight he urged desperately, squeezing his fists so tightly his knuckles turned white.

Within the mass, disjointed shadows lunged towards her, ripping through her body as if she was the consistency of gelatine. He saw the excruciating pain in her eyes as they each tore a part of her essence, the brilliant energy pinpointing the Shadowlan's position as they threw her this way and that, so she was unable to stand but unable to fall throughout the onslaught.

Finally, after what seemed like an age, Vrealâ stopped the attack by raising her misshapen hand, the command greeted with impatient growls and disgruntled shrieks as Charlize sank to all fours and vomited.

The Minae gathered closer, almost obscuring her from Christian's view – he had to crouch so he could make her out between legs that shifted with unrest – and he could see her holding her unsteady hands above her head again, an attempt to cast another spell cut short by an impatient Sirenari slicing her across the face.

A line of red spilled along her left cheek, her perfect smooth cheek, and Christian's blood boiled. He scowled at the Sirenari banished to the back of the mass by Vrealâ, listened as she clicked her tongue in annoyance, although obeyed without question, and grimaced as she eagerly licked her talon clean.

He then watched as Charlize was heaved into the air, balanced on a blue hue that put her horizontally above the mass of dead. She was still awake, her eyes wide, but she couldn't move: bound, helpless, and outnumbered.

Vrealâ stood beneath her, arms wide. She communicated with her eager entourage using a mixture of unintelligible clicks, hisses, and screeches Christian couldn't understand. But whatever she promised, it seemed to rouse them into huddling even closer together, their focus solely on the Āetis above them. She was raised higher, just out of reach of the ferocious Ghul's, and Vrealâ circled beneath a couple of times before levitating to the same height, a curtain of Charlize's hair obscuring her face.

Christian strained his neck to watch as she grabbed Charlize's left arm and uncurled it until it pointed towards him, so it seemed he stood accused and condemned for his inaction.

He deserved worse.

Back in the Marsh Village, he was the hero everyone talked about, always the first one to help. And now here he was, feeble and cowardly as his friend fought unconsciousness, her usual vibrancy dulled with hopelessness, her fingers limp as they silently begged for help that she knew he couldn't provide.

And just like that, as if accepting her grim fate, she closed her eyes – at the same moment Vreâlâ brandished an ice shard and brought it down on her wrist.

Christian fell to his knees, mouth agape. His head thrummed and his stomach churned. He could hear himself begging for the image of blood pouring from Charlize's veins into the mouths of Minae to stop spinning in his head, even as he compelled himself to look back, refusing to leave her alone.

The horde fought and crawled over one another to get their feed, a frenzy of open mouths emitting noises of impatience and greed. It reminded him of chicks being fed by their mother, a spectacle made worse because of the victim they drank from.

He swallowed another retch. Every second became more unbearable than the last. Already plagued by images of what he'd become if he allowed himself to do nothing, to bear the sleepless nights and endless guilt if he saw Charlize die before his eyes, he knew, one way or another, he had to end it.

And as she fell limp, something inside him switched.

His fists clenched, he took a step from the protection.

"Wait."

A hand appeared before him, stopping his exit, and a wash of relief cascaded through his body. With only his chest and right foot protruding, he retreated and turned to the space where the voice had come from.

"Armmos… please help her," he whispered, realising the Anima clan were not only able to fly, but could also manipulate the air so they were invisible.

The distortion only detectable by the repetition of a pattern, Christian saw that in Armmos's case, two identical gnomes sat on the floor, each holding a potted plant and smiling up at him.

He smiled back and returned his gaze to Charlize, knowing the Minae were done for. With almost smug knowing, he watched Vrealâ flip her over so her stomach now faced the floor, and then, without warning, lift her mint dress to reveal her navel. She dragged the ice shard across it, and this time, the sight of it was enough. A blind rage overcame him and he charged from the protection.

Two things happened in that instant. First, the hidden Anima revealed themselves and rushed at the dead, crying in war tones and curses as anger compelled them. Secondly, the moment Christian completely left the protection he fell to the floor, no longer confined in the spell or protected by it. Writhing in agony, a pain ripped through his stomach, its searing fire debilitating as he fought for breath, frantically inhaling and exhaling in an attempt to fight the paralysation.

All he knew, above all else, was that he had to bring Charlize to safety.

The Minae didn't see it coming as the Anima broke through them like a knife through butter. At first, they scattered, before turning to combat their attackers, revitalised by the Āetis's blood. Armmos led the siege, Charras by his side as he roared with paternal instinct and ripped two Ghul's in half with a fire sword. Another closed around his shoulders, the brute strength crushing his bones, but kicking out, he managed to release himself from the vice grip and spin around to face the threat once more.

"Dicio, Incendiī-Anima, Ambure!"

Engulfing the Ghul in flames, it disintegrated into a mass of embers instantly, and without pause, he charged onwards, reaching Charlize who lay in the twisted position she'd fallen in.

Her face white and cracked with ice, he feared the worst, urgently feeling for her pulse as he tried to find a trace of life still within her.

"It has been long since we walked here together."

Charras stiffened. His limbs – burning moments before – now froze as the familiar tone of Isalize's voice took on a crude cynicism. He carefully looked into the face of the demon, thankful that he saw nothing of his late wife within it, but for the colour of her red-ringed irises.

"It is not you who I walked here with," he replied, lowering his brow.

"But it is a *part* of me who did just that," Vrealâ reminded him.

Charras stood to his full height as he considered her. Her stature and shape was a poor mockery of the mother of his child, yet the closest Minae could ever get to it. With sadness and a tinge of jealousy, he knew that if an Ungifted or ignorant unbecome looked upon her they would see Isalize and everything that made her so beautiful.

"The part of her within you is not the part I favoured," he replied.

"Yet you loved it all the same," Vealâ said, tilting her head and taking a step towards him.

Charras cast flames that crackled up his hands, keeping the coolness of the Greater Minae at bay. Her words were a test, he knew that, but she was right. He could no more harm a part of Isalize than he could harm his daughter lying eerily still at his feet.

"Be gone from here, you know it is not time," he warned. "Even you and your master cannot manipulate the Sky's wishes more than this."

Vealâ creased her eyes in what Charras figured was an attempt to smile. "Perhaps you are right, however the fate between you and I is not yet concluded."

The words held a warning, but Charras knew of them long before. "Then be gone until then," he said.

Vealâ eyed him curiously and took another step towards him. He stood firm, his guarded composure showing no signs of faltering. It took a great amount of effort, her presence magnetic to the human essence. Drawn to the cold and senseless world of the æther, he fought the urge by concentrating on the heat in his fingers, reminding him of why the cold could never penetrate his soul.

And finally, after what seemed like an eternity, she stood back.

"Leave us," Charras uttered.

Vrealâ laughed. But it was not the bass note he expected. Instead, Isalize's giggle emitted from the hollow mouth, the familiar sound stinging like a slap to his face.

"Go," he growled.

She stopped laughing and cocked her head to one side. "No."

Incredible and frightening at the same time, the noise about Christian drowned out the sound of his struggle as he attempted to claw his way to Charlize, only knowing he had to reach her and avoid the clamour stampeding around him.

Ferocious in their dealings with the Minae, the battle soon turned in the Mage's favour, which made a path easier for him to find. Every now and then, the pain in his stomach would dim, only to come back tenfold and immobilise him in an instant, and it was all he could do to keep his focus on Charlize's pale face.

Lying in a dishevelled heap of limbs and blood, she was only a few yards away, although it seemed as if she were thousands, and Christian knew that if any Minae intercepted him now, he would be an easy kill. But he pushed the negative thought aside, promising that if the last thing he ever did was reach Charlize, then he would manage it. Somehow, he needed to hold her in her last moments.

Move, he urged himself.

Looking up through clouded eyes, he saw Charras reach down towards Charlize and hurriedly feel for her pulse. In that instant, the pain ceased, freeing him from its hold, and a sigh of relief subconsciously escaped his lips.

Suddenly, he became aware that he was safe, wrapped up in the warmth of endless peace. There was no pain, only emptiness and a swell of vast, eternal oblivion lying before him.

His tenuous link to life stopped him from falling completely, and as he shook himself from the confusion, anger replaced the calm.

It was wrong. Life secured him to earth, and it was in life he belonged.

Renewed determination forced his exhausted limbs to keep going, each movement an exaggerated effort. He stayed low and made his way through the churned up dirt, avoiding the feet of Mages who all fought around him, the heavy shouts of spells thrown back and forth, which he swiftly dismissed. There was only one thing left for him to do now.

He looked up in time to witness the conversation between Charras and Vrealâ, each of them engrossed in what the other had to say. Acknowledging his distaste towards it, he continued towards them, dismissing his loathing when, inches from Charlize, her face a picture of peace, he could finally reach out to touch her.

He wasted no time in doing so, and stretching his fingers towards her palm, grasped her cold skin.

She'd died several minutes earlier, but before he could hope to understand how he knew that, a wave of nausea overwhelmed him, the weight of death crushing him as he too fell into oblivion.

42

Nowhere

It was empty where he stood. There was no noise, no movement, no anything. Christian was nowhere, everywhere, anywhere, but none of it made sense to him. The feeling was familiar; he had walked here before, so very long ago. He was younger then, he had also felt nothing. No heat, no cold, and when he concentrated, he realised he wasn't even breathing.

Yet death was not here, here was nowhere.

Christian searched for the purpose again, the reason he always ended up here. He had to collect Charlize. He was the only one who could bring her back.

The first time he transcended into nowhere there were spirits who named him the Āetis's Arcēssere, explaining how he was descended from the Dator Vitae, a chosen line of Mages who would be irrevocably destined to aid the Āetis and bring him or her back should they pass into nowhere.

Christian knew neither why he – an unbecome – would be chosen for that duty, nor why every time Charlize died, it was up to him to bring her back again. He also didn't understand why he only remembered his purpose in death, why when he lived he couldn't grasp the connection between them. He only knew there was a need to keep her alive and well, although she was more capable of that task than he ever was or seemed to be.

A mist settled against his feet as it always did when he lingered, attempting to pull him deeper, and although there was no floor, he walked anyway, a movement natural to him.

He was being silly however; he knew how to find her.

Closing his eyes, he concentrated on her essence, calling it to him with his mind. It was as innate to him as breathing, and when he looked up again, she was there, lying in the same position she'd died in, her bloodied dress draped across her lacerated stomach.

She was further into death this time, her eyes closed instead of their usual expectant self. When they were ten, they'd considered each other for a long time before returning to the surface. She'd called him brave back then.

"Charlize," he murmured, although his voice made no sound.

Reaching again with his mind, he delved within her psyche, the blockades stronger and harder to bypass as the mist coiled about her body and dragged her further into the void.

Charlize he tried again, this time in his head.

At first there was no response, she hardly noticed his presence, dismissing him as one would a fly.

This worried him. He hoped it was not too late.

Trying again, he pushed against the defences refusing him entry and called her to him from the depths of her subconscious.

This time she heard him.

Stirring and stretching out her limbs, her eyes opened, bleary at first, but then alert and understanding.

Christian… She smiled. *My Arcēssere.*

He held out his hand.

Could we not stay a little longer? It's so peaceful here.

He shook his head and leaned down towards her, her face already showing signs of improvement as her cheeks pinked.

Memento Vivere he urged, a phrase meaning 'remember to live' as he scooped her up.

With a minor pout of her lips, she reached up around his shoulders and allowed the embrace to help her step back into being once more.

43

Connected

ᒪife was returning and Charlize could hear shouts and muffled noise ringing out around her. Blurry eyed and cold with frost dealt by the Shadowlan's, she focused on Christian as they stared at each other silently, neither moving a muscle as Vrealâ spoke above them to her father. Their hands remained connected and power surged between them, Christian lending his much-needed strength to her worn body, still sufficiently drained of blood.

"Then be gone until then," her father said.

There was a slight pause, and in that instant Charlize whispered commands beneath her breath, drawing on the strength Christian provided her.

"*Dicio, Āetis…*"

"No," she heard Vrealâ reply.

"*Pellere!*" she shouted, releasing it into Vrealâ's stomach before she could retaliate.

If surprise and outrage were emotions the demon was capable of, she would have shown them. Instead, she spat fiercely, wetting the earth with blood as she writhed within her bindings.

Knowing it was hopeless, a final screech resonated before the banishment lifted the demon from where she stood and propelled her back into death, the only trace left being a pool of blood that soon boiled to nothing.

Releasing her breath and grip on Christian's hand, Charlize looked around her as the Anima Mages abolished each of the remaining Minae. Cheers and shouts of victory soon sounded across the charred gardens, although some cries turned to anguish as the bodies of less fortunate Mages quickly became apparent, their discovery a horror befalling all who saw them.

Charlize made no attempt to hide her tears, her body too weak to contain her emotions as she scoured the grounds in search of familiar faces. To her relief, she found the faces of Tunde, Armmos, Jess, and Jade each actively helping the villagers discover and send every mound of energy.

For a short while, she gladly listened to the drone of colliding whistles, watching as orbs of elements darted into the atmosphere, her soul tired and drained. But she knew that she'd soon have to face the truth of that night.

Refusing to do so just yet, she attempted to stand, but found her body unable to support her weight. She sank back to the ground in a wave of exhaustion and wiped the moisture from her brow.

Christian seemed to be having the same trouble, his attempt to reach out and help her ending in him slouching forward and putting his head in his hands.

It was only then she realised her father stood behind her, inactive and silent. She twisted her head and saw that he stared into the distance, his expression pained and haunted. Realising he must be affected by the gardens, while also knowing better than to disturb him, she allowed him his privacy and turned back, just in time to see two stretchers flying towards her, each led by a twin.

"No arguing Charlize, just let us help you," Jess barked, hushing the protest on her lips.

She had no energy to dispute her weakness and reluctantly allowed Jess to heave her onto one of the stretchers, the respite on her legs a private relief. She looked over to Christian, Jade having aided him in the same way, and their eyes met instantly, an unspoken message passing between them. It needed no words, for both of them knew something had happened.

They were connected.

❧

The sun was almost rising when everything in the gardens grew silent once more, although Charras believed the echoes of that night would take longer to quiet. Left with loss and an abundance of questions, the Mages were headed for tumultuous times, he was sure.

A warm hand on his shoulder revealed Armmos as he took in the sight of his Haunt. Unrecognisable, the gardens had wilted to nothing but blood and mud. The dew lanterns, once highlighting a glorious spectacle, now appeared to be nothing more than mourning ghosts, while the gnome's smiling faces offered an eerie contrast to the scenes they now fruitlessly tended, their wheelbarrows and pitchforks splattered with dirt.

"It'll grow back," Armmos said certainly, although there was an edge in his voice.

Charras nodded mechanically, his head heavy with thoughts of days to come. With a sigh, he began to walk away, his dark mood unable to bear company.

"I hate to disturb you old friend," Armmos said, almost changing his mind as the power of Charras's glance struck him like a fist to the face.

He addressed the floor. "I heard a Sirenari speak part of a prophecy I have not heard before; she spoke it before I slit her throat. Now, I know it may be nothing more than the babbles of a crazed Minae, yet it seemed to be spoken with power, as if she was gloating over knowing vital information we did not; that it came from beings privy to such knowledge, stolen or otherwise."

"Speak it Armmos," said Charras.

Wetting his lips, Armmos prepared the phrasing in his mind.

"But they should never know their path,
for once realised, it shall not last."

Charras listened carefully, reciting the words in his head and finding them vague and confusing. "It could be for anyone, we'd need to hear the rest of it to make a true judgement. It would not be wise to confuse ourselves with such dangerous words, especially spoken from the mouths of Minae."

Armmos considered the notion for a while, his brow etched with thought. Then, relaxing his shoulders, he nodded his agreement.

"You are right; we have far more pressing matters than fantastical riddles to solve. Be sure you sleep well tonight."

With no more than that, he left Charras alone.

Knowing that sleep would not be something shortcoming in the nights ahead, he began to busy himself in the gardens, keeping the gnomes company while he attempted to nourish the dead soil and replenish what Isalize had both built and destroyed.

44

Forgotten

Summer came to the Haunt in a time of sorrow, a season that usually lifted moods, now merely highlighting the grief that shadowed the Mage's usual cheer. Loss was a familiar enemy, but loss within the haven of the Haunt, among the trees that protected them, seemed all too much to bear.

Six Mages had fallen, one a boy of only fourteen, his inexperience in the field of battle a price none could repay, his parent's bereavement the more tragic since he'd gone against their wishes. Only time could ever heal, while those accountable would face trial in the days ahead, especially now their Āetis knew the face of her enemy. They had to hold onto that hope, for to be without it meant suffering in vain.

One positive change that derived from the tragedy was the Āetis's quickly famed victory against the now confirmed legend that was Vrealâ. News already spread on the tongues of Mages leaving for their pilgrimage, or in the claws of owls flying to relatives in distant lands, while newspapers from the Hetairia Doman were printed and distributed only a week after the incident, the tale of bravery and triumph in the face of such grave danger celebrated in black and white ink.

Charlize knew the hype would soon fade, replaced by the darker truth that Vrealâ lived. Unable to dismiss her as a myth, or speak of her to scare or threaten at bedtime, she was very much a real monster, and very much a power to fear.

She shivered at the thought and the bench she sat on rocked slightly, causing the branches it balanced atop to bow, the spell keeping it steady precarious at best.

"You okay?"

Charlize rubbed her shoulders and nodded. Even now, she could almost feel the cold touch of ice against her skin, or the sheer emptiness in her heart as parts of her essence were broken and torn from her.

Although she would heal in time, the after effects seemed everlasting.

"How long until we're found?"

Shrugging, Charlize peered over the edge of the bench to a lonely deck below. Built into the treetops earlier that day, it was there she and Christian could get away from the constant attention, questions, and thanks they received. Barely able to breathe at times, they decided that morning to escape, only telling Jess and Jade their intentions to avoid panic, their newly self-made titles of 'body-guards' an endearing yet tiresome challenge. Their contempt and suspicion towards any who came too close was almost comical. Even Amy, who'd been keeping an unusually cool distance from Christian, bore the brunt of their protection. Jess sniffed around her like a dog would a stranger, before forcing her to perform several challenges until she was satisfied no Achak or Akuji lurked within. It was all quite unnecessary. Amy's intentions were only to thank Charlize and wish Christian well before she shyly walked back to her group of friends.

And so it was the dynamics changed, subtle at first, but soon undeniable as Christian and Charlize grew closer, she taking it upon herself to teach him as much as she could so they might figure out their connection, and he grateful for the tutelage. Her father disapproved of their spending so much time together, afraid of the gossip and false conclusions others might jump to, but he also acknowledged with a grunt that their connection was not in their minds as they first thought, although he knew no more than they about the reasons for it. Whenever they probed for further information, he would warn them that some secrets were better left unknown, before hastily making an excuse to return to the gardens he now seemed to live in, it becoming his personal burden to restore them.

A break in the branches invited the sun to blind her and Charlize put her hand up to shield her eyes, although enjoyed the warm ray as it kissed her bare arms. Catching Christian's gaze as he made sure she was unharmed, he ventured a smile.

"How are you feeling now?" he asked, referring to the energy she'd used hiding them earlier.

Casting a small flame in her palm and then extinguishing it, thus proving she still had minor strength, she managed a half smile back.

"You should watch those flames, you'll scare half the village," Christian teased, although a hint of seriousness lay in his words.

The fire had extinguished almost as soon as Vrealâ was banished, reducing the potential devastation and keeping damage to a minimum. In part, this was due to the villager's noble job of keeping the fire away, but there would be many months of repair before the Haunt stood in its former glory, while the charred wood of the sequoias would never fully heal. Almost unrecognisable, the first story took the brunt of the fire, the flames managing to lick their way past the second, although only the lower tiers sustained any real damage.

"What happens now?" Christian asked quietly as he looked towards the horizon.

Charlize followed his stare into the forest beyond, watching how the sun danced along the treetops, a waltz of shade and light wavering in the warmth. It created a carpet of leaves she wished she could walk on, and she breathed in the scent of freedom.

"You are not so blind, you have purpose. That is enough for now," she replied.

Although he wasn't sure why, a part of Christian felt excited by the prospect he had a part to play in the world he found himself ensconced in, as if the connection between him and Charlize meant the path he walked held the promise of meaning.

He leaned back and reluctantly accepted the silence Charlize regularly embraced. While he brimmed with questions, he knew he'd understand their answers in time and with patience. For now, he could content himself by watching how the sun accented the rich ebony and chocolate tones in her hair, or the way she tucked it behind her ears and exposed her cut cheek as she gathered her thoughts. It was healing quicker than he imagined it would, the scarring lighter than it first threatened, and he guessed magic had a part to play in its miraculous cure. He longed to reach out and stroke it, already knowing her touch and the way she felt, but he swore to himself he would never do so without her permission again, their respect for each other a new chapter he promised to nurture.

And he could see it when she looked at him now. No longer would she dismiss his questions or roll her eyes, huff if he accidentally insulted or scold if he did it on purpose. She accepted that he wanted to learn and believed he could reach his potential with her help. In a different world to his, that would be seen as a huge honour, but Christian was just happy she stopped talking to him as if he was twelve.

"Do you find me interesting?" she said, referring to his fixation on her cheek. With a smile on her lips, she looked him in the eye and waited for an answer.

"Mostly," he replied nonchalantly. "But I'm making sure you don't fall asleep. I don't know how secure we are up here."

"I assure you, we are perfectly safe."

"Really?" said Christian, raising his eyebrows and shuffling over so the bench teetered dangerously.

"Don't, I don't have the strength," Charlize warned.

"I think you do, you just don't want to break the rules," he pushed, bouncing up and down a little so they rocked dangerously.

Charlize narrowed her eyes and clapped her hands. The bench plummeted to the floor, the Sky their only view, and she stopped it inches above the deck so their legs pointed into the blue.

White faced, Christian let go of the wooden slat he clung to and rolled backwards to land on his feet. He watched Charlize do the same and grinned widely.

"I knew it!"

"Apparently so," she replied, her face noticeably pallid, although considerably happier as she put the bench down.

Christian put his palm up and bowed his head, Charlize placing hers against it as the familiar sensation of nothing swept along her arm.

"Mimento Vivere," he said, laughter still on his lips.

"Mimento Vivere?" Charlize mumbled, rolling the words along her tongue. "I like that."

A half lodged memory attempted to resurface, but she couldn't place or associate it, and it soon vanished among the stream of her conscious thoughts, as if it had never existed in the first place.

"What are you thinking?" Christian asked, dropping his hand. "You looked in pain."

Shaking her head, Charlize didn't have a chance to answer as the raucous yells of Jess and Jade reached them in alarm.

"There you are!" they screeched, running across a bridge to join them.

"Thought you'd done a runner on us, but we can sniff you and your bloody power a mile away," said Jess to Charlize. Then, smirking at Christian, "Not you though, might as well be dead."

Laughing, he put an arm around her shoulder. "Ever the tactful one," he said, guiding her away – Jade and Charlize following behind.

They soon reached a crossroads where three of the paths led to privacy, while the one straight ahead led to where laughter and music ricocheted through the trees. And it was there they stopped.

"Where now?" Jade asked.

Considering their options for a moment, Christian took a deep breath and stepped forward. "I know it might be risky, dangerous even… but how about coffee? I'm parched."

Charlize beamed. "Yes, wonderful idea. I know a particularly good drink called a vanilla latte," she said, unaware of the discreet glance Christian shot at Jess.

"Well then," he said, peering back at her. "You better show me all you know."

End of Book 1.

Printed in Great Britain
by Amazon.co.uk, Ltd.,
Marston Gate.